Tanith Lee, bor
of nine, and was
Since then she has produced numerous novels of a fantastical nature and several radio plays, and has twice won the World Fantasy Award for her short stories.

She lives in Kent with her husband, the writer John Kaiine, and a black-and-white cat.

'One of the most powerful and intelligent writers to work in fantasy' *Publishers Weekly*

'Unlike most fantasists who wish they could write magnificently, Tanith Lee can actually do it'
Orson Scott Card

'Restores one's faith in fiction as the expression of imagination and original thought' *Guardian*

'Bizarre imagination and elegantly decadent atmosphere' *Daily Mail*

Also by Tanith Lee

Heart-Beast

Elephantasm

Tanith Lee

First published in 1993
by HEADLINE BOOK PUBLISHING PLC

First published in paperback in 1993
by HEADLINE BOOK PUBLISHING PLC

A HEADLINE FEATURE paperback

10 9 8 7 6 5 4 3 2 1

ISBN 0 7472 4106 6

Printed and bound in Great Britain by
HarperCollins Manufacturing, Glasgow

HEADLINE BOOK PUBLISHING PLC
Headline House
79 Great Titchfield Street
London W1P 7FN

Thy way is darkness. Remember me, once, in the long and lamp-less night of thy life.

Tanith Lee, *Tamastara*

Part One

1

'Go on,' said the man. 'I know you're game for it.'

'Leave me alone,' she said, 'or you'll be sorry.'

Something in the brightness of her eyes made him think twice, deterred him, and he dropped back, swearing at her, and twisting his dusty battered hat around on his head like a change of mind.

Even so, to be sure, she marched down the side street, that she did not know. She did not think he would follow, for this street, which quickly became no more than an alley, looked dubious, as if she might have accomplices waiting to accost him. Then again he might try his luck, pounding after her and pinning her against the bricks. She did not want that, and she would kick and bite, as she had sometimes had to do before. Already her heart was hammering with the anticipation of violence – but he did not pursue. All that happened was the alley curled into another, which was simply a sort of tunnel, and now she ran down it, only hoping for a way out.

But there was no exit. No light. Grey walls went up to dark overhangs, and blackened recesses gaped on stone. Rotten peel squashed underfoot. Then abruptly came slants and turns, and slippery cobbles, and she thought, *Well, wasn't I a silly fool to dash in here* – in an inner voice that resembled her sister's – when suddenly she saw her own self in front of her, like magic. It was her reflection in an occluded pane of window glass. Beside this rose a door, which had opened inward, on a great glowing mound of *objects*.

Annie stood amazed.

It was a shop of curiosities, such as she had heard of but never seen. Even from outside she could smell its perfume, like a church, but sweeter, smouldering. It made her think of formless things, like memories she could not remember and half-forgotten dreams. Then she stepped forward and walked in. It was the end of the turbulent alley, there was nowhere else to go. Even so she guessed this was not wise. But life was full of danger.

Extraordinary. It *was* a dream. The walls seemed made of gold, and went up to a golden ceiling, where hung an octagonal golden lamp. No, it must be polished brass, that was it, and the same for the two tall rods with lily-shaped cups upon them out of which smoked a snowy vapour . . . it was the smoke which made the air so sweet. Nearby stood vases, painted and beaded with enamel flowers, and behind them, coming visible as she moved, an animal of metal as large as a horse – a tiger was it? And there a bird hung on outspread wings above the lamp, with a terrible fierce eye. And there a soldier doll in a scarlet coat was patrolling up and down. The atmosphere was full of clicks and whirrs and tiny whistlings. A mechanical pigeon preened in a golden brass cage. And here, around a stack of gorgeous bolts of cloth, a stair of silk, in which threaded clawings of gold and silver thread, Annie saw a mirror, green with age, encircled by huge snakes of ebony. There were jewels in their eyes, red as flowers. And in silver dishes under the mirror lay heaps of transparent stones, green and scarlet and blue, while from a wooden box coiled out a tail of fat round pearls. None of it would be real, for it was a fortune. No, it was glass, such as they used in the theatre.

But Annie Ember looked up, and beheld herself again, poised in the mirror above the dishes of rubies, emeralds, sapphires, turquoise. She saw these perhaps naively, but herself cruelly, and to the point. A thin and shabby girl of sixteen, her brown rats-tails pushed up under a bonnet with a wilted feather. She wore her sister's hand-me-down dress, and old boots. Her hem was torn, and though she spent most of her days mending, had not seen to this. Her pale city face had a young-old look. It was a face of sighs, the sighs of leaning back from drudgeries. An aching back, chapped hands. But for a moment, catching the gleam of the gems, her eyes were luminous and large. They had flared outside, warning off the man who took her for a whore. Now they were dreaming, still as pools in garden shade she had never known. *Is that me?*

And at her thought, a paper manikin whirled down from a wire, and doffed his hat to her.

She dodged away. And in doing so, noticed, to her right in the mirror, someone sitting behind her on a low divan piled with gold and crimson cushions.

Annie spun round. She stared.

A very old man, who was a king or a prince. But out of a fairy tale. In his long hair streaks of black remained, and his eyes were ink within and without, drawn around with kohl. He wore a golden garment, and on his feet silver slippers. From a bubbling crystal container, another snake fed itself into a point of amber at his lips. He smoked silently, looking back at her. His skin was like the smoke, almost it seemed to her *blue*.

Not blinking, he took the snake from his lips, and said, 'What will you buy?'

Annie did blink. With the brisk irritation of poverty, she said, 'I haven't any money.'

'Then why did you come in here?' he inquired. His voice was fur-smooth, it had a lilt to it she had never heard.

He must be a hundred years old. And he was a foreigner. Where did he come from? Surely she had heard tell of a place where they spoke in this musical half-laughing way, and had blue skins?

'What will you buy,' said the princely man, 'for one penny?'

She thought, *Oh, he's mad*. And then, *Or it's a trick*.

She recalled something. A beautiful word. India. It was that place. Had her long-dead mother not said—

'Only one penny,' said the prince from India, enticingly.

She glanced involuntarily about the shop again. It dazzled her. On a shelf she saw a brass rat, cunningly caught in an attitude of washing in a conceited, self-satisfied way.

'Not the rat,' he said.

'And it would cost more than a penny,' said Annie Ember, feeling her hard little pale face become even uglier.

'That would depend. Wait,' he said. 'Look at this.'

And he opened his dusk hand before her.

On the palm lay a shard of dark yellowish material. It certainly did not look worth very much.

'What is it?'

'An amulet,' said the man. 'Perhaps you would like an amulet.'

What was an amulet? Ah, yes. Something to protect you, like

the crucifix Mother had worn before her other daughter's husband had sold it.

Annie craned forward. The man stretched out his hand. She found she had taken the dirty thing off his clean hard palm. The shard looked like used soap.

'This is ivory,' said the man. 'Very old. Cut carefully from the tusk of a living elephant. Did you know such a thing was possible? Yes, indeed. And if performed properly, the tusk will grow up again, so it is not a robbery.'

'I've heard – of elephants,' said Annie. Her mother again . . . or rather her sister from her mother. Because their father had seen them, ages ago. Before Annie was born.

Then she made out the shape of the elephant that was the ivory shard. It was a tiny figure. A miniature tail behind and a greater one in front. Four columnar legs. The arch of back. The ancient head and fanned cabbage-leaf petals of the ears. But all so very small. She was used to threading needles by candlelight, otherwise she might not have made it out so swiftly.

The ivory had a perfect feel. It was like something that had had to be and must always be.

'The male elephant of this country,' said the princely man, 'he alone has tusks. The female's tusks are hidden. You must remember this. And, too, how wise the elephant is. He is the land whale, and the boulder and the mountain, and the remover of mountains. He is a cloud that brings the rain.'

Annie had barely heard him now. She was uncomfortable, for usually when anyone spoke to her at length, they wished to utilize her in some way. Even her sister. And besides, she did not understand what he said. Even the elephant looked absurd. Surely nothing could be quite of that form? Although there were plated beasts that lived in rivers, and snakes two yards long, and unicorns, her sister had said there were unicorns. But their mother, fount of this information, was dead, and all Annie had left of her was a small curl of dry hair, just as all she had of her father was his name, Ember. And her sister did not even have that any more.

'Well, I'll get along now,' said Annie.

'One penny,' he said, 'for the ivory elephant.'

'Oh no.'

She held the ivory out. It clung to her fingers. Her hand, not like his, was unclean as well as chapped, and stuck with needle pricks.

'One penny,' he said.

He is mad. Better humour him. As he raised the amber mouth of the snake of the hookah, she drew a penny out of her empty little purse, and put it on a carved table beside him.

He laid down the snake, placed his hands together, and nodded behind them at her.

She could go now.

Annie felt a moment of strange reluctance.

She said, 'What will I do with the elephant?'

'God knows that,' said the man. 'You must wait and see.'

Annie turned and hurried away through the shop, leaving the mirror and the silk, the vases and jewels, the smoking incense, and the prince of twilight in his costume of gold.

At the door she did not look back. She closed the door behind her, and went up the twisting alley, and hoped the man who had propositioned her would not be waiting, and that there would not be much trouble when she reached home without the loan she had been sent to wheedle and failed to obtain. She thought of the nasty alley and how she was hungry, and of her sister's voice, and nothing.

At last she got up into the street, and came out, and the man in the dusty hat was gone. People moved back and forth. She had not looked over her shoulder. Perhaps the shop had vanished. The ivory thing was in her purse where the penny had been. Had it vanished too?

On a wall were posters for the music hall, and a carriage raced along another road with its wheels churning up the filth. An old washerwoman barged past with her grumbling load.

Tears sprang into Annie's eyes, surprising her. She denied them.

They slid away back into her heart and left her there, hard and young, and pale and dirty, trudging home in her cracked boots.

Annie Ember lived in the slums, on Tooth Street, by the river.

It was a maze tucked into a corner of the city, the water marking its boundary. Spring had come, and the river was oily and greenish, and muck floated on it, and in the mud at its edges carrion gulls picked ferociously yet resignedly. Near dawn, dilapidated boats slid in along the tide; they had been searching for any riches the river might give up overnight, the fob watches and rings of suicides, and skeins of hair for the wigmakers from the heads of murdered women.

Tooth Street overlooked this venue. Its craning tenements were the colour of soot, the whole area seemed blasted and blackened as if by a recent volcanic eruption. The fires that burned at the street's river end would have heightened this impression, save for their gregariousness. Those without any pretension to a home lived by the fires, feeding in refuse. Here and there a kettle hung steaming from a makeshift hook. Sometimes they had killed a gull, or got a fish from the scurrilous river, and this they cooked. A bad smell soaked from these encampments that was worse than the smells of poverty from the tenements.

Annie entered a building midway along the street. Augusta House was its name. In the yard festoons of washing offered themselves limp and damp to the offended sun. Some skinny children played a game with a ball of paper and sticks. Annie climbed stairs in half-light. At each landing the window was cracked or broken and had been sealed with brown paper. One flight, two, three, four. She dwelled in the exalted position of the top floor, the head of the tower. Annie came to a door, one of several, and gave a twist and a push. There was no key used at this time of day, and by night the door was barred.

She entered on a room that was full of vague mounds. Annie looked at them, and made out as usual a lumpen settee flung with pillows and clothes, a chest from which things extruded, some chairs past their best, and piled with newssheets, a table with a cloth of holes, and set with a tea-pot and a loaf. On the hearth their own kettle faintly chirruped, and on the windowsill, before a view of the unholy street and river, stood a pot of geraniums. These were hers. A door led to another room in which was a great untidy bed, and there sprawled a young man with a white pure face and long reddish curls, reading a newspaper and drinking from a bottle. Her sister Rose's husband, Innocent.

'Is that one of you women?' called Innocent loudly, in a harsh voice. 'Bring me some tea.'

Annie took the tea-pot, went to the hearth and lifted off the kettle by its frayed holder. She poured the boiled water on to the old brew of tea leaves. On the rickety dresser she found the large cup which was Innocent's. She filled the cup with a little milk from the jug, the tea, and four spoons of sugar.

She did not like entering the bedroom, but Innocent lay there like a sultan, and took the cup from her.

'And where's my bread?'

'I'm sorry,' said Annie. Like her sister, she still spoke well, and sometimes tried to camouflage this. She had omitted to do so.

'Sorry, sorry,' mimicked Innocent, his awful, handsome face screwed up. 'Little miss fell-down-from-above. Ain't I always to have my bread? Go and get it, you lazy slut.'

Annie went back and cut a big slice off the loaf. She spread dripping on it from the bowl. Of course he always had his bread. She bore it back to him and watched him start to eat. She had an incoherent awareness of her sister's marriage, and of Innocent coming to live with them, and her mother – then still alive – not liking Innocent, but that she, Annie, a child, had worshipped him. Until she got used to his ways, and then worship changed to cautious loathing.

'And where's that other bitch, I'd like to know,' said Innocent. 'And as for you, did you get it?'

'No,' said Annie.

'Useless bloody slut. I knew it ain't no good sending you, with your la-di-da ways. You don't know how to get round these old fellers. I've taught her. But you ain't worth teaching.'

Annie felt frightened. Some threat was always being offered and she could only define it as sexual. She edged out of the bedroom, saying as she went, 'I did my best. He said we'd had enough credit.'

'Then you need to look like you can exchange something, you silly mare.'

Annie sat down on the settee, which at night was her bed, and began to pick about in the heap of rags Innocent had brought in. What might be salvaged she or her sister would repair, and then sell along the streets that led to the market.

'Not worth your keep, you ain't,' said Innocent. But he began to read his paper again. 'Bloke here,' he said generally, as doubtless he would have spoken aloud had Annie not been present, 'won a hundred pounds on a horse. Well curse him, I say. May he get growths.'

Annie shuddered with distaste, and heard her sister's weary, slightly limping steps in the corridor outside.

A moment more, and Rose came in. She wore rather garish clothes, a pink dress much darned, and a bonnet with trite roses. One item was beautiful, her lace gloves, which she had made herself.

'And here's the other slut,' said Innocent.

Annie's sister's head jerked up, like that of a dog which hears its name. Her hair was not brown, but golden, her face pretty in its dust of powder, but so tired.

She went straight into the bedroom and Annie heard the clink of coins.

'Is that all?'

'There was only one.'

'Bloody fool. There'd be more if you tried harder.'

'He was a gentleman.'

'Oh, so you wait for gentlemen, do you? What gentleman's going to go with *you* down some alley?'

'He was. He gave what I asked. Said I should change my ways.'

The sound of a slap.

'Stick to what you can do. It's all you're good for. And that cat of a sister. I ain't worked out why I bother with the pair of you.'

'Because we keep you, Innocent.'

'You want another clip? Who keeps me? Ah?'

Silence.

Annie had threaded a needle and begun on an old coat. She had skill. Had her mother taught her? She could not recall the teaching. She seemed to have been sewing from the cradle.

The young woman who was her sister came out. She smiled at Annie, despite the red blotch on her cheek, and went to the chest. Pulling wide a drawer, she removed a bundle, and undoing it, revealed a magnificent rag doll. Its face was a mask of white satin, its eyes were sewn like pansies, and its lips better than the namesake roses on the garish hat. It wore a dress of cucumber green, sewn with tiny false pearls in intricate patterns, and edged with lace. Its hair was silk, golden like Rose's own, but not quite finished.

'I'll get two pounds for her in Rustle Street, Mrs Marpolis promised me.'

'That witch,' said Innocent. He had emerged from his lair and was sprucing his appearance before a cracked mirror over the mantel. Annie marvelled idly at his beauty and his foulness so absolutely combined.

'She will,' said the sister, placatingly.

'You hope she will. She'd better. You'll please yourself, no doubt. You and your rotten dolls.' Presently he added, 'I'm off to see the Joyless Bugger.'

Which meant he would be absent the rest of the day and most of the night. Both women sighed spontaneously with relief.

When Innocent was gone, Rose unbuttoned her boots and took off her hat. The mark of Innocent's blow was fading; he had been lenient.

'Brew us some tea, Annie.'

Annie carried out the ritual with the kettle and tea-pot. Her sister's cup was only sugared once, for economy.

As they drank the tea, the afternoon faded. The geraniums turned to blood as a golden sun sank behind Augusta House into the river. The fire burned low and was replenished. Annie and her sister sewed, like clockwork, as if they had done so from the cradle.

When the last drop of dusk had been squeezed out, Annie lit two candles, and made more tea.

'Ah, let's give this a rest,' said Rose.

She stood up and walked around the room to ease her back, stiffened by sewing, one hand smoothing her eyelids and brows. She had been a beauty once, better than the dolls she made, even better than this one of the pansy eyes and bright hair.

'We've done enough. What say we play the Yesyes?'

Annie frowned over the tea-pot. She spread a little dripping on a slice of bread and cut it into two halves.

'If you want.'

'Oh, go on, you silly. You're scared of it.'

'No, I ain't,' said Annie. She corrected herself, 'I'm not.'

'Yes, no need to talk like that when Innocent *ain't* here,' said Rose. She laughed bitterly. 'Come on. Clear that table. I'll get the board.'

She went into the chest again and pulled out, from its spot of concealment, the Yesyes board, a curious concave oblong, inscribed with the letters of the alphabet and the two words 'Yes' and 'No'. With this Rose liked to experiment, setting her fingers on the little triangle, trying to make it run about the board and spell out messages. Spirits were meant to come. And sometimes the board did offer up strange remarks. Once it had said: 'Beware the parson's owl.' Once: 'Eat more larks.' And once: 'Toby forgets.' When pressed, always it would make less and less sense.

Annie did not care for the board. She suspected imps rushed in to play games with her sister. Something supernatural, not real, yet also *present*, able to cause trouble of some sort, for on one occasion the clock had fallen off the mantel during a session. But Rose liked the Yesyes. Her continual hope was that it would some day offer a possible alternative to her recent life, her cringing passion for and terror of Innocent, her guilt over Annie, and her own prostitution.

They sat by the table in the dull candlelight. Annie held her sister's hand, and Rose put two free fingers on to the triangle of wood.

Nothing occurred. After a few minutes Rose said, plaintively, 'Do speak to us. Do speak. Please. We're listening and ready.'

Rose's voice was soft and clear and quite cultured. Annie had lost this fineness, half deliberately and long ago, but Rose did not seem able to let go of her vocal beginnings. She importuned gentlemen on the streets in such a way, after all, and often they were seduced.

The triangle also, apparently.

It began quirkishly to strut along the letters, but unable to settle or decide.

'Oh, are you there?' asked Rose. 'Oh, talk to it, Annie.'

Annie was silent.

Rose said, persuasively, 'Is it Mother?'

'It isn't Mother,' said Annie. She spoke fiercely, but Rose did not notice.

Uncomfortable, Annie was hot and taut, her corset cutting into her, the smell of candle-grease making her queasy, as the half slice of bread and sour tea gurgled in her unappeased belly.

'Oh, Mother, is it you?' implored Rose.

The triangle skittered up the board. *No*.

'Ah,' said Rose sadly. 'Who then? Is it someone we know?'

The triangle stayed firmly where it was.

'Tell your name,' said Rose.

No name, spelled the triangle.

'Who are you then?' cried Rose.

The triangle oozed at an even pace, now, along the board, finding the letters and staying upon them until Rose had spelled them out aloud.

'What is it saying?' said Rose. 'I'm all confused.'

Annie bit the fingernails of her free hand.

'It says we're going on a journey. *You are going away*.'

'Oh! I thought it did. Oh – oh where?'

'*Better than this*,' said Annie as the letters met the triangle.

'Is he—' said Rose, 'is Innocent going?'

'*Yes*,' said Annie. She scowled. 'It's playing with you, Rose.'

'No, no, it's someone from Mother. We're going on a journey.'

'I don't know what that word is,' said Annie.

Rose said, puzzled, 'Ivory. It says Ivory.'

Annie started as if she had been struck.

It was an imp, an imp that knew what she herself had forgotten – the tiny creature of tusk, an animal that perhaps did not exist. Put into her purse, slipped from her brain.

Annie snatched her hand from Rose's hand, and the triangle slewed to a stop.

'Now look,' said Rose. Her tone was sorrowful not enraged. She would never fight. Annie had always fought, one way or another.

'I'm sorry,' said Annie, 'but I don't like it. We shouldn't.'

Rose tried the triangle coaxingly. It would not respond. She removed her hand and touched it to her cheek.

'It said Ivory. That was India. Mother – it said we'd go away.'

'It isn't likely,' said Annie, 'unless he throws us out.'

Rose said, ashamed, 'He won't, while I can make him money.'

'Where could we go?' said Annie angrily.

'Better, it said. Somewhere better.'

'Heaven,' said Annie, without thinking.

Rose turned to her, white as paper under her rouge. 'Ssh.'

They did not speak again until, in the black of night, Annie lay under her blankets on the settee in the main room, and Rose in the big bed, vacant of Innocent.

'I'll get two pounds for my doll. He'll be pleased.'

'He'll spend it in a week.'

'Perhaps I could lie. Tell him I only got one, and put some by.'

In the past, before Annie could recollect, they had lived in quite a big house, on a pleasant street. But Father, or someone who had been Mother's protector, had fallen to hard luck, and gradually, bit by bit, they had descended to this. Annie had one sharp memory, maybe of a Christmas, sparkling lights and candles, and a man's ruddy face. But whose had it been? Her mother she did not recall. Rose had said her hair was flowing and rich, like honey. But the curl that remained was short, grey and coarse.

On the stair, in the corridor, a step.

Both women tensed.

Then a loud commotion, echoing away all down the house, informed them it was another door, a neighbour, not Innocent arriving back.

'Let's get some sleep before he comes home,' said Rose, and, with a weary groan, seemed gone.

She had cut from her mind, or mislaid, the word 'Heaven'. Annie lay hard in the dark, and considered it. Outside vague howls rose from the lorn night.

And in her purse, where she had not looked to see, did the little ivory beast still lie, or had she dreamed the golden shop and the prince of India already? She turned her face from sleep. No more dreams. But sleep came, and she moved within it, borne away, on the mystical journey of the night.

Annie Ember opened her eyes in astonishment on the morning, as if she expected to wake elsewhere. But surprise faded. She was where she must be.

A pinkish afterglow hung above the river, and on this the pot of geraniums stood jungle black.

A noise came from the hearth, Rose busy with the kettle, her hair in curling rags, brewing fresh tea.

Where had Annie been? Nowhere. Only into sleep. She sat up. She had forgotten everything.

'Old sleepy-head,' said Rose. '*I* want an early start. He's not home yet, perhaps I can get off before he comes.'

Rose laughed. She had had a good night's rest without Innocent. Although he never troubled her sexually, he put his cold feet on her warm back, pushed her in his sleep, and pulled the quilt off her so she was left with only the blanket. His often-tipsy mutterings disturbed her; sometimes he struck out in sleep, and had once given Rose a black eye without knowing, blaming her next because it spoiled her looks. The beatings he awarded when conscious were aimed at portions of her body that would not overtly show.

Annie pushed off the blankets, stepped into her boots and did them up. She slept as Rose did, in her undergarments, and now had only to get into her corset, which Rose helped her with, her petticoat and dress.

'I finished that doll. Pity, I'll miss her. I did it by candlelight an hour ago. I woke up because the birds were singing. Those fires over by the river muddle them, poor things, they think it's morning.' If Innocent had been there, Rose would not have dared 'waste' the candle, nor would she have talked so much. Now she had finished the doll, she would be going to Rustle Street and Mrs Marpolis.

'Can I come?' Annie felt contrite, not knowing why.

'If you're quick.'

Annie tidied her bed into a settee, and did up her dress. She put on her bonnet as they drank their tea and ate a miniscule piece of the loaf, which now tasted rather stale, a usual taste.

The window was full of light. They unbarred the door and went out. On the long stairs, after all, they met Innocent, slightly dishevelled and with a sickly carnation in his button-hole.

'The mice sneaking off,' said Innocent, catching Rose playfully by the wrist. 'Who told you you could?'

'You said I was to take that doll to—'

'Don't try that trick on me, my girl. I never said that. But,' disposed to be generous, Innocent lounged on the stair, 'I'll allow it. Make sure you get two pounds, you ain't worked your eyes raw over the thing for nothing. Did you miss me?'

'Yes, Innocent.'

'Want to know where I've been, I dare say. Well, I ain't telling, but I got a shilling or two.'

Rose gave a wobbly smile. Innocent gambled and doubtless thieved. She hoped and feared that one night he would be caught, trapped, and killed like a handsome white scorpion. It was Annie who wondered how she and Rose would manage without Innocent. He did very little for them, spending his ill-gotten gains on himself and his pals, and their sparse earnings too. He badly-used Rose and had given her over to whoring, and would do the same for Annie, perhaps, permitted time or a change in her looks. He was an evil influence, yet he provided a curious backbone for their lives. His vanishment would leave a hole, a gape. Even their poor pleasures, such as this excursion, they stole from him.

He gave Rose a kiss on the cheek, 'Maybe you'll meet a nice gentleman,' and went upstairs, where he would kick off his boots – Rose would clean them later – and sprawl on the bed to sleep away his night. On then, to the world.

Tooth Street was not lovely in the spring sunlight, but here and there plants with yellow flowers had come up between the cracked paving stones. The road had horse dung on it, and both the tenants of the tenements and the campments were busy shovelling it up and squabbling.

The milk cart passed the end of the street; it never ventured down it.

'I should have bought a penny-worth. That milk'll be off by tea-time. I'm all mixed this morning.' But Rose looked lovely as the street did not, her eyes vivid and her face relaxed, smiling.

They walked to Rustle Street which took most of an hour, going up through the slums towards the higher lighter city as if surfacing through muddy water. At last they were walking the broad thoroughfares where trees grew in a wild spray of green. Ancient buildings loomed on the backdrop, columns and onion domes, and towers which the sunlight scoured to whiteness. Ahead lay the great market, and here they found enchantments, the red heaped apples and barrel-organ with monkey in purple trappings, the stalls piled with things not to be bought or even thought of. The flower-sellers were a garden, the forced roses and sunflowers, and violets thick as tapestry on the ground. They took care not to bruise a single petalled head.

A man selling whippets roared past their faces with beery breath. Rose coloured and hurried by. Annie guessed this man had had her sister.

Down a cobbled lane stood the shop of Mrs Marpolis. Its windows bulged, and there was bobbled velvet at the door.

Inside, the china figurines were a crowd, out from which masks and dolls peered with perfectly formed blind eyes. Seeing these riches, Annie wondered at their daring. How could anything stitched by meagre candlelight in the slum be worthy of Mrs Marpolis' shop?

Two lady assistants looked down their noses, their lace blouses – lace not so fine as that of Rose's gloves – and their black slopes of skirts, to somewhere at the level of the floor, where Rose was.

'May I *help* you?' As if it could be conceivable.

'I'm here to see Mrs Marpolis.'

Startled by Rose's voice and accent, the second assistant fell. 'I'll go and see if she is free to be disturbed.'

And Annie pictured Mrs Marpolis struggling for liberty in enormous chains. As Annie remembered her, they would have needed to be large.

But, 'Do you have an appointment?' inquired the first assistant, from her heights, staying the other.

Rose hesitated.

Annie said loudly, 'Of course we do. Do you decide for Mrs Marpolis who can go in?'

'Annie!' exclaimed Rose, whose plan had been as ever to avoid wrath with mild words, which it rarely managed.

Annie ignored her. She said to the assistants, 'Well, will you risk it?'

Mrs Marpolis was sent for, and came.

'This way, and enter, girls,' she mooed, waving her great hands ringed with dark jewels. Her hair was far too black, like a live crow. Her white face was a terrible mask, not like the pretty things in the shop. Enormous black eyes, in pouches of white kidskin flesh, flashed.

Annie and Rose went after Mrs Marpolis into a sanctum, and the curtain was let fall.

This room Annie had never penetrated before. A wine-red velvet wallpaper covered the walls, which were also hung with strange medallions, pictures, cameos and silhouettes in oval frames. On the great marble fireplace a fire burned heartily, and the room was stifling. Beyond the fire, in a nook, stood one solitary figurine, a pale tulip. Annie recognized it as a Madonna Rose had told her of. A small votive light burned before the Madonna in a crimson cup, throwing rich lifelike flickers over the dainty face and long blue veil. The Madonna's dress was eastern, and rich with gold, and she had a golden crown. In her arm she carried, not a holy Infant, but a plate of sticky-looking sweets. Annie gazed. Was this blasphemous?

Mrs Marpolis, inured, paid her bonbon Madonna no heed. She did not walk across the room, but glided on runners.

'Show. I will see.' Rose produced the doll. 'Ah. Fine work. And the pearls. I knew you be clever with them when I give them you.'

'I did my very best,' said Rose.

'Very fine, as I said.' Mrs Marpolis never smiled. Her mouth was large and extended, like the jaws of a beast, and behind her lips were huge white teeth. 'I am pleased. I will give you what I said. One pound.'

Rose faltered. 'Oh, well, Mrs Marpolis—'

'Or, correct me, did I promise you a guinea?'

'It was two pounds,' said Annie, 'thank you.'

'*Two* pounds? Who is this child?'

'My sister, Mrs Marpolis.'

'I had forget. So small she was, the time before. And now a young lady.' Annie held the terrible black eyes. 'And she is called?'

'Annie,' said Rose.

'Ah, Anna. I recall her now. Little Anna. Well, Anna, how is it you speak up so boldly? Were you here to know I promising two whole pounds, a vast amount, to your sister?'

'Rose told me that you did,' said Annie.

'Rose was mistooken, then.'

'Yes, Mrs Marpolis,' said Rose, 'I'm sure. A guinea, if you will—'

'She's sat working through the dark, ruining her sight,' said Annie. Her heart pounded and her eyes enlarged. She would not give up.

'Her poor eyes. Well. We must all suffer for us trade.'

Mrs Marpolis folded her fat hands in their armour on her dark skirt and looked like a statue. Another Madonna, but without any sweets.

'Then,' said Annie, 'we must go to the other lady, who promised two guineas.'

Mrs Marpolis widened her own eyes. It was the only symptom that she too was now embattled.

'What lady? This is not right. I give the pearls, and the silk, for this doll.'

'We will pay you for the materials from the two guineas the other lady is prepared—'

'Enough!' snapped Mrs Marpolis.

Rose looked near to fainting.

Annie turned towards the door.

'Two pounds,' snarled Mrs Marpolis. 'Not a penny more. You are rogues. Such women,' she said, to the ornate plaster ceiling. 'I am surround by wickedness.'

Rose hustled Annie into the street, where they stood, flushed, between distress, embarrassment and joy. 'You shouldn't have—' 'Yes I should.' 'What a turn up—'

They bought apples.

'I'll tell *him* I only got one pound. He won't expect the witch to have given me more. I can hide the rest.'

Annie licked the apple, able to be childish a moment, perhaps like Eve.

2

Innocent woke in the late afternoon, as the women were quietly sorting and sewing the rags. He announced that the Joyless Bugger and two or three other cronies would be coming to dine, and at three o'clock he gave Annie money and sent her to the pie-shop on Pastry Lane. Rose put on potatoes and cabbage to boil, and made up a gravy.

The prospect of a meal was offset for Annie, as for Rose, by the nature of the company. Even so, approaching the pie-shop, Annie's stomach growled urgently. Inside, the smells sent her dizzy. Then she had the walk back, the pie in its wrapped dish, her mouth watering, not daring even to break off a bit of the crust. She cast her mind deliberately out into uneasy seas. There was something she had been trying to remember, something that nagged at her but which she could not grasp. Beside that stood the darker, denser problem, all too well recalled, that Rose meant to cheat Innocent of half the money for the doll.

This had happened once before, when Rose had been making lace gloves and selling them to the better houses near the park. Rose had kept some of the money back, saying to Annie defiantly, 'I earnt it. And one day we may need it, you and I. Mother used to say, put something by for a rainy Sunday. And he never does. Anyway. How will he know?' But Innocent, by some murky process of telepathy based probably upon knowing Rose herself so well, deduced that something had gone awry. When challenged, Rose denied that she had 'slyly and viciously' kept anything from him. Then he had gone for her, and Annie had before her inner eyes the view of Rose hanging by her hair from Innocent's hand as he, with the other fist, smote her in the ribs and breast – places where bruises were not immediately evident. The screaming and roaring had roused the tenement, which thundered back, abusing the occupants of the top apartment, until the whole house seemed to shake, like a nightmare Tower of Babel.

Annie was afraid that this would now occur again. For Rose, even though Innocent had not yet asked her about the doll, already seemed furtive, tiptoeing about, glancing at her hellish husband under her eyelids. One should not try subterfuge with such as Innocent. At least, Rose should not. Annie had fooled him now and then. But there again, he had little interest in Annie. Innocent's interest in you was what dictated danger.

When Annie returned to the rooms, other tenants were at their doors, sniffing up the evolving aroma of cabbage and gravy. In the apartment, the Joyless Bugger, a bulging man of black moustaches, had already arrived, and soon after came the Badger, a little being in a checked cap which he never removed, and Earbone, a talkative vandal. These three stood in a line before the fire, smoking their long pipes, while the food bubbled at their backs.

Everyone sat down to the pie and vegetables, and to a large reeking cheese Earbone had produced. The men drank beer, and Rose, being pressed by the Joyless Bugger to take some sips of this, became cheerful and giggly even in the presence of Innocent.

He eyed her thoughtfully. And Annie, who had been lost in the food, felt herself change, her eyes hot and her stomach abruptly stony, so a pain began where appetite had been.

'She's clever, my Rosie,' said Innocent. 'She makes dolls now and sells them on Rustle Street to Ma Marpolis.'

'There's a canny old bitch,' said the Joyless Bugger gloomily.

The men made merry over anecdotes of Ma Marpolis, how her assistants in the shop were tied in kennels overnight, how she rode on a broomstick to raid the graveyards of the city, how she liked roast rat for her supper.

Then, 'How much she give you for the doll? You ain't said,' asked Innocent of Rose.

'Oh—' said Rose gaily, 'a pound.'

'A pound, eh?' Innocent looked round at the men. 'Not bad, eh? Not bad for a rotten old doll of rags.'

Rose laughed, soprano and sweet; you could hear she had had a pretty singing voice.

'Very nice, lovely,' said Innocent's companions.

'But,' said Innocent, in a slow, puzzled way, 'you said the old bint promised you two. Two pounds. You said.'

'She did. But then – well, she wouldn't pay me what she promised. Stuck out for one, or nothing. What could I do?'

Rose's beer-touched confidence was still high. She had not faltered. And Earbone broke in. 'She's a tough cow, that Marpolis. Can't budge her.'

'Yes,' added the Badger, 'she supplies, I hear, girls to some funny areas. I reckon your Rosie is taking a chance. You should keep her away from Ma Marpolis.'

'Yes,' said Innocent. He sighed and gently looked at Rose. 'You wouldn't lie to me, would you, Rosie?'

Rose's face twitched. Her mouth trembled. She was flustered, and could not meet his eye. 'She only gave me one pound. I told you.'

'Let's see it then,' said Innocent.

Rose got up hurriedly, and went to take her purse from the chest. She brought the purse to Innocent, quivering.

'My wife,' said Innocent to the gathering, 'you have to watch her, Joyless. She hides things sometimes, despite what the Good Book tells her, to honour and obey me.'

'They all hide things,' said the Badger dolefully.

'Too true,' added Earbone. 'My old lady hides my bacca and my beer, but I always finds it.'

'Beat her,' said Innocent.

'I've beat her blue and black, but it don't stop her. She's daft if you ask me. But then, I don't see her more than twice a month.'

'Look at this pound,' said Innocent. 'It gladdens my heart. I ain't saying two wouldn't gladden it more.'

'She only gave me the one, Innocent,' nervously over-insisted Rose.

Annie kept her eyes down on her congealing plate. She wondered if Innocent would extend his queries to her. She would do better than her sister, but probably it was too late.

'I think I'll turn you over, at bedtime,' said Innocent to Rose, and the other men laughed. 'Make sure, eh, Joyless. Nothing in her stays.'

Rose blushed violently. Although she whored, she had never lost a proprietary shyness.

Annie thought, *What next? Will he start on her in front of them?*

But nothing happened. The men resumed their drinking and chewing, their digestive asides. Annie in turn made herself eat, not wanting to waste the meal, although it felt like rocks and serpents going down.

Rose could not eat. She was trying to pretend she was guiltlessly put out at Innocent's comments on her underwear, at his doubting her truthfulness. But anyone could see she was only frightened.

When the food was consumed, Annie and Rose cleared the table, but for the tea-pot, loaf and knife, fetched the men more beer, and then washed the plates. After this the two women resumed their sewing on the settee, while the four men sat on chairs at the hearth, smoking and drinking, playing cards. Their conversation was both boring and savage, laced by terrible uglinesses of speech and desire. Had there been any point to it, Annie would have wished them all dead, but she had long ago learned the futility of wishes. Rose was nervous, and pricked her fingers till blood came and stained the ragged garments she worked on. Although Innocent saw this, he did not scold her. That too boded ill.

It was after midnight when the dinner party broke up. The Joyless Bugger, Earbone and the Badger went racketing off down the stairs to an increasing accompaniment of cries and curses from the interrupted floors.

Outside they turned to baiting one of the campments and were set on by a brawny woman brandishing a kettle and the bones of a gull. The three men ran off hooting in mock terror. Innocent turned from the window.

'Now, Rose, let's be having you.'

Annie's heart recoiled without amazement.

'What do you want, Innocent?' Rose's voice was trembling so she could hardly speak.

'You know full well. I want that pound you ain't given me.'

'But I gave it you.' Rose got up, as if getting ready to run.

'You gave me *one* pound. But I want the *other*.'

They began to circle each other, and Annie, thick with weariness, felt a grim premonition. When Innocent lunged and struck Rose on the breast – as normally not to bruise her face – and Rose fell over and began to cry, Annie spoke out quickly. 'It's in the work basket.'

'Oh, is it now?'

'She kept it back to buy you a new coat.'

'Oh, did she now?'

And Innocent lurched across and took up the work basket, upending it. He caught the pound in mid-air, amid the shower of darning thread, scissors and needles.

Innocent waved the money before his face.

'Well, Rose. Well, Rose.'

'I'm – sorry – Innocent,' said Rose, where she lay on the floor.

'Of course you are, you cow. I've made you sorry. A new coat, eh? I can find my own new coat.' And all his evil white face moved like the beak of a predatory bird. He strode to Rose and kicked her in the side. She screamed. He repeated the blow, as if he had liked doing it very much.

'Don't,' said Annie. She had started up, but she knew better than to run forward. 'If she's in a state, she won't be able to work—'

'Have to put you out, then,' said Innocent. But he turned from Rose, fastening his eyes instead on her sister. 'Not that you'd be any use. You ain't got no figure. And your face is like a coal-scuttle. Perhaps you're hiding something, too? Eh? Something Ma Marpolis slipped you.'

'No,' said Annie.

'Well, you've got no brain,' said Innocent, 'maybe you ain't hiding. Bring us your purse. I'll take a look.'

Annie went at once to get her purse. As she was bringing it to him, she saw Rose begin to pull herself up from the floor, holding her side, and sobbing noiselessly – she had been certain he had irreparably damaged Rose – but even as she felt the relief, Annie recalled that there *was* something in her purse, something she did not want Innocent to see—

There was nothing now she could do. She held it out to him and Innocent graciously accepted it.

'Couple of pennies,' said Innocent. 'All right. I'll let you off. I'll only take the one. Ah,' he said. 'But what's this?'

He brought it out then in his elegant soiled fingers.

She had forgotten not only that it existed, but how nondescript it looked. It was nothing. A piece of used soap gone hard.

She did not want Innocent to touch the ivory shard that was an elephant, that was a dream-animal of a strange smoky land, which perhaps they had told her of, when she was a baby.

'Well, what is it? Nasty thing.'

'I found it.'

'You found it. Where?'

'On the street,' said Annie. 'In the gutter.'

'Yes, that's the right spot for you, little miss high-up-nose.'

Innocent twirled the shard, the elephant, in his fingers. Would that matter? Annie could do nothing. She looked at him blankly and said, 'You keep it, if you like, Innocent.'

'Here, Rose,' said Innocent. He went to Rose, who sat now at the table, holding herself in her arms, breathing in gasps. There was blood like careless rouge on the side of her mouth, although he had not hit her there. As if addressing a whole, uninjured acquaintance, Innocent demanded, 'What's this worth? Anything?'

Rose looked at it, and her eyes fixed.

She could not dissemble. She had never done so.

'Ivory—' said Rose.

'Ivory?' Innocent was alert. 'That pig's tooth from the Indies?'

'Elephant tusk.'

'It's valuable,' said Innocent. He turned and glared at Annie. 'You little rat, where did you get this? Thieved it, did you, and didn't tell me? You ain't learned. I'll give you some of what I gave her.'

Annie braced herself, and her hand slid behind her back, scrabbling down on the settee pillows, where she had seen the scissors fall.

Innocent laughed, drunkenly, quite pleasantly. And he eased forward.

Rose said, 'No, Innocent. You mustn't.'

'Shut your row, you stupid whore. I ain't to be told.'

Rose stood up. She held on to the table, and then she let go of it, and she ran at Innocent from behind, half falling against him. She screamed with pain at the impact, and then, having begun, she continued to scream. Her hands flew up on to his head, and she started to rip out of it the coils of his fine reddish hair. Then *Innocent* screamed.

It was astonishing. To hear *him* shriek.

Both Annie and Rose were for a moment startled. And in that

moment, Innocent, howling, flung round on Rose, his fists raised up like terrible hammers.

Rose commenced to scream again and again her hands flew forward, upward, directly into Innocent's face.

Innocent's howls ascended into an atrocious squeal. And finally, at last, murmurs blew upward from the tower below, like outraged bats, the other tenants once more protesting—

But Annie did not hear them. She stared in disbelief as a spurt of scarlet ink rushed away from Innocent's head, from the face that was turned from her towards Rose. It rushed and struck the wall, the damp and mildewy wallpaper. So red.

He had dropped the ivory. It lay beside his stampeding feet. Annie could not go to get it. Stupidly, she picked up the scissors and held them like a dagger. She could stab him in the back, had better do so, before he got hold again of Rose – but somehow Annie could not take a step.

Then Innocent sprawled round. He was shrieking, swear words, shouts to God. He did not utter Rose's name nor any of the foulnesses he habitually called her. It was as if he had forgotten her. He dropped on his knees, gripping at his face. It seemed necessary that he do this, for his face was all undone, rags and tatters of flesh and red, red blood. As he struggled there with himself, and with forgotten Rose who was again tearing at him from behind, Annie caught a glimpse of something, quite wrong. It was Innocent's left eye, dangling by a thread like silk . . . out of its socket.

'Rose,' said Annie.

Rose lifted her head. She shook herself. Her face was white and pure and for an instant resembled Innocent's – as it had been. Then she turned back and snatched the bread knife from its station on the table.

'Blinded me—' screeched Innocent, crawling on the floor. And Annie saw his other eye was gone to a mass of rich ripe crimson tissue.

Then Rose cut him across the back, across the neck and shoulders with the knife.

Innocent's mouth bubbled silver and red and he fell ruined face down.

Rose stood away.

She dropped the knife.

Annie gazed as the blood ran out from under Innocent's body. Like rivers in sudden sunset . . .

And on the river, borne towards her, the shard of ivory floated, floated to her, to her feet. And there it stopped. In a daze she reached down and took it up, out of his blood. Its exquisite smoothness was unmarked, unstained.

Rose said, quietly, 'I've done it now. I've killed him. You see.'

'Yes,' said Annie. She recalled a street fight she and Rose had once passed, blood on the road, and Rose had become faint, but she, Annie, had felt only contempt, disgust.

But now Rose seemed only disgusted, and, as usual, very tired. She sat down on the chair, wincing.

'I think he's broken something in my side,' she said. And then, 'But it won't matter now.'

'He's dead,' said Annie.

'Yes, he's dead. If you cut the neck there, it kills. I think Mother must have learnt that from Father. She told me once. She was nursing you at her breast, and she told me that. You sucked up death with her milk.'

Annie dropped back on the settee. The room whirled and presently there was Rose, putting a cold cloth on her forehead. Rose had washed her hands, only her pink dress was all red, and drops of ruby were in her fair hair.

'Just rest,' said Rose. 'I'll walk down in a minute. Ask Gem's boy to go for a constable.'

'No,' said Annie, 'no, we must—'

'No must about it,' said Rose. She yawned, genteelly, behind her fingers. 'I've done a murder. I'll have to pay for it.'

'We could run away,' said Annie. She sat up although her head still swam. 'Go quickly, now.' The ivory was clenched in her hand.

'Go where? Where can we go? They'd catch us. Prison. That's my journey. And then—' Rose hesitated, surprised. She said in a sad humble voice, 'Oh, Annie. They'll hang me.'

3

Breakfast was brought in by the crippled girl. She set it down on the lace table-cloth. A dish of hot kippers, eggs in china coddlers, toasted bread and a slab of daffodil butter, green and tawny jams, the large tea-pot with its brew of leaves always fresh. The crippled girl had one leg in an iron, and a pinched leery little face. Annie thought, *Is that like me?* But she was not really interested. Not really concerned by the stunning food, though it shone before her. This irony was not lost. She would have done a great deal to get such a feast a few weeks back. To get such a feast, and share it with Rose.

The room was yellow, like the butter, as the room below was all leaden red. On a mantel fringed by a yellow shawl, a big black and gilt clock showed its round cold moon. It was twenty minutes to eight in the morning.

Annie looked at the clock. It had been only half past seven a minute ago. And when she entered the room . . . only seven. And as she had lain awake, and sometimes slept, it had been earlier. And last night – and last Tuesday – and before—

Annie checked her thoughts. It was no good. It was twenty to eight.

She remembered even so, as if it could not be helped, the crowded law court. Bad weather, it had rained. The sooty yards were full of water, and through the water the closed carriages came in like enormous black fish. Inside the building steam rose from the wet clothing of all the persons jumbled there, and a duller fainter mist rose from the gas lamps they had had to light. Ominous dark day for the trial of a foul murder.

It was odd, surely there was not an instant that could be forgotten, and yet she had indeed mislaid so much. Fragments were crystal clear – that man with the rolling voice who had called

Rose a Woman of the Alleys, with the sheep's fleece wig perched on his coal-black curls – a darling of the gallery and of the crowd, who frequently applauded him. And the judge, fat as some red vegetable, with a stupid clever face it was impossible you could believe had justice in it, although justice was his extraordinary name – Sir Montague Justice.

He sat listening, crouched there, vegetable toad, in his box above them all, God presiding.

'We have heard how this woman was beaten by her husband, my lord. But then it seems she often was in grievous error, and had earned it. What man, I say, would bear such infamy unmoved. Not merely an adulteress to his marital bed, but a common prostitute. Who sought, in turn, to lead her own sister into the same way.'

And Rose, far off, raised up also but only a little distance, miles beneath the throne of the vegetable toad god, Rose pale and still, not crying out. Meek Rose. And the meek shall inherit the earth. But oh, they did not.

No, it was the man with the voice and the curls, and it was Sir Montague Justice, these were the ones who had inherited. Power and confidence vaporized out of them, like the glim-lit vapours of the court rising from wet garments and lamps.

There had been a few who had spoken for Rose. She was hard-working. No, they did not believe she had solicited men. Yes, her husband thrashed her often. But then, men did smack their wives. What was a little correcting blow? Some women made a great deal of fuss about nothing. Some women, too, were virtuous, and did not earn chastisement. And a few against. Of Innocent's dear friends, not one could be found. The wife of the Badger had told the police she reckoned he was long dead. The Joyless Bugger had vanished under the scum.

Annie they did not convict of anything except idiocy. They thought her simple, easily led. But the constable related how he had found her on the settee, in a near-faint, her dress and hands unmarked by blood. Not guilty.

But this other one. 'She stands before you,' said the black-curled man whose name Annie had forgotten too, as one might try to forget the name of a horrible illness one had once suffered. 'You would think her nothing but a common street-walker, a fallen woman, nothing more. And yet, I tell you, just so the demon of the grisly tales of our childhood disguises itself. Strong and seasoned men blenched at what she had done. For she did not kill like a woman, who in desperation might seize some artifact and lash about herself. No, she killed her husband like a fiend from Hell itself.'

And the strong and seasoned men had described it. Innocent's body, his injured face and wrecked eyes, the effective cuts of the knife. And Rose, in her gown and jewelry of his blood, taking them quietly in to see.

There was another man in a robe, who spoke for Rose. His first case, the gallery whispered. But he related to Rose curiously. He said he would have to admit she had been a prostitute. He would have to allow them that she had committed murder in a particularly gruesome and unfeminine manner. He could only say that she had been driven to it by fear.

'Fear?' interposed the vegetable justice god, his toad face cranked forward. 'She feared him? It does not seem so. She was merciless.'

The witty curled man had questioned Annie. She could not recall how she had got up into the wooden place where she stood, only she had, and that he was there before her, glowing, as if all the lights of the city burned only upon him.

He said, 'Was your sister, Rose, good to you?'

'Yes,' she said.

'You love your sister,' he said.

'Yes,' said Annie. He seemed far off too, the whole court sailing out to sea, leaving her and leaving Rose, there in the dock.

'You would wish then to protect her?' he said.

Annie was silent.

He said, 'You would perhaps lie to protect her, although you are under oath before the eyes of God.'

'No,' said Annie.

'We shall see,' he said.

He asked her then to say what her sister had done. Annie said, 'He was beating her. He always hit her. All the time.'

'You say that he hit her all the time?'

'He did.'

'But your neighbours only recall one occasion when she had a bruise upon her face. And then she said her husband had accidentally put his elbow into her eye as he slept.'

'He hit her on the body,' said Annie. Her face grew hot with rushing feelings of incoherent helplessness. The witty man watched her so politely, patiently, attended so carefully. And he said too much. As always, when someone did this, she knew that she was being put to use. But she could not do other than she did.

'So, then, you say your brother-in-law frequently struck your sister. For how long had this gone on? Some weeks? Some months?'

'For years. Since their wedding,' said Annie.

'I think,' he said, kindly chiding her, 'you would then have been too young to judge if it began so soon.'

'She cried,' said Annie. 'I remember her crying.'

'And so he struck her and she wept. For years this happened. Why suddenly then did she find the will to turn on him and work against him this incredible act of violence? He could subdue her, you say, and did so. And yet, all at once, she is the stronger.'

'He meant to start on me.'

'You say so? And where did he strike *you*, this aggressive man?'

'He didn't strike me. She stopped him.'

The black-curled being came towards her, gently, as if not to alarm or dismay. He would have been called handsome, and up in the gallery there were women in silk gloves and plumed bonnets who had stuck their brilliant eyes upon him. But to Annie he was not handsome. He had no face at all, only a void from which issued out the voice of his genius.

'Let me suggest,' said this man to her, 'that you have been awfully shocked. Your sister, your only kindred in the world, has perpetrated a most hideous crime, before your eyes. And your brother-in-law, your only protector, is its victim. Can you say for sure what occurred?'

There was a little noise from the other one, the other robed man with the sheep-fleece on his hair, the one supposed to defend Rose. But probably no one took any notice of him. Probably not. For the question came again, in a slightly different form. Was she certain that she had seen Rose turn upon her husband in answer to his own assault.

'He hit her in the breast and kicked her in the side,' said Annie. Her voice had gone far away, like the courtroom. It did not matter what she said. There had been a doctor who had told them Rose's body was battered, and three of her ribs on the left side cracked. But it had come to be suggested one of her rougher clients had done this to her. That this very fact was what had alerted Innocent to her most recent transgression.

Why had she killed him? It was her natural villainy. For women were hysterical and uncontrolled, at the whim of their female humours. They might become wild beasts.

And men hunted down the wild beasts. How else could the earth be safe for them, and for those soft good women who obeyed them and looked to them for shelter and guidance?

Annie remembered how the black-curled man had suddenly turned from her, excluding her, and sweeping up with a graceful gesture of his arm all the rest of the court, including even pale silent Rose between her warders.

'This girl must be forgiven. Is she not little more than a child? We have heard she is a mild, diligent creature. And she is very ignorant. She does not, I venture to suggest, even fully understand the enormity of what she says, nor the weighty oath of truth she has sworn . . .'

And Annie had cried out: 'It isn't so! Rose – Rose—' like a fool, like the fool he had named her.

And the toad leaned down and glared at her, with all his power and greatness on him like a stench, and he told her sternly she might not speak and must be quiet.

Who had apparently spoken for her, for Annie herself, Annie did not know at first. But afterwards, she found that one of the women from the shop of Mrs Marpolis had done so. Which was peculiar, for this woman did not know her, to say anything.

Days went by, and more than days. It seemed for ever she was there in the courtroom. Even until the weather altered, and the steam ceased to rise and the gas was put out, and cold shafts of heartless, bloodless sunlight seared through the high-up windows.

She saw the jurors then, perhaps for the first, because the sun lighted them like a painting. But their faces were all one face, in various adornments of beard and pockmarks, spectacles and runny nose. When they looked on the wonderful man with the curls, it was as if they applauded a mighty actor, and when they raised their gazes to Sir Montague Justice, they recognized the reflection of God.

And when they looked at Rose, if they dared to, they shivered. They made mouths, as if they sucked lemons.

Somewhere down below, in a room of stone, Annie had seen Rose partly alone. They had not really said anything, beyond a few words of greeting and farewell. There was nothing to be said. But then finally Rose did say, 'It's all right, Annie. I'm resigned to it now. They've looked after me. They bandaged me and the doctor was kind. Even the others give me food to eat. I've eaten things here I haven't had for a long time. Even butter, once. I don't know where it came from.'

Annie said, 'What shall I do?' And in that question knew at last the measure of the depth to which she had sunk. For not in six years had she ever asked her sister what should be done in life, for Annie had known that Rose, poor Rose, could not tell her.

'Just be a good girl. Mrs Marpolis will help you. She sent Lucy, and Lucy promised me. She'll find you a place. That will be lovely. A nice house where you'll be warm and get enough to eat.'

Annie did not feel any importance in this, as she did not feel grief or loss. She felt a gnawing itching tearing thing, at the base of her soul. She put her hand into her pocket, and touched the ivory shard that had floated on Innocent's blood. It was nothing and it meant nothing. But she touched it.

And Rose, her sister, they did not permit her to touch. But then, the two of them had not embraced, not kissed, for years. They held hands only over the Yesyes board.

The last day came. Of course there must be a last day. The mighty actor made a speech about the fiend who was Rose. He mentioned a play in the Greek language, where madwomen had torn a king in pieces when they were drunk, and added that at least they had had strong liquor as their excuse. And probably the other one said something but Annie did not recollect. Then the vegetable god, the red toad, inclined his majesty to the jurors on their benches in the sunlight, and they gaped up at him as if before an altar. He then said clearly something the actor had not, that the eyes of victims were rumoured to imprint the image of their murderers, but that Rose had ripped out her husband's eyes. Sir Montague Justice said that never in his years of authority had he been forced to oversee such a case. He said that only God could purify such sin. Such ghastliness.

And miles away, Rose was, in a sort of upright coffin of shadow.

There was a coming and going. Perhaps an hour passed.

And then all was as before, and the jurors uttered.

The judge donned the shadow, and he in turn spoke to Rose. He told her she would be taken elsewhere, and that once there, she would be hanged by the neck until dead. He invoked God's mercy.

And Rose was drawn away, away and away, until she was only a tiny vanishing speck of pallor, that winked out like a spark.

The woman called Lucy took Annie's arm and led her from the court. Annie went in quiet, not speaking, as they had instructed her she must not. She would have liked to fill the space with raging shrieks, but she knew that if she screamed more loudly than a trumpet's blast, they had told her to be quiet and would not hear.

Besides, Rose had put it to her once. Rose had said, in the after-midnight room with blood on the walls and floor, *They'll hang me, Annie*. And all this had only been some insane flounce tied to that single absolute. A show that had no meaning. Sound and fury. And now it was done.

Almost, almost done.

Annie glanced up. The clock on the mantel said ten minutes to eight.

In the apartments of Mrs Marpolis, above her shop of dolls and masks, breakfast was always served for eight, and today no change. Mrs Marpolis had said to Annie, when first Lucy brought her in, 'You are a sensible girl. Be brave now. You do it?'

'Yes,' said Annie.

'They are fools,' said Mrs Marpolis. 'She stand no chance with them. And that fellow with his curls—' but Mrs Marpolis said no more of him. 'You stay with me a while. I place you. I am give you better luck.'

And now it was five to eight.

The yellow door blew open and in came Mrs Marpolis on her runners, in her black silk and jewelled fingers.

She stared at Annie, and then she raised her glittery hands.

'Hark,' said Mrs Marpolis.

Annie's head darted up. Her heart sprang into her gullet. She stood, and in her ears she heard the city bells sounding, the bells that sounded in these high streets, for eight o'clock.

They waited, and the chimes rang out, one and two and three, four and five and six. And seven. And eight. And then the silence fell, thick as a blanket, down, and down.

Mrs Marpolis' hand flashed fires as it crossed her bosom for the Trinity of love and forgiveness.

'It is over,' she said.

But nothing is ever over. Nothing is ever gone. And in her mind, which had no notion how it must have been, Annie beheld her sister falling like a flower from the chain of time, falling on and on, now and tomorrow, world without end.

Mrs Marpolis sat, and dished a kipper on to a pale china plate.

'You will be brave,' she said. 'Eat. We survive.'

And Annie took the plate, and with her knife and fork severed a piece of the coppery fish, and put it in her mouth.

As she tasted it, the clock on the mantel also uncannily chimed. It was always a little late; she had forgotten this too. But it did not matter. For again and always Rose fell through the dark. Annie ate the kipper, and watched how Rose fell on and on.

Part Two

1

It was a journey. She was going away: the imp had been right. And for Innocent too, and for Rose. But they went in different directions. Innocent to Hell, and Rose . . . into the dark. And she, Annie Ember, where was she going so fast, carried by the great wheels and the hoofs of the horses – where?

At first she could not see out. She was in the middle of the other passengers, squashed down like a parcel. A big woman with a basket on her lap, and several large men in smothering coats. The coach filled with pipe smoke and breath, and the windows offered only glimpses, the smutty walls of the city, its distant white buildings, an onion dome above a silver stretch of river as unlike the river by Tooth Street as day to night. But the city fell aside, and long lines of red brick houses were there, their chimneys smoking, and parks held in by walls of privet. These too were whirled away.

Annie stared much of the time, besides, at her own feet, clad in stiff new boots. She had been dressed in a plain flat fashion, her hair washed with green soap, plaited and put up neatly into a new drab little hat. She was to change her ways, and her clothes were the forecast. She was respectable now. Aloft, her small tin box, secured by string, contained surplus underwear, handkerchiefs, a brush and comb, curious items that did not seem truly to belong to her. On her knees her own basket held the pot of geraniums from Augusta House. She had taken these up the evening Lucy conducted her to the shop. While in Annie's purse, with four shillings shiny from novelty, there was the other thing. She did not know why she had kept it. Probably Mrs Marpolis, so generous and insistent, would have purchased a piece of ivory gladly. Maybe a guinea would then have been added to the shillings. What was ivory worth? But Annie had not offered it to Mrs Marpolis, the shard of murder and shadow. She had picked it out of Innocent's blood, and the blood had not dyed her hand. It was as if the ivory had instead washed her clean. Dreadfully, emptily clean, like a blank slate.

Annie Ember did not think of that as the coach plunged away along the road from the city, out into the unknown country beyond. Annie had become generally practised. She had closed a door inside her brain. Behind it – there the shadow continued. But she did not even dream of Rose, Rose in her hat of flowers. Rose who was falling. No, it went on, but there was no need to see.

Annie saw her feet and the new boots.

That was all.

And she heard the rumble of the coach, and sounds flew in, the roars of the city, presently the notes of the world beyond.

Greenish sunlight patterned on the windows, just visible through the cloud of human fog.

The big woman began to dip into her basket. She took out pieces of buttered bread and a strip of meat. Later she took out an apple, and later again a cake. These she fed to herself as if inserting material into some automatic contrivance that pulverized matter.

The men slept and snored, and next the woman slept in gusty troughs of breathing.

In the evening the light slanted and turned to thin bronze. The coach stopped, and they were decanted at an inn.

As the violet afterglow eclipsed the sunset, Annie stood before a timbered rickety building, which seemed to have been erected in the middle of a park, but this was the country. All around the trees were set, like flickering golden nets. Whispers passed through them and high up the birds flighted and sang. Then the veil of luminous mauve shade swam down through this foliage of leaves and wings, and a vast unearthly darkness filled and swelled the trees, as though they had become some other amalgamated creature.

Annie lay in a tiny creaking room, sharing the bed with the big woman, whose heat inflamed the mattress, sheets and pillows. A bird sang in the night, too, for a little while. It turned Annie towards sadness for a moment, and then she did not listen any more. When she fitfully slept she dreamed of the trees fading and swelling, metamorphosing in the dusk.

The next day they were off soon after dawn and a breakfast of greasy ham, swarthy bread, and tea. However, as the morning passed, all the men left the coach, and eventually the woman, too, who had till then gone on producing from her basket cakes and bread and butter and apples, devouring them slowly and thoughtlessly, her eyes round as two marbles.

Alone in the coach, Annie sat beside a window and gazed out. She felt that she must. She had learned to look at things carefully; just so she had studied the alien evening trees.

So she beheld for the first time in her life wide fields with only the hint of growth on them, and arching vines and shallow stands of unborn hops, and whole spooned valleys of fruit trees powdered by blossom, as if a million butterflies had settled there. And the woods furled over like tents, the celadon green shimmer, the green umbra that was a dark vein, quivers of light pierced through like arrows.

It was beautiful. But it had come too tardily. She inertly saw it was not like a city. It had other rules, unusual traps and disguises.

A lightning of blue – some vibrant bird had dived above the carriage. A young fox was playing on the verge – she thought it a wolf, although wolves were seldom seen now. Rabbits whipped through the bushes. Other rules. Other disguises.

And it was too much. She dropped asleep at last. Only an hour after, the coach stopped.

'There's your road. I'm to put you off here.'

Annie got out of the coach, her basket in her hand. The tin box stood against the grass and wild flowers. The coachman pointed. 'Two miles. You'll come to it.'

He left her, and the iron-footed horses, of whom she had been exceedingly cautious, galloped away.

Mrs Marpolis had told her, it was a big house in the country. Out of the city, where she might now be known, tarnished with death and law.

Hers was to be an excellent employment. Hard work, oh yes, but Annie had always, Mrs Marpolis knew, been accustomed to that. And here there was security, and the hope of advancement.

She found girls for these houses, these rich and out of the way domains. They must be young women of sound character, and tough, strong young women, sensible. Mrs Marpolis trusted that Annie appreciated this chance, and would embrace it readily.

Like an open door at an alley's blind end, where else was there to go? And what was there to lose?

Annie did not care.

Something in her said, *Yes, get away. Leave it behind.* But *that* would go with her. So she thought, *It's easy*. You did what was easy as opposed to what was awkward, since so much was unwieldy, comfortless, awful. If it was easy, you obliged.

And then the new clothes came, which Annie hated, but put on. And the shiny shillings she could not believe she would ever spend.

'You must work, and have no credit. One day you are repay me all I give.'

Annie nodded. She did not think Mrs Marpolis expected repayment. She was paid anyway, presumably, by those who sought their servants through her.

'And your speech is well,' said Mrs Marpolis. 'And your sewing very fine. I tell them, you can make lace like your sister.'

'I can't,' said Annie.

'So, you can do other things.'

Her task was to be, primarily, that of a scullery maid, and Annie had seen in the city the sort of work this entailed, back-breaking and ceaseless. But so all work was. What odds? Rose would have been pleased. Rose would have liked the plan, Annie in the country, the green woods and fresh air.

Close the brain's barrier upon Rose.

The road curved nonchalantly, and once the carriage and its snorting clattering horses had gone, no other traffic moved on it but for Annie and the bees crossing to the clover.

Massive trees lined the roadside. By day they were steeped in shifting mists of green, and the arrows of light lay still now like spangles on the ground. Through gaps in the trees, Annie saw the hills. The day was warm, and the smell of country musks, liquors, moulds and fruitings hung about her, sometimes making her sneeze, making her certainly wary, for all the clues had altered. No soot, no sewage. None of the hostage air of the city.

Her box was not heavy. She held it by its string, and the basket of geraniums. She did not know why she had brought these. Suppose she did not go the way the man had said, but wandered off into the green, among the clover and bluebells under the trees? But that was the jungle. She would not leave the path. She was not a fool, even if monsters, thinking her one, had spared her life.

The gate appeared up a lane which led off suddenly from the road.

You could not miss the gateway.

It was of arched white stone, and on its top was a pillared, domed crown-like architecture. The gate itself was of iron in the form of lily flowers and birds with fanning tails.

Annie got off the road and went along the lane to the gate. She looked through it. A hillside in a sheath of lime turf went flowing up into a forest of woven boughs. A drive cut through from the gate, and the trees came down a little further on, to droop above it, as if lazily inquisitive.

A strange house was inside the gate. It was of one storey only, and several doors of it gave upon a verandah that ran its length. It was not an English house. In a field behind, a solitary brown and white cow stood, thoughtfully grazing.

A woman was stationed in one of the doorways, gazing hard at Annie.

'Ember?' said the woman. She was dressed in a charmless flat dress like Annie's own, her slavish hair piled up. She had the general look of an enemy.

'Yes,' said Annie.

The woman called, 'Gate! Gate!'

A fat dirty boy, like a city boy but for the colour in his face, came running from the side of the house. He pelted to the gate, and undid a section of it, just wide enough for a single person to pass through.

'Take her up to the house, like you were told,' said the woman on the verandah. The boy gawped at Annie, and, his back to the woman, shot out a predator's red tongue.

'You come uv me,' said the boy.

Annie went through the gate, and the boy locked it up again. He pocketed the key importantly. He was nine or ten years old, with apple-blossom cheeks and beastly little eyes.

'Go with Sebby,' said the woman. 'You shouldn't have come to the big gate, but I knew you would. Take her over the hill, Sebby,' she added. 'And watch out for the hunt.'

'I us watching for it, Mother,' said the boy. He had seemingly lost interest in Annie, she was only a chore now.

He trotted off the drive away from the bungalow-house, and up the hill towards the trees.

Annie went after him. As she stepped on to the lime grass, the woman called harshly, 'What have you brought geraniums for? Are you mad?'

But Annie pretended she had not heard.

The beastly boy had now gone up among the trunks, he was chugging along, looking back to see how she flagged, but Annie did not flag.

On the slope's brow, she glanced back again, but the woman had gone in.

'You from the city?' asked Sebby, rudely.

'Yes,' said Annie.

'They us stupid there.' He danced over and abruptly slapped his podgy hand on to her bottom. As he pranced about her to see what she did, Annie spat into his eye.

Sebby fell down and rolled about, rubbing his face.

Somewhere in her brain, something – but Annie had shut the door.

Presently Sebby got up.

'Won't you let me?' said Sebby. 'If you let me look up your skirt, I'll give you a pound.'

'No,' said Annie.

Sebby shrugged. He walked now, out of breath. 'What's your name?'

Annie said nothing.

Sebby said, 'You're Ember. Missus says you us.'

'Then I must be.'

'Missus us quick,' said Sebby. 'She had me. But I split her. There.'

The trees broke wide, and a colossal vista spread like a painted wing. It made Annie giddy, momentarily frightened, and she stopped in her tracks.

Sebby stopped too, his hands in his pockets. He was not ragged, but she barely saw him for a minute.

The green swept away into blue-green and so into blue. It was only distance, yet it was magical, seen in this way. The land fell, through oaks and pines, chestnuts and birches, and somewhere there amid the trees a wide runnel of water sparkled. Beyond, was a valley. And in the valley something spangled like the river, but it was scarlet and gold, white and silver, and behind it the green-blushed blueness of other hills rose entire into the young blue sky.

'The big house,' said Sebby. ''Tis a funny old pile. Like in a picture book.' Then Sebby seemed to extend forward, all his upper torso on a spring. 'Look! Us they. 'Tis the hunt.'

And over the vista, between the wash of green and the wash of green-blue, threading the trees, Annie could make out a line of brown and bloody red. Men on horses, flying forward.

'They found,' said Sebby. 'But you us stupid. You don't know. They hunt them foxes, they do. They catch un and rip 'em up. They gave Mother the ears, once. The bugger us in her garden.'

Annie did not know what he spoke of, only that he spoke of death. She heard dogs barking and baying now, and realized that the forefront of the brown stream was a flood of hounds. But she had heard of this – the hunting of wild beasts.

'Goo-on!' yelled Sebby, pummelling the air. 'Catch the bugger.'

Annie wanted to slap the horrid child across the head, but knew she must not. Like the fox – had it been a fox and not a wolf she had seen at the roadside? – she must try to survive.

'Ladies like fox coats,' said Sebby. He turned as the hunt of death melted into the woods, with a vague echo of broken stems and branches, a faint mad cry. Sebby winked. 'Not very toothsome, us you?'

'No,' said Annie, 'and I'm spiteful too.'

Sebby looked intrigued, but then reconsidered.

'Come on, you're slow.'

He went part tumbling and half running down the hill, and Annie again followed.

The green wine of the air swilled off, and the trees repeated their shade, to obscure the way.

They crossed the damp river at a shallow juncture, by a humping railed bridge. Ferns rose round it, and at its further end, a mossy carven stone lifted high up, seven feet or more.

'Know what that us?' asked Sebby. He winked again. ''Tis a *thing*. A governor's tassel.'

Annie spared no special look. She had seen the male penis, here and there. This stone did not remind her of it.

Under the hill was a low wall, and in it a second ornate gate, made in a pattern rather than an image of birds and flowers. They went through, and trod, Sebby to his shoulder and she waist-high, through grass, buttercups and other wild flowers, over the roots of trees. The ground dipped and then lifted. And there before them was the big house, from the picture book. Mrs Marpolis had not told her anything.

Annie ceased moving, and put down her box.

She stood, and once more Sebby stood too, perhaps willing to allow her scope for doltish bewilderment. Proud yet mocking, he said, 'You've never seen the like. Sir Hampton Smolte's house. It us the talk of the county, Missus says. I usn't born when he did it. Nor was you.'

Somewhere, deep in Annie's mind, the wisp of a voice said to her, *Like a raja's palace*. But it was the voice of the dead, and until now Annie had never known what the phrase could mean.

The house rose out of a cultured wilderness of gardens, where lumps of bronze and marble gleamed and blazed, and points of burning white and red. The building of the house itself was long, and low, of two storeys only in parts, and elsewhere of one storey alone. Its flanks had a creamy texture, but this then was fronted over by a sort of complex pastry-work of deep scarlet fretted with lavender, and pure ripe incredible gold. Where there was a roof, it too was coloured, red or plum, and along the house-face ran stripes of tall windows held in pillared scarlet arches. Even the glass was caged in lacquered screening. Above rose domes like white icing sugar, encrusted by red and mauve sugar embroideries. While at apparently random intervals slender stalks of masonry had pushed up like weeds, with gilded turrets of smoke blue and indigo.

'There,' said Sebby. He squinnied at her thoughtfully. 'From the Great Hinde,' said Sebby. ''Tis meant to look.'

'India,' Annie said, but without sound.

And, 'Like a rajee's palace,' concluded Sebby, mimicking the phantom voice that had brushed inside Annie's skull.

Then, her allowance of wonder used up, Sebby waddled away,

and so she must go after, skirting the banks and terraces of gardens, treading down a pleached path, into a tunnel of yew trees, through the dense mounds of which the mosaic of the house still flamed on the right hand, but drawing away as they descended farther into the valley.

Presently they passed into a swept yard, where astonishingly a huge bronze spoked wheel stood on a plinth, a bronze being caught inside it, many-armed.

'There's the stable,' said Sebby. 'And down there us your kitchen quarters. I us off now.' He raised his face. 'Give me a kiss.'

'Go away or I'll bite you.'

A complaisant expression of belief crossed Sebby's features. He broke into his bumbling run at once, and was gone.

Annie put down her box yet again, and paused for a few minutes in the midst of that large plain yard, under the wheeled shade of the unknown god. In his fists he held discs and blades, bows and rays. He was terrible, and shining, and his shadow black as night.

Over the yard wall she noted what must be the stable buildings, also long and low, and white, but with rose-red domes and a gilt clock high up inside the face of a golden sun.

She heard no noise but the throb of bees and the sing-song of grasshoppers in the park. She shut her eyes. And when she opened them it seemed to her she had entered another world, and now she knew it. There was no need or will to move. But she must.

When she left the yard, she found a brown-walled garden and glasshouses, and so another corridor between thick yew hedges. At the end of this she almost stumbled on another boy, but thin and angular, sitting like a spider in the hedge. He leapt up and scrambled away at once. She had seen no one else, but now a high female discord shrilled in her ears.

As Annie emerged from the hedge walk, she came on to a paved space. Another portion of the palace was here, but less fantastic, its lattices more sullen and clotted, and only one token russet dome above like a burnt strawberry.

Two girls in the livery of servants, dull stuff dresses and bibbed aprons, were shaking a beast of orange velvet, shaking it fearlessly, despite its claws and the snarling head so packed with teeth. Cinnamon dust blew from its striped pelt. A tiger-skin, dead and helpless in their clutch. They laughed as they smacked it.

Then their heads swivelled and they saw Annie.

They let the tigerskin droop.

There was no welcome, rather they seemed to detest her on sight, as if she was more work for them to do.

And the tiger lolled its mask and looked at her over its shoulder too, in the aura of cinnamon motes, with cold glass eyes.

The housekeeper's room was not oriental, nor picturesque. She sat in her horsehair armchair before the black-leaded fireplace, on the mantel of which stood little pictures of people, perhaps old friends and lost family, perhaps nostalgic, but seeming menacing, an army of demons she might call to her aid.

'Well, Ember, you look a sight, and no mistake. You must be tidier here.'

Mrs Beare was a bony woman in iron stays, her waist nipped so tight she might be liable to snap, her heavy face conversely too big for the rest of her. She wore a dark silk dress and her eyes were a little crossed, which made her only the more ominous.

She had told Annie that Clarrie, the kitchen maid, would instruct in forthcoming duties. Annie must be obedient to Mrs Rope, the cook. The master's male cook she was to avoid. He would not require her services.

'You can go now to your room, which Tiff will show you. Make yourself presentable, since this afternoon Madam wishes to see you. We understand you are able to do fine sewing.' Annie waited. 'Well, you may speak.'

'I can sew,' said Annie.

Mrs Beare raised her thin, chewed-looking eyebrows, and one eye bored into Annie while the other waited patiently alone.

'Madam will decide. You know who I mean? Sir Hampton's wife, Lady Flower. I will say, girl, it's unusual, but you have a chance here of improving yourself, and your station. Work, work is the key. The Smolte house is a big house. We have only two pairs of house maids and they're never idle. Below stairs you'll be busy. Tiff is a good three years younger than you, and she's been with us three years. You must take your lead from her. Mrs Rope is your superior and you will respect her. If you are in any problem, you may come to me.'

When Mrs Beare said this, her entire face compressed itself, so that everything, even the cross-eyes, slipped inwards like sea creatures into a pool to hide.

Annie nodded.

'No,' said Mrs Beare, 'you must drop a bob. Do you know how?'

Annie curtseyed. She had seen others do it, in the porticoes of rich houses, and once or twice on the stage, when she was very young, before Rose married.

'Yes, that's good enough. It's a courtesy you accord to me, and to your mistress, Lady Flower. Now, hurry along.'

In the next room, up in the attic, Annie was to sleep in a bed narrow as a pen, and beside her, in the two other pens, Tiff and Clarrie. Otherwise there were a wash-stand and a jug, a cupboard, a tiny window which looked out upon an angle of another wall the colour of biscuit, with a long greened pipe run down it, but on the upper edge of roof, the glimpse of a cake of dome, cream and crimson, played over by goldenness . . . And then the country sky, spring blue, with its dapple of tender clouds.

'Did you sleep in a bed before, you?' asked Tiff.

Annie took no notice.

Tiff pinched her arm and turning, Annie slapped Tiff's cheek.

Tiff darted away.

'You're handy.'

Annie stood by her unpacked box, and geranium basket.

Tiff said, 'You can't keep your old box here. It'll be stored in with the lumber. They uv got some things in this house, I can tell you. Are you eighteen? I'm twelve, see. I been in this position since I was nine. What do you think of the house? They don't believe it in the village. Lest they've seen it. I wish I us an upstairs. I'd get to clean the metal things. And the rooms up there. 'Tis called the palace. The master us a sir. He us a hero in India. Do you know what India is, you?'

'Yes,' said Annie.

Tiff was small, and reptilian, made lean and maybe stunted by her sixteen or seventeen hours of work a day. She spoke curiously, half as Sebby had, and half in a strained wincing way.

As she left the room, she kicked Annie on the shin and flipped herself aside. 'Too quick for you then.'

Annie washed in the cold three inches of water the jug contained, and put on her prize, the dull grey dress of the house and its crackle-starched apron. Her hair she rebraided tightly – unbound, it fell sheer to her knees. Perhaps she should cut some of it off, now she must be so tidy. But Rose had always said her hair was good. For Rose, then, not yet. She put on the silly cap like a doily, and looking at herself in the small round mirror, Annie cackled with pure scorn.

But she had never slept in a bed, before the shop of Mrs Marpolis, and the inn, and this bed was her bed, even if it was so narrow.

She must be careful not to fall out on the floor. Tiff might spring at her throat . . .

And finally, away from the first rooms, and the large kitchen with its lit black engines and copper implements, the staring moulds of fish and ducks, the long scrubbed tables, and fat furious Mrs Rope, drinking her yellow beer and cursing among the mounds of chopped spinach.

Up, up, a brown and horrible back stair smelling of bad soap, and rats – something like the city after all, but not exactly.

And then prim Clarrie pushing open a mean little door. And saying like all of the others, these emissaries in chaos, 'Go along there.'

So Annie went, and after a passageway with one window that gave, also, on a wall, she found another door, of black smooth oak, and opening it, there was Mrs Beare, out, as Clarrie had said, of 'the old Beare's Den'. And Mrs Beare said, 'Yes. Straighten your cap, Ember.' And led her forth into – the house.

There was a carpet. It was green, woven with flowers and birds . . . And on the wall a green paper, and there a goddess, a four-foot goddess standing on a lily. And she was gold—

'Don't dawdle, Ember.'

And a latticed window like a shell of light.

And a door with gold beasts on the panels.

Mrs Beare knocked harshly. Her appalling tortured little waist quivered.

'Yes?' called a voice.

Annie listened. She thought, *The city*. For the voice was properly a rich lady's voice, yet it was the city's voice, too.

And then the door gave, and they went, Annie last, into a pale and blooming room, with two columns up which two plants of green lacquer curled, and with a sofa between them like a heap of rose-petals.

The mistress of the house was sitting there. She glanced up.

Lady Flower was fat – or voluptuous, and possibly both. Her face sat on a neck, and on a chin, but there it was, pretty, and like corked perfume, still sweet but past its beginning. A cloud of ginger hair billowed from her scalp, kept prisoner with ebony combs. Earrings of polished green rain dropped out of the cloud.

All about the white wallpaper, painted with pink birds in bushes of vast fronds, bamboo and orchid, held her in its nest. There were too many pictures, and a heap of books lay on a table, of which Annie saw a title: *Her Secret Revealed.*

What was the secret of Lady Flower, for she had one, who did not? Was it only the secret of her filigree youth now floundered in a pie of flesh.

'Well?' said Lady Flower.

'Madam. This is the girl, Ember.'

'Ember? What kind of name is that, for God's sake?'

The fat hand surged into the air. A ruby and a diamond ignited.

Then the eyes of Lady Flower passed over Annie's. Wan scorched blue. Oh, they had seen great heat and light. They had stared long distances. Her face was shrewd, but her eyes – no, the eyes were shrewd too, once they had focused.

'She can sew, isn't that it?'

'Yes, Madam.'

'And can you, girl?'

'Yes, Madam,' reiterated Annie.

'Ho. Well, I must see some of your work. Do you know any verse? Can you read?'

'Yes, Madam.'

Lady Flower gestured to the book, *Her Secret Revealed.*

'Take this. Read me a piece. Where you like.'

Annie raised the book. She opened it at its gaudy silk marker, and now so near, she smelled spice upon her mistress. Perfume not stale but only strange.

'"He entered the room in trepidation,"' Annie read, '"and finding her at the piano, her fair delicate arms decked with pearls, he was struck once more, and freshly, by her charms. Could this woman be his wife?"'

'Enough,' said Lady Flower. 'You read poorly. But you speak very well. Where were you schooled?'

'By my sister.'

'Ah. Well. We shall have to see.' There was no betrayal of anything. Did this woman know what had become of Rose? Surely . . . 'My daughter may sometimes want you. She's a fastidious girl,' said Lady Flower, her lips growing solid and stiff. She picked up the book from where Annie had replaced it. 'Ember,' she said. 'Whose fire went out?' And she laughed coarsely like a man in drink.

Annie felt a wash of hatred lash through her. It was comforting, familiar.

Pandemonium reigned in the kitchen all afternoon, with the creation of dinner. It was a furnace of heat, and this was spring, summer not yet come.

The evening meal tonight would be served at six, instead of eight, for the master of the palace was off on business in the town, and would dine at his club there.

'No filthy stinks tonight,' said Mrs Rope, as she went about the line of pans, and peered and poked.

'She means those curries,' said Tiff to Annie, scissoring with a sharp elbow.

The curry kitchen, it seemed, was out across a courtyard, in the Indian way, and a good thing too, for even so the smells ran in and soured the air, making the maids nauseous and Mrs Rope doubly infuriated.

'Good English food,' growled Mrs Rope, stirring a cauldron with a muscular wooden spoon.

Clarrie and the vegetable maid chopped herbs and rubbed the spinach through a mechanism with a handle. The vegetable maid had also tied up a bunch of greens with string from a canister, and put them in a steamer.

Tiff scurried up and down, fetching this, wiping that, and Annie had been cast into the scullery, where, plunged to her upper arms in the deep stone sink, she washed the endless crocks.

'You'll be at that until midnight,' opined Tiff.

There had been a lunch or dinner of cold meat and pease

pudding. In the afternoon came a tea with a resonant black cake off which Tiff and Annie were served the tiniest wafer. There was a steward, who took his meals with Mrs Beare in the Beare's Den, but the upstairs maids appeared, and a footman called Pocks, and a gardener covered in earth manifested and was sent off to wash by the enraged Mrs Rope.

The maids chattered and were constantly shushed. They all four cast at Annie unkind glances, as the first two of them had already done over their tigerskin. They were not, it seemed, supposed to speak at meals. No one was save for Mrs Rope, the gardener, and the silver maid, which beautifully named soul was a sturdy woman of Mrs Rope's age, in charge of the china and service of the family table. Nevertheless talk went on in spasms.

Countless others of the household were mentioned, although not present. The cook of the curries, Rawlings, was spurned, the gardener's boys, who ate in the yard, castigated, and Lady Flower's personal maid obscurely reviled, with sidelong eyings of Annie, to see if she were uneasy or impressed.

But Annie was only tired out, tired in a way she had never been before, by the intense kitchen-heated country air, the herd of new and opposed faces, and the journey that had preceded her tasks. She supposed she would get used to it all. She would have to. She felt no insecurity, for her world had always been unsafe. Here, presumably, it was actually to be more benign, although she doubted it. 'Annie would be careful of Paradise,' said Rose.

She did not, of course, once think of Rose in any deep or wounding way, even when Tiff said to her, 'Any sisters or brothers, you?' Annie said only, 'No.' And before the tea was done, Tiff had spilt boiling liquid on Annie's hand, only a sprinkle, but Mrs Rope roared and Tiff was banished to clean the larder floor.

Beyond tea, Mrs Rope, engorged with cake and tannin, took over the gale force of dinner. She did so with a frightful anger, cooking into her roasts and pastries a tirade of maleficence. She did not swear – she had the same foolishly enunciating voice Tiff tried to adopt, and more successfully – but she called her crew by everything short of obscenities. They were kites, pigs, cursed, motherless heathens, and lug-lollocks – which, it turned out, meant half-wits. The vegetable maid broke down in tears at length at having her spinach vilely criticized, and Mrs Rope, spinning like a brawny top, flung a wet dish cloth Tiff had just brought in, straight into the crying maid's face.

Annie washed the pans and more pans were brought her.

In the intervals of shouting, Tiff could be heard whistling under the slabs of butter and round brown eggs in the larder. It was cool there.

The pans bubbled and the vegetable maid snivelled quietly.

There was a worm in the potatoes. Mrs Rope spoke ill of the gardener.

As the light condensed, oil lamps were lit, the heat grew, and when the dinner hour came close, the noise, clatter and activity increased to panic. Mrs Rope called God's angels to witness that she was beset by she-hounds with slop for brains. The maids raced. A dish was smashed, and Annie dragged over from the scullery by Clarrie to sweep it up.

On the kitchen table then, she viewed by lamplight the mound of hot and cold food that was now in waiting, and it almost made her crow, as she had done at the sight of herself in her uniform.

The ice-pail was inspected last, and a satin ice cream drawn out and tried by Mrs Rope. She thumped down at the table and called for a flagon of beer.

'It's done,' she said. On her sweating face was a grimace of victory.

Annie beheld next two maids flying along with the dishes on a trolley, along the wide corridor which led back to the house. The corridor was glassed in with windows on each side, and the lattice-broken panes of westered gilt flushed over the women as they ran, and over the food. They would give it up at an inner door to the footman and the silver maid, and the overseership of the steward and his assistant.

A silver soup-tureen, a silver dish of pickled things, toast on salvers, tumblers of butter, a fish like a nacreous leaf—

Mrs Rope gestured at the oven.

'See to that before it burns.'

Clarrie bent to a pit of fire.

'Ember,' said Mrs Rope, 'fetch more beer.'

2

The dining room of the Smolte palace was on the ground floor, and ran on its west side into the orangery. It was a scarlet room, with rounded red pillars, ringed, like the arms of giant maidens, with silver and gold bands. On the ceiling was a painted sky, not English, a dull, swart blue, fringed by the tops of painted dark green palms. And on the walls fearsome heads seemed pushed in through holes, the muzzles of bears and horned deer, and under these other things in glass cases, striped jackals, mounted wolves, a hooded cobra coiled about a stone. On the floor were the skins of tigers and black panthers spread out in pools of fur that shimmered and smouldered in the half-light.

The candlelit dining table, which could seat twenty-four, and now sat four, was isolated in the middle of this sea of sunset shadows and dead beasts. On the table were spread three coal-red Indian carpets, and on these the Smolte china lay, a service brought back in a crate, like so much else. Over the white ground, edged in gold, tea-coloured rajas hunted and moon-skinned damsels played amid the flowers.

At the window darkness had begun to blush, coming in over the English park and changing it, but to what? One window was ajar . . .

The table burned up brighter, but it was mostly silent.

Two women and two men, the closest of kin, the silver utensils shining in their hands and the gold-stemmed goblets of claret crystal.

Someone spoke.

'By God, what drink is this?'

The steward moved from the mahogany sideboard where, between dim gilded images, the food and drink were spread.

'It's the red Sir Hampton recommended, Mr Rupert.'

'It's muddy. Go and fetch something else.'

The steward, Churton, straightened. He was a big barrel of a man with a small head – a curious reverse of the housekeeper, Mrs Beare. He seemed immovable, and the younger man at the table guffawed loudly.

'Ma, *you'd* better tell him to go.'

Lady Flower, who in her youth had gone by the name of Flower Bell, frowned.

'Don't call me Ma, you cheeky wretch.' Something in her voice when she said this – Annie could have classed it once again: the city. The lower city at that. Then to Churton, Flower Bell Smolte said in her lady-voice, 'You'd better do as my son says, Churton. Don't make a fuss. Mr Rupert must have what he wants.'

Churton bowed, and putting away the despised decanter, he crossed the room, through waves of fur and the snarling watchful paralysis of jackals.

'Something with flavour,' added Rupert. He sat back and put his head down on his hand. 'For God's sake, can't I even have a glass of wine without a scene?'

'Now, Rupert,' said Flower, Smolte's wife. 'Be nice.'

The younger son snorted again. 'Vain wish, Mama.'

He was ginger-haired, like his mother, and stocky, fleshy, as she was, and, even at her verdant start, had been. He had her mouth, which was too full for him, and her nose, which was too small for him, but her eyes, which were wide and blue, he had missed. Urquhart Smolte had the eyes of a porker.

Flower's other son did not have any look of her. He was dark-haired and very pale, slim and graceful; his well-shaped hands had none of the bluff scars – riding, hunting – of his brother's. As he sat with eyes downcast, the faint air of lassitude about him was not unattractive. He was handsome, his features good, his lashes longer and blacker than Flower's had ever been, even after applications of burnt cork.

Flower looked at Rupert. His health was uncertain. The blame for that was in the past, like so much else. He must be given in to. Damn that bloody butler. She did not like Rupert upset. Rupert was . . . difficult. And of course, she preferred him. She had almost lost him. Urquhart was a buffoon. He spoke like a gentleman and acted like a pig. Look at him now, stuffing his ginger face with fish. Her own hair – spicy blonde they had called it once – gone to that absurd colour.

A vague rustle of muslin made her aware of her other child, to her left.

'Elizabeth, I've said before, you're not to feed that thing at the table.'

Elizabeth Willow Smolte glanced up into her mother's eyes. Her own, like Rupert's, were black, and down her back flowed raven black curling hair in studied undress. Elizabeth Willow wore white. She always did so. On the table by her plate, amid the historic china and coloured glasses, sat her cat, lean and evil, a peculiar dark tabby nearly black as Elizabeth Willow's blackness, but with long, pale eyes.

'She won't eat, Mama. She's only had a butterfly today. I saw her catch it.'

'Horrid animal,' said Flower. She remembered a gown she had had, patterned with butterflies. He had liked that. Her husband. Then.

Again, silence sank on the lighted island of the table, and all around the stealthy dusk crept on, and all the creatures of the room morphed into it, but here and there a gem eye glinted.

Flower did not like the room. It reminded her, apparently, of the Indian night. She had never grown accustomed there to the going of the sun. It was a blaze of radiance in red and gold, and then came one minute of an afterglow like beaten brass. And then, pitch black. And in the black, monkeys hooting, snakes rustling – did her daughter's dress sound like a snake now? – and there was too the deep quietness that sometimes came, when some unreal pagan god seemed to pass, those insane cruel gods of India, masters of lust and murder, revenge and wickedness.

The silver maid and the footman were clearing the dishes.

Something else was brought in under a cover. It must be the wood pigeons she had asked for.

Surely this succulence would tempt Rupert? He hated sensible food. He would only eat the scalding, numbing curries that his father craved. Urquhart the pig, of course, would consume anything.

Churton re-entered the room with two bottles which he had brought from the cellar. He sidled past a stuffed panther by the orangery door and came to the table.

'Madam?'

'Go to Mr Rupert,' said Flower irritably.

Rupert looked at the bottles. 'That should do.'

Churton produced a knife and cut the wax from the first bottle. He eased out the cork, and the liquid pop echoed in the wide room.

Candlelight blinked in ranks of eyes beyond the campfire of the table.

A rife rotten smell involved the air.

'Christ—' said Rupert. He jumped up, half gagging. Churton stepped back from the bottle, his assurance marred.

'Gone bad,' commented Urquhart unnecessarily.

'Get it away from me,' said Rupert. He thrust off from the table and strode to the one open window that gave on the upper lawn. He stood there, his back to them, breathing. 'I won't be served filth from the drains.'

'Now, Rupert,' said Flower. She gestured the obnoxious wine off the table. 'Sir Hampton will deal with this.'

Elizabeth Willow giggled softly.

Flower glanced at the window. The candles played on the glass of the orangery doors, as if fireflies had assembled. Nearby, the great elephant's foot table with its polished nails caught the light oddly; she did not care for it, never had. She had hated elephants.

'Rupert, come back and sit down.'

'In a minute, Mother.'

Flower was hungry. The maid hovered with new potatoes green with parsley, asparagus in spears, a purée of spinach. There was always everything here, from the busy hothouse. Flower indicated that the steward should uncover the dish of wood pigeon.

The cover was removed.

'Oh,' said Elizabeth Willow, 'look, Kitty.'

From the browned buttery breasts, the tiny trussed legs of the pigeons, something rose up. It was like a little mechanical thing, buzzing and humming. It glimmered purple, with a dot of red, another eye—

Flower shrieked. Insects alarmed her. And this was some sort of beetle that had been *cooked* into the dinner.

On a blur of wings it lifted from the steam and circled round the candles.

Flower clapped her hand to her mouth. Urquhart stared.

Elizabeth Willow and the cat attempted, each of them, to trap the beetle in a paw. But it evaded them.

'Oh, catch it, Kitty!' cried Elizabeth Willow. Her eyes shone. The room was full of shining eyes.

But the beetle was away, around the candles, up into the air. It flew to the open window and over Rupert's shoulder, out into the darkness of the night.

Rupert had turned. He said, 'And you expect me to eat that now, do you?'

'Oh no, Rupert. No,' said Flower, angry and dismayed.

'This vile bland tasteless food you like, and you can't even keep insects out of it. There's no reason now, Mother.'

After all, his handsome face was not flawless. The eyes were a touch too small, too close together. One did not really notice, only that he was not perfect, as he had seemed to be.

Urquhart said, 'I don't care. Give 'em here.'

The maid helped Urquhart to wood pigeon and potatoes.

'You will speak to Cook,' said Flower to Churton. 'This is disgusting. I can't sample it. Urquhart, you're a pig.'

'Yes, Ma. But it's still very good.'

Rupert pushed wide the glass door and went out of the scarlet dining room, into the dark where the beetle had gone.

The orangery ran west, its south-facing windows filled by conservatory plants and by the eponymous orange trees in painted tubs. Above soared the domes and minarets with which Sir Hampton Smolte had decorated his folly, weightless in the night.

Along the lawn, on a plinth, was the small Shiva, dancing, in one of his many hands a skull, torso wound with a cobra.

Rupert leaned down, ran his hand across Shiva's back. The bronze was smooth and black. Spiritually, it meant nothing to him, naturally, but in other ways . . . It had danced in the garden, the other garden, *there*. He had been then of the same height as the statue, which had at that time rested on the parched tobacco grass of the lawn. In fact the 'lawn' was a misnomer; mostly it was bare sear earth, and out of this desert grew the astonishing lushness of the plants, the rhododendrons, the two true oranges, the pepul tree with its enormous writhing trunk high as a house.

He had been five or six when they brought him away. He could not recall anything of the passage home. He became ill on the ship and nearly died, they said. But all that was merely an omission.

Rupert gazed away into the night of the English park.

He could still remember the scent of the Indian night, powdery and dry, yet intrinsically wet with *darkness*, and over it the smell of actual water sprinkled on the swept floors, the cow-dung burning in the nearest village. Some nights garlands of lamps flowed through the black, or firecrackers erupted. And sometimes an odour blew from the river a mile off at sunfall, burnt meat, and Rupert's mother would hustle him into the low hot house.

The heat. He was always cold now. No wonder he was never really well. This bloody damp dripping English climate, its tepid failed summers.

Something slipped by him. But it was not a creature of Indian night. Only his sister's vicious cat, going off to hunt in the park.

Rupert lit a cigarette. It made him cough, and he walked farther away from the Smolte palace. So his mother did not hear and come to chide him.

There was a new girl. His mother had told him about her. She could sew, that was the excuse. 'She speaks like a lady,' Flower had said, as if she would ever properly know how a lady spoke, other than her own theatrical impression.

He had been trying not to think of the girl. It made him feel a little sick, and his hands trembled.

In the rose garden, among the hoops of briars where the buds had not yet come, he coughed so painfully he cast the cigarette away with a curse. He found the marble bench with the Indian handmaidens carved at either end, and lay down between them.

Rupert shut his eyes, and waited in darkness.

He conjured up the hard mattress in the mosquito-netting. Too hot even to bear a sheet, despite the movement of the punkah, which in any case would soon cease as the lazy servant fell asleep.

He could not sleep himself. In the other room his mother and father, and the new baby in the cot, Urquhart. Sometimes noises, his parents, he knew now, engaging in sexual matters.

Then he had been puzzled. Not frightened, exactly, not anxious. But something.

The night anyway was full of noises. Insects, animals. Far off a jackal howled.

Then she would come in, the Indian woman.

It was strange, he did not really recollect her face, only her sinuous sombre shape, the dyes of her saris, magenta, cobalt, river yellow.

'You must go to sleep,' she would say, in English.

'Can't,' said the four-year-old child, as he always did.

'You are a bad boy,' she said. And presently she would put in upon his tongue a bitter sweet that tasted dimly too of her smoky fingers, the umber of her breast where she had hidden it.

She would stay until the feeling came, then she would suppose that he had gone to sleep. But no, he had only gone upward into the feeling, out of his body, out of his skin. The delight—

'Christ,' he whispered now. He turned on to his face on the hard marble. A peacock screamed in the jungle, but it was only his waking dream.

In the beginning, she had been Florrie Ball, but at sixteen luck, and an admirer, had got her on the stage. There she became Flower Bell.

She had no singing voice, but she had had personality. This, with the explosion of gingery blonde hair, very tight corsetting, and a glimpse of black stockings under white petticoats, had given her an income. She had, too, coupled with whoever was useful, even once allowing an amorous manageress to slip her hand inside a low bodice. With men, ever fearful of unwanted pregnancy, Flower Bell had tried most fairly harmless patent contraceptions known to woman. Only once had she fallen, or perhaps anyway there was some other cause. Certainly a dose of something from the quack had brought her on. She had been sick all day, but up on the stage by evening, kicking her heels and telling the gallery her *'Sweetheart was Bonny'*.

She had had a lovely skin. India had ruined her skin, and her hair. India had not been her friend. But friends were an illusion anyway. You could trust no one. Girls stole your stockings and your men, and men themselves stole your body, or at least got it as cheap as they could.

Hampton Smolte had come to the stage door one night when Flower Bell was out of sorts. She had told the old boy who kept the door to 'send the cheeky blighter off', she only wanted to get to her lodging and put her feet up. But then Hampton had bribed the doorman and appeared in her dressing room.

Flower took a good look at him. He was young, not more than five years her senior, and as bonny as the fellow in the song. Black curling hair, brown eyes like a cow's – daft for a man, but so great and warm, and lashes a girl would kill to get. Tanned skin, and strong, a lovely figure. And in his red uniform. A soldier of the Queen.

She did not know how, but he had more money than she would have expected a soldier to have, even the officers. He explained, he had done well in foreign climes. They had an oyster supper, the kind of food she liked; she noticed even then he toyed with the meal, though he outmatched her in the wine. They drank four bottles between them. He saw her home in the lamplit morning, over the river in a carriage, and he kissed her. But something made Flower Bell resist. 'I won't say I'm a daisy,' she said. 'But I'm not a naughty girl, either. Don't you think it, Captain Smolte.'

What had made her do this? Had she been in love with his pretty eyes? Perhaps. Her heart fluttered when, undeterred, he came back to see her on the following night.

He was a little veiled about his family, and it occurred to her he had got himself up the ladder of the military world in clever ways, just as she had got herself up to the stage. She had been a duchess in a play by then, and learned a sort of aristocratic voice that almost fooled, that sometimes did fool, the undiscerning.

And he had money. He gave her a ruby ring and Flower Bell was beside herself. She would have to have him, despite his tales. He told her he had found a treasure in India.

She was fortunate, or so she thought. He desired in the way he drank, after a glass, he must go on. And so at last he married her, in a poky little church with a scatter of nobodies, and some of her quieter theatre acquaintances in plumes and sentimental tears.

She did not at first go with him to the fairy tale land of treasure and large-clawed beasts with which he had regaled her.

No, she spent a ghastly year in a lodging, living off the money he sent, which after all was not enough. And she wondered what she had done, if she had been a proper ninny. But then he came home, and oh the night, the nights they had of it. The suppers and the wine, as at the start, and the glorious sex. She had never known a man who could bring her to such a shrill wild peak. She did not know why. It was not his looks, it was not his strength, nor, really, was he a wonderful lover, only strong, eager, sometimes too quick, so she must struggle under him to her own release, but always it came, like a storm. It was India on him, then, since India was magic. He had convinced her. He did not tell her of the stinks, of the heat, of the biting things, of the press of dark tribes whose land it was – had been, for anyway, the conqueror had it now – no, he spoke only of marble pavilions, golden towers on sunsets of flame, and of the silken rivers down which wreaths of marigolds drifted. Of tiger hunts, elephants, and parrots.

It turned out he did not even care for India himself. He was bewitched, that was all. Once he had her there, he was one moment reviling everything, the next gone off on some mission into the inferno and the dust.

The voyage out had been awful, so cramped and boring. The weather too calm or rough. Dredged up into another boat, they entered the land on a wide brown heaving river, as unlike the rivers of silk as she could imagine. Corpses and crocodiles floated in the water, and Flower did not know which was the worse.

It seemed he had left the army. Yet he was a soldier still, in administrative work, with men under his command, a pernickety official to advise. And there was an interest in lucrative indigo.

The house was low and long, overcast with heat and shadow, and when the rains came, the monsoon, the noise of it almost drove her mad.

There had been a local raja, and once or twice she had seen him, unbelievable in gold and pearls, upon a painted elephant having vermilion ears and silver feet. And there had been tiger hunts, and she was gifted a carcass, and was surprised this appalling beast was after all so small. Marvels, but too late, too unlike the stories.

India angered Flower. And in India too, unavoidably now, children were inserted into her, carried by her in the cumbersome pall of heat, thrust out in humiliation and agony, while the monkeys screeched at her cries, and poisonous snakes were extracted from beneath her bed of labour. Rupert, and Urquhart. Sturdy western names. There was a nurse, an ayah. Flower did not care if she gave the brats her shady milk, Flower wanted to preserve her breasts – not realizing they had already been spoiled for ever.

She had been pregnant with Elizabeth on the journey home. They were rich then for sure, and about to gain their title. But embryo Elizabeth, tilted and tossed by the tempestuous sea, had womb-grown into a curious child. Or possibly it had been the trouble beforehand which subtly infected her. The Little Mutiny, as it was called. Flower had never before been so terrified. Seven villages . . . That wash of native faces, all crazed, one face repeated, and shouting in the torchlight – some heathen festival had sparked it off. Something with an elephant. She had never understood, or cared to.

Hampton Smolte called up his men, and with their rifles they fired over and over, gunning down the seething crowd. It was done in a night, perhaps in a few hours.

Flower remembered the ayah weeping, and that she had struck her. The ayah then ran away, like a serpent on legs, her black tail of hair flying at her back.

Flower, Lady Smolte, came out of her reverie and saw her maid moving across the brocade curtain. But this was not worrying, for Luksmi, though she might retain certain elements of India, now left behind, was a Eurasian, more like her English father, a common lout who had been in Hampton's small army, than her long-forgotten melanic mother. Luksmi, in all but name, seemed simply an ugly Englishwoman. A liverish pallor, darkish hair, a long flat nose – these were the only hints of her commencement. Flower had taken pity on Luksmi. Luksmi was her one good deed. Luksmi was a Christian.

'Put those earrings away.'

'Yes, Madam.'

'Must I tell you everything?'

He might come to her room tonight, this ample bedroom with its Indian frescoes she did not like, and over which she had hung popular paintings of kittens and young girls in arbours. The bed had columns like those of some temple in the jungle. But there it was. He too had finally only hated India, yet he had tried to bring it here with him. The extraordinary house, the pastes and curries – dear God, she had only been too glad to suffer the last of those on the boat. Yet Rupert wanted them as well, would eat nothing else.

Would Hampton come up? Sometimes she missed him. Her appetite for sex had faded . . . it was his company. But he had been at his club in the town: billiards, and the special dinner they would make him, like his Rawlings, hot things and rice. And the wine and the port.

'What are those shoes doing there? Put them away, Luksmi.'

How noiseless the night beyond the windows. Out into the park that beetle had flown, just as insects had flown up from the night dishes *there*. Bugs in the rice, snowing into the candles. The horrible blister flies, and white ants which ate the furniture and clothes. Yet India had sighed upon this night, too.

Beetles. Bad wine.

He would be angry, Hampton. Would he?

Elizabeth Willow was in the music room at midnight. It was a capacious, exotic room, designed seventeen years before like all the rest of the Smolte palace. Elizabeth Willow was one year older than the house. But she had not been planned, or designed. She had merely biologically *become*.

This was a room of silver and blue, silver moulding crusted about its chandelier, and on its ornate ledges were arranged figurines and balls like roses, all of pure ivory, that shone in the light of the candlestick Elizabeth Willow had brought in with her. To one side was a gleaming harp with an Indian head on its upward crest. On one wall rested a row of Indian instruments, a bina, a sitar, a little drum. At the centre of the room, on the blood-red and indigo carpet, a piano stood.

Elizabeth Willow soundlessly traced the ivory and ebony keys. She was not permitted to play at this hour, for sound carried all over the caverns of the palace-house. Nevertheless, some noiseless music came, for Elizabeth Willow began to dance, over the polished floor, up and down, a sort of waltz which was not, her slender arms upraised.

She had no thoughts, this girl. Had not needed to have them, perhaps. And yet, she had a sort of waiting. She was not like her brothers, romantic, crotchety Rupert, piggy Urquhart, who used their days in brooding or rude exercise respectively. Not like her mother, who read her saccharine novels and pined over old posters of her triumphs on the boards of the city.

Not even like her father. Elizabeth Willow was, in fact, mostly like her cat. Supine or rapid, instinctual. The tutors of her youth had thought her simple, but been too canny to say so. She had learned very little, only to read and to play, very inaccurately, the piano. Her voice was fair, but she had no ear, could carry no tune. She was a creature of rhythm and impulse. And cruel. They had found that early. The governess, for example, whose fingers had been broken by the desk-lid in the schoolroom. And Elizabeth Willow's other ways.

Elizabeth Willow danced in the blue and silver music room, under the silver starred ceiling. The room faced north, towards the wooded hills, and had the long glass windows common to the house. Would something come from the hills, or from some other direction, around the gardens with their topiary and trellises of Persian roses, their fountains and bridges and statues from India, or in imitation of India? Would something come and cross the grass, and move into the open latticed glass doors of the music room?

Something did come, but it was low and small. The light slid on its black tabby back.

A tiny panther out of the jungle Elizabeth Willow had never seen, but which Rupert had told her of, in childhood.

'Here, Kitty,' said Elizabeth Willow, 'what have you brought me?'

Kitty had brought a dead shrew. Kitty had played with it a long while, up in the meadow under the woods, until all life was irrevocably extinguished.

Kitty set the death before her mistress.

Elizabeth Willow picked it up, and sniffed the bitten fur.

'Clever Kitty.'

Kitty never allowed herself to be lovingly touched. She leapt up on the piano, causing the keys to respond, the black and the white. She sat upon the piano's top and glared, and Elizabeth Willow returned the kill, which Kitty then devoured, up on the shining piano lid, and drops of blood, still warm, buttoned over its mirror.

Within the house there came the softest noise.

Elizabeth Willow turned and glided to the inner door, which she opened only a crack.

There by the unlit stair that led away into the back areas of the house, Divy the housemaid was standing with Pocks the footman.

'It's only the old cat jumped on the piano,' said Pocks. 'It always does it.'

Elizabeth Willow pressed her black cool eye to the door crack.

Pocks took Divy's silly pointed face between his hands, and putting his face against it, seemed to begin to eat her lips.

Elizabeth Willow was interested. She watched carefully.

Suddenly Divy drew away.

'No. It's wrong. You mustn't.'

'Course it isn't wrong. Don't you like it?'

'Yes.'

'Come on, then.'

Elizabeth Willow watched until Divy again abruptly disengaged herself. There seemed, in the low light of the lamp they had put down on the ground, no blood upon Divy's face. Nevertheless, she ran up the back stair and that door fell to.

Pocks sighed, and, picking up the lamp, went off on his rounds, assisting Churton to lock and bolt the palace.

Elizabeth Willow crept over to Kitty and observed the cat tearing at the dead shrew.

The action was similar.

Elizabeth Willow pushed Kitty away and bent herself to the kill. But she did not like its taste and Kitty spat from the far end of the piano.

Pocks came in at the door.

He swore. Then quickly apologized.

'I didn't know you were here, Miss Elizabeth.'

Elizabeth Willow struck one key of the piano with her finger. It had blood on it and now the ivory showed bright red, as Pocks went by with his lamp, to lock the outer door.

Elizabeth Willow ignored him.

'That cat'll be in trouble again,' said Pocks cheerfully as he came back.

And Kitty, turning at once, lashed out, scratching Pocks across the cheek.

He yelled. His face was fearful.

'You mustn't say things about Kitty,' said Elizabeth Willow. 'She understands every word.'

Urquhart came up the stair, into the annexe, to the room under the solitary gas lamp. Up here it was neither quite the servants' quarters nor, decidedly, the main house. There was a bathroom, a concession and a treat. Also perhaps a cordoning off. And there the door, with a panther of brass running over it. How suitable.

Adjusting the bottle of wine in his arm, Urquhart knocked politely. He was always polite to her, for she was not a lady, and appreciated courtesy.

Her soft voice came at once.

'Enter, Sir.'

She was always polite in turn, fawning – until later. Then she changed.

He opened the door and went in.

At once – somehow it never reached beyond her door – the pungent smell of incense from her little shrine, where the candle flickered in its pink shade, and the fresh flowers stood, and there were sometimes miniature cakes, and in autumn fruit from the vines and canes. And forbidden drink in a bronze cup.

She sat on her bed, which was utilitarian, like most of the room, a servant's bed, lacking even a curtain.

She wore a linen nightdress, trimmed with cheap lace. Her hair was in a plait that reached down to her knees . . .

'Is it all right, Luksmi?'

It always was. Even at the times when, with other women, you must abstain, she did not care. She had said, red with white, sacred, the colours of the Integral Unity.

Luksmi stood up and made her obeisance, the gesture he had just a fleeting memory of, from before, her narrow hands together, raised before her ugly sallow face. Above and between her eyes was a faint smudge in the flesh of her low broad forehead, the mark of some esoteric knowledge, she had once told him. But then she had told him too of a child born in the village, in India, having on its legs the scars of crocodile teeth, and this child recalled a life before its life, and of dying in the crocodile's larder under the river—

'Ready for bed, old girl?' he said.

Two glasses, cucumber green, stood on a mosaic table that was hers, not of the house. He poured the wine, and she, rising up like a snake, drew the coarse linen off her body.

He had seen her all his life, practically, when one day, he *saw* her. Her breasts first, covered up but so proud and full. He had ogled her breasts for weeks, that year he was sixteen. Sent away to school before, he had known nothing but the suggestive horseplay of boys. He still liked to fight and fondle men, but the bodies of women had a different allure.

Luksmi's face was unlovely, but her neck was a column like firm, unyoung white marble. And then her cream body began, which was beautiful as the statues in the garden. High and impossibly large and firm, the two breasts, with nipples like the blue-brown buds of lotuses. Round, the belly and the hips, but taut as a dancer's, as the dancer her mother had been. Her waist tiny, his hands could contain it. The bush of her genital hair was not like the hair upon her head, but jungle black, the rukh itself, with tigers therein.

She undid her hair from its plait and it slipped over her like a veil of smoke.

Urquhart grasped her and easing her down on to the bed, possessed her at once.

She was always lubricious, ripe, easy. She put her feet, of which the soles were pink like coral, up on his back, and kicked him lightly. He came in seconds, in a flurry of bursting pleasure.

Lying then, his nose in her hair, smelling the incense offered to immoral Krishna, and Shiva, and Vishnu, he recollected running barefoot over the hot earth under the brown shadows of the ferns and trees. And a woman had screamed and scolded him, thrusting the protective shoes on to his feet. A great rosy flower hung by his face, and he saw a serpent under the tree.

'Do you miss your India, Luksmi?' he asked her.

'It is gone. They are kind to me.'

But they were not kind. Next to the shrine was a small plaster Jesus. He too had been included in the Hindu pantheon.

Urquhart believed that *he* was kind. He would have done a lot for Luksmi, if he could. But it was not feasible. Not yet. She could not even wear the perfume he had bought her. Ma would throw her out if Ma knew what they did.

'Do you love me?' said Urquhart.

'Yes, my lord.'

Later there would be longer games. She knew many.

He snored gently into her pillow and Luksmi lay still. She showed no sign of anything, for in her heart she knew all things are earned, nothing is to be escaped, or forestalled. Nor is anything eternal but the soul. And the lights flickered before all her gods, who were all one, all wonderful, unspeaking, non-participant, but present.

The night lay thick on the countryside, its fabric seldom broken by any solitary rural light. Above the stars, not like those of the Smolte music room. And on the Smolte park and woods, like the blackest of the black keys of the piano, sheer darkness.

He knew his way, even in occult night, and the horse knew, and knew better than to commit any mistake. Even drunk, he was in control, of the animal, and of his own big body. Sir Hampton Smolte, maker of all this.

Black hid him, even maybe from himself. Riding, he might have been young again. And the park . . . that might have been some other place, though it did not have the scent of it, or the sounds.

Something scuttled over the broad drive, a vole perhaps, or a wild pheasant. Just so the jungle chicken of India had been wont to burst out across the path. Nag the snake had another noise, deadly, like a little shifting of the earth itself, skin sliding over skin.

The day's business – stocks, city trade – had been facile, and the evening had been fair enough. They did him a decent curry, not as good as Rawlings' jobs, but satisfactory. The wine was very good, thick and sonorous. He had won at billiards, and since they had been betting on it, earned a wad of cash that amused him, as his fortune did not. But then, there was a twist to his wealth. It had come out of India.

The drive wound through the woods, and emerged on the sweep of hill, curling down towards the house.

Lights still burned there, awaiting him.

He reined in the horse. 'Stand, you brute.'

Sir Hampton Smolte looked down upon his palace.

It had seemed to him once that not a raja of the plains or hills would not have been envious of this jewel. For it had copied what of the East it fancied, and added the luxury of the west. And yet, he hated the house, too. Was vainglorious of it and ridiculed it. The 'kennel' he would call it to his acquaintances in drink, or the 'hut'.

He had built it in order to hate it, had brought India away with him so that he could continue to despise her.

Away in the dark he could hear his river now, tippling over its stones, near the bridge with the lingam. The river even could not sound the same, for the Indian rivers would soon be awash with rain at this time, and later dry and thin, oozing over into beery pools where the women pounded endless garments, singing in high heartless voices.

Smolte punched his horse lightly.

'Go on, Caesar.'

They crossed the river, and at the bank's edge lay a cast shoe. Someone had been unlucky in the hunt today. Serve them right. He let them make free of his land, and got scant repayment. The aristocracy of the county looked down on him, though they were mostly penniless. Well, let them rot.

There had been no foxes to hunt, *there*. They had hunted jackals, and at other times gone after tigers, panthers, spotted deer, bear. The year he had come back to England, there had been a wolf hunt hereabouts, but you seldom saw a wolf now.

The lamps of the house drew nearer, spreading their golden fog up the hill to meet him.

He remembered beaters shouting in the jungle, and the tiger springing out like an arrow, straight up on to the elephant, which squealed in terror and pain. They had had to shoot the beast. But it was a tusker, and the ivory had been presented to Hampton Smolte. He had shot a rogue himself, at Kalachandra, in the forests. It fell in the midst of its charge like interrupted thunder.

Light moved up over Smolte's body and face. He was heavy, thickset and fattening, his long legs like sausages in their tight smart breeches. His face was yellowish, the complexion one brought home from abroad. In scoops of flesh, the large brown eyes had lost their density, the whites yolky and flushed. His hair had thinned. He was not the man Flower recalled. His face had a bias now to it, as if it had at some time slipped between two expressions at variance. None of his scars were visible; his clothes contained them.

He rode aside and down into the court where the wheeled Indra rose up, and through into the stable yard. The carriage house was in shadow, but an oil lamp burned on an upturned bucket by the stalls, and there Darius sat, cross-legged in that improbable way of the holy men, one bare foot tucked into his groin.

'How's the foal?' demanded Smolte. His voice was sludgy but the words quite clear. He held liquor well, a tankard.

'I'm pleased with him,' said Darius.

'Are you, by God? Then he must be a fine one.' Smolte illogically resented Darius' possessive care of the horses. As if they were Darius' own. But what could you do, he was expert at his work.

Darius had come back with Smolte, from the Indian world. Darius was not an Indian, but some English type, flawed by Celtic origins. And in India he had taken on an Indian name, was fluent in Hindustani and the Moslem tongue. He took from each culture what most appealed to him, and seemed to know too much. Coming to his native land, Darius had gazed about in an alien's way, his seeming surprise tempered only with the acceptance taught him by naked men garlanded by marigolds.

Darius rose easily from his crippled position, and held Caesar's head as Smolte's stones swung off him.

'He's not happy,' said Darius softly. 'They've not fed him right.'

'Oh well, you'll see to it.'

'So I will.'

Darius did not look like a foreigner. He was thin and tall, had grey eyes and polished fair hair. The tan of the East had left him merely pale.

Not saying anything more to his master, Darius led the horse away into the stable, where he would rub him over and cosset him.

Somewhere in the straw of the mother's stall, the foal made a sprightly noise.

Smolte walked back along the yew avenue, out of sorts, for Darius rarely failed to annoy him. He crossed the rose garden and the lawn before the house, coming up to the orangery door. It was open, but Pocks, who should have been waiting for him too, was not at his post.

Smolte locked up the door, and marched between the tubs of palms and orange trees, into the scarlet dining room, where the gas lamps now burned low along the walls among the heads and horns.

The man paused. He looked around.

The room seemed to hold the ghost of something, like a chord of music smitten forth half a second before.

He glanced, here, there. Tigers glared down, impotent, the dead bear. The panthers and jackals were caught as if, a moment earlier, they had been at play together.

But the table resting on the elephant's foot was solid. *That* would not gad about.

Smolte thought again of the elephant that the tiger had clawed, and the elephant he had shot for its tusks. He did not permit his thought to go further. And yet, for an instant, there drifted before him a face so beautiful that it was like agony.

He lifted his head and said aloud, 'Get out, you bitch, you slut.'

And she was gone, and only Flower his wife was upstairs, where he might visit her. She was available. There would be no trouble there. But he did not want Flower. Had never wanted Flower, save as the screen between himself and – India.

He turned off the gas and the room dissolved away. There in the English gloom at two o'clock in the morning, the jackals would not dare to sport. The panthers would stay still.

He knew he had come home like some nobody. The horse abstracted, no greeting at the door, locking up himself. Gone the obeisance and proliferation of the other country, a slave for every task and act, the titles of *Sahib* and *Lord*.

No, he would not bother Flower. He would have a brandy or two and get to his bed. He would not dream. He did not dream. He felt alone as he climbed the carven stair, up past the statues and the temple bells, into the green corridor. Alone in his palace in the calm of the dark.

And Annie was alone also, down in the servants' wing, the last pan scoured and just now put away.

They had left her two candles, one of which was almost done.

She lit the other and went out, over the kitchen, to the long corridor that would return her into the house.

She was so weary she could barely move, could hardly see. The wisp of the candle-flame upon the glass of the corridor did not alert her. Anything might be out there, pressing close, but she had no strength to spare for unease.

She found her way up the back stairs, and ascended. It went on for ever, this climb. She was so tired she leaned on the wall and for a minute she slept, standing up, the candle lethally drooping.

Then she forced herself on. She had memorized the way. In four hours they would wake her – she must begin again.

'Poor old Annie,' said Rose, sympathetic, nearly real, in the hollow of her ear.

When she crept into the attic, Annie beheld the other two asleep. Tiff coiled up hard, and Clarrie on her back, mildly snoring.

Something crunched against Annie's foot.

She looked, and the candle shone on a broken pot, some earth, the wrecked stems of her geranium, its flowers scattered. Clarrie had suggested the geranium be placed on the window sill, but someone had knocked it off. Tiff probably.

Annie picked up the smashed plant and held it in her hand, but it seemed miles away, as the courtroom had done, as Rose had seemed, and then become.

It was useless attempting to hold on to anything. And yet, she laid the geraniums on her pillow by her head. Their curious edible oily smell was so familiar, and especially strong now, in destruction. As if dying had caused some innate surge of life.

Rose said, 'There's a whole garden. Find some earth and plant them again.' And then, 'Go to sleep. I'll get up to let him in, if he comes home.' And Annie knew Rose meant Innocent, and that it was no good listening to Rose.

3

Up in the thorns the roses bloomed, peachy pink, carmine. They had come out of Persia in the sixteenth century, grown in the rust soil of India, and now they were here.

But not resembling Rose, not even like the fakes upon her hat. Tended like queens.

Annie had not seen the rose garden again. She had not been near the front of the house at all. But three roses were brought into the kitchen, to be candied. After all, queens in jeopardy.

Mrs Rope had gone for her lie down after the servants' midday dinner, and Clarrie set Tiff on to the pans. 'You come with me, Ember. Bring that basket.'

They went through the lower yew walk, to the kitchen garden.

It was a large oblong space, walled in by brick, up which ran vines and the espaliers of fruit trees. Amid the rows of greens lurked bird and mouse traps, one of which, from the state of its apparatus, had obviously claimed a victim. In the shade of a fig sat the dirty gardener on a stool, smoking his pipe. He looked at them idly under a crunched straw hat.

Clarrie and Annie cut thyme and sage, and Clarrie bent over the early summer vegetables.

'Go and ask him for some earth for that plant,' said Clarrie. 'Quickly now.'

Clarrie seemed to have developed a slight, forgetful conscience over Annie. It was Clarrie who had poured water into a glass and put the broken geraniums into it. It was Clarrie who chased Tiff into the scullery to assist with the endless pots and pans.

But Annie approached the gardener only because she had been told to. He did not seem a likely proposition.

'I'm to ask you for a pot of earth.'

He did not look at her. He picked his nose, then wiped his

fingers on his jacket. With the same hand he extracted a melon seed from his waistcoat and rubbed it on his face. 'Uh.'

Annie said, 'I'm to ask now.'

'What's it fur?' asked the gardener.

Annie said, too pessimistic to employ subterfuge, 'For a geranium.'

'Bugger uff,' said the gardener.

Annie guessed he would not have spoken even to Clarrie in this manner. But Annie was only the scullery drudge.

She went back to the herbs. As she expected, Clarrie had forgotten already.

But when they returned along the walk, the gardener's skinniest boy was in the hedge, and seeing them come, as usual he leapt out and bolted off.

'He's dumb, that one,' said Clarrie. 'Should be in a hospital.' And then, 'Where's your earth?'

'He wouldn't,' said Annie.

'The old beast. As if he owned the place. Run over to the stable. Ask Dari for some droppings. That'll do. But you can't keep it in the bedroom, mind.'

Annie was loath to go, but she had decided from the first that all commands here were safer obeyed. And so she went back down the walk, and by the glasshouses, to the wide yard, where she had stood the first morning, under the image in the bronze spoked wheel.

At the entrance to the yard, Annie halted.

A man was there, leading round and gently round a young and leggy horse the colour of a chestnut. His movements were so careful, so considerate, they astonished her, and the unbalanced ambling of the foal was full of humour, correspondingly carefree. Presently she saw they were passing in and out, in and out, of the statue's shadow.

Although she had made no sound and she had not thought he had seen her, the man quietly said, 'What is it that you want?'

Annie did not know what to say. Her request was bizarre, in any case doubtless futile. And the strange procedure with the horse seemed more important.

But the man led the young animal towards her.

'Don't be alarmed, now,' said the man. 'He's only a child, he is.' And then the foal softly put its nose into her bosom. Annie was startled but did not draw back. There was nothing threatening. 'A lover of women,' said the man. 'He won't hurt.'

Annie touched the foal's face with her fingers. He was prickly soft, his nose hot as the sun on her shoulders, but more friendly. He smelled of country things, of his mother's body he had left not so long before.

The man had fair hair, and he stooped a little from his height. Behind him, the statue plaited the blue sky in its interstices.

'Indra,' said the man, nodding back at it, 'the warrior. He's there to watch for the horses. That's his chariot wheel he's in. Now, they sent you, so you must be wanting something.'

'Dung,' said Annie.

The man threw back his head and laughed.

'They never sent you for that?'

'It's for a plant.'

The foal took its face from Annie, and scampered on the leading-rein. 'Hush,' he said to it, and then, 'And who of them has a plant?'

'It was mine,' murmured Annie. 'It was broken. Only a geranium.' And wished she had not said so much.

Beyond the coroneted head of Indra was the stable roof with its domes, and clock, which suddenly struck for three.

'And did you bring the geranium from your home?' he said.

'I must get back.'

She turned. And he said, 'Fetch me the flower, and I'll put it into some earth for you.'

But Annie thought, *What is he after?* She hurried away. The foal made a little liquid rippling noise, and she heard him say, 'There now. You want your mother.'

His voice was full of cloudless distances. He must be Darius, the peculiar one they sneered at in the kitchen. A madman they said, but clever with Smolte's horses.

Mrs Rope was by the range, red-faced, and shouted at Annie, and soon after they began on the long preparation of the eight o'clock dinner, the sweat running off them in their burning Tartarus.

Despite the heat of the kitchen, the long, long hours of deadly work, the scrubbing and grinding, peeling and chopping, the washing of stone floors, and ceaseless emptying of slops, Annie felt a new strength come on her as the summer pressed into the year.

The air, Rose would have said, suited Annie. No city smokes or reeks, the doors and windows always open – save when Rawlings prepared his curries. And the food, though the others grumbled about it, was more than Annie had ever seen, let alone been given to eat. Meat and new vegetables, soup she herself had stirred, just-baked bread, cake smoking from the oven, fresh tea, cold lemonade from the ice-chest, and now and then a snippet from the incredible meals that went upstairs, fish and chicken, slivers of beef, blancmange and trifle, and melting ice cream. Even the curious curry aromas did not offend Annie, although she sampled none of these.

'Look at the great thing,' said Tiff, 'you uv puffed out, you. What'll we do uv her?'

Though her hands were raw, the skin of Annie's face, and of her slender body – glimpsed in swift undressing behind the attic screen – was white and clear. She had colour in her lips now, if not in her cheeks, and gradually, as she grew quicker at her work, with longer periods of sleep, the rings went from around her eyes. There was left only a little darkness about the upper and lower lashes. And this Tiff had accused her of putting on for beauty, with soot, so a threatening Mrs Rope hauled Annie to the window to be sure. But then Mrs Rope slapped Tiff, calling her a stupid mischief-making lollock.

Tiff herself did not often inflict injuries any more, she had maybe become tired of it, and of Annie's returning blows.

Annie paused in the sunlit kitchen yard, a bowl of peas in her hands, the closed walls round, the trees above. She thought, *I'll be here for ever*. And her heart beat slowly with resignation. It was as if a spell had been put on her. She did not question or object. Life did things to you, as it would. It was only that she heard Rose's voice less and less now. While, though she was too tired to dream, through the shut door in her waking brain, there sometimes thrust a ghastly image, a shape that fell . . . But she could slam the door, or if that was not enough, twist the hair at her temples until the pain put out the light of Rose's hanged descent.

'Don't pull on your hair that way,' said Clarrie sharply. 'That's what poor Brown used to do.'

Brown had been the fifth housemaid. Something awful had happened, creating a sort of saga for the kitchen. One night Brown had been taken ill, and her screams had filled the house. 'A horrible noise it was,' said Tiff, with relish. Madam had had the doctor brought, and Brown was rushed away, but she died. 'It was the Typhly,' declaimed Mrs Rope. 'Gone in a night. She never got it from my wholesome food.' 'Awful, the screams were,' chorused Tiff. 'She was in the upstairs,' said Clarrie, shuddering. 'Taken poorly up there. Madam said she was walking in her sleep from the fever.' 'They were generous to the family,' added Mrs Rope. 'More than she was worth, if you ask me. She was a slummocky wench.'

At the end of the first month, Annie was paid her wages, with the other below-stairs women, by Mrs Beare in her Den. Annie put the shillings into her purse and hid it again under the mattress. She did not inspect anything that was in the purse. Did not think about anything there.

Nor did she take the geranium to mad Darius in the stable, although it continued, in its murky water glass, to put out leaves and red flowers. It was odd, the plant, it had always flowered, it seemed to her now, even sometimes in winter on Tooth Street. Where had the geranium come from? It did not matter – where things came from, or went.

Rawlings was in the kitchen arguing murderously with Mrs Rope. He brandished only his big tanned fists, but she had got hold of a meat cleaver and hefted it.

The curry cook had been an army man. He had served Hampton Smolte when he was in the regiment, and after at the station at Kalachandra. Rawlings had learned the secrets of the natives' devilish cuisine, and knew himself a master.

The hair now bristled on his scalp which showed through like a shelled nut. His burly muscled body twitched with rage.

'I tell you, I'll have my saffron and my ginger, be damned to you, you bloody fat woman.'

'And you'll keep a civil tongue, you doss-house jack.'

It seemed spices had gone missing. It was only a pretext. Whenever they could, like lovers, these two would come together.

Now Rawlings filled his big ribcage for a roar – and stopped, his sunburnt monkey's face turned to stone.

'Well, speak up, you lying rascally son of a coddled turnip!' bawled Mrs Rope.

And at her back Churton boomed like the bell of doom.

'Mrs Rope, be silent, if you please.'

Silence was. Churton pointed quite across the two warring heads, directly at Annie Ember, labouring, a soul in torment, cleaning the range.

'You, girl. You are to be brought up to Madam's sitting room in half an hour. Be presentable. Control your hair.'

This room was incredible. It was soft white, like the fruit creams from the ice-pail, and it was in one of the towers, with windows on four sides, four *rounded* sides. And in front of them, pierced marble screens. Sunlight came through in golden droplets that shone like bees on the floor of marble paving.

In winter the room was cold and damp, and Elizabeth Willow moved elsewhere. Annie did not know this.

She saw the daughter of Sir Hampton Smolte sitting in a white dress on a window-seat, heaped with oriental cushions sewn with spangles, gilt flowers, glass gems – or were they real?

The cat lay nearby. It did not move. Nor did Elizabeth Willow, only watching with her dark bright open eyes.

'You work in lace?' said Lady Flower.

'No, Madam.'

'I was told that you did. Well. All right. But you can sew?'

'Yes, Madam.'

'There will be things for you to do for my daughter.'

Flower showed Annie Ember a carved cupboard of 'things'. Cut-out white clothes not yet stitched. Annie nodded. Obedient.

Then Flower lost interest and went away. So it seemed. Before she did so, she had said Annie should have some of her daughter's old dresses, and put out three over a sofa. They would fit Annie, she could see, for Elizabeth Willow was too slight. Flower had said too there was the old bathroom, under the tower. Annie was to come up here on four afternoons, after the servants' dinner. And remain until five o'clock. She might take a bath in the bathroom, and then put on one of the dresses, before going into the sewing room – Mrs Beare had shown her? – where she would stitch up the new clothes. And her hair. It must be regularly washed. She should brush her hair. There was a lot of it and it was not tidy. Perhaps leave it loose. A young girl . . . it was the fashion, Flower had said, nearly coquettishly.

But then Flower was gone, and Annie stood there bewildered.

The cat did not stir, but Elizabeth Willow went over to a chest against one of the window screens. She opened a drawer.

'Look. Do you know what these are?'

Annie was not sure.

'No, Miss Elizabeth,' she said, for Mrs Beare had told her how she must address all the beings of the upper house.

Elizabeth Willow dangled the skein of whitish objects, not so pure as the tint of the room.

'Come here.'

Annie went closer. She did not like to. For Elizabeth Willow was like a person made from paper, strung with black hair and stamped with eyes, dressed up and caused to move. She was not exactly present. Yet, she was a cipher of the daunting authority of the house.

In the drawer were silk chemises and petticoats of lace, but a pallid inimical smell came up with the perfume of the lavender sachets.

Elizabeth Willow slipped in her hand again and drew out a shrivelled matted ball.

'See?'

Annie did not understand. It was a dead and partly desiccated mouse.

'They're bones. Bones,' said Elizabeth Willow with a pale incarnate joy. 'I want you to stitch them on these underclothes.'

Annie stood there.

'Well?' Elizabeth Willow's eyes let fly a tiny shaft of random venom.

'Yes, Miss Elizabeth.'

'Along the lace,' said Elizabeth Willow, 'so I can wear them.'

She plucked a blue-black feather from the drawer. 'Kitty caught a crow. I know she did. They said they shot it. But it was Kitty's kill.' Elizabeth Willow stroked the feather into her hair. It became one with her hair. 'I'd like a hat of feathers.'

Annie stayed very still, and out of the chest, in nimble white fingers, came the skull of something small, that had had a beak.

'Sew it on. On this—' Elizabeth Willow pulled a silk shift from the chest. 'Here. Over the heart.'

Annie said, 'The stitches will have to go through the holes.'

'Oh, that's all right. Mama says you'll do pretty sewing.'

Annie took the heap of garments, and her hand was filled with fragile bones.

They were beautiful, but an odour clung to them, the physical life which had been.

'Go away now,' said Elizabeth Willow.

Outside Annie stood on the empty landing, above the stair carpeted in white – velvet it looked – and on the wall a painting on wood, lovely girls, Indian girls, dancing under a foliaged tree.

Annie went down the stair, and walked along the passage, and there was the bathroom, door standing ajar, narrow and bare, a tub, no more, yet it was porcelain. Here she was to bathe, and down below was the sewing room, Mrs Beare had already shown her, a chamber of dilated tawny shades.

Upstairs ran a rilling laugh.

She's mad, thought Annie. *Their Darius isn't. But she is.*

She was in the house. It was all about her. These people seen and never seen, spoken of below. Flower with her airs. The lord, Sir Hampton. Rupert and Urquhart, vague talk of sons. And that girl, Elizabeth Willow. Crazy.

What was she to do now? Sew? Well then, she would wash in the tub and put on one of the white dresses. Brush out her hair – she had never, ever worn it loose.

Annie felt a complex excitement. And a fear.

Suddenly she too had been loosed, here in this palace of the Smoltes. And, brushed by the other one's insanity, had it galvanized her also?

Annie went into the bathroom and *slammed* the door. She bolted it, and, going to the taps, turned them on in a sort of fright.

Which was justified. Cold water streamed, and steaming, boiling water too.

She threw in the plug and let the tub fill.

Annie had never in her life immersed herself in such a lawless chaotic *biblical* element. A *bath*. To *bathe*. She listened ironically, instinctively, for Rose, but no whisper came.

Through a high slender window, latticed almost shut, thick afternoon light fell poached and dim.

Cool water . . . Was it a wickedness? Was it to invite some threat? The day's heat pushed her. This was a chance – easy.

She undid her unpleasing grey stuff dress, the apron of servitude, and dropped the insulting cap on the floor. She freed her plait. The tresses soaked down her body. Long, greenish-brown . . . Annie shook her hair. She undid her stays, always awkward, and took off her petticoat and drawers. Everything fell on the floor, where she had cast the other garments, and that clutch of bones. Forget them.

Annie got into the tub.

The water was . . . like silk. Silk.

She snuggled into it, and in an anger of pleasure snatched up the soap – creamy and of an apple scent. She soaped her body, alley-cat face, long throat, slim shoulders, firm arms, rounded breasts, more full now than they had been. She soaped her narrow twisting waist and almost fleshless belly and buttocks. The curve of hip. Between her thighs, that forbidden place, and the soap caressed it. Her long legs, their thin ankles and the high-arched feet. She dived under the water. She was a naiad. She had heard of them – water nymphs. Rose had told her—

Down. Beneath the surface. Warm coolth. In a pool. She could *drink* the bath, soap and all. What would be wonderful would be a glass of lemonade. But there was none. And she must stop soon.

She came up, and into her hair she worked the delicious edible soap. Her hair was growing, it was thicker and stronger. It would have to be cut, she could not manage it. But, not yet.

Oh, this must be wrong. Hurry – no. Be wrong. Oh, yes.

She lay back in the water, and heard a bird singing, deep in the fairy gardens of the Smolte palace.

She could stitch bones. So what? The nasty Elizabeth Willow need only be placated.

Annie dipped down again, under the water, and came up once more, gurgling and laughing. She raised her arms and smelled the delicacy of her young skin rinsed by the soap of the rich.

She dare not linger any more. A moment more—

Yes, a moment more, to enjoy the vision of her, the girl in the tub. He did not want her to stand up, to lift the towel they had left her, to get dressed, not yet.

She was better than the other ones.

She had a face that had sin in it, and her hair was between wet and dry now, flossing out in an acorn aureole above, dark as seaweed below, meandering on her flesh.

Her flesh. White and pearly. The breasts so exact and high. Sweets for nipples. And at her groin the brush of a brown autumn coppice.

Rupert, standing in the small chamber above the bathroom, looked through the chink. He felt himself swell in almost-readiness. He pressed his forehead to the warm plaster.

What was her name? Ember? Annie – Annie, that was it. *Anna.*

Not pretty, but better than pretty. White face and red mouth. The large limpid eyes. Sensual. A soulless mermaid.

Yes.

On her journey to the sewing room, Annie lost her way. She turned a corner and came out on a landing above a crimson carpeted stair. Up above the ceiling soared, painted blue and hung with brazen bells. On the walls were carpets. And at the stairs' foot, a palm man-tall in an urn of brass.

No one was there. Below, reflecting in the burnished floor, only a large ivory elephant on a basalt stand.

Something about it made her stomach turn over, and then she recalled why. She went quickly back, and along the corridor, and after two more turns, located the carved doors to the sewing room.

She sat down on one of the yellow couches, by the sewing cabinet Mrs Beare had shown her, and undoing it, she found again the myriad implements. How unlike the work basket of Rose. Here the cottons and silks were arranged in rainbow gradations, and in drilled rows were packets of needles, cushions of pins. On a dainty rack hung scissors with ivory handles, and little ivory thimbles, painted with the tiniest flowers.

Annie had never used a thimble. Her scarred thumb was proof of that. The ivory would not really have to touch her.

She threaded a needle and reached among the garments.

On the mantelpiece a gold and ivory clock told her that she had been a long while in the bath. Her hair slipped over her shoulders down the bodice of the young lady's dress.

There was ivory everywhere. She had better get used to it. It was very clean and white, not like—

The bird and mouse bones were more like the ivory that Annie had been given for one penny. She picked up the skull of the bird. Perversely, she began to sew it on to a silk shift, exactly as Elizabeth Willow had instructed.

As the needle moved, the barrier shifted in her head, and something fell. Annie reached up, and taking now a hank of her shining hair, pulled hard on it.

'No, don't,' said a man's voice. And then, barely audible, 'Why do you want to hurt yourself?'

Annie jumped up. Although she had been told to come here, she was instantly on guard and electric with guilt.

'Why, what a look,' he said. 'Am I so frightful?'

He was not. Tall and elegantly slender, clad in a gentleman's pale grey. His hair was black and he was handsome. She knew him from descriptions.

'Mr Rupert,' said Annie, putting down the words like too-sharp knives.

'And you must be the girl who sews. Anna. Sit.'

Annie did not speak. She sat.

'Well,' he said, 'I came to see you. That is, I heard you in here and I was looking for company.'

Annie still did not speak. How had he heard her, had she been noisy? She was not company for him. She was the drudge.

'Do say something, Anna. You're making me uncomfortable.'

Annie said nothing. She lowered her eyes and began to sew, cunningly transposing another garment over the evidence of sewn bones.

The man, Rupert Smolte, came into the room, and shut the door. He advanced immediately to the other couch, and sat down facing her. 'Do you mind if I smoke, Anna?'

'No, Sir.'

Why ask her? What could her wants matter?

He lit the cigarette and she smelled the perfume of its tobacco, rich accessory, like the soap that now scented her body.

'This house,' he said presently, 'I suppose you think it's quite grand. Or do you think it's entirely, hideously vulgar?'

Annie looked up once more and met his eyes. They were narrowed, black, in fans of sumptuous lashes. In the apricot shadow there he looked so handsome that he too was like the house, impossible.

'Go on, Anna. Answer frankly. You won't? Why not? What do you think we are? Aristocrats? Never, I assure you. A jumped-up soldier's family, and my mother a chorus girl on the halls. Just talk to me, for God's sake.'

His boldness made her bold. He dared her to be, and since his very presence was a sort of challenge, she must sneak out of cover and try what he was at.

'Why should I have an opinion,' she said, 'Sir?'

'*Why*? Because you're a woman not a vegetable. Look at you. A very narcissus. And you speak beautifully. You could give my bloody mother a lesson or two. Anna—'

'It's Annie,' she said, 'Sir. Annie is my name.'

'All right. If you want. Whatever you want, Annie.'

Oh, that's his game. Probably he tried all the new maids. Was it even arranged by his mother – the chorus girl – the bath and the dress, the loose hair?

'I think I must go back to the kitchen,' said Annie.

'To your charming pots and pans. No. Stay and talk to me.'

He was the power here. He could do what he liked. And she, Annie, what should she do? If she pleased him would it help her? No, more likely drag her down. She had seen the girls in the city flung into the workhouses to give birth, in squalor amid the rats, to the children of their betters.

But neither could she fight him. He was not a lout of the back-streets. *Leave me alone or you'll be sorry*.

She could not say it, here in this house.

What then, in Christ's name, was she to do?

A flit of panic was masked in her lowered eyes. She began to sew steadily, and when the needle bit into her finger, she did not flinch, only moved her hand so no blood should go on the white, white dress.

'You see,' he said, 'I'm not like my family. My awful vulgar house-ridden family. I'm the weakling, the useless one.'

She glanced again. Despite herself, his voice had begun partly to fascinate her. He did what they always did, he spoke too much, the surest sign of the coming wish to use, and yet, it was a melodious voice. It was – how obscenely strange – melodious in the way Rose's voice had been. Exactly like that. The same fashion of lifting and sinking. Like Rose.

'I've nothing to do,' he said, 'but sit about like an old, old man, and remember. Do you have memories, Annie? Of course. But my life stopped, *was* stopped, when I was a child.'

He coughed. He turned and mashed out the cigarette angrily in a brass dish on the table.

'Well,' he said, 'not for long.'

Annie looked. He was making her respond, as a clever actor will. But in the shadow he was very pale now. His eyes, infused with pain or fear, were larger. In turn he lowered them.

'I'm a coward,' he said. 'I don't want to die.'

Annie had stopped sewing.

'Yes, that's shameful, isn't it, Annie. I should be a brave man. I shouldn't mind it. Oh, but Annie . . . I do mind. Wouldn't you?'

Annie said, 'Everyone dies.'

'Yes, how true. What a little viper you are. But you've got thirty or forty years of shimmering life in you. It's safe for you to say.'

He held her gaze. She had never seen anyone like him, except on heights, in the distance. Something in her had quickened, and she crouched above it, ready to leap to her feet and run away after all. *He's making a fool of me*. But: *I must listen*.

'Annie, your face is suddenly full of kindness. Your eyes glow with it. What a gentle girl you are, really.'

It's a lie. She knew she did not seem the way he described her. It was another enchantment. He was making her into what he said. Resist then.

'I'm sure I'm very sorry, Sir,' she said, falsely, in Rose's soothing way, not now like him, or herself.

'Yes, be sorry. Please.'

He coughed loudly, perhaps for a minute, filling the treacly air with sound. She was perhaps meant to be startled, but then she had heard coughing before, coughs worse than this, the body that must produce them too exhausted to make much noise. Yet when the seizure left him he leant back, as if exhausted. His eyes were shut now. She must stare at his face and be ready to look away at once when he opened them.

On the mantelpiece the clock struck five.

Annie's stomach twisted so violently it hurt her.

He had sat up abruptly, and stared at her now.

'What is it? You don't like a clock striking?'

'No.'

'Poor Annie,' he said. 'And now you must go back to the infernal regions of Mrs Rope.'

She began to put away the needles and shut up the sewing cabinet.

'I want to see you again,' he said. 'What do you say?'

'What can I say?'

'Say you don't mind.'

Annie's face lit with a flash of fury. He saw it, and his eyes avoided hers a moment. But only a moment.

'I can't say anything, Sir. I can't make *you* do anything.'

'No,' he said, 'that's true. Better say yes, then, Annie.'

He rose, as she did, and caught her hand.

'You've pricked your finger,' he said. 'Fall into a sleep, Annie, and I'll climb up all the thorns and kiss you awake.'

He leaned over her, and she smelled the scent of him, male and washed clean, the expensive incense of tobacco, starched linen, and the tang of cedarwood.

Annie felt giddy. She wanted to strike at him, kick out, and fly. She gripped herself in terror. She was more afraid in those instants of her own self than of him.

Then, he touched his lips to her forehead. He was cool.

'Give my curse to Mrs Rope.'

He let her go, and she walked stiffly from the room. Like a noble lady, he thought, upright. Unwilling to admit that anything had passed between them.

'That's not nice now. I won't have it in here,' said Clarrie, pointing to the geranium growing slimily in the muddy water. 'Look what it's done to the tumbler. I'll have to ask Mrs Rope for another.'

Out from the seven o'clock morning kitchen, Annie bore the geranium towards the compost behind the hothouses.

And in the lower walk she thought, *No, I won't*. And she went instead into the yard, under the bronze statue whose Indian name she had been told, the god in his chariot wheel. In the court beyond, two horses looked mildly from their stalls at her, and Darius appeared with a bucket, which he set down.

'Good day to you,' he said.

'You said you'd let me have a pot of earth for this,' said Annie, with awkward animosity. She was ready to have him shout her away, but the fair-haired man only said, 'Ah, yes. I remember.' And took the wet and curdled geraniums out of her hand. 'They have fine roots on them now.' He did not add that weeks had gone by since her first request.

Annie watched him go off with the plant and the bucket. Maybe he would only feed the geraniums to the horses, which seemed rather interested in them.

She turned and walked out of the stable yard, and back through the first yard, and on into the walk.

In the kitchen she began upon the pans angrily. She burned with anger, and only the hard spine of common sense kept her from snapping at prissy Clarrie. She did give impertinent ratty Tiff a clip round the ear. For some reason Tiff burst into raucous tears, and then Mrs Rope bellowed from the kitchen.

Rage of course was futile. Annie was in the trap. What could she do? Run away and starve, or die of assault on the road. She had no home. She was no one and nothing. She banged the pans like cymbals, and Mrs Rope roared that she was a beast of Babylon.

At one, after the servants' dinner, Mrs Beare evolved in the kitchen to remind Annie she was now meant to go up and do her sewing for Miss Elizabeth.

Annie obeyed, mounting through the house with a furious step, that became hesitant and anxious when she had gained the upper regions. She shunned the bath, and only put on there the lady-dress, not undoing her hair, shaking now either with anger or nerves, she did not know which.

All afternoon, until the striking of the clock for five – she had grown used to it already, it was not like the clock of Mrs Marpolis – Annie sewed in that hot room. But no one came in on her. There was no hint of him.

When she went down again she felt leaden, washed out, as if her personal city had been awaiting an invasion with muskets and cannon, but the enemy had failed to show his scarlet banners. There had been no gunfire. She had not had to fight.

'Don't dream, Annie. This table needs a scrub again.'

Somewhere in the panic before the upstairs dinner, Annie was visited by recollection of Rose, how she had been over Innocent. Afraid, enamoured, resenting and eluding, ever-aware, as if he were omnipresent as the notion of God.

But Annie was safe down here in Hell.

Last night there had been a kind of dullness, like the numbness of a blow before it begins to smart. The anger too would fade. She was helpless. Better get used to it. She could, possibly, trick him. He would lose interest eventually. There were other girls, and women of his own kind. But then, did he only grow tired of the chase when he had brought the victim down?

After their dinner had gone up, and the fuming curries got by worse-fuming Mrs Rope, the usual devasted aftermath swamped the kitchen.

Only the business of the pans went on, but now all would be tidy by eleven o'clock. Annie had grown adept, even though Tiff stayed to help when made, more hindrance than assistant, and stealing little things, bits off cakes and spoonfuls of the lidded preserves, skittering round the kitchen and the larder like a fly. 'Don't you tell, you, Ember. I'll poke your eyes out if you do.' Annie never answered these threats. She could kill Tiff simply. She could kill anyone, she supposed, if she must. But then, to kill brought a penalty.

In bed, no longer numbed, Annie could not sleep. The attic room was like the kitchen oven, the sheet was fire. On the windowsill, emptiness. He had fed the geranium to the horses. They lay now, with flowers in their stomachs, slumbering.

But horses did not lie down to sleep. And there was something else, very big, standing and sleeping also, in a forest where enormous vines and shoots towered upward with the trees—

Annie woke. She heard Clarrie snuffling and Tiff in her obdurate silence.

I will sleep. Don't dream, Annie.

Without dreams, Annie slept.

The next day came, and the next afternoon, above in the sewing room. She finished a dress for Elizabeth Willow, and had to tell the housekeeper. Also, untold, Annie sewed the bones of mice on to a petticoat. She worked at this with a twisted mouth. She thought, *He'll walk in and see*. But Rupert Smolte did not walk into the room. Not that day, not the day after. And these were the four allotted days, and they were over, until the following week.

Annie felt strengthless. Her anger and nervousness had wrung her out. Tears of tension pierced her eyes like the needles her fingers.

He had not come. He had lost interest after all. That was her luck: she had been spared.

A flatness hung on her stale and tiring fifth day. Only the pans, the floors, the stupid squabbling madhouse of the kitchen.

She could not sleep again that night. She thought of how he had held her hand and leaned over her. Fits of heat and cold rushed across her flesh, like the water from the white bath.

She detected something, some foolish sensibility. *Acting like a lady* . . . Annie Ember had no time or space to be susceptible.

Yet, she could not sleep. She dozed until the burning light of earliest morning rayed through the window, sliced the wall. Then she got up and the stale and thankless day began again, ran on and on, and finally ended in the repeated climb up to the attic, longing to sleep—

I must sleep. She searched for Rose's murmur, but Rose did not speak to her now.

She had never mourned Rose. Or, that was wrong, she had mourned for Rose from the second Innocent had died. Perhaps she had mourned for Rose all her life with Rose.

No, not Rose's voice. His voice that had seemed to her to have, so wickedly, the same inflexion.

'Can't you sleep, Annie? Even after you pricked your finger. Why not pretend? And I'll kiss you awake.'

His lips on her forehead had been nearly cold, but then he was ill, he had said so.

Well, the rich could afford their sicknesses.

Clarrie snored. Tiff did not even seem to breathe. The room was airless, suffocating.

Annie sat up slowly, and raised her arms above her head. She stared into the dark, and let the mental door give way, and watched Rose fall. And fall. And some water left her eyes, moved down Annie's face, but she felt this was not grief. And anyway, she dared make no noise.

They had left her an oil-lamp, on the scullery shelf, and by its light Annie scrubbed the last pan. Tiff had gone up an hour before, and the others much earlier. It was midnight, Annie suspected. The influx of extra pans had come late, some supper dish. Annie did not question.

As she swilled away the disgusting water, she heard an odd and threatening sound. The kitchen door that gave on the yard was being unlocked. Mrs Beare had seen to it earlier, as she always did. Perhaps Churton had unusually come down for something, avoiding the house, or Rawlings, who now and then prowled the outer courts, after his own bowls and pots had been seen to.

Annie dried her hands and took the lamp.

She walked out of the kitchen and stood there, to face what had arrived. In the dark golden light of the lamp, her face was savage more than tired. Her eyes had their shadows again. They widened.

'My God, a tigress in an apron.'

Her legs began to tremble, and there was a sinking heaviness in her stomach, her loins, as if she must drop on the floor. She held up the light staunchly. Her enemy, Rupert Smolte.

'Don't say you're glad to see me. Obviously you're not. The scouring and scraping are preferable.'

'What can I get you, Sir?' said Annie.

Her voice was firm. She had learned early to evade, hide.

'Oh, nothing.' He glanced about. 'And here she works away her days.'

'I've done now,' she said.

She put down the lamp again. They had told her to douse it and light instead a candle for the ascent to the attic. She went to the candle box, and suddenly he was beside her. His shadow sprang up on the wall, covered her. Instinctively she stepped away, from him, and from the shadow.

He was in his shirt, no jacket, nothing gentlemanly but for the ruffle of the linen. He was hot tonight, she could feel the heat of him.

Her heart ran like a hare. Was there to be an escape?

'Then if you'll excuse me,' she said.

'I won't excuse you, Annie. I'm lonely. I want you to come into the gardens with me. You'll like them. They're very pretty. Full of curiosities my father lugged out of India. You'd like to see, wouldn't you?'

She said, 'I'm not allowed.'

'Yes you are. I allow you.'
'You'll get me dismissed.'
'Nonsense. Stop talking like a prim little maid. Take off your apron and that dunce's cap. Take down your hair.'
Annie swallowed. Never in her life had she felt this terrible compound of fear and excitement. She said, 'I won't.'
'What?' He laughed. 'You'll defy me? Cruel Annie. Let me tell you how silly you appear. Have you ever realized? But with your hair loose you look like – not a lady, better than that. You look like a girl who is the daughter of a great magician. A nymph who lives in a tree. Acorn-coloured hair. Oh, Annie, to please me.'
'Why should I please you?' she said. Now her voice cracked, she could not help it.
He said, seriously, 'It would be tolerable for me if someone did.'
'Am I to pity you, then?'
'You might.'
A flare of temper spangled through her. She said, before she could prevent it, 'Oh yes, pity you, with your great house and your fine clothes and nothing to do but torment *me*.'
The lids and marvellous lashes had almost shut his eyes. They glimmered out at her, through the lamplight and the dark.
'Is that what I do?'
She put her hand down into the candle box, and he caught her hand again, and drew it out. He raised it and held it against her head. 'Take off the cap. Take down your hair. I'll undo this scullion's apron.' And he moved behind her and his hands were on the back of her waist, untying the apron quickly, neatly. *Done it before.*
She pulled the cap off and threw it on the floor. His hands came up and went into her hair. 'Wonderful hair,' he said, 'such quantities yet so soft.'
She slid away from him and undid the plait he had already loosened. The hair cascaded down her. She felt its weight almost as if she were naked.
And then, the lamp went out. She gave a low cry.
'And you're afraid of the dark,' he said. 'Christ, you don't know what darkness is. English darkness is nothing, Annie. Nothing lives in it, you see. Take my hand. Come on, take it. In a

minute, when we're outside, you'll see by moonlight.'

His hand was cold, although his heat had scorched her. There was alcohol on his breath, but clean, almost aromatic. He led her out, and the yard was dimly blue. Above the walls a half moon gave its light. After the oppression of the kitchen, how cool the night, and the scent of horses and trees, and faintly of flowers, which increased as he took her into the lower avenue.

Annie did fear the dark, the moonlit dark perhaps more especially. She had known the nights of the city, and huddled indoors. Here branches wove against the dark blue luminous dome of the sky. Anything might be abroad, beyond the yew hedge.

But she feared him more than the dark. He had made her speak imprudently, insolently. He had made her throw down her shield.

They did not cross the outer stable yard, though she heard the horses moving as he negligently guided her aside, through a narrow place in the hedge. The glasshouses glinted above, under the moon, and then they came down long mossy steps into a grass well of shadow. Water shone, in a stone trough, but they went by.

Great tangled arches passed over them, and the singing odour of jasmin replaced the sour tints of compost, vegetables and greens.

They moved through a walled passageway and came up steps again, on to a wide lawn.

A shoulder of the house reared high, jewelled above with smothered curtained lights. The minarets and domes were less believable than ever beneath the fey and umbrous filter of the moon.

Then there were tall trees, which massed and shut off the house. The smell of roses now.

'We can go this way, but the thorns will scratch you. Put up your other hand to guard your face.'

They traversed a funnel of needles and attar. The thorns scrawled her sleeves, the back of her hand, her hand in his, his hand.

They came out into the rose garden through the tunnel of flowers and claws.

He let go of her hand at once, as if he detested it. This

disorientated her. How cold her hand had become in his, while the rest of her was at a different temperature.

A breeze blew from the moon upon her face. She could hardly make him out, hemmed in among the briars, only everywhere the mooned splash of the faces of roses lifted as if to be kissed.

'Look there,' he said, 'do you see Nag going up the arbour?'

Annie stared. Something vast and coiling, sheened silver, twined. 'Is it a snake?'

'A cobra. But it's stone. And there, a tiny goddess in the grass.'

Annie turned her head slavishly. A nude woman of voluptuous proportions, *her* hair wound like a crown. She had four arms, and in her four hands were items too small to be discerned.

He said, almost irritably, 'Come along.'

She went after him, through the garden of roses and snakes and goddess, and into a second garden where there was again the shine of water, but everywhere. In a tall basin huge lilies had closed their cups; they were not like the roses which wanted the moon to kiss them.

All around, the towered hedges, and the breath of flowers, and the cup-closed dark.

'Do you hear how silent it is?' he said. 'Imagine a night full of things chattering and shrieking, the buzz of insects, frogs croaking. Howls. Whispers.'

Rupert leaned on the support of a lacquer bridge that crossed the pool to a six-foot Shiva Blue-Throat dancing on a stand of verdigris.

'There is a god there,' he said, 'gazing at you, Annie. If we were in India, you'd have felt his presence immediately.'

He took a little flask out from the lattice of the bridge, where he had previously fixed it. He drank down a mouthful of the bitter cloying laudanum. He thought of the woman coming in, in the dark, and how at first she had had to force him, how he had struck at her.

The medicine did not soothe, or else it was the memory. He coughed rackingly.

Annie listened to him cough. She went to him and struck him quite hard on the back, as she had seen rough women do with their children.

The moment she had done it, though, she darted away in terror.

She had overstepped some final bound, and did not know why, or what had made her do it.

The coughing had choked off. He said, 'You little bitch, you hurt me.'

Then with a sliding over of the confused panes of darkness, a rush and crackle of plants, he fell down into the grass, straight down – was gone as the night folded over him.

Annie stayed motionless, and ominously now, now Rupert's form was no longer between them, she saw the gleaming Shiva reflected in the face of the pool. A being poised on one leg, many armed, whirling – yet static. As she was. In the dance of making and unmaking, creation-destruction.

Annie lowered herself to her knees, and crawled to the spot where Rupert Smolte had vanished. Either he had fainted or he dissembled, probably, certainly, the latter. Yet she was not sure. She hated him yet wanted to touch him. Wanted him to be unconscious so that she might run away – and dreaded too that she had harmed him.

She found his arm, outflung. The pulse in his wrist hammered as her own did. She reached out her other hand and found the arch of his ribs and the heart galloping under it. Between the grass, the moon made a mask of his upper face, the eyes closed like death, the lashes black as the ferns of the garden.

In the pool a fish jumped in a ring of gilt.

Rupert Smolte caught her by the waist, and pulled her over, down, to lie on the surface of his body.

She held back her head and struggled, but his grip was like iron. Although she had the survivor's strength, it was no match, in her young underfed shape, for his. And she could not attack him. Dared not, could not. Would not.

'The moon's in your hair,' he said.

'Let me go.'

He roped his arms around her waist. Her back could not resist any more and she could only hold herself away by her hands clutching at the ground, and finally she was finished. She dropped against him as he had dropped on to the hard earth. She felt every inch of him under her, the thin adamantine frame of him, its heat, the knot of lust at his groin. She had lost, was lost. Let him get on with it. It would soon be done.

But though he held her pinned to him, he did nothing more.

Possibly minutes passed.

At last, she raised her head. Her face was close to his. She stared at him and he stared back at her. Intolerable endless brevity.

And then he let her go.

'Well, there you are, free.'

She lay on him a moment more, then rolled herself aside. Nausea enveloped her. The shame of night.

'You can go back now. Back to your darling kitchen.'

She did not know if she could find the way. She would have to.

He stood up as she did, and the nether dark where they had been flowed off from them.

'I can still feel your flesh against me,' he said.

It must be true, for against her own body his still pressed hard as rock, there, not there, insubstantial, like a dream.

'Tomorrow,' he said, 'you'll learn you're to help my sister with her dress. Then, when she's sent you away, you'll come to me.'

'No,' said Annie.

'Yes. Liar. You're mine.'

And he reached out again and effortlessly took hold of her. He kissed her mouth with closed impatient moving lips, her throat and even the fabric of the scullery dress above her breasts. The world seemed to spin off from under her. She fought him and he grasped her hands. She had not fought him as she knew how to fight. *Liar*. She buried her face against his shirt and he pushed her away.

'Go to the sewing room tomorrow,' he said. 'I'll find you there.'

She thought of Rose. *Yes, Innocent*.

She said, 'Yes.'

He said, 'Say *Lord* to me. Say, *Yes, Lord*.'

She hung her head and said, 'Yes, Lord.'

He turned from her, as if he had thrust her out of the rooms of his mind.

Annie retraced her steps through the sorcerous garden of water and the mystic garden of roses, and in the tunnel of claws, her hands were scratched again as she should have scratched out his eyes.

4

'Wake up, Ember!'

One minute she was deep in darkness, and then shaken out into her body, in the coppery morning light.

Clarrie let her go. Tiff stood sniggering.

'You should have been up long before,' said Clarrie. 'Make haste now. You'll get a telling off from Mrs Rope.'

Annie got out of bed in her coarse nightgown and dressed behind the screen as they left the room.

While she did this, the episodes of the prior night came back to her, in portions. When she washed her face and pinned on her retrieved cap, Annie had collected them all. So, despite the warning of Mrs Rope, she stood for another space in front of the mirror, thoughtless, tranced.

She ran down through the back of the house, light-footed, queasy, and in the kitchen after all Mrs Rope, presiding at the tea-pot, did not shout. It was a day like the other days. And utterly dissimilar.

At noon, when the servants were sitting down to their dinner, Mrs Beare swept in and inclined her big head at Annie. 'You're to go up as soon as you've eaten, Ember. And at five, go in to Miss Elizabeth. Tonight Madam wishes Ember to remain upstairs, so don't expect her back, Mrs Rope. You're lucky, Ember. Make sure you are a credit to us.'

Annie got up and bobbed, and when Mrs Beare had gone, Tiff dug her fork into Annie's arm. 'Miss Fancy.'

Annie took no notice. She picked at her food, and Mrs Rope decreed the heat had upset Ember's appetite, and had her given a quarter glass of beer, to toughen her up for her busy evening above.

At twelve-thirty, Annie went up into the house.

She had wondered vaguely if any of the below-stairs staff knew more than they said; there was such connivance at work it seemed to Annie only a fool would not guess at something. But no remark had been made, and Tiff was merely jealous and nasty, as usual.

Annie went first to the sewing room, and there lay the pile of clothes, stacked ready, as if legitimate. The chemises and shifts with bones she had concealed at the bottom of the stack, and now she fingered these too. A weirdness lay on everything, so that everything must be re-examined.

When the sewing room door opened, Annie froze, her heart in her mouth. But through the door came Lady Flower, in green flounces, her emeralds in her ears. Annie bobbed.

'I see,' Flower said, irrelevantly. She stared at Annie, frowning. 'Have they informed you of your new duties?'

'Yes, Madam.'

'You're to work here until five, then go up to my daughter. You'll help her with her clothes. This will be excellent practice for you, Ember. Perhaps something can be made of you.'

She knew. Oh yes. Her eyes were fixed on Annie but did not once look at Annie. The eyes of Flower, Lady Smolte saw purely necessity.

'And tonight . . . you'll go on with your sewing. There's plenty to do. Be industrious. Some dinner will be brought you.'

'Yes, Madam.'

'Go and take your bath now,' said Flower, imperiously, the trace of lower city suddenly quite decided in her voice. 'Wash your hair. A girl can't wash her hair too often. Don't pay attention to these old wives' tales. I never knew a girl catch cold from *that*. And you're healthy, Ember. Yes, I can see that you are. I know the signals. Good skin, teeth. Well, go along.'

A procuress, then, Lady Flower.

Annie walked to the bathroom, and there were the three white dresses they had given her, hung up ready. And the scented soap, and another soap for her hair, and there some essence in a bottle. Annie uncorked and sniffed at it. No whore of the ordinary street would smell like this . . . She filled the bath full of water and unclad herself, and stepped in.

This was for him. Every stroke of her hands, every creamy lathering, was for him.

It was as if he watched her, and she grew hot and buried herself under the cool water.

After the bath she put on the essence and a dress. And the scent that floated now from her body alarmed her. Her wet hair dried in the heat of the afternoon as she sewed up the seams of the ultimate gown in the sewing room. No more to do now. Nothing at all.

She sat playing with the coloured silks, the thimbles, not minding them, not thinking.

Not thinking of anything, for the images that erupted in her mind were solely animal.

She should run away. Everything terrible she had seen on the city streets might become of her. But he wanted her. A kind of fever blossomed in her, rising a little with every second.

At five, she stood like an automaton, took up the finished clothes, and went along the corridor and up to the Smolte daughter's chamber in the tower.

No one answered her knock. The door stood wide.

Under a window the cat was spasmodically toying with a dead robin.

Annie had never seen a bird so near, but dead, it looked unreal.

Elizabeth Willow was not in the white room, nor did she come from any of the other doors that opened from the landing below.

Annie put the clothes on the bed, and observing this, the cat spat and hissed at her.

Annie stepped away, and out again, and down the stair. More of a pretence went on then even than she had surmised.

Presumably she need only go back to the sewing room – and he would appear, as he had promised. She hesitated. But all about were the walls in their gilded paper, and fringed curtains and latticed windows showing the gardens where, last night, he had drawn her to an enclosure more profound than that of any room.

At that instant a woman moved into the corridor and approached her. She was a foreigner, with a flat snake's face, and her hair in an unbecoming bun.

'You are Annie? Follow me.'

Annie followed her. A demarcation line had been reached, by the use of her first name.

Despite the medley of emotions now boiling up in her, Annie noticed the woman had a beautiful way of walking, and she held her head high, as if she were proud not of herself, but of life. But then Annie lost track of that and could only feel.

They went up and down stairs, across landings with ebony doors having brass or gold pictures on them. Lamps with vermilion tassels hung above, and brass bells, and on the walls passed paintings of Indian scenes, carpets, cases of stuffed birds – yellow, turquoise, green – unlike the dead robin in everything but surcease.

They crossed eventually into a passage with a polished floor, and reached a door on which was a brass tree.

The woman turned there and gazed at Annie. The unattractive darkish face was calm as a pool at dusk. The dull eyes had a light in them, you saw, a far-away shadow of some soft fire.

'I will come to you later,' said the woman. 'I am Luksmi. I will not forget. Remember, I will come.'

Annie said bluntly, 'Why?' knowing that the fire in her own self blazed up, visible, past subterfuge.

'There will be things to do, later,' said the woman.

Annie said, 'What things?'

Luksmi said, 'We are slaves.'

'No,' said Annie.

'Remember,' said the woman, mysterious and gentle. 'I will come.'

Then she left Annie and walked with her dancer's walk along the passage and out of sight.

And Annie turned squarely to the door with the tree and knocked on it sharply.

No one answered, again. Nothing. There was utter quiet, only the inexplicable susurrus of the house itself, as if it slowly breathed. Smells of beeswax, musk, the aroma of her own scented skin.

Annie did not knock a second time.

She had been brought up here – a *slave*, a slave, what else? – and now there was the door – but she could open the door.

He had not met her where he had said he would. Nothing had been as she had been told it would be. That was part of a plan, to bewilder her – lest she grow stronger and resist?

Annie closed her hand over the brass doorknob and turned it.

Beyond was a wooden panelled chamber. On a round table, a monkey crouched, with life-like crystal eyes and an enamel orange in its paw. Over the walls were guns, knives, two hundred pieces of the cutlery of death. And Rupert stood by the window, whose ochre blind had been pulled down between ox-blood curtains. He was leaning there, and as she came visible to him, said, 'Look at that, Annie.' In a rack in front of him lay a sort of deadly musical instrument, a gun-metal trumpet five feet or more in length, ending in a stock of white tooth. 'An elephant gun,' he said. 'My father used it. Come and touch the ivory, Annie.'

But she saw only him, and she walked into the room and up to the gun, and poised there, waiting.

'You don't understand,' he said, 'do you? Do you even know what an elephant is? A massive charmless brute. It takes something this size to puncture its hide.'

She put out her hand and laid one finger on the stock incestuously made from the tusks of the beast it killed.

'Do you like ivory, Annie?'

She looked up into his face. Today the countenance of this man was lax, but she recognized the texture – that of craving desire. She wondered if he would instantly push her on to the table and possess her, squashed against the indifferent monkey.

But he only moved away from her, glanced from her, opened another door and beckoned her to go after him.

The sitting room, presumably his, was bathed like the gun room in the ochre light of drawn blinds.

The details of the room, awash in this light, did not clarify themselves. She could really see, properly, only Rupert.

'Look, there's some food here. Cold things, but you won't find them cold. I want you to try this.'

She did not want to eat. Her heart seemed to have filled up her chest, there was no margin for air, let alone food.

He lifted a decanter from a table and poured out two glasses of red wine. 'Have this first.' She took the wine, because he gave it to her. She absorbed a mouthful – it was bitter, metallic, leaden, and too warm. She swallowed it somehow. 'Now this.' He held before her, in his fingers, a doughy bready substance, on which some cooked vegetables rested. It had the smell of the curry meals which Rawlings prepared, and doubtless Rawlings had prepared these too. Annie took the morsel of unleavened bread and bit into it cautiously. The flavour was strange, sweet like Mrs Rope's holiday cake, yet savoury, peppery, sullen. She swallowed it also and her throat burned, so she drank at once from the goblet of wine.

'How obedient you are, Annie. Are you doing all this to please me?'

Annie found she could not look at him any more.

Instead her eyes roved round the chamber, but nothing would adhere. It was a welter of forms, impressions, swathed in the decayed blond glare of blinded westering sun.

'Drink some more of the wine. Eat a mouthful of that. It isn't spicy, scarcely.' He put a plate now – one of the glorious painted plates from the upstairs service – into her hand. Little flowers of curry, coloured pickles, he had set them out for her, as if to tempt a child. Annie thought of Rose chewing violet cachous. Rupert wanted her to *taste* of these things. No one had ever tempted her before.

Well, she was to be his whore, she must please him.

She ate some more of the food. Its savour sung up into her brain, and the wine had begun to affect her slightly, as she had known it would. Two things she had never had in her life. And the other, unknown, element, his love-making, surely, soon. But he did not seek proximity with her as he had yesterday, only handed her a plate, refilled her glass – a blue glass like an ink bottle in which the wine was black – moved around her. As if she was in a wizard's circle.

She turned abruptly and put her hand on his arm.

He said, 'Not yet, Annie. Are you so eager?'

She averted her head. *She* was not to attempt *him*. She must be docile. A slave. A hot blush, worse than in the bath, suffused her from her scalp to her thighs.

'If you knew,' he said, 'what it's been like, waiting for you. I wanted you to be here so much. I could only think of you.'

Was this true?

No, she thought. *Yes*. Across the gap between them, she felt him trembling now, as she did, and put down the plate.

'Finish your wine.'

She tilted the glass into her mouth and drained it.

He had taken her hand, removed the glass. They were seated on a sofa, and the room swam under the yellow river of the light.

'You want to please me, don't you,' he said.
'Yes.'
'More than anything? Say, more than anything.'
He had made her call him *Lord*. She said, 'Why do you want me?'
'Oh, Annie,' he said. 'Stupid Annie.'
Well, she was stupid. She wished to press herself against him. She yearned to be his. And like the swimming incoherent room, afterwards was not of any concern, yet.
'Take off your dress,' he said. She reached back for the hooks, and he said, 'No. I'll do it.'
Then he undid the garment, and peeled it down her body, and drew her against him in her petticoat and corset.
To be this way with a man. Had Rose ever felt— Forget Rose.
She wanted him to kiss her, but he did not. He bent back her head and gazed into her face and his eyes seemed to sear hers out so she shut them. He unlaced her corset and his hands went round her ribs, up under her arms. He had her breasts and she heard herself make sounds as his fingers rubbed against their points, squeezed the mounds of them. Then he slid down her and he had drawn off her boots, and wrapped his hands about her ankles.
Annie raised her lids. The room swelled and condensed. She was drowning, in the wine and in his need of her. She tried to slip down to the floor, to be with him, but he stayed her.
'See, a garland,' he said.
She glanced again. How silly . . . She laughed.
'You love me,' he said. 'You'd do anything for me. Slaves,' he said.
He slid his palms up from her ankles, over her legs. She flung back her head and the room wheeled – flight. She was flying not drowning.
'You see,' he said, 'when she came in, I couldn't sleep. It was her work to see that I did. And so she wanted to give me something.'
'Who?' whispered Annie.
'Ah, the Indian woman. The ayah. A kind of nurse, Annie.'
'Yes, I know what an ayah is.'
'Ssh,' he said. 'Let me tell you.' He held her thighs fiercely and looked up into her face, her parted lips and fast shut eyes.

'I struggled with her, Annie. I fought her. It was a battle. I hurt her.'

'Yes,' she said.

Rupert got up. He pulled Annie upwards with him. And then, since he had tied her ankles together with a silken tasselled purple cord, he partly carried her out of that room into another.

This second room, not his bedchamber, lay at the centre of the suite. In it there were no windows, only plain white walls, darkened now in the miasma of a lit candlebranch. He shut the door.

The bed – there was one – was a four-poster, and round it hung the yellowish gauze curtains of remembrance, mosquito netting.

Rupert raised Annie and lifted her right arm up against the right hand post. There he tied it with another purple cord, tight, binding into the knot a skein of her long brown hair.

Annie's eyes opened only a fraction. She tried to ask what he did. No words would come. Languorously she observed as he bound her left hand, her hair, to the left hand post. And as he pulled then the rest of her clothes from her body, at length cutting off her drawers, leaving her naked as an icon of ivory in the candlemurk, she watched.

'Beautiful Annie,' he said. 'My darling.'

He gagged her with a purple scarf.

Her head drooped. She hung heavily from the cords.

Somewhere she heard her own voice, inside her now, under the gag and the laudanum-drugged wine. It was shouting at her, but she could not reason why. He would make love to her soon.

Rupert Smolte took up, from the top of a small carved cupboard, an ivory rod that had on it three ivory claws.

Going to Annie he held her left breast in the fluttering golden gloom, then scored down it with the ivory.

Annie's eyes opened, the lids like shutters flying wide. She did not scream.

He drew the ivory up, then down, her body, over her upheld arms, her bosom, over her stomach, and three thin threads of darkness, criss-crossing, like the wine in the blue glass, followed.

His eyes were narrowed now to slits. The sweat stood on him like pearls.

He gasped and tossed the ivory aside and ran back to the chest and brought a stick, an ivory stick.

He struck her. He struck her across the arms and breasts, over the upper belly, on the waist and stomach. He moved the stick against her groin, rubbed it there, outside her body, then slashed across her hips and thighs.

On her cross Annie struggled. The screams could not get out of her, they roiled in her belly, stuck.

Rupert sank his face into the fur of her loins, he squeezed her body between his hands, then stood away, and coming to the back of her, kneeling on the bed, he lashed her across the spine and buttocks.

The scream which came was like a squeal, like the noise rabbits made, they said, in traps.

At the sound of it, he sobbed, and mouthed her, her bruised and bloodied flesh, rocking her against him. When he came about her again, there was blood on his face, hers, and he was white as something nearly dead, a panting, starving face. Who was he?

'I mustn't be too quick,' he muttered. 'Not spoil it.'

He turned from her, and went to the table where there was another decanter of dark wine. He drank from the lip of it, and she saw. He kissed the decanter, not her, kissed the wine, with her blood on him, on his cheek.

What had happened?

The pain was all over her, flaring up as if she had caught fire.

Like Innocent, with Rose, he had not marked her face.

Annie's bladder let go a trickle of urine, and she felt a dim swirling embarrassment, and her head fell back again. She heard him say, 'You're so lovely, Christ, oh Christ—' And then, 'I hit her and made her bleed, I bit her. But then she managed me. I had to take it. The opium.' And then he said, 'Christ, too fast.' And he drank again, and then, looking back at her, as if remiss in courtesy, he said, 'You too. Yes, have another drink, Annie.' And he came to her and she saw both his hands had something clutched up towards her, in one the decanter, and in the other a type of flail . . .

He eased the gag from her mouth, gently.

'Here.'

She crushed her head away from the wine. She could smell the drug in it now, for this was mixed more powerfully.

'Yes,' he said, coaxing, 'take some.' He lifted the flail and tickled with it her neck. The strands were leather, and here and there were minuscule teeth of metal, all caught in an ivory handle. He showed her, the handle. Seven skulls of ivory. He put his cheek against hers, so after all her own blood was on her face. 'Beautiful Annie. My goddess.'

Something in her mouth. Words. She said, 'Then get down on your knees and pray to me, you bloody rat.'

Rupert tilted his head away to look at her. 'What?'

'Pray, to me. Get down. You can whip me after. Bloody worship me first.'

His whole face began to shake. The shaking was over all of him. He slithered down her frame, pulling his face over her lacerated body, and knelt there at her bound feet.

She looked down on him, his bowed head.

What had he said – the ayah had *managed* him.

'Pray,' said Annie, or the voice which had possessed her.

And Rupert began to splutter phrases, some English and some not, grasping her knees, and as he did so the final spasm overwhelmed him. She knew what it was. She knew as he writhed against her, cries bursting out of him much louder than her tortured tiny rabbit scream. It went on and on. She thought he would never stop, and then he collapsed backward, crashed over on the floor.

He seemed properly dead now.

She flew above him, still hanging from her ropes. And suddenly her left hand slid free and fell too, useless, against her side. The cord had given way. If he had been nearer she would have reached and pulled out his hair, torn out his eyes, but she was too far. She vomited, and the vomit soiled her further. On the floor lay the flail, which might have killed her.

Dependent from one arm now, she slept the sleep of the damned.

It was Luksmi who woke her this time.

'I am here. I will care for you.'

The candles were out and the only light came in from the other room, morose and choked by shadows.

Annie tried to curse Luksmi, but Luksmi only undid the cords and laid Annie down on the bed, the netting pushed aside.

'There are salves I know. These will help you. You will have no scars. You will get well.'

'Is he dead?' Annie asked. But Luksmi did not apparently fathom her slurred and almost noiseless speech. And in any event, of course he would not have died. He lived on, and Annie too. Annie too.

Part Three

1

Riding up country into the jungle-forest after the rains was, he concluded, his punishment. He had done enough favours and oiled enough palms, they did not do anything else to him. Only attached him to this wretch Withers, and sent him up into the green hell of the rukh. Hampton Smolte's exploits at the age of twenty-one had been risky but lucrative. Betting on the morning races, gambling in rank little rooms at midnight, turning a blind eye to this, saying he had been here, or there, when he had not been, supplying a little opium, and now and then enabling an officer to reach the prohibited and dusky arms of a clean local tart. Even so, a dishonourable discharge from Smolte's mode of living, the army, was partially in sight. And this jaunt, they had said, those friends of his who had cooked up for him a temporary captainship, was just the job. Get him off the hook and out of the way.

Withers was presumably being sent out of the way, too. A lazy appointment that entailed a pension, something between an overseer, a collector and a judge, but really nothing of anything. The place itself was nearly off the map, a forgotten station in the depths of the jungle, somewhere needing something official but not costly. And that was Withers, and his escort of servants, and the twelve soldiers, five of them Eurasians at that, led by Captain Smolte.

Withers had eyed Smolte in his own special, unlikeable way, a sort of leer that was also a sneer, so you did not know if the man was more liable to feel your bottom or pinch something from your pocket.

'Well, you're a fine figure, Smolte. You'll just do me.' And then he had eyed the straggle of 'troops'. 'Trust 'em, can you?'

'Yes, Mr Withers,' said Smolte, who did not trust a man of them, nor Withers either.

'That's all right then.'

Smolte's appearance at that time was an asset to him, and he knew it. Good looks, well-kept uniform, an exact seat on a horse. He could have done well with women, but they were all married. The native girls he would not touch. He could see they had a certain primitive grace, some of them, but their greased hair and coffee skins did not appeal, nor their hot smell of spice and incense. Come to that, he did not much like the food of India either, preferring eggs and kippers at breakfast, potatoes, beef or tinned meat at dinner. Although he liked to drink, Smolte rationed himself. He had seen men die in front of him of claret and Indian sunlight.

Despite Smolte's misgiving, Withers did not apparently incline to sodomy. His long wrinkled fingers were kept about his long wrinkled person. Withers' clothes, though not bad, soon partook of the look of his skin, drying, fraying and crinkling up. From his head flopped grey dry hair. His expression was habitual. Smolte came to see Withers looked at everything in the same fashion, leering and sneering, sizing it up, mocking, and ready to cut and run.

The journey was on horseback, and Withers slipped and slewed about, slapping at insects, constantly marked by bites and blisters. Seeing a snake draped over a bough, Withers had choked and pointed, as if it was the first snake, the damned snake out of Eden. 'Well, man, shoot the bloody thing.' So Smolte had shot the snake out of the tree, and one of the Eurasians had run over with his stick and beaten the rest of the life out of it. Smolte ventured an opinion that snakes were common. 'Yes, bloody beasts. My boys killed them in the verandah every morning for three weeks. Woke me with the row.'

Smolte wondered if he would have to kill every snake that Withers glimpsed.

They saw nothing else of any immediate danger. Sometimes there came the scrape of a boar's tusks, but Withers did not seem to know what it was. Deer passed like shadows. Monkeys were only a flash of dark on light.

When they started, the rukh was still steaming from the last of the rains, but after the first days, this haze lifted and the autumn heat began to simmer. The forest was the green of all greens, tones like unripe banana, like English oak leaves, like the heart of a rotten emerald. Stands of bamboo rose to the ceiling of vines. It was more a net than a wood. In parts they moved nearly in blackness, and in others shafts of greened amber light tore through, solid, like bolts. There were tracks and paths, nothing very helpful. By some miracle, slipping, slapping Withers was not unseated by the bumps and tussocks, the things that rattled up or down and startled the horses.

They camped at night, makeshift, canvas and mosquito webbing, the Indian cook making a to-do over his fire. Smolte and a pair of the men would shoot jungle fowl for supper, or the small rat Withers considered a delicacy. But it was all curried up, made into a mess.

'Don't like the food, eh?' said Withers, as they ate over the oil lamp in the swift dark.

'Not too much, Mr Withers.'

'Well, Smolte, I tell you, you'll be addicted to curry soon. That's how it is with India. You loathe it, then you take to it. Then you can't get enough.'

To construct formal conversation, and perhaps to cover any rumours Withers might have picked up, Smolte said that he had hoped he might be back home, in England, before too long.

'No, no,' said Withers, 'this is the country for you. You can make something of yourself here.'

This was partly a fact. In England, Smolte had not had prospects. The army had been a chance to get away from the earliest mishaps. He had then found he could trick the army quite a lot, in India. But it would have been different at home.

Withers began to talk about the deserted station they were heading for. 'Know anything of the area, Smolte?' Smolte did not. 'Well, I won't mince my words. There's a lot doing there. I tell you, I was after this one. Had to pull a string or two to get it. Ignorance in high places, or they'd be more careful of it. Of course, there's the plantation. But I don't mean that.'

Smolte felt a slight smart of tension run down his back with the sweat. But he only pulled a burnt moth off the lamp. Withers said, 'There's a fortune to be got at Kalachandra.'

For some reason, maybe because of the notion of money, even if it might be mistaken or totally spurious, the name of the station struck Smolte for the first. *Kalachandra*. Black Moon. But why look for sense in native names? They related usually to superstitions, and the myriad heathen idols, under which India, of course, tottered. He had heard the raja who maintained his palace in Kalachandra was a Moslem. It was they who had India before the English, and were murderously resentful sometimes now, and sly.

Withers said, 'When I say a fortune, I'm not joking.'

'No, Mr Withers.'

'I can see you believe me,' said Withers, with one of his obnoxious insights, 'you're dissembling so grimly.'

'I don't want to offend you,' said Smolte, 'but there's talk of fortunes and treasure, and God knows what, all over the continent.'

'And with good reason.' Then, like a smirking child, Withers changed the subject, leaving Smolte to dangle. But Smolte was too canny to press him.

The journey went on, and they had four more days and nights of the stewing green rukh, before Withers said any more. This time they had come by a village and found the local hospitality bungalow, as run-down a wreck of a spot as could be conjured. Here the Indian cook had an argument with the black old man who claimed to be in charge, no birds were available in the jungle, and they were served up – by the old man, who had won – a terrible tendrilous piece of mutton, and glutinous rice on which was sprinkled a ton of ginger.

Withers ate all this, and drank his nightly half pint of brandy, warm as blood. He sat gazing off across the clearing beyond the bungalow. There was occurring, visible through the gap in the forest, the peach-rose afterglow of Indian sunset, an extraordinary light that could be missed altogether if you sneezed twice, or had reason to rummage for something. Almost instantly the lid of darkness began to close, and the fires of the village down the slope blew bright as the fireflies that might come later.

'A week more,' said Withers, 'and we'll get there. Get to the river at any event. It's a fine sight. He's built his palace on the bank, or his forebears did, on a rock. And there are temples. Have you seen the building here, Smolte?'

Smolte shrugged.

'Well, it may affect you. Forget the cities, all those new bloody pillared English piles going green in the rains. These people built up out of the earth, like moles.' Withers lit a cigar, and then turned to Smolte and offered him one. 'And take a glass of this, if you want. It's a good bottle even if those filthy fellows have jolted it.'

Smolte accepted the cue politely. He poured himself a small measure. Drinking in little tended to irritate him, he liked to have excess, or preferred nothing. But he must be wary, here.

'I'll tell you what,' said Withers, 'there are stupas, and these three temples along the bank. But what you want is what's out in the jungle beyond. Twenty shrines, so I've heard. And every one with something in it worth having.'

'Is that so, Mr Withers.'

'Come on now, no pretence. Shall I tell you why? It's the way they love their gods. Their gods are like their mothers and fathers. More than that. So they put jewels on them. And gold, Smolte, and everything precious. This raja now, he's no Hindu, but he keeps ten elephants. And he dresses *them* like queens. Caps of gold and silver hung with rubies. Diamonds on their toes.'

Smolte said, 'It sounds exotic.'

'Yes, and I've got you dribbling too. I'll say now, straight out, what I'm after. You're a likely chap. I need an army here, nothing much, just to keep the peace, you understand. Fifty men, say, and a strong officer in charge who's interested in seeing me through. It'll be a cosy post, not much to do. Kill flies, eat and drink. Take regular pay, I'll see to that. Scour the forest a bit for jewels. And keep the raja happy. But he's a crawler. Thinks the English must be given presents. That's lovely as far as I can see. What do you say? Do you care to come in on it? Can you find me my little private army?'

Smolte could. He had his own liaison with human dross and its underworld, the potential mercenary sub-army, those who had fallen from the ranks, those who had evaded, but were still vital enough to do a piece of work.

But he was not prepared to leap into Withers' arms. Smolte had not seen this fabulous place yet. Withers could be unhinged.

'I'd like to help you, Mr Withers, but I'm not sure I'd be the right man.'

'Better at getting kicked out of the regiment,' said Withers sweetly, 'going home on the underdecks with no pay.'

Smolte said, 'Thank you for the brandy. I'll go and check out my men now.'

Withers laughed. He seemed to think he had achieved what he wanted.

Smolte was uneasy. He lay awake and heard the abominable shrieks of the monkeys. Not only Withers bothered him. He had not had a woman for a year, and this was more irksome to ration even than drink. He thought of an English girl, naughty, plump and white, with pale loose hair, in her stays with her breasts popping, and gave his seed angrily to the Indian earth.

When they reached the river, there was supposed to be a boat, and it came. It was an old steamer, and up aloft had been fixed a brown sail. A contraption. But it went.

'You come with me,' said Withers. 'I want you to see this.'

So Smolte gave the men over to Erskind, who was able enough if a perfect idiot, and got into the boat. A native by the name of Gal took them upriver.

At first the course was narrow, the jungle hemming in on both sides, and closing fast behind them. The water was yellow as paint.

'Look,' said Withers. 'Bloody crocodile.'

Did Withers wish Smolte to shoot it? In any case, it looked more like a dozing log.

Then the river widened. It became vast, and the farther bank vanished. The reflections of the jungle were green in the water, and water hyacinth grew in the channels, misty blue flowers that wanted to choke the world.

They saw a panther then. It was out in daylight for some reason. It showed like ebony in the sunlight, and suddenly was gone. Withers now did not object. He gave Smolte another cigar. He gave Gal a cigar.

Hours passed and Smolte drowsed. It was pleasant to be a lord, taken upriver. He hoped Erskind would look out for his horse.

It was sunset when they came to Kalachandra, and the sun was away inland, falling out again into the river in pools, like spangled saris thrown into the water. Black tree shapes broke the ripples, were broken by them. The water, where it was not red and gold, was like honey, and the sky was red as a woman's painted mouth.

On this, jet black, Withers' vaunted palace appeared and the mounded stupas, and the ruinous temples with their spires like beehives.

'This is Jarashan's boat. He expects a visit,' said Withers. He winked revoltingly. 'You'll see something now.'

The sun died, and was left only in torches burning up on the rock. The palace was high, and down the banks before it fell the ghats, rock platforms like those of some curious giant insect. Here the people burned their dead. There was a faint smoulder there in one place, like a broken rose.

Withers grinned.

'Roast pork, eh?'

But Smolte could smell only the antediluvian smell of the river, the cooling clicking jungle, and the spice of human cooking somewhere away along the bank.

The beauty of the red sunfall, even now soaking away in the blotted ink of night, laid hold of him abruptly. He was not open to it, and it made him uncomfortable. He reviewed meeting some petty prince, in his weeks' soiled uniform, with Withers leering and fleering ahead of him.

A light became, like a buttercup, in a high window of the raja's palace.

The building had towers, minarets, a shape that was both Arabic and of the Inde. There was sitar music, trailing, a scarf in darkness. And the palace melted into night.

Smolte took in not much. A walk up from the river, a terrace, an entry. A long wide corridor with many delicate holes through which the darkness seemed to whistle. A lighted room, barbaric, torches everywhere. No, there an oil lamp, but in the shape of an Indian nymph, of black bronze.

Withers' raja, Jarashan, came in behind his servants, who moved round him always like butterflies.

He wore brilliant blue. He sat, and his guests, cross-legged on the gilded cushions.

There were paintings on the walls, of flowers, of stars.

They were served sweets and sherbets.

Jarashan was a handsome man, blue-fawn skin and blue-black hair. His eyes were luminously dark, hiding everything. It was as if he lived, was, dressed and jewelled as a prince, in a sort of game. But they were expected to play it also.

Some girls appeared and danced. They were a whirl of bitter green and scarlet and mauve, with ankles clacking and nostrils twinkling gold.

Withers watched them lasciviously, but that might only be needful courtesy. His sex seemed leached out. Smolte felt nothing. The colours hurt his eyes. He guessed himself to be slightly feverish, and made a note to take a dose of quinine tonight.

Jarashan declared they were welcome, that he was glad of them. He said that God had brought them safely through the rukh.

On a wall was a painting of Jarashan's ancestors hunting sambuk, tiger, gazelle, even small lions. Jarashan detected Smolte looking and said, 'These frescoes were done in the time of my grandfather. I do not hunt. But you, Captain Smolte, will do as you desire.'

'I'd like to go after tiger,' he said. He felt almost drunk, and wondered if there was opium in the sticky juices.

'There are many tiger in the forest. They are sometimes a worry to the villages.'

Jarashan, playing his game, spoke flawless English. He spoke to his servants in Hindi, and in Persian, in the manner of the aristocrat.

Withers said, 'I love these sweets.'

'Have more. You must take some, Mr Withers, when you go.'

Withers somehow insisted on their being shown, then, a room with a large complex carving in it.

'This is the god of Beginnings,' said Jarashan, calmly.

Smolte thought Jarashan was to be relied on less than a cobra.

The statue was in buttery, viscous marble, and flowers had been laid before it, pure white orchids. It was, he imperfectly knew, the elephant god, Ganesa, balanced upon the mouse-rat which was his vehicle. Ganesa, with the broken tusk – he had flung it at the sky – a plate of sweets in his hand, and he sat a lubricious damsel, a handmaiden, in his lap, and she about to feed him.

Ganesa had a man's corpulent form, the head of the elephant, crowned and beautified. He was smooth as satin.

Withers mooned over it, maybe looking for jewels.

'See, Smolte, dateless. Old as the river.'

'He is good to us,' said Jarashan. 'Lord of Beginnings, Maker and Taker of Obstacles. The Mountain which Moves.'

'But,' said Withers flirtatiously, 'you are not a Hindu, Sir.'

'Oh, all the gods are emanations of the One. God has many forms. Even the Christians' Prophet has spoken the Truth.'

'The raja is lenient,' said Withers to Smolte, loudly. 'He permits the worship of all gods.'

'My sister,' said Jarashan, 'had a Hindu mother. Am I to dismay my sister?'

The visit took too long. Withers and Jarashan fell to discussing ancient poetry. Smolte felt his eyelids drooping and his stomach hard with impending looseness. They left late, and met the men and horses below the rock, and thereafter came the ride of two miles to the station, by which time Smolte was shivering, his bowel boiling, and all the creatures of that day, Withers, panthers, crocodiles, elephants and rajas, were mingled in his brain.

The station was a desolate monument to desertion, but Hampton Smolte did not see anything of it for several days.

The fever was a bad one, and though he did not lapse into delirium, he was so weak that even getting up to use the chamber-pot became a nightmare. All day he shivered and at night he burned. He had never been ill in India before and had put this down to his own clever organization of himself. The sickness exasperated and humiliated him. And Erskind slinking in like an old nanny, and Withers leering round the door, or sat in the cane chair, watching Smolte as if to take notes, made everything worse.

Finally Withers told him a priest had come; Jarashan, hearing of Smolte's ailment, had sent him.

Smolte objected, but then the priest walked in anyway. He was a Brahmin, clad in white, his head shaven.

'I said no,' said Smolte. 'Get out.'

The priest paid no attention, only came up to him and, drawing out of a satchel an object of baked clay, lowered this on to Smolte's upper body.

Smolte knew enough to grasp that, while he did not care for the Brahmin, he in turn was defiling the priest, one of the scholar-magician caste. So he gave in. The clay object was a hand, and the Brahmin used it to touch Smolte, presumably for purposes of diagnosis, in lieu of flesh. And that was to preserve the Brahmin.

The priest did not say a word. Presently he went out, and next the Indian cook bustled up with a smoking dish of curry. Withers followed him in. 'You're to eat this.'

'If I tried I'd puke. Take the muck away.'

'Well, the holy fellow gave him the recipe. I've been told he's saved men from the cobra bite, and once revived a boy who had drowned.'

'Be damned to him,' said Smolte, past caution.

Withers said, 'If it was me, I'd give it a try. You're tough, but if you go on as you are, I'm not going to answer for you.'

They left the puddle of food by the bed.

Smolte turned his head and looked at it through the fever blur. It was on a painted golden dish, or a dish inlaid with gold. The smell was all over the room and soon he would be retching. He would have to get up, damn them to Christ, and throw the filth out of the window.

Something then made him roll over and dip one finger in the dish, and put the finger in his mouth.

The searing caustic heat of the spices seemed to lacerate him, not only gums and tongue, but skull and brain. Yet as the upheaval faded, his mouth watered. By God, he *wanted* the stuff.

Common sense told him if he ate it he would be done for. But there again, Withers was right. He was in a poor way.

He tried the food once more, and got through maybe a quarter of the dish.

Smolte felt so hot then he was sure it was the end. He lay twisting on the string cot, moaning in an agony of fire. After about ten minutes, a fountain of sweat burst out of him and he fell back drenched, stunned, and suddenly it was as if a cool wind blew upon his body. He thought some extraordinary weather change had come about, and in the midst of wonderment and relief, he slept.

When he woke up, it was night and the fever was gone. He ate the last of the congealed curry, and now it did not seem so virulent. He slept again.

The next day he was strong enough to get up and go out into

the verandah of the barracks, and look at the trees poking through the buildings of the station.

Withers said nothing, but was intolerable, sneeringly gazing at Smolte through knowing sidelong eyes, as if he had the advantage now.

There was a mall at Kalachandra, but trees had come up all over it, just as they had thrust through the public bathhouse and uprooted the bandstand. Vines had smothered the half-built English church, and squirrels lived there, and mongooses pounced in and out of convenient holes.

The barracks had survived rather better, and Smolte set his twelve men, unwillingly, to clearing it, with the help of the gang of natives sent by ever-helpful Jarashan.

The station was on a rise, and under it was a curious barren plain, flung down between the walls of the rukh. The plain was strewn with rocks, where jackals roamed wowling at night, under a dandelion moon.

There were five or six villages, one a mile off on the coil of the river, the rest inside a day's ride. A road led to the largest village, which lay up against the raja's palace. This road had been kept in repair, a task that must be seen to every week, for the jungle was hungry and possessive, it loved the things of man, to cover and devour them.

There were bungalows on the edges of the station, inside the crumbling vine-roped walls. Their thatched roofs were full of flowers, and in their amok gardens the frangipani grew, smothering the air with its cake-shop sweetness.

Smolte did what Withers wanted, clearing up the barracks, making itineraries of what was needed. When Withers wished to prance off to a village, Smolte and five men would go with him.

There was nothing that particularly impressed Smolte. The villages were poverty-stricken, yet oddly ample, living by their fields, buffalo and goats, women in the yards, spinning or pounding grain, stirring rice. The food which everywhere was offered, Withers ate with his normal greed. Smolte found he did not mind it so much. Sometimes an echoing flavour would sift in his mouth and he half wanted to finish the dish. But he would not accede to them for anything, these shadowy people. On their dark, the colours their women wore were almost an assault, blood and orange and magenta, and their arms, even here, were littered with glass bangles, while now and then a jewel blinked at the nostril or the ear. And Withers would point it out to him. But Smolte would be away soon. Back to the colonial cities, and then maybe . . . home. He had had enough. He did not feel as he had, as if he could shrug the country aside. It had put upon him its silken paw.

Withers showed him too village temples of mud-brick painted white and pink, with terracotta offering bowls standing before the three-fold gods, Brahma, Vishnu, Shiva. Withers licked his lips, but said, 'Nothing *here*, of course.'

To come at the secret temples was apparently a matter of exploration, raking through the green muscles of the forest, tearing up trees, digging pits and hauling off great stones. Let him keep it, the bastard, the mad dream and the unpaid labour.

When it was near the end of Smolte's term, and he was already beginning to get ready to clear out, leaving Withers only the specified four men, under Erskind, and the bevy of quarrelling servants, Jarashan invited Withers, and Smolte, to a feast.

'They have the elephant festival here,' said Withers, 'and the harvest's coming. They start to celebrate early.'

Smolte would have been glad to miss the feast. Though he had begun to like the native food, he retained tales of poisonings, malign princes glad to see the English off. Withers, guessing Smolte's train of thought, as, infuriatingly, he sometimes did, remarked: 'Jarashan has a taster. There's sometimes trouble, unfriendly tribesmen coming into the area. They don't approve of the prince's unorthodox religious views. They have a unique cult of Ganesa here, you know.'

'The elephant,' said Smolte, woodenly.

'Ganesa's more than that. I tell you, if he could do what they say, I'd be down on my knees to him. But there you are. Jarashan's a Moslem who embraces or allows other faiths, and he has enemies outside his kingdom. There have been five attempts on his life. All foiled. But the food is checked over, in front of you.'

They rode the horses back to the palace, along the afternoon road and up a stone causeway through the jungle. It took over an hour, but in the palankeens they had been offered by his highness, it would have been nearer three.

The peachy westering glow was shutting the jungle into blackness, but when they came out above the village, the whole sky was rosily gold. The village, which Smolte had not taken in before, was quite huge, an embryonic town, an anthill of mud-brick, arterial earth streets, wells and markets and washing, poured up towards the ghats and the river. Above, the palace on its rock seemed to grow from the ground, blue and green ceramic tiles catching the sinking sun, and flickering like nacre, its towers aureoled with light and circling birds.

This palace was, it now seemed to Smolte, something of a city in itself, but antique and ruinous, although more elegantly and irrevocably so than the English station below. Red-bloomed trees burst from dark pagodas, and the pavilions of some lost king's women, that lined the way into the prince's courts, had become tall heaps of foliage, pierced by occasional marbled sequins of daylight. In one place was a colossal cistern, the water long turned to a marsh of lotuses. Purple vultures rose from distant walls and vanished in the core of the molten sky.

Below, the three temples lay along the river bank, thick gold as honeycomb, amazing with carving. And down beyond, the ultimate river ran, like an answer, the same shade as the sky but cut with silver by some little boats.

They entered a long wide passageway, framed by marble screens through which the light sprinkled. As they moved along it, an elephant trumpeted imperiously, not far off.

The room they were taken to was larger than the first visiting chamber, which anyway Smolte did not properly recall.

There were no torches here, but ranks of candles, already lit against the sudden declension of night.

Red walls, painted over by incredible gardens, were broken by the long arched windows, these fretted with the marble screens, through which very quickly darkness made black patterns.

The floor was marble, polished by the feet of dancers.

They sat on chairs now, at a long table of mahogany, the raja's compliment to their western tastes. The candles blossomed in the arms of apsaras, and a yakshi under golden boughs.

The raja Jarashan came in last in long strings of pearls, and was benign to them. Smolte watched him with care. But now Jarashan seemed only more royal, more faultless.

The dishes were borne in. And there was the taster, a fat, happy man, who tried everything with joy.

'But you've had trouble, Sir,' said Withers, as the taster scurried to intercept the painted golden plates, the sauces and saffroned fowls, the bright bowls of baked nuts, pickled fruits, breads. 'Is he never nervous?'

The raja gestured graciously to his taster, who said to Withers, beaming, 'Dharma.'

'He trusts to fate,' said Jarashan.

They ate. Smolte ate. The food filled him with hunger, he could not get enough, and had to restrain himself. He was not going to plummet into the dishes like Withers. The prince's cuisine was superb. And, although he did not drink any of it himself, Jarashan had a fine red wine brought to them, French it might be, though there was no mark on any of the bottles. And later, with the achingly sweet delicacies which followed, port was served, and black sugared coffee.

Withers and Jarashan had begun to talk poetry again, but Smolte, rather than bored, only found himself stupidly glad to be excluded, so that he might revel in the meal, and let his eyes go round the splendid inimical room, with its carven ceiling, whose intricate knots and chandelier-like garlands startled him. At the centre was a panel like a carpet, mosaic, border within border, and at its heart, a rose.

Jarashan said, 'Captain Smolte, you are so kind as to take an interest in my modest salon.'

'Elaborate work,' said Smolte. He would not bring himself to fawn; there was too much magnificence.

'So? But we have our ruins, too. And like these things, the state of my small kingdom. Mr Withers will have told you, there are those who come into my forests and mean no good to me.'

'So a trained army, when it was hard by, was of use to you,' Smolte said callously.

'Yes. The English have been my friends. And now, I have a favour to ask of you, Captain.'

Smolte leaned back and looked this prince in the eye. Smolte's own eyes were dark, but not so dark as the lenses of these people.

So black and shining, holding the light in specks, like fish in a pool. What went on behind those eyes?

'I'm your servant, Sir,' said Smolte, coldly.

'You are too kind, Captain. We are near to the great festival of Ganesa. My sister . . . I have mentioned to you my sister, whose mother was a Hindu woman. My sister wishes to go into the forest, to offer at a temple there. Only a pair of hours' distance from my palace. But – there is perhaps some danger.' From the tail of his sight, Smolte could see Withers on the edge of his chair, almost falling off it indeed, with excitement. 'Could I beg an escort from you, Captain? Yourself, a chosen number of your men, to protect my sister on this venture.'

Smolte frowned. And bloody Withers piped up, 'Sir, it would be an honour. Yes, yes. Smolte will be delighted. His men are idle. What better.'

Smolte said nothing.

Jarashan smiled. He said to Smolte, persuasively, 'I assure you, my sister takes her religion very seriously. This is a journey of importance to her. And thus, to me.'

Withers repeated his vows. 'Of course, Sir. Consider it done.'

Smolte said, 'I can't detail men—'

The raja interrupted, with vast grace, as if he sang. 'The temple, though ruinous, is of note. It is very old, and has, they say, hidden treasures.'

Withers made a little noise.

Smolte thought the game, this time, had gone far enough. He raised his head, and the raja murmured, 'But here is my sister. Forgive me, I have permitted her to come in, to ask you the boon herself.'

Two girls had entered, and got down on the ground in the weirdly royally servile way they had. Behind them into the room walked another woman, young as the night.

'My sister, Sitavaina,' said Jarashan, softly. 'My father's daughter, the pearl of this house.'

Smolte looked. He tried to clear his eyes, but they were clear. He tried to hear something that was not audible.

The girl was dressed in silver, silver tissue, sewn with silver thread in wafts and streams, that caught the light and brought it to her and left it there upon her body, while the room went dark.

She was the colour of the shade upon lit bronze. Dark, smooth. Her hair was smooth, lacquer black with a running fire along it of blue; it fell to her knees, as water falls over silence. Her eyes were large and were like the moon in a way that was not to be understood, for they were blacker than coals that keep the fire in them but hide the fire. Her face, her lips seemed shaped by a master sculptor, as did the form of her, long and supple and curved, the rounded breasts and tiny waist wound in the weave of the shining sari, and the snake's curl of her thighs. On her silver and her darkness glistened gold. Shells in her ears, a hammered necklace at her throat. Her arms were golden ringed, and her narrow hands.

She stood there, as if the world could only wait upon her, and it did.

And then she made the gesture of courtesy, bowing behind her raised pressed palms. Her nails were the pink of roses. A golden flower slid on her forehead.

'Speak,' said Jarashan, 'let them hear, my sister, how cleverly you use their tongue.'

And the girl raised her face, but she looked away into the room, or into the night beyond, which had made her.

'Without protection I may not go. I want only to lay flowers and cakes before the Lord Ganesa. My brother forbids me, unless soldiers are with us.'

Sitavaina, that was her name.

He sat and waited for her eyes to come to him, but they did not. He felt it as an emptiness in his belly, just where the sight of her had smitten, like a blow.

But she was an Indian woman. A heathen, an animal, a shadow.

Withers said, 'Of course, Madam. You shall have your escort.'

Smolte found he could not speak.

He took a gulp of the port, and the servant behind him leaned to refill the glass. How much had he had?

The girl was regally bowing again now. Drifts of smoky hair rimmed with blue phosphorus and silver veiling. The little gold flower moving. Her breasts under the tissue.

Her eyes lifted and touched, after all, the eyes of Hampton Smolte. Only a second. Yet something passed into his body, like the sting of an insect, the bite of a serpent.

He felt fury, and banged down his glass. It was a trap. Some sort of ploy or plan—

'Steady, Smolte,' said Withers, between a leer and a flurry at the crack of glass.

Jarashan's face was only very still. He said, 'My gratitude is great.'

The girl had gone. How? Had she disappeared into thin air?

Smolte said, 'I can spare six men. That should be enough, with the guns. There won't be any trouble.'

Smolte thought, *She didn't see me*. He puzzled what he would seem to be to her. Reddish and unclean, a pig in a uniform – is this what they saw? He had heard tarts laughing in the brothels behind the officers' backs.

Then some champagne – where did he get *that*? – was brought in, and Withers and Smolte drank the champagne, and dancing girls swirled, and a sorcerer put a crow into his mouth and brought it out alive from his ear.

What had she seen when she looked at him?

And he, what had he seen?

'Doesn't keep his women in purdah,' said Withers, chattily, as they rode back through the night forest. 'Lets them learn English, French. They read western novels and bloody books on history. But she's the favourite. Did you note her jewelry? Even better than his. You could say he's in love with her, but only in the purest sense. The mother was a beauty too, it seems. What did you think?'

'The girl? Indian women don't appeal to me. I can't judge.'

Withers lit a cigar, and it made another spark of light pursuing the torch of the escorting soldier. All around the rukh pressed its black and stealthy face. Unseen tigers trod through the bamboo, hunting the moon.

'No eye for quality then, Smolte. I'm disappointed in you. And he was. He expects any man, if he's a man, to appreciate Sitavaina. He'll think you're a bottom-boy. My God, I'd have liked a try at her. But she's not for us. Perhaps for nobody. Her brother and Ganesa. Too good for any man.' And waxing lyrical, drunken Withers began to quote poets of the English language, his unmusical voice going on and on.

What listened in the undergrowth? Insects crisped the air.

Deer fleeted from a pool as they passed. And somewhere, a mile or two off, a tiger gave its choking bark. That shut up Withers. He began to look round and want to get back.

Smolte rode in silence. He felt light, and curiously bitter, as if life had done him a rotten turn. He had had enough.

Sitavaina.

She walks in beauty like the night . . .

It was only that he had not had a woman for so long. And not seen a white woman since he came up into this god-forsaken jungle.

Smolte did not let himself think of her. Or if he did, he tried to see only her darkness. Even the Indians praised the fair-skinned women of their race. The gold-adorned plates of the raja had on them men painted sombre and women creamy.

Black as a raven.

No, not black. Like bronze, or sandalwood, satin-smoothed. Like dusk. Amber flushed with blue. Impossible to find the colour—

Think of the fantasy woman again. That girl he had seen once who sang on the stage, heavy-built with big breasts and that flamy haze of pale gold-fox hair. What had been her name? Bella something. She was what he wanted. A woman like that. Pull her on his lap and fondle her big tits and up her frothy petticoat where the black stockings ended.

You could not touch this girl like that. You could not even think of her like that.

And yet, somewhere in the jungle-forest, in a green cave of leaves, roll her slender dark satin body free of its garment among the orchids, crush her under you, pierce her as the kings pierced the women in the carvings of the temples. Couple like panthers.

Smolte woke out of the daze of half-sleep. He had come in a dream, like a boy. India had had him, played a trick.

He thought of her blue-black hair and his rage turned to a kind of pain. What would it be like to put his face into that hair? Did she smell like the other dark women, spicy and tinderous? No, it would be amber and dusk, flowers, water.

He was stiff again.

Smolte thought of the big-breasted English music hall actress, and tried to come. Flickers of pleasure quivered through him. Not enough. He dropped back into sleep, dreamed of the architraves of the forest, hollow temples with red, ruby-eyed gods, crows flapping out of their mouths and bellies, Withers running from a tiger, and a tiny elephant swimming in a lotus marsh, small as a mouse.

Jarashan said, 'Please drink, Captain.'

And the servant bent forward with the bottle.

'Thanks, no.' Smolte moved his glass away. 'I'm here as a soldier, not your guest.'

'But always, my guest,' said charming Jarashan.

Smolte said, 'You've suborned Her Majesty's army, Sir. That's enough, isn't it?'

Jarashan widened his eyes. A million lights from the fading day shone there. 'Suborned? But this means something villainous, does it not? Surely, your *chivalry* – that is the correct word? My sister, Captain. You will guard her like a jewel.'

'Yes, Sir.'

Smolte stood, a man of iron in his red uniform. He had spent some time upon himself. He had bathed in the peculiar Indian manner, the jug sluicing over him, cursing Withers' Indian servant, warm water that felt icy. He had washed and pomaded his hair, shaved, pared his nails. Well, he had to. This bloody prince.

Jarashan waved the servant back.

'Something else, Captain?'

'Nothing. Thank you.' God knew, there might be opium or bhang in the food or drink.

Jarashan sat on his couch. He had not invited Smolte to sit. Jarashan, on whom the fading light lingered, said, 'You are a soldier, Captain. But what is your dream?'

'My – dream—'

'What would you wish to be?'

Smolte said, 'I don't know, Sir.'

'No? Truly? Perhaps you are wise. The circling wheel lifts us, and we rejoice, but then we are cast into hells where demons chew upon our bones. I will tell you,' said Jarashan, 'when I was only a boy, I dreamed one day I should be a merchant. I would travel the whole earth, and here and there offer my wares, which would be fabulous. Diamonds and emeralds, turquoise, gold and silver. And I would sell these items for a pai. And why, Captain Smolte, would I do such a thing? My father, I may tell you, sent a priest to read this omen. The priest said, it was another life. But my father, a Moslem, would not listen. What do you think?'

Smolte swallowed the dryness where the wine had been. He said, 'Excuse me, Sir. I don't know.'

'And I do not. And yet, it has been, or it will be.'

The doors, flowered with gold, opened, and another servant bowed to the earth.

She was ready. They were to leave now.

Outside, in a yard of the palace, the sky flamed like topaz and then the night was there. And Sitavaina.

He had marshalled the six men, four of them natives. He did not want them to see her, and *he* did not either. She was in a palankeen, the curtains of sequined gauze drawn fast. Slaves carried her. There were women too.

One of the white soldiers muttered, and Smolte told him to close his mouth.

They went through the vast ruddy torchlit gate, and down into the rukh.

The forest. A place of darkness and the breath of the gods, of raging hunger and of roaring beasts, the realm of great terrors.

But I can never be fatigued, if I am with you. The tearing thorns are muslin. The cruel wind is perfume.

Heaven with you. Hell away from you.

Ah, where had he heard those words?

He could not even see her, in her litter of curtains.

Two of the men went at the front, with guns and torches, and he had set four, with torches and guns, at the back.

He rode, armed, by her palankeen, among the lamped slaves on foot.

They had brands too, the people of Jarashan's palace. Gold fire flamed on the black face of the jungle. Things woke and squalled. Even birds flew up.

And there was music, for it was a holy procession.

He was out of his depth, as if in the sea.

The smells of incense, flowers, night, trees.

Suddenly he leaned down and said to the curtains of the palan-

keen, 'Are you comfortable, Madam? Everything is all right.'
And the voice came, 'I know it is. You are kind, Captain.'
The slaves knew the way, through the forest, through the dark.
And eventually, they came to a hill, up against it, and here everything stopped.
There was the noise of insects then, frogs, the voice of the dark.
He looked at the hill, and the man who ran forward with his torch illuminated it.
The temple was a cave. It went into the side of the mounded earth, and through a drapery of creeper Smolte glimpsed the stalactites of incredible carving.
But then, the curtains parted, and she came out.
She wore the tints of roses, blush and faintest yellow, and on her was all the gold of India. But she *was* India. She was like a goddess, her black river of hair covered by a mist of rosy saffron, and on her feet soft loops of gold. A star burned on her forehead. No, it was a diamond. *No*. It was a star.
Never in his life, never, had he seen one like her.
Sitavaina.
She went into the temple, and in the silence where the music had been, he put his men about outside.
At the entry to the cave he paused. A torch had moved before her, and her women after. And suddenly now a cloud of the night itself rose up from the cave, into the arches of the forest. Bats.
The soldiers did not like them, but the Indians laughed.
Smolte stared forward, and through the wheeling of a thousand wings he glimpsed carven pillars, drops of stone made into filigree.
'Sahib, take off your shoes.'
Smolte looked, and saw a man in white, who bowed to him.
Yes, you could not go in with your feet protected. Spiders and scorpions and snakes were there, and every disease under the sun. But you must walk barefoot before these gods.
Smolte called Crew, who, looking scared and stupid, pulled off the boots from Smolte's feet.
He went into the cave. After her.
The pillars were shaped with a hundred forms. Women, trees, men, towers, elephants. His eyes could not hold them. And everywhere, like icing, the droppings of the bats, fresh sculpture upon the old.

The jungle had come in too, and roped the cave, the vast creepers, the roots of forcing trees. Paving cracked and uplifted. Court behind court, each barred by a veil of vines. But there the light of the torch, ahead, and now the song— He tried so hard to understand.

> Oh you, whose back upholds heaven,
> Oh you, who makes and takes the rock and the shade,
> You, you, whose eyes are the fires and the joy of life.
> You, who know, who are, who will be.
> We are here upon the plain,
> Give us the joy of the plain.
> Take away our fear, wipe away our tears.
> Let us fly forward in the chariot
> To kiss the face of morning.
> You who are the mountain, remove the mountain,
> You who are the rain, bring water,
> You who are the knowing of being and the world,
> Give us the sweetness,
> Lord of the Here and the Now.

But he did not understand.

And so, he parted the vines, and looked through into the sanctum of the cave temple, to where she was.

It came to him, harsh and far off, that Withers had been right. There were jewels there. Blazing like comets.

The image was like the one he had seen, occasionally, in other shrines, and in the palace of Jarashan. It was a man whose head was that of an elephant. But it was twelve, thirteen feet high.

Four armed, it held a silver dish, a silver axe, a golden crescent and a golden flower. It was of pinkish tawny marble that gleamed, as if streams of honey ran down it.

Ganesa, Lord of Beginnings, Lord of Hosts, Maker and Remover of Obstacles. For a moment it had a fearful power, its naked glaucous sheen, the fact that the bats, though they had covered all things else, had not marked it.

But then he saw the golden collar, the dishes and weapons and other attributes, and its diadem of gold set with rubies and pearls, and the sapphires in its eyes.

And then. Then he saw Sitavaina.

She stood before the image, lifting up her arms. She offered cakes and flowers, as she had said; her head-covering half slipped from the midnight of her hair.

If anyone had come in that instant to harm her, he would have died for her. If she had turned and seen him, he would have been born in that moment.

But no one came. And she saw only her god.

And then he beheld it was an idol, and jewels were on it, but he thought, damn Withers, so what. And he saw she was an Indian woman, and he had only to wait, until her silly, blasphemous ritual was over, and then he would take her back, and tomorrow he would go down through the rukh, to the city and the sea. He could go home.

She caressed, with one finger, the lowered trunk of the elephant god. He saw nothing but her. Nothing in the world but Sitavaina, who was a shadow animal-woman of the heathen dark.

Then the musicians, who had gone in, began to play, and it seemed the sapphire eyes of Ganesa winked.

And out in the forest the bats flew, dispossessed, until all of humanity should go away.

Smolte stamped his foot, silently, and a scorpion withdrew into its crevice.

He went out, to the mouth of the cave, for his boots. For his life. For himself.

2

Flower sat on her pink sofa, the tea service before her. It was exquisite English china, but the pot was full of vehement Assam tea. Flower rubbed her ringed hands, as if to plane them down to girlhood. They were coarse now, her hands, they had grown more vulgar as she ascended higher. But there was still the sparkle of the diamond and the ruby.

She was not looking forward to what came next. However, it had to be done. It was necessary that she kept Rupert in mind of her, her part in what went on, the care that must be taken.

Flower did not feel, herself, she had done wrong. No, hers was a protective role, that of a clever woman who must arrange things.

And what was a bit of fun? Men had perverse tastes, most of them, she had learned that early enough. And so, her son was a little rough. Well, it could be dealt with.

She had realized how his activities must be handled after the scandal in the city. He had gone there and been very unwise. Flower was indignant. What else could a common whore expect? Flower had herself paid for the woman's nursing expenses, and she had spoken to Rupert, a difficult conversation, for she had not wanted really to talk of it, her own son's sexuality. She had let him know, nevertheless, that these urges were better indulged at home. And she had made it her business, and the business of that witch, Marpolis, to see he was supplied.

There had been three girls. The first two ran away. God knew what became of them, the silly little hussies. The third girl, who had been given the position of a housemaid, had seemed more sensible, and her long dark hair had been to Rupert's taste. Sarah Brown. But when he had done with her what he wanted, she too had flown, and this time out into the midnight house. Her screams had torn through every room, from the cellar to the attic. Until somewhere, Rupert had caught her up. He had not then, he said later, been able to restrain himself. Dragging her back into his apartment, he flailed her until both she and he lost consciousness. Sarah Brown had been in such a condition that all Flower's gifts of cunning and income were needed. What became of this girl too she did not know, or care to know. She was living with her well-paid-off family, probably, and said to be useless, a mental case. So far as the house knew, Sarah Brown had died of typhlitis.

Flower had warned Rupert this time.

He said, stonily, 'I'm not a fool. It won't happen again.'

And, seemingly, it had not.

This girl, Ember, was damaged but not badly.

Now, with a flinching prurience, Flower meant to find out the lie of the land.

He knocked on her door, loudly and rudely.

'Enter,' said Flower. She sat up behind her tea-pot.

Rupert came in.

He wore his most sullen expression, eyes cast down. He did not like her interviews, naturally. He had told her long ago that how he pleased himself was his affair. But obviously, now, it was also hers.

'Good afternoon, Rupert.'

'Yes, Mother.'

He sat facing her and stretched out his long insulting legs. He was, she thought, far more handsome than Hampton had ever been, and yet Rupert had a ratty, shifty look to him that Hampton did not have either. Hampton's cruelties were blunt and crass. Rupert she did not trust. He had been a strange child. There, she had let the ayah see to her progeny. And it was only Urquhart, a noisy and annoying infant, who nevertheless always ran after Flower, tugging at her skirts with jammy hands.

Flower poured the tea. Rupert drank his black with ginger and a lot of sugar. He reached too for the plate of candied fruits.

'Please wait a moment,' said Flower.

'Mother, don't be so petty,' he said, 'you can lecture me just as well while I eat something.'

'Lecture?' She raised her sandy brows, darkened by cosmetic. 'No, I congratulate you.'

'On what?' he said. He stared at her morosely.

Flower did not grow flushed, but she felt an itching start inside her bodice like prickly heat. She said firmly, 'You behaved yourself. You were restrained.'

'*Was* I?' he said. He lowered at her, then looked away, a dull blush after all flooding his face. 'Is this necessary?'

'I find it quite as distasteful as you. But there it is. It's what you like, and a gentleman must have what he likes.'

'Must you always go on like a bloody third rate actress sipping gin?'

Flower said, 'It taught me a thing or two, Rupert, being a third rate actress.' She drank the scalding tea, not in his Indian way, but with milk. The milk here was safe. 'Insult me if you must, but I want an answer.'

'What answer for God's sake? You want to know what I did to her?'

'Be quiet,' said Flower. 'I'm not interested in what you do, so long as you're sensible. And it seems you have been. Will she suit you?'

Rupert put down his eyes again. He said, 'Yes.'

'And will she stand for it?' said Flower.

'Oh yes.' He smiled, and his colour changed again, but he added, 'Master and servant.'

'That's not what I asked you.'

'We're matched,' said Rupert. 'Your abominable city trollop has found a gem.'

Flower said, before she could stop herself, and with aversion, 'You mean that she likes it.'

Rupert got up and turned his back to her.

'Shall I throw the cup at the pretty wall?' he asked.

'Sit down. Don't be a fool. I pay for your scrapes, and your father knows nothing of it—'

'Let him know,' said Rupert. 'Do you think he's never bent a whore over a chair and thrashed her? If he never did it to you, then maybe he never fancied to.'

Flower's temper swelled and she held it down. He had had tantrums as a child. It was never any use to shout. The ayah had shouted in the beginning, but then she had another way. Oh, Flower guessed at the opium the woman had slipped her son. So what, it kept him quiet. He took laudanum now, and the doctor did not object.

'You've made your foibles my business,' said Flower. 'Your father's requirements are nothing to do with you.'

'Nor with you, I should think, any more. He's past rutting.'

'*Rupert—*'

'Unlike my brother, that pig Urquhart, who'll stuff anything that will stay still long enough.'

Flower got up.

'I've had my say. You keep to your side of the bargain, and I'll let you go on with the girl. Now you can take yourself away.'

'Oh, thank you, Mama.'

'You should thank me. But I know better than to expect it.'

'Do you? That's splendid.'

As the door closed on him, Flower had herself the desire to fling something at the wall. But those days of liberty were gone. Here you did not mark the paper or chip the blasted columns.

After Rupert, Flower had the other difficult session to accomplish. She finished her tea and then picked up the novel she had selected: *Within Two Hearts*.

Before the mirror, Flower stood, and bore with what she gazed at. She had been a beauty, but she had been spoiled. She put the diamond earrings into her ears. Money always spoke more loudly than words.

The room faced north-west, and so now the warmth of the hot day was coming in there and slants of heady westering sunshine. The window looked behind the house, over the trees towards the hills. A nice view. And the room was also nice, plain but attractive, done in an English way, with chintz, and even a bowl of flowers on the table.

The girl was sitting up in the bed, in the lacy bedjacket Flower had seen to. The girl looked sallow, but not ill. Sullen in fact, as Rupert had, and her eyes kept down.

'Well, Ember. I hope you're feeling better.'

'Yes,' said Ember.

This was no time to reprimand her for lack of civility. But it would evidently have to be watched.

'It seems,' said Flower frankly, 'that you've been a good girl. An intelligent girl.' Had she liked it? Flower could not tell.

Perhaps Ember sensed her own coming power. Yes, she would have to be watched. 'You mustn't imagine, however,' said Flower, 'that you can take on any airs. Oh no, Miss.'

The eyes did come up then. They were so heavy, leaden, as if chains of the brain must be used on them to make them move.

For a second Flower was alarmed. Was it after all worse than Luksmi had told her?

'You must eat up the food they give you,' said Flower, 'make yourself strong again. There'll be no more below-stairs work. You can see to the sewing now. That will suit you, I should think?'

'Yes,' said Ember. Her eyes sank, too heavy to be lifted any longer.

'And here is a book you might care to read,' said Flower, putting down the novel on the bedside stool. 'I think you'll be gratified by it, Ember. There's nothing amiss in doing yourself a kindness. We must all get on as we can.'

When Flower had ruffled out, Annie lay motionless on the pillows, and the mellow summer light stole over her face.

Some time had passed, some days, since Luksmi had brought her here, all across the darkened house with its small gas flames burning at intervals like glims in a fog. Luksmi had wrapped Annie in a robe of silk, and when it was taken off again, it had been patterned with red.

She had been naked in front of Luksmi, but did not care. Luksmi had bathed her over, and then stroked some bluish ointment on her skin, over all the lacerations, punctures, rips and broken seams. It had hurt so much that Annie had wept, but Luksmi dried her face gently and guided Annie into the bed, where she lay in agony and a roll of darkness came and carried her away.

Annie dreamed she had been run down by a carriage. Rose was bending over her, her sister, saying, 'Hush, it'll be all right. I'll sew it all up, Annie.'

And then Rose did sew up all her wounds and the pain was awful, getting worse and worse, but then it faded.

Later she woke and Luksmi gave her a drink and Annie slept again.

Then Luksmi was there with a mirror, and Annie saw that Rose had indeed sewn her together very well, or else the ointment was magical. She was healing, some of the lesser wounds almost gone, the worst fast closed.

Then the bed was changed, and she was allowed to sit up in the bed in a linen nightdress and over it the bedjacket with its ridiculous festoons of lace and ribbons. Luksmi brought Annie trays of food, soups with cream and little pies, a glass of white wine, a peach from the hothouse.

Annie made herself eat. You must always take what you could when it was available.

Maybe five days went by, and after those Luksmi showed her the white dresses hung up in a cupboard, and how her tin box had been brought, and with it Annie's purse, which they had easily found hidden under the mattress – and Annie felt ashamed at not finding a better hiding place. On a reflex, Annie had opened the purse, and it was empty. Someone – Tiff? – had stolen all her money. Luksmi had seen and listened to Annie's silence. Luksmi said, 'If you have lost your pay, do not be distressed. They will pay you again.' Then the dark white thing dropped out on to the coverlet. Luksmi said, 'But they have left you something.'

'No,' said Annie, 'it's mine.' She did not know why she said this. Nor why she next said, 'It's ivory.'

Luksmi came and looked down at the ivory. Her odd face, with its dingy skin, and the peculiar freckle above her eyes, took on a stillness as if her inner tempo had stopped. She said, 'May I look at it?'

'If you want.'

Luksmi drew up the ivory and held it in her hand before her face. She observed it for some while, and Annie lost interest, if she had been interested. At last Luksmi said softly, 'There is a tiny hole, above the neck of the elephant. This can be worn about the throat.'

Annie took no notice.

Luksmi said, 'It has protected you already, although you have not asked. I will find a chain that you may wear it.'

'No,' said Annie.

'Heed me,' said Luksmi.

'Why should I?' said Annie, and for a moment some deep and awful smouldering thing, like the hurt of her wounds come back in full, dredged up from the centre of her soul.

But Luksmi did not reply, and in the evening she brought a

thin, thin black chain of some unknown metal, and threaded the ivory elephant on to it, and then fastened it around Annie's neck. Annie said, 'I don't want that.'

'It is a thing of great good luck.'

'I haven't been lucky,' said Annie, for she was almost asleep.

'You have been through a gate,' said Luksmi.

What nonsense, Annie thought. She thought: *He stopped. I made him*. But she would not think of Rupert. One more image to be shut away.

In the afternoon, when Flower bundled in, Annie was awake, but still not thinking of anything. It had come to be simple merely to sit, her mind nearly a blank, over which canvas wandered vague suggestions, impressions, all dissolving consolingly to nothing.

As Flower entered, Annie saw only an enemy, and to Flower's words she had no true response. She wanted Flower to leave her alone, that was all, and Flower did so. While to and of the dancing of the diamonds and the craftily chosen dress, Annie gave no attention, kept no recollection.

She knew, of course, exactly what Flower had said and meant. Annie had been 'intelligent' in the matter of Rupert. Annie had done what he wanted. Now she could sit in the upper house and sew. She would have elegant clothes, she would be cosseted. But this was horrible, and as soon as she could, she must go away, because . . .

But *because* would not solidify in her mind.

The light passed richly over her face on to the wall. It shone through her like glass. She was as still as glass and as the wall. No need to move.

Luksmi came at six o'clock with the special tray, and Annie wondered for a moment if Mrs Rope had prepared it, perhaps thinking it was for an ailing Elizabeth Willow. Soup with sherry, a chicken breast and potatoes, a syllabub, an orange.

Annie ate diligently, and it took all her energy. The food consumed, she lay back exhausted.

'I have seen,' said Luksmi, 'jackals eat as you do.'

Annie laughed. Luksmi came from India, where Annie's father had been.

Luksmi picked up the novel with the insane title from the stool, and handed it to Annie.

'I don't like reading. And that's rubbish.'

'Not all,' said Luksmi. 'She gave it for a purpose.'

And Luksmi turned the pages of the book before her, and there, inside, were three folded bank notes.

'You are paid,' said Luksmi, 'for your misery.'

Annie took the money, the leaves of the white tree of horror, in her fingers.

Now she was a paying proposition, like her sister Rose.

And he – he would want her again.

Annie Ember walked into the outer yard of the stables. It was daytime, hot. She had no idea of the hour.

Against the Indra statue of bronze, a flower grew, red as a victory, up and up and through the segments of the wheel. She went by, and into the inner court.

Darius was there with one of the horses, a big roan. Through the smoke-black mane Darius was rubbing handfuls of rice, over and over.

He and the horse turned and saw her there.

She wore the lady-dress, and her hair put up as Luksmi had done it, elaborate, as if she were someone.

'Good day,' said Darius. He touched the horse upon the cheek, and left it and came over.

'What did you do,' said Annie, 'with the geranium?'

'Ah, the geranium.'

'I gave it you. It's mine.'

'So it is. Well,' he said, 'didn't you see?'

Annie waited. Her face was cold and old.

Darius looked at her.

She thought, *He knows. Maybe they all know. I'm Rupert's whore. He is violent to me.*

But it was not pity or contempt in Darius' face. What then? She did not comprehend.

He said, 'I'll show you, Miss Annie.'

How did he know her name? But then, he knew. And *Miss* Annie. She had gone up in the world, up high on her cross.

A silent screaming roiled in her, but he had taken her back into the first yard, and the horse quietly followed. It shook its head.

'The Indian women,' said Darius, 'rub rice through their hair.

Their hair is the best on earth, and so, I do it for the horses.' He pointed. 'There your flower is. I gave it to his care.'

It was the geranium, in a great black pot, and it had grown huge and climbed up into the bronze wheel of the statue. The flowers were blots of fire, and the vast green hairy leaves entwined with the arms of the god. It was a monster. Yet, it was beautiful.

It was no longer Annie's.

'Wait,' he said, 'would you rather I put it in a bit of old soil, and let it perish?'

'I don't care.'

'Ah, but you do. Never mind it. Snap off a stem, and I'll make you another plant. It's grown so fine, it will spare you its child.'

She stood and looked at the geranium, which had struggled in the cage of its pot at Tooth Street, above the festering river. Now it was a tree, a vine. It was the god's.

'What is he the god of?' said Annie. It was as if another used her voice. For what did she care?

'The god of heaven. Of the lightning. The god of warriors.'

'Soldiers,' she said.

'Each,' said Darius, 'with the soul of those who fight.'

Annie said, 'My father was in India.'

'Was he so?'

'But I don't know where, or what he did. He was a soldier. And he died.'

Darius stretched out his hand, and then put it back.

He said, in his musical mild voice, 'Don't cry. It will all come right.'

She laughed.

'The wheel,' Darius said.

'The wheel of the chariot?'

'Of life. It turns. And lives follow lives. We pass through everything, all happiness, all pain, and in the end are free of it.'

Annie said, 'My sister's dead.'

'Ah, is she dead?'

Annie sat down on the ground of the yard and put her face into her hands. She cried as never, since a baby, had she cried. And the horse came and dropped its warm nose on her shoulder.

Darius squatted down, about two yards away.

In the hot day sun, Darius and the horse stayed by her, as she cried. But she thought, *No, no*. Why did she cry? There was no use to it. Yet the tears poured. And she could smell, with their salt, the geranium which had grown up in the chariot wheel of the god.

'I will say something to you,' said Darius, presently, when she was quiet, 'about death. I was in India, where your father was, and where *he* was, Smolte. And there was a tiger hunt. The tiger is a creature made of day that moves by night. He's the colour of marmalade and striped like the bars of a furnace.'

Annie raised her head. Darius said, '*Their* house is full of skins. Smolte would go into the rukh and shoot these beasts, for their pelt. The whiskers of the tiger, even those can kill. There was a ranee once who slew her husband, by cutting up one whisker of a tiger and putting it into the fellow's food. It's so vital, it tears like steel. And these beasts, whose whiskers even kill, men hunt. And they found this animal by a watering place. And Smolte raised his gun and shot him. But the tiger leapt up and was away. Then they said *Go after*. For a wounded tiger is worse than all the devils in hell. But no one would go. The Indian men, by God, were too canny, and Smolte too much a coward. So, I was sent.'

Annie sat back. She leaned against the wall of the yard, and touched the prickly velvet nose of the horse.

Darius said, 'I found him in among the thickets. His kill was there, a spotted deer he'd almost eaten, and he was lying before it. He was fiery as a sunset when it dies, and he was dying too. The bullet had entered his brain, but he was too perfect to know at first. So he ran. But death came after him. There was shade in that thicket, and so I could see into his burning eyes.' Darius sighed. He too lifted his head, and spoke only to the statue up above. 'I saw a tunnel there, in his eyes, go back through darkness into a golden place. And at the front of his eyes, he was, golden too. And the gold of him blew backwards, back down the tunnel of the dark, into the gold of his kind. His body he left, and he went away. I saw the flame go off from him, out of his skin, up into the air. And then he was dead. For this, for my bravery at stalking him,' Darius said, 'they offered me his ears. But I won't have the skin of a king to line my floor or put upon my wall. He went back into the soul-place of all tigers. And he will live again. He lives.'

'But Rose won't live,' said Annie.

'Ah, was it Rose? Sweet Rose of May . . . Don't you know,' he said, 'she is alive. She's in the air and looks at you and says, Poor Annie, why can't she see?'

'I can't.'

'Never mind it. If you were blind, the rose would still be shining on the tree.'

The horse made a laughing noise. Annie got up.

She did not trust Darius and his luminous voice, nor Luksmi. They had let her suffer, say what they might.

He watched her go from the yard, and back among the funeral yews.

Through the house, over the green and crimson carpets, through vaulted polished dark and between columns, to the door.

She knocked for, summoned, she must.

No one answered.

She did not knock a second time.

He was not in the gun room, and her eyes swung round and took in the rifles, the pistols, the elephant gun, the knives with hilts of ivory and inlay. The static monkey.

Then she went into the further room, and he was there.

Do you like ivory, Annie?

It was round her neck, and she had forgotten, but as she entered now, in her white dress, her hair undone, she recalled.

'How sumptuous you look,' he said.

He sat in a chair by the table, and on the table were the curries and the ochred meats, the things he liked.

Had her father liked them? Who had he been?

A man with the name of Ember.

Annie went forward, and Rupert raised his glass.

She had been infatuated by Rupert. His looks. The aura she had thought was his. *Rose's vocal rhythm*. And he had seduced her too.

But *this* was Rupert, she saw it now. His *evil*.

And in the other room waited the claws of ivory and the flail of metal teeth.

Annie went to him, and she struck him hard in the face, so

violently the chair went back, and he nearly fell out of it.

He rocked there. She had hurt him.

His eyes burned but not like a tiger's eye, these were the eyes of some dark sump, some abysm.

'Kneel to me,' she said, 'kneel down.'

She thought, *Someone has told me what to do.*

Rupert Smolte went to his knees before her on the carpet. He took the hem of her dress in his hands and brought it to his lips. His saliva stained the cloth. 'Annie,' he hissed, '*Annie* . . .'

3

Not much before one in the morning he rapped at her door. But she had guessed he would come, and sat up waiting, playing patience at the lacquer table.

It was a fact, she still knew when he wanted her. That was all that was left of their earlier passion. Even so, it was a useful knack. For herself, Flower no longer missed the thrills of lust. She had come to associate them with what followed, the carrying and bearing of children. Hampton, she suspected, had a doxy in town. But nevertheless, now and then, he sought out his wife. He still found something in her big white body that excited him. She felt better for his visits, more womanly, younger. And particularly after Rupert's nastiness, she was glad to prove her son in error.

Hampton swung into the bedroom, its glittering oriental hubbub which Flower had tried to domesticate.

He had been drinking at his club, with the men who thought him good enough for that, but not for the sociability of their houses. They hunted over his land, and allowed his son, Urquhart, to ride with them. Urquhart indeed they partly accepted, and Rupert too, if Rupert had wished for their company. But Hampton was the nabob, the little man who had got his jumped-up place from foreign knavery. And Flower was his slut wife. The scatter of county ladies might call on her once a year, near Christmas; she had tried hard to please them, and then tried not so hard. Flower told herself she had no use for such persons. She missed her former friends, trustless though they had been, loud people, gaudy, lugubrious and merry by turns. How long since she had seen any of them – seventeen years or more. Not since the last child, Elizabeth, born in the city with the mercy of ether.

Hampton took off his coat and threw it over a chair.

'Damnable evening.'

'Oh, dear me,' said Flower.

'I lost five pounds.'

'Well, I don't suppose you'll notice it.'

'Don't suppose I will,' he said. 'But I prefer to win.' He put his hand on his necktie, and said, 'I hope you're not too tired.'

He was, she thought, a regular coquet. She said, 'No. They've laid me a little supper next door. Will you try something? There's cold duck, and some white burgundy.'

It was her small exercise of power, to show that she had known he would come. To show she could order for him things he liked.

Hampton Smolte nodded.

She thought, *The old fraud. He's just as happy to sit down and eat as to straddle me.*

They went into the sitting room and she arranged his supper. He drank at once, and thoroughly. She had made sure there were two bottles of wine.

She watched him. She was brooding tonight. She considered how he had altered, seeing him vividly as if they had been parted for years. He literally was not the man she had known before. Not only had he thickened, lost his hair and his physical charm, but something in his nature had changed too. It was difficult now to recall him as he had been, or rather accept that this earlier Smolte was the initiative of the later model.

When they had eaten, he would undress behind the screen and put on a nightshirt. She had not seen his upper body since their days in India. He was sensitive about the scars, the awful one notably. It was true it was dreadful, and the wonder had been he had not died of blood-poisoning on the spot. But she could have put up with the hideous pucker of dead purple tissue, he was the coy one. Once she had come in on him and seen him looking at the scar in a mirror. He had shouted and sworn at her, his hand across the place, and his face like a lunatic's, frightening her.

But she would not think about that. There was something she wanted, and now the house was settled, she intended to see if she could get it. The idea, begun by a letter she had received over a month before, had somehow grown up in her. It had intrigued, suggested spiteful amusement.

'Now Hampton,' she said, 'do you remember when I was a girl, there was a chap, name of Oxway? He had a troupe of animals. There was a bear that could dance. It made you laugh.'

'No, I don't remember,' said Hampton Smolte. And in his mind he saw a bear dancing on a marble floor under the pillars of a raja's palace. Round its neck was a golden collar. It had been trained by coaxing, and when it had danced, it was given sweets.

'Well, Oxway has made something of a stir. He has a gang of monkeys now. They can do anything. He's shown them off before royalty. They wear clothes and top hats and what not. It's a scream.'

'Oh yes,' said Hampton, idly, drinking, 'I saw something about it in the paper.'

'Well, what do you know but he's written to me. And he's offered to bring the show here.'

Hampton looked at her.

'Monkeys,' he said.

'Precious Indian monkeys,' she said, sprightly. 'What could be funnier, here? And we could invite our high and mighty neighbours. They'd come running, it's a marvel and all the fashion. They couldn't afford to refuse.'

'You underestimate them,' said Hampton.

'No I don't. You only know the stuck-up men. But the women are another matter. They say the Queen has nearly seen Oxway's troupe.'

'And what is *nearly seen*?'

'Don't split hairs, Hampton. I should love our neighbours to come grovelling. Let them see how we are, the money we've got, when they live in their derelict mansions that let the rain in, not two pennies to rub together.'

Hampton tucked down his chin. He looked stubborn.

She selected for him and lit his cigar. As she bent over him, he fondled her breast. She had kept on her corsets and her frilly things. He had always preferred her half-dressed, even in the old days; finding her in a flurry of petticoats and lace had always seemed to fire him more quickly than mere naked flesh.

Presently they went to bed. The procedure did not vary, and now, though he was slower, Flower pinched and tickled him, urging him on to a finish. She had been used to pretend to her own pleasure for some years after she no longer felt any, but now she did not trouble. He did not seem to mind, so long as she was willing, and when he was done he always politely thanked her. And after about ten minutes, got up to go away.

'Why not stay here,' she said, 'this bed's big enough. I rattle in it.'

'No,' he said, 'you need your rest.'

He inclined to sleep alone, although she wished him to remain. She did miss that, the warmth and solidity of his body against hers. Even in the terrible heat of India, she had liked to have him there. But this Smolte was not that one. This Smolte got up to go.

'Well, you might let me have a bit of entertainment,' she said. 'And to see an old friend. What friends have I got?'

'Now, Flower,' he said.

'Well, tell me, who? Lady Craven, who drives up every few months to nose about. And the village wretches, who think they can be my equals, or betters, I should say.'

He was weary. He looked heavy and old, far older than she. He would give in in a minute.

'And this act is an utter scream.'

'Yes, Flower,' he said. 'Let me think about it.'

'Do think of it, Hampton. For poor Flower.'

And she thought suddenly, *Why am I importunate? Do I give a damn for a herd of smelly monkeys, and that rogue Oxway – he'll probably pinch the silver.*

But something had made her do it. And now it was between them, the exercise of her will and his.

Mrs Rope scanned through the steam of the afternoon kitchen. She shouted, 'And to think of it! As if I haven't enough to do, with only a pack of half-wits to help me. And now, to be told to make a dinner for a tribe of monkeys!'

Divy, the housemaid, who had come down to scrounge cake, was ill-advised enough to giggle.

Mrs Rope erupted into torrents of fury. She told Divy that Divy was the daughter of a sheep, and if she had ever done a stroke of work, which Divy had not, Divy would know that an imposition had been imposed, a crime effected.

Then lunging round in her ferment, Mrs Rope saw Annie Ember in the doorway.

Mrs Rope closed her mouth like the brick traps in the kitchen garden. Plainly, Annie was now an agent from upstairs.

'What can I do for you, Ember?' asked Mrs Rope.

Annie was pale and straight in her dress, her hair done up as Luksmi had taught her. Annie said, without inflexion, 'I'd like to speak to Tiff.'

'Tiff,' said Mrs Rope. 'Where is the brat?'

'With Clarrie fetching carrots,' said Divy.

Mrs Rope said, 'Will you sit down, Ember? There's tea left in the pot. Or a glass of beer, maybe.'

'No thank you,' said Annie.

She went straight through the kitchen and out of the door into the yard. As she walked towards the lower avenue and the walled garden, Divy ran after her.

'How are you doing?' said Divy. 'You've gone up, and no mistake. All that sewing.'

To Annie, Divy's face looked fly and complacent. Surely, surely the whole house knew what Annie actually did. It was true that she sewed sometimes, the daughter's white dresses, a table-cloth, a handkerchief. But mostly she did not sew. She sat in her chintz room and attended, until called, on him.

'Well then,' said Annie, 'I sew.'

'Oh, hoity-toity,' said Divy. But Mrs Rope bellowed and she ran back towards the kitchen.

Just then, Clarrie and Tiff came through into the yard from the garden, with baskets of carrots.

When Tiff saw Annie her bald little face grew furtive.

'Annie,' said Clarrie.

'Yes,' said Annie, 'but I want to speak to Tiff.'

Clarrie said, 'Don't keep her long, she's the larder to do over.'

Tiff said, 'I uv going in. I usn't got nothing to say to you.'

Clarrie said, 'Don't be saucy,' and went by, going in herself, leaving Tiff behind in the yard.

Annie stared at Tiff, and Tiff wriggled.

Tiff said, 'Did you hear, you, they're to have monkeys play in the house, and we're to be let watch behind a door.'

'You took my money,' said Annie.

'Ooh, you liar,' said Tiff. She screwed up her face.

'Out of my purse,' said Annie.

'Well, I didn't. But you've gone up. 'Tis Master Rupert's fancy, you, Divy said.'

So, there it was. Of course.

Annie said, 'I've got something else for you, Tiff.'

And she shot out her hand, and stuck a red-threaded needle from the well-supplied sewing cabinet into Tiff's arm – in as far as the eye, so only the thread hung free.

Tiff screeched. She went the colour of peeled potatoes and pulled the needle out by its crimson thread, and then bent over and was sick on the paving.

Annie turned and moved again into the servants' kitchen, and through it. They looked at her, as clearly through the open door came the noise of Tiff's retching.

In the passage, where the windows were, Annie walked in a stilted dream. She flexed her hands. Well, her sister had been a murderess.

Her face, which she could not see, was like something carved, with large blind eyes. Tiff had been fortunate. It could have been worse.

On the sign-board of the Bird-In-Hand was a curious vision. It was a raucously coloured peacock, perhaps slightly inaccurate, and standing up, violet and green tail spread, on the great stone hand of an oriental statue. Corry Pulger, who had had it done, had seen a few years' service at the Smolte palace, and by his insolent accolade had maybe hoped for custom from that quarter. Fairly regularly he got it, too, in the shape of Urquhart Smolte, while once in a blue moon Sir Hampton would stop off, generally already quite full, to top himself up with wine or beer, on the route home.

Tonight, however, the visitors were a little different.

Corry Pulger had opened up the upstairs sitting room, and there the lady sat in her worn trimmed velvet cloak, and round her throat a necklace of diamonds Corry had heard were glass, the real item being in pawn. Lady Flight had taken a lemonade, but out in the meadow Lord Flight and Lord Bobb were cooling themselves with brandy and aerated water.

An arm of the river ran beside the inn, and here from time to time even the gentry would come to fish. Lord Bobb was peering in at the clear brown water.

'Not a trace of the damn things. Something's ate them up, if you ask me.'

'Perhaps a chimpanzee escaped from this to-do at Smolte's.'

'Oh, they're not chimpanzees, dear fellow. They're macaques.'

'Thought that was a bird.'

'It's not,' said Bobb. 'An Indian monkey.'

'And what do you make of it?' asked Flight, a tall lean man whose arms seemed constantly in his way.

'Well, I'll go and see. The chap will attempt anything to make us look at him. The least we can do is spare a glance.' Bobb, short and round, saw a garnet ring rise on the surface of the sunset river. 'What's that? No, it's gone.'

'My wife,' said Flight, 'insists that we go, because Lady Craven is going. And it seems my wife owes Lady Craven some favour, and so doesn't want to put her out by cold-shouldering the Smoltes, since Craven is to be there, and if he lowers himself so must we. Women are the devil.'

'Bless 'em,' said Bobb. He was unmarried.

'But now she's worn out,' said Flight, blinking up at the sitting room window. 'I've forced her off here to get a respite. But she'll have one of her heads for days.'

'I wish I'd brought my rod,' said Bobb. 'There's something down there, but it don't look like a trout.'

'Best drink up and have another glass, and get on our road,' said Flight. 'They dine at eight. Too early by far.'

'Well, they're bloody scum,' said Bobb. 'I'm only going to look at the damn monkeys. No doubt nicer than the Smoltes. The woman's a bloody tart, and the daughter's got owls in her tower.'

'Urquhart's all right,' said Lord Flight.

'There you see the action of a good school. But the other one's a bounder.'

'Artistic type,' said Flight.

They eyed the river and drank their glasses.

The upper window gave birth to the coiffured and feathered head and shoulders of pale Lady Flight, hampered by perhaps unreal diamonds.

'Do you think we shall be late, Edgar?'

'They dine too early.'

'The sooner we arrive the sooner we can fly,' said Lady Flight, appropriately.

The county had been of the same general opinion as Lords Flight and Bobb. Many had languidly refused an invitation to the Monkey Dinner, as it came to be known.

Those that arrived did so out of curiosity, or because, despite their contempt for the Smoltes, they did not quite wish to alienate them. One must be careful of money.

Mr Wetherall indeed appeared with a cloth-wrapped package, and drawing Hampton Smolte aside, suggested that he might want to look at it. 'Genuine oriental piece,' said Wetherall.

The reception room was in a hot royal blue, and it too had a frescoed ceiling, a sky that seemed greenish by comparison, stitched with long-necked birds.

Those who had so far not entered the Smolte palace glared about, between laughter and astonishment. But this had always been the reaction, and the Smoltes paid no attention to it. At the beginning, aristocratic sightseers had come to look the house over. They had stared at the minarets and domes, and declared that Hampton Smolte's horses would have complained to him about the domed stable, had they been able to use tongue or pen. In his grounds people had marvelled at the heathen idols, and one lady, examining the lingam phallus by the bridge, had asked if this was the representation of some god too horrible to be otherwise visualized. He had not enlightened her, for though he was then bursting with hate, which sometimes he mistook for vigour, Hampton Smolte had returned to England yearning for safety. He had been gallant in India, and he was rich. He did not want to make enemies.

This motive was still on him, at such moments as these, the glamorous room full of awkward people who were his superiors. His hate had settled with eighteen years to a sort of normalcy, he barely noticed it now, and his hopes of solace had perished, leaving him almost relaxed.

The black and white of male evening garb was here and there a decade out of date, and generally shabby, except in the case of smart, smarming Doctor Gry, who gained cash through his patients' numerous illnesses. There he was, shaking his finger playfully at a bored and slouching Rupert, in a jacket almost as good as Rupert's own.

The women's garments were better, but not, probably, as sleek as their owners would have liked. Added bows and ruches had assisted last year's gown, and sometimes, over a drift of scent and powder, would flow the dim whisper of moth-balls.

Which made Hampton Smolte recall the invalid reek of the dresses of the city ladies in India, new dresses, those, but ones which must be packed in camphor and wintergreen, to keep the white ants from devouring them.

'Look here, Smolte,' said Wetherall, unwrapping his parcel. Out came an ivory figurine. 'What do you think?'

'Yes,' said Smolte, unavoidably sensible of his momentary strength.

'A Hindu idol. Hideous thing. But you collect the elephant's tooth.'

'I did. I shot down some of it myself.'

'Yes, bloody great animals. But, can I interest you?'

'Well, let me see.'

Smolte took the ivory. It was of English make, and the material itself perhaps not Indian after all. The image was a fanciful Krishna, rather Greek.

'What do you think?' insisted Mr Wetherall, leaning back as if to replace his social height – which had toppled – with inches. But Smolte was the taller.

'I can have someone look at it,' said Smolte. 'If you leave it with me.'

'Oh – ah – yes, then. Good thinking. You'll let me know?'

'How much do you want for it?' said Smolte.

Mr Wetherall blushed. Smolte was a bloody shopkeeper.

'Eight guineas,' snapped Wetherall.

'Shouldn't think it would go to that.'

'Well, then, don't bother with it.' Wetherall snatched the ivory back. 'Can't waste your time.'

Across the room, Mrs Wetherall carefully did not look at what her husband was up to. She counted her pearls like a rosary. They were not fakes, like Lady Craven's. But Lady Flight's necklace was definitely real, it flashed so crudely, just like their hostess's garlands, those vulgar diamonds and faceted beryls.

Doctor Gry said mincingly to Rupert, 'And you must be sensible with the sedative, Mr Rupert.'

And Rupert did not hear, although, because his damnable father or idiot mother had inflicted this situation, he did not stalk away, as yet. Rupert knew, in the inner room of his mind, that was not like the inner room of his apartment, where the netting was, and the other bed, and the strigil of ivory, and the flail, Rupert knew his father had rule over him, for now.

Major and Mrs Plimpley were looking at the cabinet to which Flower had led them. They bent forward across their respective corsets, and beheld cups of brass and gold set with pearls less regular and more costly than Mrs Wetherall's.

Flower stood chirruping. She wore black silk, so slimming, and her fantastic green and white necklace, earrings, bracelets, and in her hair a tall black feather in a diamond claw. She was pleased, and full of the bubbles of the champagne she had already drunk, and the wildness which was soon to ensue. She and Oxway had talked of it all morning, and Hampton, who had at first frowned, had given in as he normally did. 'If he can keep control,' Hampton said. And Oxway had cried, 'Sir Hampton, my life on it.' Yes, it would be a rare old meal and no mistake.

Flower glanced round, and saw Rupert departing from Doctor Gry, and Urquhart talking away to Craven and Flight, Urquhart who was an oaf, and got on so well with these lords and ladies.

By a window, pallid on the gilt lattice, Elizabeth Willow sat like a white imp, feeding something from the kitchen she should not have been given, to her snarling shadowy cat.

Flower thought, *Where will she get a husband?* No one eligible had come. In fact, there were ten guests only. All borrowers, inaccessibly lofty, trapped by Flower's scheme. The fools. Elizabeth would have to settle for someone from the proper world. But God knew who would fancy her.

The maids went about effectively with the wine and cider-cup. Churton presided. *We're grand*, thought Flower. *Bugger the lot of them*. And, *Just wait and see*.

Against the wall, the huge ebony clock, with the gold sun and scene of a tiger hunt, struck eight.

Flower raised her decorated head.

And there, precise to the instant, clanged the dinner gong.

Smolte led them through with Lady Flight, shabby as a failed Cinderella, and Flower bowled after with Lord Bobb.

'Not wed yet, your lordship?' said Flower.

'Alas. Who would want a fat dull bachelor?'

Prefers his doings with little boys, thought Flower.

In the red dining room, under the palm-tree heaven, watched by the beasts on the floors and walls, they sat down at the long table, where now twenty-four places were laid.

And as the guests were seated, a breath of consternation rose. There were empty chairs before which the silver and gold lay ready, the pleated napkins and five or six goblets. Who would sit here? But they had realized.

'Oh surely, Lady Flower—' protested Lady Craven.

But just then, the door from the orangery opened, and in they came.

The monkeys. There were eight of them. Three males, five females.

They had been dressed like ladies and gentlemen for their evening. No expense spared. The females wore gowns of taffeta and silk and lace, the muted yellow of a butterfly's wing, the blue of twilight, the limpid green of mint gin. On their heads were dainty ornaments of beads, feathers, rosettes. They were impeccable in white evening gloves, and bracelets of rhinestones. Two carried fans. The males wore faultless black and white, starched shirts and fashionable cutaway jackets, neckties of grey satin and the softest cream, simulated pearl studs. On their hands, too, white masculine gloves. One had a monocle, and one a military medal on a mauve ribbon.

They had been dressed . . . And out of this their heads rose, with brushed fur the shade of blond smoke. Their perfect faces were like masks, so ancient, so clever, so lawless – yet so calm. Their eyes were round sherry pools under the sculpted arches of their brows, and through their delicate ears, subtly pointed as those of exquisite demons, the broad lights of the room glowed milky apricot.

They walked to the table in a sedate and simple way, upright, soundless, only their dresses and starch rustling. They smelled of clean aliveness, of hair and fruit, and of French perfume and pomade.

'How charming!' exclaimed Mrs Plimpley, in a stupid hysterical manner.

They were, but not for her: she was affrighted.

And the rest of the visitors sat locked in stillness, as the eight monkeys took their seats, beautifully, and stout Oxway, well-dressed, and with an exactly straight countenance, came after and took his.

There was only one immediate and honest reaction.

Elizabeth Willow's cat, which should not have been brought to the table, had flattened herself to the floor, ears back and whiskers bristling. Then with a yowl, Kitty shot away and directly up a red velvet curtain, to the pelmet above.

Flower would have cursed, but not in company. Besides, she was amused. Mrs Plimpley and Lady Craven would undoubtedly have liked to follow the cat.

The monkeys had watched the cat's escape serenely. They showed no inclination to pursue.

Flower spoke up. 'Don't get in a dither. They won't hurt you. Will they, Oxy?'

Oxway smiled beneficently.

'I can assure you, ladies and gentlemen, they are under my complete control.'

He spoke, not like a lord, but better, like an educated actor.

The diners, all but the monkeys, squinted at him, but no one else spoke.

Then, Major Plimpley turned to the female monkey on his left, in her blue silk gown. 'Good evening, Madam. I trust I see you well?'

The monkey looked at him, with her marvellous eyes, then dipped her head, courteously.

The Major laughed loudly, and Wetherall and Urquhart joined in.

Doctor Gry, a mimic on most occasions, turned to the female monkey in lemon on his right. 'Pray won't you take a little water?'

And this monkey woman gazed at him, and slowly shook her bedizened head.

'Why, they know English,' said Lord Bobb. 'I suppose they don't talk it?'

Oxway said, 'No, my lord. They're the best of guests. They say nothing.'

Urquhart fired off his buffoon's laugh again. He said, 'Why haven't I got a monkey next to *me*?'

The human women, Lady Craven and Mrs Wetherall, who

were either side of him, appeared affronted.

Rupert said, 'Yes, that would suit him better.' And Lady Craven gave a vicious little titter, flirting at Rupert over the table, thinking him handsome. But Lady Craven was too old for Rupert's tastes, too anglicized. She would never know. She knew very little.

The food was being served. Churton, and the maids, passing up and down the table.

The Smolte board was impressively laid, white lace cloths over the red carpets, the second Indian service, which included finger-bowls of gold, the glasses of green and wine crystal with golden stems. The two golden candlebranches, made for an Indian prince, were in the form of golden nymphs, with eight white candles apiece. Two golden epergnes, holding rusty and blancmange-pink roses, with greenery trailed along the table.

It was oyster soup. The guests were given it, in the glittering plates, and the monkeys too.

The monkeys detached the pleated napkins and placed them on their laps. As the others began cautiously to take the soup, they also did so. They were lovely.

'Look at the things,' said Lord Flight. 'By jack.'

The speech-emboldened humans began to converse. They spoke of weather, of sport – the shooting and riding after of animals. Lord Bobb introduced the idea of the novel, and Flower was called upon by him for the plot of the current sensation. Lady Flight attempted to speak of the classic novel, and was driven out.

A local fish was brought, with a madeira sauce. After it came a saddle of beef with redcurrant jelly, and a salad of cress, lettuce-hearts, fennel, cucumber and hard-boiled eggs.

By the end of this, the guests had settled, and the decorous monkeys had become almost acceptable.

The monkeys ate flawlessly. And though they were not given the beef – Oxway had declared meat and wine were not good for them – they ate of everything else, sparingly, neatly, sweetly.

Lord Bobb and Plimpley had fallen to assisting their female monkey companions to water and bread, waving the servants jollily back, and Urquhart, sat between two ordinary women, continually voiced an outcry, and abruptly had started to get up and go to the nearest male monkey with the medal, the far side of Lady Craven, in order to feed him pieces of beef, although Oxway protested.

'No, Sir,' said Urquhart, 'confound it, I shall.'

'He will bite you,' said Oxway at last.

'Let him bite. He's a fine fellow.'

Lady Craven said angrily, 'Please desist, Mr Urquhart. He may bite *me*.'

'No, Madam,' said Oxway. 'My males would never insult a lady.'

And on his cue the male turned to Lady Craven and offered her a small bow, but she shrank aside and Urquhart handed the monkey another slice of meat, which the monkey ate.

'What's this fellow's medal?' asked Urquhart.

'The order of the palm,' said Oxway. 'He was a great climber in the wild.'

'By Jove, so it is,' said Major Plimpley peering across. 'A palm tree done on the metal.'

On the male's other side, Elizabeth Willow sat demure. She had paid no attention to her cat, lowering above on the pelmet, where now she had sunk into a sort of stupor of watchfulness. Elizabeth Willow put her hand into the monkey's plate, and offered him a round of white egg. The monkey took the egg. Elizabeth Willow put her hand instead on to the monkey's face, and the monkey turned and looked at her.

'Elizabeth,' said Flower sharply.

Elizabeth Willow removed her hand.

When the sorbet – pineapple, rum, champagne – had come and gone, the roast was brought in. It consisted of two hares, very lifelike, with raised ears, back to back on a bed of artichoke, among flowers of carrot and iced butter. They had grape eyes, and were praised. Only Rupert looked away from them in disgust.

Hampton Smolte, who had gone along with the desultory hunting talk, and a discussion, diagonally across the table with Lord Craven, of wines, now raised his head. And Churton brought to him a dark curry, and to Rupert another.

'Look at this,' said Lord Bobb. 'The old habit. Don't it get stale, Smolte? You've been at home a long while.'

'Curry is an addiction,' said Rupert.

'So many things are,' said Doctor Gry, gaily. 'Certain foods, drink, tobacco. And even some medicines, I fear.'

'Eat your dead hare, Sir,' said Rupert. He turned now to the female monkey between himself and the doctor. 'Here, pretty lady, have a mouthful of this.'

'No, *no!*' cried Oxway. 'I plead with you, Sir. It could kill my beast.'

And indeed, the monkey had turned her face away, and flickered before it her little lemon fan.

Rupert laughed coldly, and left the matter.

But Urquhart, now constantly moving about the table, getting in the servants' way, blundered up to his father's plate at the table's head, and hefted off a forkful. This he offered first to the female monkey in mint green – she refused – and then to the next female monkey, by Oxway himself. 'I protest,' said Oxway, looking now alarmed. 'Flower—'

'Ma won't stop me,' said Urquhart.

'Hampton,' said Flower, 'make him stop it.'

'This is your jest, Flower,' said Hampton Smolte. She had never seen him look so swollen, so witless. His revenge? Her irritation mounted and she partly rose.

'Anyway, she won't have it,' said Urquhart. The monkey in tawny lace had pressed a lace handkerchief to her lower face.

Urquhart moved away. He went by Elizabeth Willow and made a mocking sally on her – 'Will *this* monkey have it?' – but Elizabeth Willow pushed him off.

Then Urquhart came back to his male.

'Here, old man. Try this.'

'No,' Oxway said again.

But the male took the fork of curry nimbly out of Urquhart's hand, and raised it. He ate the mouthful.

'My God,' said Oxway.

He got up, and Lady Craven too sprang from her seat. 'This is too much.'

The monkey gave a sudden cry. It was like the voice of a hurt child.

Oxway ran to him and, picking him straight up from the chair, held him to his big body.

'Silly, silly lad,' said Oxway. 'Didn't Papa say? Now see. Here, drink this water. Drink it, drink. Do as I tell you. Don't I always know best?'

Oxway persuaded the monkey to drink deeply from the crystal

carafe of water which he had grabbed off the table. The monkey went on crying and drinking. Oxway rubbed it, through its perfect dinner jacket. And Oxway shot a look of loathing at the table, but none of them saw.

Even Flower was laughing, for Lady Craven would not come back until her husband angrily insisted, and Mrs Wetherall had had to be fanned. Urquhart was laughing like a fun-full mischievous boy.

Oxway carried the monkey to his own place, and sat there with him on his knee. Finally the cries subsided. The monkey laid his head on Oxway's breast.

'You see,' said Oxway, 'we take them from their jungle, where they play over the ruins of the houses of gods, and we make them perform for us. But they're delicate.' Then he looked at the monkey, stroking the resting blond head. 'Are you better, my love?' The monkey looked up and kissed Oxway on the cheek. Mrs Plimpley, who was now tipsy, and Lady Flight, exclaimed cooingly.

Doctor Gry said, with slimy perspicacity, 'You have no children, Sir?'

'None,' said Oxway. 'I prefer my beasts.'

The monkey got down and went in a seemly way back to his chair. Urquhart leaned rudely over the back of Lady Craven's chair and chucked the monkey under the chin. The monkey looked about. He did not bite, though Oxway had jumped up again. The monkey only stared at Urquhart, through centuries of day and night, worlds of freedom and captivity. Then the monkey turned away, and touched his medal with one finger.

Elizabeth Willow said in her high clear voice, 'Urquhart couldn't climb a palm tree.'

Urquhart said, 'Shouldn't want to.'

But he sat down and was quiet, hungrily eating his roast hare.

When the iridescent jelly stuffed with strawberries and melon arrived, the monkeys ate their portions so that nothing was left, but the others were flagging.

The women, the monkeys, and Rupert, did not touch the savoury of braised chestnuts and ham. The monkey with a monocle removed a lawn handkerchief and polished the glass.

Flower said, 'We'll go into the orangery now. You men have your brandy.'

And the monkeys rose with the ladies, and Oxway too, and he led his tribe off so they should be ready for what came after.

Lady Flight said to Flower, 'Well, it was quite a witty joke.'

'Wasn't it?' said Flower. She prevented Elizabeth Willow from calling her cat. 'Let it stay for the port.'

Mrs Wetherall had produced her smelling salts.

In the orangery, among the trees and ferns and brass elephants with ivory inlay supporting vast urns of lilies, fruit and ices were brought to the ladies.

Mrs Plimpley said, 'I thought it wonderful,' with the look of a matron who has just been relieved of her stays.

'Order in court!' shouted the judge, banging with his gavel on the little wooden box before him.

He wore a sheepish yellowish wig from which clouds of powder rose, smothering his crimson robe and making him scratch furiously. The judge acted just like a monkey, which he had not done during dinner. Then he had been a gentleman with a monocle.

When the laughter died down, the prisoner was called for, and she came in with her wardress. The wardress wore a stern dark dress with many flounces, huge keys rattling at her belt. But the accused, a beautiful lady reckoned to have poisoned her blameless husband, had on a white satin gown, a plumed hat, and primrose gloves.

The judge ogled the lady poisoner. Then he shook himself and clouds of powder came again. Everyone in the court, except the murderess, sneezed and turned somersaults, with strange ease in their restricting garments – and the wardress was seen to have a petticoat redder than the judge's robe.

Other than the judge, the accused and her guard, the small courtroom was filled up by a lawyer in flowing black curls and another in flowing cerise ones, a lady witness clad as a maid in cap and apron, and two other ladies who comprised the inner audience of the trial. These were fashionably clad, but were presently found to have bags of oranges which they sucked or flung at the lawyers, when occasion prompted them.

'Order!' howled the judge. He pointed at the murderess. 'You are accused of a dreadful crime. Your innocent spouse who you slew with doses of arsenic and banana.'

The outer human audience laughed again very much.

They were relaxed now, Flower Smolte's guests, because the monkeys were finally in their proper place, up on the little stage, performing. And doing it so cleverly, too, and behaving exactly like monkeys at last, into the bargain, scratching and sneezing and bounding about, pelting each other with fruit. Arsenic and *banana* indeed!

Oxway threw his voice brilliantly, now in a high falsetto, and the lady murderess raised her primrose paws: 'I am guiltless.'

'Nay,' said Oxway, baritone for the judge, 'you were seen, slipping from his room, a smile of cruel triumph on your lips.'

The monkey with black curls rose for the defence. He gestured magnificently, and when an orange was cast at him, caught it, and shoved it thoughtfully in a pocket of his robe. While he spoke, council for the prosecution played with a large snuff-box.

'The lady is without blemish,' said the defence. 'It is true, whenever she went near her helpless husband, he grew worse. It is true that she emerged from his door and was heard to remark: *Now he's done for, the rascal*. But this might mean anything.'

The prosecution upset the snuff upon the witness, who sneezed comically and then bit him. The prosecution bounded into the arms of the monkey audience, who hit him with oranges.

The witness was called. Still furiously sneezing, she said she had seen her ladyship put arsenic into the master's soup.

But the judge had fallen asleep and snored.

The audience had to wake him with an orange.

Then he scratched vigorously and called for soup.

The murderess, turning to the human audience, gave a cackle.

Behind the Smolte dinner party, at the double doors of the bright green drawing room with the stage, and two snakes painted up the walls, Smolte's servants stood, also allowed to watch, choking on their glee not to annoy the aristocratic guests.

Mrs Rope was at the front, on a chair, and beside her a chaired Mrs Beare. Churton presided with Pocks in the room.

Behind Mrs Rope and Mrs Beare the others crowded in order of presidence, and at the very back stood Annie Ember, but not Tiff. Tiff was not well.

Annie looked at the slim blond monkeys. Although she might, she had found, have been in the second row with Divy and the housemaids, she had declined. She had not wanted to come here, but they had seemed to think it was a treat. And Flower had even come to her and said what a lark it would be, as if she, Annie, were Flower's confederate, which in a ghastly way she supposed she was.

Annie stood with her hands folded on the white dress, her hair done as Luksmi had shown her. She was pale as ash, ludicrously pale as the powder clouding from the monkey-judge's wig.

This was the second trial she had seen.

Did Flower know of Annie's past? Was this Flower's final edict, the ultimate manner of showing Annie she could not escape?

No, there was no need of that. Probably Flower knew nothing. It was a coincidence.

The judge . . . that man whose name had been *Justice*. And the man with black flowing curls, not defending as the monkey did, but damning. And the crowd in the court, and the witness, herself, oddly translated between two times, in cap and apron.

Rose had not been dressed so grandly when she stood in the dock. Nor had she been allowed to say anything. Would the monkey in white be found guilty? It seemed not, for the witness maid had gone out and come back with a plate of soup. The Smolte audience rocked with mirth. Not Rupert, of course, Rupert would not laugh at this. But even Hampton Smolte was amused, as he drank his brandy. And that one called Lord Bobb seemed almost unhinged.

As the soup went by the murderess, she tipped into it something from a rhinestone wristlet.

Never in his years of authority, the judge had said, had he been forced to oversee such a case. Only God could purify such sin. She would be hanged by the neck until dead.

Annie turned and went silently away from the servants in the door, from Smolte's audience.

She walked out through the orangery, and out through that door, the first she found, and down into the garden, which surely she was forbidden, as Eve had been forbidden Eden.

The darkness had come, but it was soft, and the air softly cool after the heat of day. Above, stars glimmered, soft too as if their points were caught in a veil. A moon rose, smoky, ivory colour.

She went into the water garden deliberately, the place he had drawn her to and where he had fallen down, and brought her down on to his body, the birth of a desire she did not understand, now for ever destroyed, the beginning instead of horror and guilt.

And here she could smell the adjacent roses, come now to their summer effulgence. Roses, roses.

Rose would be rotten by now. She would be bones in the prison earth. A skull. And on the fleshless stalk of her hand, perhaps, the marriage ring of brass no one could be bothered to steal.

From the house, faintly, for she had left open all their doors, wafted their laughter. As if they laughed at her. But they laughed at the monkeys. They laughed at the trial. At the murderess. At Rose. Yes, they laughed at Annie, Trample her down, chain her in cords, cut her, beat her, and then laugh. *Don't you like it, little girl? Say* Lord *to me*. And then, kneeling on the ground, *Annie . . .* And the flail turned back on him. He was now the one that Luksmi tended. Annie was safe. But for how long? And through *what*?

A gust of shame enveloped her.

She crushed her face into her hands.

But night leaked in about her fingers, and the moon, the crystal stars caught like ornaments in black hair.

And looking up, she saw across the slide of water the god, Shiva, in his endless dance. He was dark bronze on a greenish pillar that glowed as the water did, and the moon had pencilled in his form with thin white lines. Round his lower throat was a band of gleaming blue enamel. Life and death, lust and chasteness. A garland of black at his waist was a belt of skulls. Darkness and the light of truth. He held a trident, a javelin. How did she know anything of him? Rose must have said these things, long ago. Rose whose skull was in his girdle.

Annie thought of her unknown and faceless father, and Shiva there in the night.

If she had had the words, Annie would have cried out to Shiva, feeling the power of him as Rupert had told her that she would. She would have screamed for justice, for balance, for an answer. But she had no words, she only stared at him, over the glistening stretch of water.

And a breeze went through the flowers, and from their crowns lily petals fell, fell by the statue of the god who danced. So that in the dark, he seemed to move then and the dance was real, making and unmaking, until all the petals had fallen and lay on the surface of the pool. Then he was still once more.

She heard furious laughter again from the house, in that moment, and the loud cry: *Guilty! Guilty! Guilty!*

A sense of terror came to Annie, but she did not run from it.

She stood before it, as in the onslaught of a gale, and so it pressed through her, by a thousand broken apertures, over the garden, and away.

4

All the guests had gone, but oddly, he was one of them. They had had a large dinner, and then played a charade, and then cards. Lastly, whisky and water, and then the gharries came, and the carriages, but he had his horse, and rode off through the blackness of the night.

Distantly, the village blazed with tiny lamps, like a fairy grotto at home, at Christmas. It was the Festival of Lights.

But he turned on to the forest track. Where was he going? Back to the colonial city. Ah, but it was the station now, the old station and the bungalow where Flower was, her white body with its ginger muffs of fleece, waiting.

As Hampton Smolte dreamed, in the clutch of night, so Flower dreamed a few rooms away of dancing on the boards, eighteen years old, but they were a rotten audience, laughing at her seriousness, not applauding when she kicked up her skirts.

And Elizabeth Willow, who had liked the monkeys, dreamed she had gone after one into the park.

But Mrs Rope dreamed of a splendid dinner she was making with the help of an army of angels, and Divy and the housemaids dreamed of liaisons with young men, or with Rupert Smolte, of whom they knew very little. And Pocks dreamed of penetrating a woman, who was Divy but was not, and Churton of addressing a meeting, and Rawlings of a cauldron in the compound where he had cooked for Smolte, and Mrs Beare thought her dead mother was in the house, ordering her about—

But Oxway dreamed he was a penniless boy on the city street and someone had given him a stone for bread.

Urquhart ran over the hot earth, barefoot, and he could smell the rhododendrons and the castor oil bush, and the smoke from the fires by the river. He chortled, for no one had stopped him, and reaching the pepul tree, he looked up into its coiling muscular boughs. The leaves were silvery and they stirred, though no breeze was blowing. Urquhart put up his fat hands into the tree, and pulled his body and his feet after.

He climbed.

Once, a being had sat under this tree, imparting wisdom, but Urquhart did not care. He climbed up and up, and knew that from the upper height he would see the thatched roof of the house, full of strange flowers, and the ayah in the compound, combing rice through her hair.

The heat was deep and scented like balm.

If he climbed high enough, would he see the ghats by the river, and who had burned there?

Something roped Urquhart's waist. He strove against it but it tightened.

He glanced down.

A vast snake, black silver, had coiled out of the tree and gripped him.

Urquhart struggled, and so he saw that all the boughs and branches of the pepul tree were really snakes. The great boughs were cobras, and the little boughs were adders. They wriggled and stretched towards him, and he felt their terrible facile little stings.

Urquhart screamed for the ayah. '*Luksmi!*'

But Luksmi did not hear, and the cobras went on squeezing at him and striking from their spectacled hoods, and the adders bit him, and he knew if he had worn his shoes it would not have happened.

As Urquhart was struggling, and Elizabeth Willow chasing the monkey, Rupert Smolte entered a cemetery, and found all the tombs glaring open at the black sky.

Crows perched on the domes of the graves, but they did not attempt the corpses. The corpses were all bones. Rupert kneeled down, and touched the skeleton of a folded woman, round which long skeins of black hair had woven themselves.

Hampton Smolte had paused in a clearing. A slender necklace of water fell to the earth. It had a silvery, oily sheen.

* * *

Flower tossed her skirts and showed her frills and the audience hooted. Something struck her hip and she saw it was a decayed orange. They were throwing fruit at her, the beasts.

Elizabeth Willow ran into the depths of the park, and how tall the trees were, and full of owls.

The monkey had gone, and Elizabeth Willow dropped down on all fours, and ran swiftly, for she scented a shrew in the undergrowth.

Rawlings stirred the cauldron of scented curry and dark meat.

'Put in more ginger,' said his advisor, and Rawlings did as was suggested. 'More, more,' cried the voice.

Rawlings threw in handfuls of the powder.

'Now cumin,' said the voice. 'Be quick.'

Divy fell back under Pocks and felt his hot body mastering hers.

Mrs Rope cuffed an angel angrily.

Churton had forgotten his speech.

Mrs Beare was very small in a pinafore and she had lost her temper.

Tiff dreamed she had lost her *skin*.

'Well, I'll follow you,' Darius said. But he knew he was unwary. He knew he would be led into the clamorous deeps of the rukh, and left there. Yet he could not deny.

The early mists were all upon the trees of the jungle, on the vast spires of them, the spiked fans of bamboo and congregations of vines. Into the green tapestry he went, and before him the slender girl, playing on Krishna's pipe of gold, sweet melody, under a canopy of birds.

She was pale, and the hair flowed down her back.

She would lead him on and on, until he did not know the path— Oh, he had heard the stories. And then she would become a tree, and he would never find his way from the place.

But Darius did not care. There were gold rings on her ankles, and in her hair were stars not hidden by morning.

Rupert lay down on the earth and the ghoul of bones crawled

over him, and something scraped and caressed, licked and chewed at him, so he looked down.

Seven skulls were on him, on his male member, milking him.

He fell back and gave himself to this torturing pleasure in the vale of tombs.

But in the sky was a goddess, black as pitch, and her eyes were skulls like the skulls that made love to him. She opened her mouth and out dropped some yards of fire, that were her tongue. She leaned over him, Death the Woman. She leaned down through the skulls.

Elizabeth Willow knew the shrew had got away from her, into some hole too small for her to enter.

And in the sky there was a noise, like wings, so she looked up and up.

All heaven was moving. Something tremendous swept upon her, and Elizabeth Willow, no longer predator but prey, scuttled over the leaves to find some hole.

Flower cursed them. They were not throwing oranges but bats, stones, snakes, and turds.

Annie moved through a jungle of the night, lit by the lamps of tigers, and in the trees peacocks had opened their tails with the moon many times over on their quills.

But Annie saw herself. It was *not* herself. This was her mother, wandering far into the forest, called by the pipe of a god.

Under the trees, a man stood waiting.

He was not a man, but a demon, smoke-dark, poised there, his long hair flowing down his back.

He was beautiful, but the far side of death, he could inflict great pain. He was a servant of some buried hell. Yet he called to Annie's mother, and Annie's mother went to him. They lay down in the grasses and he pillowed her head on his blue-brown hand.

Hampton Smolte saw that the waterfall was a single tear, falling again and again, down the silken face of something unseen.

And as he watched, a shadow came from the jungle, having a serpent attached to its face and feet like the trunks of the trees. It was an elephant, indigo in colour, and it swam up the tears of the fall, up into the world. And there it swam out into the golden river, through sunset and dawn, black now with wet, and its eyes were flame. The air was full of screaming—

The curtain fell, but it was made of creepers. Flower could not get out. She ripped at the curtain, but flowers caught hold of her feet. Her chosen name had doomed her.

Beyond the trellis of smothering green the monkeys screamed and shrieked like devils out of hell—

A turban unwound and unwound, miles of cloth, and under it was hair of fire that streamed and screamed—

Rupert thrust up from the bed and was awake, but did not know where.

The sheets were wet and foul. He had succumbed to pleasure, but also soiled himself, as if a tongue of flame had indeed entered his body.

The shrilling noise did not stop, however. It went on.

Hampton Smolte threw himself out of his bed, swearing and full of a younger strength, that suddenly left him.

He pushed the dream aside.

His house was full of screeches and pandemonium.

Flower woke and screamed herself. The cries of her dream had spilled over.

'More spice,' said the voice.

And Rawlings, craning to see, beheld a severed warrior's head in the pot, telling him what must be added to make the dish, of which it was the main part, tasty.

Several servants were outside the dining room, in a cluster, Churton at their head with a lamp. He was nervous, and seemed to have some cause.

Behind him, large Mrs Rope, her hair become a schoolgirl braid, and herself wrapped in a sack-like dressing-gown, and nearby a couple of the maids, though not Divy, and Pocks looking stupefied.

The awful, demoniac noise proceeded out of the scarlet room beyond the doors – which stood ajar. No light was there, nor much in the hall, the gas having been turned out with the nightly locking-up. It was now past two in the morning, the hour of Fall, doubt, the descending soul.

Beads of sweat stood up on Churton's forehead.

'I wouldn't go in,' said Mrs Rope, above the screams.

He had no inclination to do so.

What was in there, in Smolte's feverish dining room?

The weird shrill cries rose and sank, causing weirder echoes high in the painted ceiling. Now and then would also come the sound of movement – the *furniture* in flux, or a thin tearing noise.

One of the maids, who had gorged herself on cheap pamphlets of the uncanny, whispered loudly, 'It's a polterghost, that's what it is.'

'Be quiet, you barrel of sawdust!' said Mrs Rope. 'It's some animal.'

'A monkey,' said a voice.

The servants reacted as one, for it was the voice of Hampton Smolte.

'I was, Sir, just about to—' stammered Churton.

'It's those apes of Oxway's,' said Smolte. 'The fool had them caged upstairs, but evidently not secure.'

He too had a lamp, and was clad in a red dressing-gown, as if purposely to match the invaded room. Under his left arm was a stick from India with a heavy silver knob, but ready in the right hand stuck a pistol.

'Oh!' exclaimed the maid who had not spoken. 'He'll shoot the poor things.'

'So I will, if I have to.' A strange lull came, as if the creatures in the room had heard. Smolte strode directly to the door. He looked florid, from the dose of brandy he had taken very fast before coming down. He said, 'Churton, you'll follow me. Hold up your lamp, and if you can, light some of the gas.'

Churton shrank in his bulk and his little patent-haired head quivered, but he had no choice. He went after Smolte.

Smolte crashed the doors wide, and a bolt of screaming exploded from the dining room.

The thick light of the two big lamps swept in.

'Merciful Jesus!' exclaimed Churton.

He tottered, and the lamplight reeled.

Smolte said, 'In God's name—'

And the polterghost maid let out a shriek of her own.

There truly were demons in the room.

They were on the long table, cleared now of its feast and china, and on the red curtains, which they had rent to rags. They hung as if in mid-air, up on cabinets and from brackets, where they had climbed. They had the bodies of naked monkeys now, smooth with hair, but the heads of panthers, bears, horned deer—

And with these heads, which they had wrenched free, held before their own, with slender articulate monkey hands, they leered at Smolte, out of the jungle of the darkened wrecked room, whose ornaments they had scattered, whose wall-covering they had defiled. The panther eyes gleamed and the eyes of the bear glowed like blood, alive again, with monkey life.

And then, up from the floor, a tiger came springing with a concentrated manic noiselessness – sprang for Smolte as long ago— And Smolte fired headlong at it.

The shot was like the breaking of an ebony pane inside the ear.

Portions of consciousness went from all of them, these men and women; they staggered, as if the bullet had gone through each and all – save Smolte. He stood upright, congested and cursing. In fact the shot had dashed wide and struck an ivory object still intact, now in many pieces.

But the tiger dropped and crouched, and one saw it was a monkey in an orange skin, the snarling head upon its own.

Silence, and in the silence, soft chittering.

Then someone ran along the passage shouting.

This was Oxway. He burst into the room against Smolte.

'Don't shoot them – I beg you – please—'

'You bloody mountebank,' said Smolte. 'Look at this havoc. You'll get the bill, you may be sure. And a pretty penny it'll cost you.'

The monkeys were settling. They let go of the precious heads, which rolled on the floor. They sat.

Oxway, pale and laboured, gaped at his tame and charming troupe, who had become vandals and demons.
'What possessed them?' he asked.

Part Four

1

Darius had not been his name in the beginning. But then, he had seldom been called by name, it was *Boy*, or *Beast*. Those were his names, for eleven years.

His father was a soldier, and his mother that soldier's woman, but this was all that was known. She left him a few days old at the foot of a charitable institution, in the hill station, where for a time he was scrubbed and beaten and taught of the love of Jesus Christ, which love no one in that house had permitted to touch them.

Outside the walls of this place lay the hot wet green world, and palm trees sailed to the sky, or beat before it when great winds blew. The outer world was not like the inner world, and one day Darius who-was-not-yet-Darius took himself from one to the other. He was only five, and he could not have said properly why he did so, except that he followed a band of curious people he had seen go by on the road.

They were white, this clan, and they were itinerant. They passed through the upland stations in search of work, in reality in hope of scrounging, while in the native areas of the land they merely took and thieved. They regarded the indigenous Indians as heathen savages, and themselves as good fine superior stock, forced by necessity to a rough life. They were drunkards and brawlers, knowing nothing, wishing to know nothing, the rubbish of the earth, horrible children with the wants of an appalling maturity.

Darius they took on because he could read, which they could not, and because he knew some Hindustani, also since he was so small they might train him to break in where they were too cumbersome to go.

Six years he was theirs, but he never learned to be as they

were, and so he was a poor robber and a useless pickpocket, and only sometimes could they employ him to get pity from some rich and kindly Moslem, or foolish white memsahib, pretending Darius was their starving little boy. They cuffed him a great deal and he was beaten by the men's belts, especially the belt of the man called Fog. But Darius had grown up with cruelty. He steeled himself to endure, not grasping what he did. He learned to be a trickster, cunningly excusing himself this way and that from thieving from the villages they skirted, or from the shrines.

Fog, who had been a soldier too, towered over Darius' years with the band. A large shapeless log of a man with bundles of arms and legs, done up in a stinking shirt and dun-grey coat. Sometimes Fog would black his face and put on native dress, his greasy reddish hair tied in a turban. But he did not pass, of course, for any of the tribes of India, though his eyes were dark, and he acted as if dumb. It was a sort of game with him.

The other men in the band deferred to Fog, and the women made up to him, but the women were pathetic ruined articles, kept for sex and to cook and mend. Twice one was pregnant, but the child never arrived. Their method of living killed it outright in the womb, while the mother, with an incredible, impossible sodden toughness, survived.

Darius watched them, or rather saw them, go on at their crimes, their drinking of arak – which they scorned even as they downed it – their pillage. He saw them tramp, in their boots, into holy places, and seize the offerings of fruit and cakes, and he saw too how the priests in those places allowed this, with dark pure looks, just as they allowed the monkeys to steal from them without chiding.

Sometimes they came on a city, and here they would wander into its sinks and alleys, creeping out at dusk to beg from the white women borne in jampuns. One night they murdered a soldier in a brothel, for his wages, which were slight enough.

Darius did not think of running away from the band. He read filched English newspapers, months old, to Fog, and once one of the men sodomized Darius, but Darius simply endured. He knew no sense of waiting, yet presumably he was.

Out of the welter of this past he could afterwards pick only shame and pain, and had he not learned to put away from him the evil of unkind memory, he would have wept in after years for those times with them. It was, too, as if he did not properly see the world in those years, for all he had got out into it. The views and vistas, the sweeps of hills in garments of sal and jacaranda and champak and green rain, the peacocks clustered at the stagnant pools, the red daq trees and strawberry-and-cream magnolia, the notes of birds and squall of hunting cats, those came later. But somehow he could always remember the colonial houses with their stiff columns and thatch, and the mask faces of white men, and the hot women gasping in their stays under sunshades.

When he was about eleven, they reached a town or large village, and the band were drunk. Out of the swift twilight opened up a river of smooth blue water, and above were the burning ghats, where the Hindu people brought their dead, to anoint, and free the soul. On the platforms of rock many harsh yellow fires were crackling, and in spots music rose gently, to honour the separation of the spirit from flesh, its union with the Eternal.

Darius had beheld such a spectacle before, but, perhaps because one of the women, Maira, had given him some drink, he seemed to witness it for the first time.

Fog spat. He had drunk copiously, and now he swaggered towards the platforms.

Impelled, Darius went after.

On the nearest terrace, a white-wound woman sat, her head upon her copper hand, and above the lit pyre of her dead husband, three other men, one of whom had poured the clarified ghee upon the dead. No outline of the body was visible, it had gone like the sun, and where the sun went, into the secret heaven of elsewhere.

Darius stared, and the smoke filled his eyes with tears.

But Fog got on to the terrace and he too stood above the fire.

'Puh! What a stinking thing. You filthy heathen bitch.'

At first Darius did not realize what Fog was doing, but then a stream of fluid, hissing and fierce, rushed down into the fire, which cracked and shot up sparks. Fog was pissing upon the cremation, putting out the flames with a reeking blue ray of water dense with arak.

The widow sat impervious, and the three men, perhaps her sons and the sons of the dead, also stood still, and the dark night came and gathered them to its darkness.

But Darius ran forward, and seizing Fog's drunkard leg Darius yanked him crashing over, and when he was down, Darius kicked him, as Fog had often done the others, in the groin.

Then Darius pulled a still-bright brand off the fire from out of the blackened marigolds and lace of black skin, and tried to relight the dying embers.

The four people only looked at him, they did not move. He knew it was no earthly use, their perfect ritual had been polluted in unthinkable ways.

But then the woman got up. She shook her head at Darius, and he backed away. He backed into Fog, who was recovering and blundering to his feet, and so, before Fog could take him, Darius ran, down from the platforms of night and fire, off into the forest. And all the while, the sweet face of the woman was before him, shaking its head above the smoke of ruin.

He heard Fog lumbering behind some way, and the band trailing shouting in the rear. Maira had sometimes been kind . . . But they faded from Darius, and he was at last in a trackless silent chamber of trees and umber.

He was not afraid now. He knew that he was free. And curling up under the ferns, he slept, believing he had been forgiven.

His life began that night; he was born in the forest out of sleep.

He found, as he had always seen, that it was possible to go about India asking, and the door being opened for you. He did not starve or want. Villages gave him shelter, and the jungle itself. Sometimes he saw the lords of the forest pass, the tigers and black panthers, the tree-roped hordes of monkeys, the wolf and wild dog, the elephant, the mountain which moved. He bowed to them and they let him be. And among men, he was circumspect, yet easy, finding they did not harm him, though sometimes he guessed his colour was unlovely to them, or even lovely – but then not in the way of a human thing.

He learned from pandits under trees, and from women washing clothes upon the stones, from wandering white cows whose flesh swung on them like a curtain, from the morning and the evening. He lived a year in the household of a Moslem prince who never once saw him. He was a beggar in a city, rubbed with clay to look dark – not to fool or mock, only to make himself more aesthetic for them, those who gave. But they noticed his grey gaze, sigil of low distant hills and lakes in a cool far country. Still they gave.

And he saw, too, the great City of Light, which had begun before Rome, where the alleys, narrow as a needle's eye, went down to the river, and camels passed through them.

In that city Darius, and he was called Darius by then, watched the huge artery of the river in the saffron light, how it was strewn with lagoons of marigold and pink lotus, while on the bank the men in black rags, like carrion crows, attended the fires of the dead. And he saw the fires on the river also, the night of lights in the city of lights, when music rang across the water.

But one noon he met with Hampton Smolte.

He had learned too, along with the aspirations of the spirit, some ordinary matters, and by the age of about thirteen – he never knew for sure what age he was – he had gained a knowledge of horses and other animals, even humans, and of ways to treat them should they fall sick.

Thus he had been called to a house near a port, a building of ill-fame, where the empress of the establishment had a pet mongoose, far dearer to her than her girls. The mongoose had slipped into a lack-lustre state, and Darius, who had sometimes fetched sweets or garlands to the house for a pai or two, was summoned.

He stroked the mongoose over and dissuaded it from biting him, and soon ascertained someone had given it something bad to eat. So he dosed it with oil, and when it had cleared itself, gave it a potion made up for him in the bazaar. By midday, the creature was bright as a star, jumping all over its mistress's head, nipping at her nose-ring, and searching for non-existent snakes about the well. 'My beloved, my baba!' cried the empress, looking out. She then put a fistful of silver into Darius' hand and told him he should drink and dine in the kitchen below.

Across the court from the kitchen was a door into a dim sand-coloured room, where men, and white men among them, came to consume palm-liquor and oddly-made whisky.

As Darius ate his rice and bread, he saw into an edge of this room, and presently two soldiers entered that had an upright air to them. Their uniform was spick and span, and they sat with authority, and were waited on by the servant as if they were kings. They inquired after particular fellows who frequented the brothel, Stiggins and Connaught, and some others known by nickname only. They told the servant there was something good in the offing for these men, and for the servant too, were he to assist.

Darius observed the soldiers with a little muted interest, for their insignia was absent and something was not quite exact with their burnished uniform. Now and then private armies were formed about the land, even armies of white ruffians to serve those very princes subdued by the English. Probably this business was of that nature.

When Darius had finished his meal, the kitchen boy brought him a mug of whisky, a great treat, and Darius smacked his lips and made a performance of taking it; then, when the boy had gone, poured it down a hole.

As he looked up from this, the world hesitated in its turning.

Another had come in through the front door of the brothel drinking-shop. He was a big unwieldy man, of a beige complexion, and murky brows, his head in an untidy cabbage of dirty turban. Though he had aged quite an amount, and got on him the peculiar lax fat of drink, Darius knew him well. It was Fog.

Fog sat down and called for booze and threw some coins on the ground. Then he kept very still, and while he drank, he regarded the two soldiers under his lids, their smartness and their brimming drinks.

When one of the men, the taller, handsome man, got up and walked outside to the alley, Fog also got up, in a stupid fumbling way, and slunk after.

Darius waited a moment, to see if the second soldier would be aware of a plot, but he only forged on with his drinking. Darius recalled the soldier murdered years ago, and he too rose and went after Fog.

In the alley, the handsome soldier had been urinating by the wall, and Fog had set on him and encircled his neck with one bulky arm, a thin knife pressed into the victim's back-ribs. Strangely, Fog was keeping up his act of being an Indian, and quacking away in a sing-song, as unlike the musical rhythm of the native as could be, that the sahib must give up his money and his pistol, or he should be sliced to the heart on the spot.

The soldier did not move, and Darius had an idea he might have a trick or two of his own maybe, but then again, Fog was violent and half-insane, and one should not always wait on chance.

Darius ran forward, light as the mongoose he had cured, jumped, and punched Fog in the ear. Fog, drunken, fell over – exactly as he had that other time on the ghats – and Darius leaned over and took his knife.

The soldier had turned and he looked down on Fog and he said, 'You want my pistol, vermin? Have it then.' And he shot Fog point blank through the head.

Darius felt as if the bones had dropped right out of his body. He went dizzy and shut his eyes, and he thought, *He was my father*. A wicked father, a curse, and yet Fog had stood in the place of a parent, and now there was a round red-black hole in his forehead.

The soldier said, 'You saved my salts, boy. That's good. We whites must stick to each other.'

Darius said, 'Look where the paint is running off him with the blood.'

'By Christ,' said the soldier, 'I've shot a bloody Englishman.' Then he grinned.

Darius laughed with pain. He had in fact seen death of many kinds quite often. Yet he marvelled even now that a man could think any other man a reasonable candidate for murder.

Above the alley, a narrow window with an iron lattice had crowded with girl faces, frightened amid their veils and cheap glass gems. Just as quickly the window cleared and no one was there. No one came to see.

The soldier spurned Fog with his boot.

'You knew the bastard?'

'I've seen him about,' said Darius.

'Well. I owe you something. What will you have?'

'Thank you, nothing.'

The soldier said, 'I'll tell you a house where you can find me. I might have work for you. You're handy. What can you do?'

'Nothing,' said Darius, for he felt a long-ago fear.

'You're the boy who's good with animals. The old bitch-ma told me about you. Can you cope with horses?'

'No, no,' said Darius.

'Come on,' said the soldier. 'Do you want to rot in these rat-warrens? You know some medicine too, don't you? I can offer you a sound venture. Perhaps more.'

Darius stood in a floating weakness. This man had just killed his past. As the soldier explained where he was to be found, and pushed on him after all some money, Darius listened and took note. He was in the hand of Fate.

Then the other soldier came, and said, 'You shouldn't have shot the bugger. Now we'll have to pay the madam.'

'For what?' said the handsome soldier. 'Let her squawk. She'd be in more trouble than I would.'

And they went from the house, no one stopping them, and Darius left too and went down to the navel of the city.

In a dim wooden cave that was the underside of a boat, he sat before a priestly man naked but for a thread on his breast.

This man told Darius that Karma had brought the soldier to him, that he must go with the soldier if the pattern was to run true.

'How long will I be with him?'

'God knows. Only God.'

Darius said, 'But I was free.'

'None are free until the flight into Eternity. Turn from it now, it must then be done at some future time.'

'He is corrupt.'

'He does not,' said the holy man, 'yet know.'

'Can I prevent his destruction?'

'You know that you cannot.'

'Can I change him?'

'You know that you cannot.'

'I will not go to him.'

The holy man said nothing, and Darius crawled out from the boat into the evening light, and walked up the canalled walls of the city, painted with gods and warriors, to the lodging of the soldier, Hampton Smolte.

The conches were sounding from the Hindu temples at the coming of the rains when they set out, for Kalachandra.

It was an eccentric time for travel, but there had been delays. In England, Smolte had married, he had hung about, apparently not wanting to return. But then he had come and done the work that was wanted, gathering up the makeshift army, conducting it away through the forests.

After a time, Smolte left his army in the charge of the former soldier Erskind, and he, Smolte, went up by river. There was a functioning steamer now, and on this the indigo would come down. There had been a lot of talk about the indigo, and the jewels in the jungle shrines, and the rich raja who gave presents.

Darius was the sice, the groom for all the horses. Smolte's men left him be, save when they had an argument. Then he was always mild, sensible. The horses loved him. Odd stories clustered round him. That he could mesmerize serpents, that he was not afraid of tigers, that he had been glimpsed drinking at a water-hole among the deer. He looked older than he was, already tall, thin as a pin, his hair like raw fair silk, his eyes worlds off. They said he was a bit simple, the sice, the horse-boy.

But he was Smolte's property too. Did Smolte have him? No, Smolte had a buxom wife he had not wanted to leave. Maybe then Darius was Smolte's bastard. There was something, for though Smolte took little notice of Darius, some link lay between them, as when Connaught had tried to beat Darius with a riding-crop because Darius said the mare must be walked not ridden that day, and Smolte came and shouted. As when Darius was seen sitting, looking at Smolte up on the rise among the trees, gazing into the end of day.

But when Smolte was gone on the river, they learned in their own way to respect Darius, for he was not to be trifled with. He knew a sappy bark that could heal a cut, and how to silt up dysentery. And you could not hit him from behind, he knew, and was there, or he was away, or if you troubled him, he had a blow like a mule's kick he could deliver, but he was reluctant to do this.

Darius was odd. But they got to Kalachandra with him, and at the station they let him go to the stable of the barracks and keep charge of their horses.

He would lift his head, hearing the elephants two miles away in the courts of Jarashan's palace. Fireflies would sit in his hand.

The English 'resident' of the place, Withers, said, 'There's a bloody boy knows something. Yes, he knows these forests.'

Darius was to grow for six or seven years amid such things, but he had the rukh, of which he alone was not afraid.

He wandered out into it, along the chartreuse paths, which was not so blessed, for later Smolte deemed him a tracker and took him hunting.

Hampton Smolte wrote to his wife once every two months. He sent her virtually nothing, for he had given her already the ruby Withers, tempting, had dispatched to him. In England, Smolte had been driven half mad by Withers' letters, showering on him like those of a lover, detailing feasts with the raja, and Jarashan's gifts – a diamond ring, a golden tea service, French champagne.

Hampton Smolte thought he knew the game that Jarashan had played. He had meant his own sister to ensorcell Smolte, so Smolte must come back, and bring his mercenaries with him. And then the raja would have that extra safety, better than his mustachioed bodyguard, an English army, of whatever sort, close by.

In England, Smolte had gone straight to the music hall, straight to see the voluptuous white woman, dancing. That night her hair shone like rosy gold. His concupiscence flared, turning him to a thing of iron and red blood that was fire. This was what he had wanted. This white flesh.

He pursued Flower Bell, and he had her. He rammed himself into the rich cushion of her. She was his talisman. She kept the dark away.

He believed he was quite better then, and partly looked about for some scheme in England that would bring profit. But there seemed not much, and all the while Withers wrote him these whining sneering letters. And Flower too was costly, with her oyster suppers, all the telling gifts.

It was when he began to see he would be a dolt not to go back, that he married Flower. He tied himself to her. But then he could not cumber himself with her on the errand of making Withers' little army. Alone, he returned to India, and he did what was wanted, not a long job but a complex one, skimming men from off the garbage heaps before they were rotten, testing their metal, accepting or rejecting them. And then the trek into the jungle in the storms.

When he reached Kalachandra, Withers greeted him like a libidinous uncle, and there in Smolte's quarters was a small statue of Shiva, pure gold, from Jarashan the prince.

For some weeks he drilled his men, had them beaten when they drank at the wrong hours, plied them with the old tale of riches. He went with Withers to look at the indigo along the plain. The rows of rangy shrubs were beginning to flower pinkish-purple. The plantation was small and possibly erratic, its workers milling about as soon as the overseer was seen, with the look of having been otherwise dormant. Still, Withers spoke in rupees.

He did not speak of the temples in the forest for a month, and then it was in the terms of 'patrols' – Smolte should take patrols out. Smolte did as Withers wanted, and found nothing beyond one empty ruin full of scorpions, creepers and bats.

The army of sixty-five men was all right. They had shaped into the proper mould, obedient where needful, languid otherwise. Though ruffians, they maintained appearances. The sice was good too, and useful in other ways, with his knowledge of various cures. Smolte had brought the boy because the boy was white, and had witnessed Smolte's killing of a robber. In the beginning Smolte had felt he had been generous to Darius, but later Darius irritated him. He was a bit like those youths one heard of, brought up by monkeys or wolves in the rukh. He came and went like shadow, sat in the contortions of holy men, did not eat meat, wandered about the forest as if it were a street. Withers had said Darius, on these occasions, should be followed. 'He knows something. He'll find something.' But following Darius was not easy, for one or two of the men had tried it for a laugh, and lost him.

Smolte worked at his military duties, sat long hours with his feet up, smoking Withers' cigars, drank brandy and ginger, rode, hunted, dozed, ate curries and birianis and unleavened breads packed with soft nuts. He did not sleep well at night. The slick heat of the last of the rains, the boiling tumult of falling water, held him in a cradle of unease.

For this, he had come here. And see, after all he would not

get rich, even though the small presents accumulated. Smolte had merely been caught by Withers' lunatic obsession. And, as before, Smolte began to want England, and found that he regretted tangling up England with his marriage to Flower Bell. Yes, he regretted the marriage, even as he rubbed himself over the memory of her flesh. He should have let her be. There were other girls of her type. Yet he had been afraid, had wanted to put up the barrier of that white body. But it was all a mistake. There had been nothing to fear.

In truth, why had he come back to India? Some bewitchment . . . No. He was only a fool.

Withers said, 'Our prince wants you to take a battalion and go show him their glory.'

Smolte thought, *He read my mind*. Perhaps Jarashan could do this, waiting for the moment of Smolte's deepest disillusionment, then beckoning.

'Jolly party,' said Withers. 'But I'm not invited, it seems. They make their own protocol, these devils.'

Smolte remembered Withers and Jarashan reciting their Persian and Greek poetry, and considered there had been some falling off.

He chose the fifteen smartest men and got them along the road, that was not so pristine as it had been, on the horses Darius had turned into mirrors. The uniforms were the best, if you did not know too much of how they should have looked, and as with young brides, what had not been to hand had been borrowed off others who had it.

All the time they rode towards the prince's palace, Smolte ached, from head to foot. He wanted to shout aloud.

When they reached the large village-town, brazen in the daylight, he barely saw it, though Jarashan's people came out and brought their babies to stare at the red-coated troops.

More trees had grown up in the courts, and again he heard the elephants – Stiggins nearly jumped out of his skin, and Smolte was able to berate him.

In a wide yard they went through their paces, creditably enough, with a few manoeuvres recollected from fine English city drills. The prince stood on his yellow balcony under a poppy sunshade, and when they were done, he smiled and waved.

'Pretty bugger,' remarked Berry. 'I've heard he's got some

sisters or wives – best-looking black women in the whole country.'

This time Smolte looked at Erskind and Erskind informed Berry that if his cake-hole was not kept buttoned he would be very sorry.

After their parade the men were taken away for some sort of treat, and Smolte another, through the usual corridor of marble screens, down to a garden place.

Massive arches went up on pillars carved with scales and lotuses. A blazing terrace stood open to the sun, and there on a slender table perched a sparkling and fantastic board and figures, a chess-set made of ivory and ebony, inlaid with silver, and with gold and silver pieces. Smolte stopped still, looking at it where it flashed. The golden elephants had castles of ruby on their backs, the silver infantry had shields of diamond, the cavalry and archers were smothered by pearl and topaz.

Jarashan waited in the shade. He too had rubies about him. He said, gently, 'A token for Mr Withers. Do you think he will care for it?'

'I'm sure he'll eat it,' said Smolte.

But Jarashan only laughed pleasantly.

'Come down into my garden,' he said, 'you will find it cooler.'

They descended, only the raja's steward stepping quietly after them.

Birds rang in the trees that sprang below the terrace, and the dark green shadow swallowed them, nearly as hot as the sun. Then there was a wild half-overgrown grotto, where water fell in a thin silver chain, and stone cisterns of flowers received it. Up against the tree-riven rock sat a rose stone Parvati, garlanded with jasmin. There was gold on her diadem, and under the blossoms a necklace of flat gold crocodiles, snout to tail. In one hand she held up a golden shell that glistened like a flame. Her form was of course extraordinary, the large round breasts, the tiny waist, and broad hips in their beaded apron. Smolte felt a spear of tingling lust pass through him. He looked away.

They sat on benches where cushions had been laid. The steward nodded and a bush gave out small boys who served sherbets and candies, and river-brown whisky for the Sahib Captain.

'You have done exceedingly well,' said the raja. 'Where did you find such peerless troops?'

'Here and there, Sir.'

'And no doubt they owe much to your tutoring.'

Smolte prudently kept quiet.

Jarashan said, 'How safe we are now. Who will dare to annoy us?'

The curve of the breasts of Parvati glimmered between glowing and melting away. Under her lifted arm an arch gave on another garden where there were mango trees. The sun shone between these straight as a lance. A blue peacock strutted suddenly out into the arch and the sun and burned there a moment.

'There is always beauty,' said Jarashan.

Smolte thought, *Does he expect poetry now? I'm not bloody Withers.*

'We must tread carefully,' said Jarashan. 'There is so much that may be lost in an instant.'

She would be married and gone away. In more than a year, what else? This would explain why even Withers, that monstrous old gossip, had not talked of her. In any event, she would have aged. Indian girls did so quickly. By thirty they were hags. But she had been . . . fifteen, sixteen. He thought of her face, could almost see it, up in the shade, like another bloom of the garden.

Jarashan spoke in Persian. Then he said, 'Forgive me. It is a verse – let me see: *Kill not the ant that steals the wheat. He dies like us in pain, and O, his life was sweet.*'

And into the arch came a compote of girls and grandmothers, in the red and rose and amber veils of India, some with their faces hidden, some not, all sprinkled with gold and jewelry, all gazing at Smolte and laughing like bells.

'Ah, they are bad. Pardon my women,' said Jarashan. 'They are curious always in the matter of the English.'

Then the women parted and only the sun was there, but the sun was a woman.

She leaned to feed two peacocks and at her touch they spread their fans and the turquoise feathers were emblazoned by the sun so they became on fire, and so did she. Her black hair poured down, but she was black light.

There was a dam in Smolte's body, forcing flame into his genitals, and his heart up into his mouth.

It was Jarashan's trick. Jarashan meant him to see. He must be bound, still, so he should stay.

They had not married her off. Jarashan would not. He loved her too well.

She straightened, and she was Parvati among the peacocks of Shiva. Her sari was like embroidered smoke, and through it he saw the faintest smoulder of her darkness. She turned a little, and was gone, and the bell-laughing women went after her.

'My sister, you remember,' said Jarashan.

Smolte said, 'An honour, Sir. Your people won't offer hard liquor to my men, will they? I can't allow it, I'm afraid.'

Jarashan smiled his secret smile. He loved, and all men must love. All suffer, as perhaps he did.

'The princess won't marry then?' said Hampton Smolte.

'Her only lord is her god.'

'Ganesa,' said Smolte.

'To whose presence once you conducted her.'

Smolte struggled with the pressure inside him. He was young and fit, but wondered if he would now succumb to apoplexy as so many had. And then the ludicrousness of it struck him, and he said, 'I'm married, Sir, myself. Did I say?'

'Mr Withers has mentioned it.'

Smolte felt the fire drain out of him, as a rain cloud moved abruptly up across the sun and all the gardens dulled.

'If I stay, I'll send for her. The men want their own women too, to comfort them. It's natural.'

'Quite so.'

Kill not the ant. Did it lust and love, did it go away and deny, and return and find all as before? Crush it then. Crush it out.

He would never be free of her now.

They found a temple when the rains had finished. Rather, one of Withers' unreliable native searchers told him of it, and four of the patrolling soldiers then located it, and, for a wonder, owned up.

There had been a tiger, a man-eater, in those parts, and Smolte ostensibly went to deal with it. He longed to shoot the creature, heat and lead going into its thick fur and bone. But the tiger eluded them.

The temple was up above a muddy green pool, and at first it looked only like a crinkled rock rising from the vegetation.

They hacked a way in, and there, in the arboreal crepuscule, was a host too absorbed to notice them.

Carved lovers entwined along the walls, their couplings no less erotic for the fluency of their postures, or the creepers and flowers that had half smothered them. There from a knot of leaves a silky stone breast with eager tip, and a stone hand that caressed it, there a head thrown back in joy, there a sculptured penis pressed into the hungry stone plum of a mouth. In the centre was the lingam, still vaguely dyed from ancient offerings, but no one had entered here for twenty years or more, save for the bats and snakes. A brown snake hung indeed as a garland on a nymph's breast, among the mummified marigolds. Sunflowers had cloven the floor, and flowers tiny as the dots of i's, so frail, so strong. But elsewhere there was what at first they did not quite believe, ropes of pearl and emerald, rubies set in anklets of green gold, the wink of the diamond and spark of sapphire. On the stone phallus itself, twisted in with the vines, buds of silver and rainbow opals.

Smolte's men cavorted, loudly jeering at the lovers on the walls which had aroused them, playing with the gems, clambering to get them, trying to dig with knives the precious stones out of the eyes and ears of love.

Hampton Smolte hated the temple. It should not have existed.

But he recalled that other shrine, where she had gone. Ganesa in his gems and metals.

The men were sworn to secrecy by their own outlandish oaths, and later Smolte came back with an equipped despoiling party, and with Withers.

Withers was extremely quiet. He passed under the statues, his wet eyes blinking only with the arousal of monetary greed. 'I told you, Smolte. And there'll be more. We'll be the richest gentlemen in England.'

Five days after, the tiger killed a child near one of the villages, and Smolte, going out at dawn, found it. He experienced no terror as the animal bounded at him out of the maw of the jungle like a sunflower of death. He shot it down and it collapsed lifeless. It was old, and had only two teeth; it had turned to men since they were more simple to take. The village gave Smolte the skin, which was quite good. It seemed a relief to him, to have fired back at this being which had pursued, and now brought down and devoured him. If he must stay, he might have revenge.

2

When she had been in India some years, Flower still impatiently marvelled at her presence there. However, she did not try to pretend she was instead in England, for attempting to cut the garden into a different shape, or stuffing the bungalow with imported or substandard heavy English furniture, was no use. Besides, her England had been a place of noise and ebullience, irreconcilably unlike the sounds and silences, the hubbub and quiescence of the East.

After Hampton had escorted her up-river – the colonial cities, the phosphorescent sea left far behind – she had been startled by the desertion of the station. There were women there, but they were not her sort. And for the native people she had, and kept, a kind of reluctance. They were all right, she did not object to them. But to see them as in any way like herself, and the other whites, let alone as friends or allies, was not possible for Flower.

The bungalow was solid, near to the outer wall, which had been repaired. It had some furniture – English – and native carpets on the wall; the wooden floor was constantly swept and sprinkled with water. Brass objects stood about, and garden blooms that were preposterous crowded in earthenware bowls. Beaded curtains veiled the verandah, and beyond was a trellis thick with foliage and flowers.

In the garden they had put crushed sea-shells on the paths to deter the snakes, without much success.

Flower had very little to do, and this pleased her, for she was soon big with Rupert, and in the heat did not want to assay anything. She lay about and ate sweets. She learned to take tea black, having seen how the goat was milked.

Her day was punctuated by meals, by the noise of the well-bullocks hauling up the water sack, sometimes a squeaky bugle from the barracks.

She had a carriage pulled by a bullock in which she could ride about the mall. She did not often use it.

Withers she thought a nincompoop, half-crazed, probably drugged with bhang. He seemed to her very old and his sleering ways only made her want to slap him.

The ayah infuriated Flower.

Flower could not pronounce her name, and called her *Ussi*. Ussi would brush Flower's hair, iron her personal garments, take care of the child, and later the children.

She seemed to Flower herself like a rather stupid yet cunning child. So they all seemed, the sweeper, the lamp-boy, the bullock-man, the cook. When Rawlings, the white cook from Smolte's garrison, came in to prepare food, Flower felt happier, although she did not like his dishes any more than she liked the other muck.

The ayah sewed, and regularly lost – or stole – the silver needles necessary in the humidity. Insects proliferated, every year there were more. Over the walls the beasts shrieked in the jungle, and a couple of times she was taken to a dinner at the raja's dilapidated palace, and saw his elephants, painted like harlots for some festival.

Hampton gave Flower jewels in India that amazed her. Then she became weary of them, for everything was so florid there, the orchids on the table, the village women in bright red, that an emerald rope was only like the rest, and might vanish when they went home.

Of course, they talked of going home.

Late evenings, when he sat with her in the verandah, the oil lamps dashed by moths. Then, he spoke of it. A few years . . .

Nearby the ayah would be crooning some weird chant to the child. Below a jackal snuffled through a rubbish heap. England—

Flower's husband had been snared by India, Flower saw. His skin was now dark, and he smelled of the curry he ate, and later fed to her boys. But Hampton was not often with her. There was the plantation, which was always failing, and Withers always wanting something, excursions into the forests, drills.

But then, in the hot nights, they coupled.

And once or twice, the scent of a flower, the stars above, the first music of rain, the mist on the canopy of the jungle – Flower sensed the life of the land, which might touch her, too. But she would not have it.

She did not nag him. She was too clever. And on the boat they had warned her, men went insane in India, you must be cautious. They had told her also that mulligatawny soup was proper on Sundays, that the boy must always shine the master's boots, and of the woman whose hair was eaten by rats, and the raja who had once beheaded his singing girl at a banquet, because a sahib had mentioned he did not care for her voice.

Flower did not nag, and she did not moon or regret, and she did not hate or love the country she was stranded in.

She waited, for she had realized enough to see that they were growing wealthy.

But also she watched Hampton alter. His looks began to sink, his skin grew more yellow and more flaccid from the daily tots of brandy and whisky. In the sunset, when he came back to the house, she would hear his harsh voice shouting at his horse. He was full of anger. Even in sex, was rage. She accepted she was useful, a more adequate form of masturbation. She had lost him, if he had ever been hers. But she did not know why, or wonder why, for she did not greatly mind. He would provide, he was a sound bet that way. And since she did not want any more children, she schooled herself to feel no pleasure – she understood quite well that a passionless woman was less likely to conceive. As his bouts of love-making grew more and more peremptory, that too became more simple. She pretended.

She looked at him from a distance or through a screen. And when he shot tigers or put on a little parade for his brown prince, Flower praised him. And she left him to the power of his India as she left her unwanted sons to the omnipotence of Ussi. She dreamed, and read the expensive novels sent for her up the river. She tried to preserve her skin and hair and body against the Great Return.

Eighteen months after Urquhart had been born, Smolte told her she was to pay a call on the women of the raja's palace.

'What for?' said Flower. 'So they can stare at me and paw me like a lot of monkeys?'

He gave her one of his smoked-over cloudy looks.

'You'll have to, Flower. He's a prince.'

'And I'm English. That's that.'

She was still irascible. She had had a nasty time of the birth – a krait snake had been discovered under the lacquered bed-frame even as she heaved and screamed to get the child out.

Smolte leaned on the verandah post.

'It's an honour. You haven't any choice.'

'Oh haven't I.'

'I tell you you haven't.'

Flower sniffed. 'I suppose that wretch Withers wants me to go. Price up the jewelry on the princesses' necks.'

'There's only one princess.'

Flower had heard of this woman, unmarried they said. So presumably horribly ugly or deformed. The gossip of the native women was misleading. Flower had re-christened the princess by the partly phonetic similarity, *See-the-Viper*.

'See-the-Viper,' said Flower now. 'Will she be there?'

'She speaks excellent English,' said Smolte. He had turned his back and lit a cigar.

'Oh, you've met her. I thought they were kept hidden.'

'No. He likes them to come and go.'

'And to gawp at English women.'

'You weren't asked before,' he said.

'And why now?'

'I mentioned you.' He paused. 'She was with her brother and she asked me how you were.'

'Nice of her. She's the wise one, no brats. Is she ugly?'

'Just dark,' he said. He was staring off through a gap in the trellis at the garden boy watering the blackened lawn. 'An Indian face. That kind.'

Flower did not know how she really felt. She was tickled by a slight curiosity, as she had been about the raja. But all the gaudy magnificence and the ruinous palace had seemed to her like a stage-set, and one too where she did not act the main role.

In any case, there was no option. So she went.

As she swished that day across the compound to the road, she saw her elder son standing in the garden with Ussi. They both looked odd, in a fashion Flower could not fathom.

Rupert appeared certainly too dark, tanned like a native himself, and Ussi was like a shadow, her black pig-tail down her side. The boy carried a small terracotta god-toy the ayah had given him. It had a fat belly and an elephant head, a nightmare thing. There had been a clay bullock-cart, too, with gilded wheels, but Urquhart, crawling, had already smashed that.

'Cheer up,' said Flower, 'your ma's only going to see a princess.'

She travelled by her own awful bullock-cart, on the hard-cushioned seat, and her back ached horribly all the way. Some of Smolte's soldiers accompanied her as an escort, but her husband was off on other business. He should have come with her. Flower ached and sweated, and began to feel nervous.

At the ochre palace she was taken into a court with marble pillars and painted rooms let on to it. On the brilliant cushions sat the wives or relatives, God knew what, of the Raja Jarashan, and if See-the-Viper was there, Flower did not guess. These females ranged from young to very old, but Flower had been told that twenty-five was ancient for an Indian girl. How could you be sure?

They all got up and salaamed, or whatever it was they did, and Flower greeted them with a stiff aching little bow, wanting to sit down.

And then, out of one of the inner rooms, walked a girl in honey-coloured muslin with a drifting embroidery of silver.

Flower had never judged an Indian woman pretty before then, but this one she could see was extremely beautiful. Her face would have been her fortune, even in England.

The woman nearest to Flower said, in spaced English, 'Mrs Flower, this is the sister of the Lord, Sitavaina.'

Flower curtseyed, and winced.

'Please sit,' said See-the-Viper, and a sofa had been placed, and Flower plumped down on it with an inner groan.

Then See-the-Viper sat on a cushion, and there was an exchange of courtesies. How was Flower, how was her baby, did she require anything they might supply, she need only say and it should be hers. And what had she named him? – they could not pronounce it and burst into giggles – although not See-the-Viper.

See-the-Viper was so beautiful she could not, perhaps, laugh, as the surface of a sky-pool cannot break.

Juices were brought, and cakes. Flower enjoyed these and she started to eat. She thought, *I'll take a wager he likes the look of her, for all he doesn't seem to notice her*. Flower was only amused by this. Hampton could no more think of an Indian woman in a physical way than she could entertain the notion of a black man.

As Flower put the cakes and sweetmeats into her mouth, crunching up the nuts and seeds, she began to sense that See-the-Viper was in fact attending on her. And so when the other women got up, by twos and threes, and went away, Flower wiped her lips on the silk cloth, and readied herself.

They want something.

See-the-Viper asked if anything else might be given to Flower.

'Thank you, no. And now I'll be pleased to hear what you have to say, whatever it is. Let's not beat about the bush.'

The young girl had such poise that Flower's words seemed to fall into a crater and evaporate.

She's dark enough, thought Flower. *He was right there.*

Sitavaina said, 'I have wanted to see you, Madam. To see his wife.'

Something in Flower went hard and motionless.

She felt the flush dry out of her face.

She said, 'You mean my husband, Hampton Smolte.'

'Yes,' said Sitavaina, simply. Her black eyes, which were like polished onyx and had no floor, looked at Flower with a serenity that might be an affront.

'And why, may I ask?'

Sitavaina smiled. The sky-pool did not break.

'You must pardon my interest, Madam. You are the only wife my brother will permit me to behold.'

Flower was not mollified. Obviously the riff-raff of the station would be out of See-the-Viper's sphere. But the way she had spoken . . . *to see his wife*. There was an intimacy. Of some kind. But what could it be? It could be nothing.

Flower drew in her breath. She said, 'Well, here I am.'

'And I must now ask you,' said the princess, 'for the kindness of your heart.'

Flower tensed again, but just then one of the women came back, leading a child. The picture was strangely reminiscent of the image she had on parting of Rupert and Ussi under the pepul tree. But this was a small girl, about four, with spindly legs. And this one was not *sufficiently* dark. No, she was muddy pale and her hair an unbecoming greyish brown. A half-caste, thought Flower with distaste.

Sitavaina held out her hand, and the little girl ran up and took this exquisite hand and held it, staring away beyond the fat young white woman, up to where a golden-earringed dragon cannon lurked on a roof.

'Excuse me now,' said See-the-Viper. 'I will be plain. One of your husband's men has sired this child upon a girl of the palace. We may not keep her. I inquire therefore if you will take the child into your household.'

Flower's mouth dropped open.

'What about the father?'

'He is a drunkard. He does not know.'

'Well, your slave needs seeing to,' said Flower righteously. 'Loose morals—'

'You must understand,' said See-the-Viper softly, 'she was too afraid to deny him. He had watched her dance, had spied upon her. She was very much distressed.'

'And now won't keep the bastard,' snapped Flower. 'Well, I don't want it.'

'Then I must entreat you, as a great favour to myself and my brother, the prince.'

It was to be forced on her then. Obviously, the child would profit from an English upbringing, however unconventional. And they did not want this mark on them of her colour.

'I'll take it as a servant, if I must,' said Flower, coldly.

Sitavaina did not remonstrate. She only said, 'She is called Luksmi.'

And Sitavaina touched the child quietly on the head, and Luksmi looked down, and directly at Flower after all.

She was not a pretty child. The worst of both bloods had got into her. Hr face was flat and between her eyes was an unpleasant birthmark.

'What can you do, Luksmi?' said Flower in a starched tone. 'Can you see to clothes?'

'She has little English,' said Sitavaina. 'Perhaps you will teach her.'

'There's a fellow in my husband's army, Darius, the sice. He's taught some of the native soldiers to read English.'

'And then she will serve you,' said Sitavaina. She spoke gently in her vernacular to Luksmi, and Luksmi saluted her gravely, and came over and stood by Flower like a small unwanted docile dog.

After which See-the-Viper's slaves or servants brought Flower some incredibly coloured silks as a gift, and a silver box with a pearl. She had often pondered if they knew how Withers and Smolte plundered the forest shrines. There had been three discovered while Flower was in India. Probably they did. How could they object? They feared the English, and it was right that they should.

And now she was saddled with this other brat.

When they rode back, she had the child put up behind Stiggins on the outriding horse. It was probably his mistake. He had a native mistress. But Stiggins did not know, and only scowled, and the child sat awkwardly for the two hour journey, her little, not-dark-enough head bowed under the branches and green parakeets.

Perhaps every six or nine months, he had seen her. Only so often, through all those years. At first, as if she knew – did she know? It must be so common for her, to be wanted – he had not seen her at all. And then, because Flower had come to be with him, he thought it was that, she was flighty, jealous even. But she was not, not Sitavaina. Nothing so lovely could be entirely human, and she was not human. She was enigmatic. But it was not a game.

It was Jarashan who made her come in, presumably, Jarashan wanting to see Smolte in the net. Let him see it then.

Smolte stared at her. He stared and she, so purely, remotely divine, let his glance, his glare, slide away.

And while Jarashan, he thought, relished it all, and Smolte burned, she moved like a slender cloud between the earth and the sun.

Maybe she spoke to him fifty words, in all that time. And once, once only, she had raised her eyes and looked at him, across a chamber that dissolved to dust. But her eyes were only mystery. She wished to see, but offered nothing.

She was Kshutriya, of the Warrior Caste. Did she invite him to battle? She did not age at all. He did – he saw. She could have prevented it . . .

He would gallop to the bungalow down the mess of road, and

take Flower, plunge into her whiteness to scald out the shade.

But when he heard she had asked for Flower, then something in him quickened, yes, even after the years of vacuum. Why would she want to look at Flower, if not because of him?

And even when Flower brought home the child, and the child was given over to Darius and the ayah, and learned to mend and brush hair and see to powder and soap, even then he believed there had been that behind it. Especially since Flower said to him: 'She told me she wanted to see your wife. What did *that* mean?'

'It means he won't let her see the other wives. If they are.'

'So she said. But what else?'

Then Smolte had slapped Flower's behind and said, 'Got you cross have I, little woman? I must make sheep's eyes at your Ussi next.' And he and Flower went to the bed and copulated under the mosquito netting, but neither Flower nor he, in their different ways, forgot.

Meanwhile Withers, Smolte imagined, was finally going quite mad. He spent all day at windows of the barracks or his house, staring after natives, soldiers, Darius with the horses. 'He's off. Where's he off to? He's found something.'

Smolte wondered if they had pillaged enough. They would be rich. It might be time now to leave Withers. The indigo was going downhill, for a fact sluiced out by the rains. Smolte had two sons. They would need to go home, and why not he?

He knew why not.

She was the reason why not.

And now this: *She wanted to see your wife*.

The world curved towards harvest. Along the fields the crops blew, and all the fruits shone in the trees. At the dawn streams the women bawled their song of love to the sun.

They hunted tiger, he and Erskind and the bodyguard of the raja – for Jarashan did not hunt. Smolte had shot quite an amount, bear, panther, tiger, wolf, a rogue elephant, many deer, and so on. He had pride in the skins, the heads, tusks and horns. Even in the snake he had bludgeoned in the garden, with the silver mark of a god upon it. That had been stuffed in a city and sent back to him and reared now near the small Shiva on the lawn, where Flower cursed it. The Shiva had a cobra too, but that was bronze, and orange flowers fell over it that were steeped to make a tea.

Despite his own reticence, Jarashan loaned out his elephants for a grand hunt, every year or so. It was bizarre, for the elephants were dear to him. 'It is his friendship to you, Sahib,' said the bodyguard. More likely the ordinary crawling.

That morning the beaters moved as always, in a black pack, banging drums and squalling with their flutes, shouting, driving the tiger to a centre.

When Smolte came out above it, he was miles high on the elephant, the dark one they called God's Kiss.

God's Kiss was fearless, and on the way he had plucked boughs off the fig trees. Now he stood like a rock.

Smolte took aim, and in that instant the tiger leapt, leapt, and scored the elephant from his ear to the sensitive tip of the trunk.

As the tiger fell back, Jarashan's man shot it stone dead with a bullet under the brow.

But God's Kiss cried loudly, splitting heaven, and then sank to his knees, almost toppling his driver and Smolte from the barricaded seat.

The elephant kneeled weeping in the fern.

Smolte saw the tears, thick as jewels, fall from his eyes.

There was utter outcry. The Indians ran in all directions calling on Allah, calling on a million other gods or names of God, and Smolte said to Erskind, 'The damn thing's down for good.'

'I'd finish it, Smolte,' said Erskind. 'It won't be any use now.'

And Smolte went to the bodyguard, a big man with a black moustache, his head wound in a white turban with a ruby. This fool was crying too, and Smolte said, 'We can't have this.'

'He is wounded. He is wrecked,' said the bodyguard. 'We must bring men – how shall we bear him?' And the mahout lay sobbing in the bushes.

'For God's sake,' said Smolte. And he had them give him the huge gun, the elephant piece brought out because there was always a danger of these beasts roaming wild around Kalachandra.

He put his foot on the side of God's Kiss and the elephant looked at him through its peculiar tears. Smolte put up the barrel and fired.

The elephant rolled over and crushed the riding-box. It lay like an enormous stone, an obstacle flung into the jungle. Its trunk rippled, and became inert.

Birds rushed screeching into the clear blue sky and then there was a silence.

Smolte turned. Somehow he had been searching for Darius, but Darius had refused to come. Darius had been on many tiger hunts, he had never refused before, although he had said he did not care for it. 'Be damned to you,' said Smolte, 'you're my gun-boy. You'll do as I want.' Today Darius had not been anywhere to be found, and so was left behind.

Why seek for Darius then? Nothing more needed to be done.

'His nerve was gone,' said Smolte of the elephant. 'Lord Jarashan wouldn't thank me for leaving him poor breeding stock.'

They gave him the tusks, later. They were a splendid pair. The bull was a beauty for all he had not had proper courage. Jarashan never referred to this incident.

But when the elephant festival came, only eleven of his elephants walked out on to the earth streets of the town. Smolte was present to see, Jarashan had invited him, so he had had to go. He watched the eleven beasts, and each had been dyed a different shade of colour – azure and navy, emerald, crimson and rose, yellow, purple, marigold, turquoise, ink black and whitewash white. He could not help asking himself what colour God's Kiss had been done, went over and over it in his brain, the absurd heat and noise and dust making him an imbecile. He could not think. There were no other colours.

The elephants were hung also with cloths of gold and silver, and had head-pieces of gold with tassels of red and orange, mauve and vermilion. Their toes were varnished silver. On their backs in the gold houdahs rode the mahouts, twirling sunshades like coloured flowers, and the air was vociferous with conches and drums.

When it was over, the row went on in his head half a day and a night.

In his bed with Flower he eventually slept and dreamed of the weeping elephant walking down through the town in a garment of mist, painted and dyed the tints of everything Smolte had ever seen that had a colour. And this made him nauseous, woke him, and he got up and drank brandy in the verandah. Flower did not stir.

It seemed to him that, as Darius would have claimed to, he, Smolte, could hear the noise of drums and cymbals from Jarashan's town. He knew they would go about all night, with music and torches, and in the streets of the villages too – probably that was where the drum-beat came from, the nearest village. They would carry a huge image like pink Turkish delight, decorated with necklaces and earrings, garlands, a golden headdress like a tea-pot among stars. And they would hide, from the image, the sky, under a canopy, and their own heads too, for Ganesa had an old quarrel with the moon.

Smolte stared away into the dark, and he seemed also to glimpse the firefly lights. But he was only tired. So he went back to the bed and lay by the big body of his wife, and had no more dreams, for he did not sleep.

Tomorrow, she would go into the forest. *She.*

Every year, near or during every festival, the same. Like that first time when he had been coerced into providing her escort.

But now it was not in his charge. He and Erskind had trained a native battalion of the raja's men, and it was this part of Withers' army which accompanied Sitavaina, to protect her. For years Smolte had led them to the palace, and given them ceremoniously to Jarashan for that night, and then feasted, while she was taken to Ganesa. None of them, she or her retinue, would come back till dawn. What went on? Well, he would never know.

He considered it. It was, after all, like a dream. He saw her dancing before the god of marble in that hidden cave of whose existence and contents he had never spoken. Her hair swept the floor before the statue. Did her beauty rouse it? Did Ganesa come alive?

Smolte rose at first light and went riding. When he returned in broad daylight, Erskind met him on the mall. Withers had disappeared.

'He's off somewhere, or gone to look at the indigo.'

'No, the overseer was in. Withers isn't there. There's nothing left to see.'

'Then the old devil's slinking round the station somewhere,

digging under stones—' Withers had begun, surreptitiously, to do this.

'I've got them off searching. You know how he is about snakes. He could make one come and bite him just from the fuss he makes.'

Smolte went in to the barracks and put his feet up on the table, and smoked one of Withers' cigars, and had some glasses of whisky. Then he reviewed the native battalion, the seventeen men who would be going to the palace.

By the afternoon, there was no sign of Withers.

Smolte did not give a damn.

The feast was as usual plentiful, chickens prepared in butter and stuffed with almonds and spices, solid gold dishes with the delicate curries Jarashan preferred. He had not, Smolte, liked this food, but now he could not get sufficient, could have made himself sick, unable to stop. And yet, tonight he did not gorge himself, not on the food nor on the red French wine, the bubbling champagne. He took just enough to keep his countenance.

Smolte had explained Withers had problems with his stomach. To tell the truth would be to invite more of Jarashan's false solicitude, and loyal suggestions for measures of search. Withers did not matter. He was a puppet, and he had lost his head or his mind.

Girls danced as they ate, pointing fingers and jewelled toes. But they did not remind Smolte of her. He wondered if, had he asked, one of these creatures would be supplied for him. Always Jarashan coaxed him to rest the night in the palace, and always Smolte declined. He had never forgone the notion of treachery. A serpent in the pillow, a gifted girl with a knife. It was better to get back to his fat white wife.

Jarashan spoke of hunting, to please Smolte presumably, and Jarashan did not refer to the death of the elephant Smolte had shot in previous months. Jarashan did not utter any poetry.

Nearby the taster sat on the floor, round and smiling. Jarashan had said that, although the English presence had made him safe, it would be an unkindness to deprive the taster of his function. Perhaps he feared Smolte in turn. Yes, he feared Smolte. The Englishman must be appeased, fawned on. He must have always what he wanted.

When Smolte left, the night was dark. No moon was present. Black Moon Kalachandra did homage to Ganesa. In the town beneath, lights played up and down and the horns sounded and the clash of bells.

Smolte rode over the causeway, and turned, and looked back.

The palace grew up for ever from the rock, bulked black on black, and in its windows saffron lamps and luminous red glooms. Among the wild gardens he heard things move through the leaves, squirrels springing from marble lattice to copper minaret. The elephants were silent, maybe sleeping, lying down as they would only do in contentment.

When he looked again out to the jungle, he saw, as he had seemed to in the verandah of his bungalow, a flight of lights far off, down among the trees.

The procession had gone out late, or lingered on the way, and so was still visible to him. Sitavaina and her escort, her women and her slaves; moving towards the temple in the black velvet wood.

Smolte sat on the horse, and up above in the building, a woman laughed, as if at him.

There is a time for all things. Years may go by, ages of morose acceptance, of not knowing, of achieved ignorance and solid codes, but then – the time is there, and all is new. As if one world had slipped over into another, where things are probable that never have been so before, where roses are blue, and night as bright as morning.

Smolte pulled the head of his horse around.

He rode down into the jungle, going the way that she had gone.

They made a circle amid the trees, about a hundred feet off from the hill, their torches burning, and their lit faces under the white turbans dark as a paler night.

He was challenged, but when the man saw it was Smolte, he saluted, and let his captain by.

Smolte tied the horse close to the hill, against a great sal tree.

Then he went on, and at the entrance to the cave, one sat, as before, and Smolte said, 'I know,' and had this man pull off his boots. There was no other pause, they did not, could not, stay him.

He went in.

The forest, as long ago, must be full of the bats which had fled out. A very few remained, fluttering dimly high above. There was hardly any light. Smolte could not see the carvings, or the vines which roped across his face, the spider webs which broke in sticky nets.

But then, over the succession of courts, the glow of torches came again.

He got into the shrine through a tunnel made in the vines by the women's slighter passage.

And the torches blazed there on the carven bat-encrusted pillars, and on the idol of white wine molasses, its marble flushed as if with heavenly ichor, the sapphire eyes. Those eyes. They looked down upon Smolte, at him, and they were full of all the perception of a thinking clever immortal being, which knows all and forgives all but lies.

'Well,' Smolte said quietly. 'Ganesa.'

On the altar were heaps of flowers and cakes, cups of golden ghee, and little lamps that curdled up a rounded secret light unlike the sharp fire of the torches. And there were fresh jewels too, he saw the acid wink of green and vivid red . . .

But they, they were not there, the women. They had gone on, beyond the god. He heard their laughter suddenly, as he had heard the woman laugh above him in the tower of Jarashan's palace.

'Well, Ganesa. Do I pass?'

Smolte grinned. Ganesa would let him by, for the elephant god was the god of the world and the wants of life.

The torches made Smolte hot. He undid the formal military jacket he had worn for the palace. He put his hand on a curtain of creepers and went through into the place beyond.

He felt light now, but steady. Certain.

There was a funnel of stone. Something slid over the floor. He did not care.

The hint of flame was there again, before him, and he had come to the last depth of the cave, a rocky room that dropped down in steps. And on the steps the lamps had been set, and they filled the whole chamber with a smoky straw colour glow, that rocked in the pool of water at the stair foot.

Flowers on the water, white and crimson. Incense in the air as in the shrine. And in the pool, the women bathing in the water made sacred by the proximity of the god, and perhaps to enchant him. All the women, naked, and the surface of the pool aswirl too with their long black tidal hair.

And Sitavaina, naked. Sitavaina with her black hair falling down into the water, which came only to her thighs. As she moved, lifting the hair away, her body was made of darkness, with gems of light upon its edges, on the nipples of her round breasts, the silk of her skin, and at the point of her belly the night itself curled waiting.

The men had not stopped him. They had not known what went on. For this they would not have allowed him to witness.

A girl bringing an unguent from the steps beheld him, standing there in the entrance of their sanctuary, his red jacket undone, and the world of life's wanting in his face.

She screamed, thinly.

Then the others turned, and saw him too.

And Sitavaina.

She stood, not covering herself, her body gleaming, her hair flooding down. There was a golden necklet on her throat. No other thing. She said, 'Captain, you must go away at once.'

'I won't go away,' he said.

'This is a terrible thing that you are doing,' she said.

He laughed now. He said, 'No.'

The women were frightened very badly. They shivered and shrank.

She said something to them in her own language, and they cried out, protesting, but she said it again. And then they scurried out of the pool, snatched up their coloured garments, and ran away through some other exit in the stone wall. Leaving only her in the lamplight, and him.

She had made it so that they were alone together.

He walked down the steps to the water's edge.

She said, 'I will dress myself.'

'No,' he said again. 'Let me look at you. I've wanted to see you like this. And how could it be? But now I do.'

'You must allow me to clothe myself,' she said.

'But I don't.'

He stood there, and she stood in the water. She did not look at him. She looked into the distance. And slowly she drew her hair about herself, and she had so much hair, so heavy and so silken, that it covered her, clothed her, to the water's surface.

And somehow, by doing this, the hair revealed to him in the lamplight two or three slender chains of silver in itself, that were not adornments but the first coming of old age. He had never noted this before. And now it broke his heart.

'Sitavaina,' he said. 'You're all I want. My beauty. My darling.'

Then she did look, into his eyes.

She said, softly, 'Is it that you love me?'

'By Christ – yes, I love you.'

'I take your love as a great gift. I will treasure your love, and I thank you for it, though I do not deserve your love.'

'Take my love and give me yours in return. Give it me here and now, Sitavaina.'

'That I cannot do.'

'Yes you can. You're a woman. You've lived without a man. Or have you? Don't you believe what your temples say – man with woman? Making love.'

'It is not for me,' she said. 'I have never wed. I am not here for that purpose.'

'Look at you,' he said. 'For what other purpose? Christ, let me show you.'

'I will try to help you, but not by doing that. That is not for me. But I will be with you whenever you wish, or never again, if you will prefer that.'

Smolte stepped off the stair of stone, into the water, and he caught Sitavaina in his hands. She was warm and real, slim, smooth, and impossible.

'I must have you now,' he said. 'I've waited bloody years.'

'Let me go,' she said.

Her face was close before him, her jewelled eyes and sweet fruit of a mouth. And he drew her against him, and her body touched his, and he put down his face and found her breast that was a girl's breast, so full and high and firm and wonderful.

'If you do this,' she said, still very low, 'my brother will kill you.'

'Not him. He wouldn't dare.'

'He will do it.'

'Why? He wants you for himself?'

'He loves me purely, but more than life,' she said. 'As you do not.'

'No, I don't love you purely. I want to have you, girl. Now and here.'

And he pulled her from the water with a vast strength that elated him and swung her round and down so she lay on her back along the steps among the lamps.

All his flesh and blood had gathered into a tremendous throbbing and engorged turmoil, that centred at his penis, and which he must bury in her, in the glory of her, or he would go insane. He tore open his clothes, and spread himself on top of her. She did not struggle, and her face was still, but in her eyes there flared now something.

She wanted him. Of course. She had always wanted him. This was their moment.

But her thighs were like steel, they would not part. He forced his hand between them.

'Let me have you – I will have you—'

Then her whole frame became charged with life. Her face lost its blankness, her body writhed, her hands flew up at him – and he pushed them down and held them either side of her head, and drove his knee up between her legs and brought the burning shaft of his penis up against the night hair of her sex, and finding her only by this, as if that sightless worm must know the way, he began to cram himself inside her.

Sitavaina shrieked. Her cry struck on the roof of rock, smashed there and wheeled off in pieces.

He jammed and crushed himself into her, deeper and deeper, and the whole hill seemed to heave at his thrusts and he was blind with pleasure, shouting, feeling her breasts against him, and then she too reared up to meet him and he let go her hands. Her mouth came like wet fire on to his chest.

For a second of excruciating delight he felt himself burst inside her and there was no pain only the galloping of the spasms, but then agony swamped him, sickeningly, in his chest, his groin, his brain, black and savage and without limit, and he flung back and saw the blood gouting from his right breast, as the semen had jetted from his phallus.

And her face was under him on the stone, the face of a tiger, its lips veiled in scarlet, and her eyes were not human, nor animal, but those of demons.

'What – what in God's name—' He heaved away from her. He

clutched at himself and cried in terror.

And she, rising up like a snake, spat out before him the male nipple she had bitten from his chest.

Must get away from her – he must fly from her and from this place—

Great rolling masonry of rock, pillars, trees, the god lurching down to club at him with its shining axe – and night – and pull closed the red jacket that would not show any blood – and someone snatching at him, and boots, but he would not stay – and here the horse, and he was on the horse, and away, fly away, escape from the demoness – but the black of the night was pain and the trees were pain – torches – gone—

Smolte fell over the horse's neck. He was not quite conscious, nor quite dead.

He wept, and slavered. He vomited over and over.

The forest mocked him. It reeled and sang and lamps flashed in the upper boughs, and beasts scenting his blood stalked after, but demons unwove them.

'Darius,' said Smolte to the horse. 'Find Darius.'

The horse moved on. It would be lost. He would die in the demon-haunted jungle. Vultures would pick at him and jackals tear him open.

Withers ran cackling through the trees. 'This way!' Withers squealed.

Blood ran all over him. It was in his mouth and nose. All he could taste was blood and vomit and tears and terror.

The horse found Darius, as a dog would. It made its way back through the forest, and in those hours of madness and the unconscionable, no beast attacked it, or its semi-aware passenger, no pitfall gaped. They reached the station, and were discovered.

Smolte was delirious. They could make no sense of anything he said. The frightful wound shocked even the harder men, and Darius was brought to the bungalow, where a grey-faced Flower rushed at him: 'He'll die, won't he? He'll just die on me, here in this foul bloody place!'

Darius put her out of the room. With a white-hot iron, he cauterized the pulpy sludge on Smolte's chest. Darius had seen the mark of teeth. When Smolte's shrieks had ended, and

Darius had mixed up and applied his salves, he must confront Flower once more.

'What did it to him?'

'A bat, I think,' said Darius. 'In the jungle.'

'He'll die,' said Flower. 'What'll I do?'

Darius said, 'Pray, perhaps.'

'Pray? To what? That won't help me.'

That night she packed her things. Her boxes and trunk stood in mute judgement, and it was the ayah and the child, Luksmi, who bathed Smolte's head and carried away his puke and excrement, and assisted Darius with the medicines.

And once when Rupert stood scared outside the bedroom door, Flower struck him. While Urquhart, oblivious and toddling noisily about, broke the Ganesa toy.

Sitavaina.

She goes down into the pool and bathes away the blood – she knows the kind god will allow it – *his* blood and the blood that has poured from her, the wound he made. Then, when she is cleansed, she puts on her garments, and goes from the cave, by the darker way, so she will not pass by Ganesa to harm the beauty of his shrine.

Her women come to her, and she mildly puts them aside. She does not speak. She speaks to none of them.

And outside she is placed in the palankeen, and they bear her back to the palace, playing their music, and only all the women silent.

Night goes over and day lifts up the sky.

Sitavaina does not eat or drink. She does not speak, she speaks to none of them. She lies still on her crimson bed with a gold-sewn pillow under her neck. She gazes into the distance. When the women come to her she does not look at them. If they lean close, gently she puts them aside with her hand, like a woman holding back a veil.

Her brother is told on the third day.

Then Jarashan comes to his sister. She does not look at him. She does not speak.

He questions the women. They tell him, fearfully, what they know.

He is with Sitavaina a long while alone. What he says to her no one knows save the crows which perch above the roofs.

Then he goes from her.

The days continue to flow by, like a procession on a river. There is a huge silence, only sometimes the murmur of priests chanting, and the little bells.

She will fast until she dies. It is a long, painful and arduous death.

Some women begin to wail in the palace courts, and are hushed. The silence comes back. The crows sit upon the roofs, and a vulture like a purple guard.

She does not contemplate annihilation. For she is a mote in Eternity. It is only that what she is has been irrevocably changed. She must go back and begin again.

Presently terrible pain commences, the agonies of death by starvation. But she does not groan, she does not speak, she says nothing.

Gradually the flesh melts from her, and her loveliness pares down to the bone. Strands of hair fall from her head. Her nails fall out. Her women weep, but in utter silence.

Her brother does not come to her now, cannot bear to see.

The days and sunsets pass, the endless nights which have an end.

On the forty-second day she is lying on her crimson bed, and they are fanning her softly, and from a hole in the fabric of Being, out of nowhere, a cobra appears in the court.

The women huddle away, not able any more to cry aloud, they have gone so long in dumbness.

But Sitavaina turns her head, and stretching out her arm that has no strength in it, she beckons.

The cobra comes. It has been sent by heaven. It is an act of blessing and mercy that she shall not suffer any more.

The cobra glides like a dark spill of night over the court, up into the open chamber, up to the crimson bed. She does not speak, she holds out her wasted arm. The cobra wraps about her arm, over and over, a bracelet, and then uncurls on to her breast.

The women hide their eyes, and when they look again, the cobra is gone and Sitavaina is arching upward in her death-throe. But her eyes are full of light and she cries out: '*So humm.*' *I am.*

Then sound is reborn and the women scream and sob.

But Sitavaina is empty, and now her silence is complete.

It is strangely easy to remake her body's beauty, once she is gone from it. They comb out her wondrous hair, of which there is still a quantity, and put into it ornaments of gold and silver, and on her forehead an emerald. They clothe her in scarlet silk thick with gold embroidery and spangles of gold. They henna her hands like a bride.

She is carried through the town below the rock, to the ghat above the river, where they lay her on a bank of lotus and orange marigolds.

Priests shout and sing.

In the forest the bul-bul speaks, and the coppersmith bird beats his maddening rhythm. The river coils beneath, pale umber, and the sun begins to go and the river is red.

Then the torch is out to the pyre and the flames go up among the flowers towards her body, and the gold melts and drips and the scent of burning perfume rises.

And then, after all the sounds and silences, there comes a fearful cacophony, that of a bull elephant trumpeting.

They stare up towards the courts of the palace. But the notes do not start from there. They bellow out of the jungle, whose black heart is closing on the night. And from the black heart blackness rips its way, thunder that moves.

In the hot streets of the sunset town, where the people are standing and the incense going up, they look to see and scatter aside with exclamations of fear. A huge darkness tramples past. It steps upon the flowers, and touching against the walls of earth, cracks them. It is black, enormous, glistening as if watered by the falling light. A mountain which runs.

And as it looms up on to the ghats, there too the watchers drop away from it, the little forms of people, the priests in their white, the howling women, the lord with his twisted, eaten face.

This animal is God's Kiss, surely, the perfect one, killed by the wicked, come back from death.

But was God's Kiss, even, king among elephants, so huge?

He is black and his back upholds heaven. His trunk is living power and his legs are pillars. His eyes are red as the fire in the air. His ears are the world twice over. His tusks white swords.

He stands tall as the sky, above the blazing pyre of Sitavaina, and noiseless now lets down the cobra of his trunk, and sluices up the flame. He fountains this out upon himself, and is for a moment an elephant bathing in a river, but the river is fire. And he burns.

The elephant burns above her as the sun burns out. His skin shears off in a carnival of scarlet, and then he is white, all white bones, a skeleton larger than the eye can hold. And then he is only an outline of silver ash, and she is golden ash, and they mingle, the fire sinks. The sun is gone and so are they, and there is only the voiceless dark which is the cauldron of beginning, the void that *makes*, the shadow cast by what is to be.

One of Withers' natives tearing out of the jungle in the night, rushing along the mall, squawking. That was their warning.

Erskind, Berry, and slovenly Crew came to Smolte's bungalow.

'What, are you daft?' said Flower.

'No, Missus,' said Crew. 'Get your infants and come on. The only safe place is the barracks, that's for sure.'

And Erskind crashed on Smolte's door, and Smolte was there, sitting on the side of the bed, in his nightshirt fat with the bandaging beneath it.

He had been mending, the fever was gone and no poisoning had set in. Darius had been useful. But Smolte was weak, stupid. Nothing could be done with him. He had cried like a ninny, a baby. Flower had had no patience.

And now what would he do?

'It's the villages,' said Erskind. 'They're up in arms.'

'That Withers,' said Flower. 'What's he been at?'

'No, it ain't Withers. Withers ain't never been found,' said Crew.

Erskind said, 'Nazeem comes running in. He says there was a funeral on the burning ghats below old Jarry's palace. Some wife of his, I suppose. And they say an elephant comes out of the woods and broils itself on the pyre. Lot of nonsense, but you know how they are.'

'How are they?' said Smolte.

'They took against us, Smolte. That beast you shot – it must be that. The raja's behind it, of course he is. But the word's gone round. All the villages. Every man-jack. It's a bleeding mutiny again.'

Smolte stood up. He raised his head and gave a sort of cry.
Erskind started back and Crew looked nervous.

Then Smolte turned to them a yellow, sane and rational face. He said, 'Collect all the men together, and break out every gun. The women must come into the barracks. Turf those others out. We can't trust them.'

'The native battalion?'

'Who else? Get to it, man.'

Flower said, 'Do you mean our own servants—'

Smolte said, 'See to the children.'

'Give me a gun,' said Flower, 'I'll use it.'

'You don't know how,' said Smolte. 'Go and fetch the boys. Crew, help me get dressed.'

Flower stumbled away and went into the bedroom where Rupert slept under the mosquito net. The ayah was not there, and Flower reached in and shook him. The child opened his black eyes and stared at her, and Flower felt a plunging wave of nausea bounce through her belly. 'Come on, up now. We're going to Father's fort. Won't that be nice?'

'Tired,' said the child.

'Yes, and drugged silly,' said Flower. 'Up you get, or do you want the black men to come and chop off your head?'

As Rupert pulled himself from the sheet, Flower went to the little room where she had been sleeping during her husband's sickness. Fat Urquhart lay snoring, and she grabbed him with distaste. Damn the ayah, she should be here to assist – but then the ayah must not be trusted.

As Flower led her children on to the verandah, two of the soldiers went past her and Smolte appeared, dressed and with his pistol.

'What about my things?' said Flower.

'You'll have to leave them.'

She scowled with temper, and felt the plunging of her stomach again. She knew what it meant. He had managed, the wretch, to get her pregnant again before his accident.

Smolte left her. He was firm, striding, his eyes wide and full of hardness, so she would have admired him had the circumstances of the night, and of all their life indeed, been different.

Then Crew skulked up to escort her through the station streets.

As they crossed the compound, Flower saw the ayah standing there against the rhododendron.

'Get out, Ussi. Go and join your precious friends. You can't come with us.'

The woman wore a white sari, as though she were in mourning.

She stared up at Flower, hefting the lumpish child, and the other, Rupert, pinioned to her fat ringed hand.

The ayah said, 'He is an evil man, your husband.'

Flower said, 'Hold your tongue.'

'He has caused this thing,' said the ayah. 'It is the raja's sister who has died. She died by fasting. And the god sent the elephant to her pyre.'

Flower dumped Urquhart on the hot dark earth and went to the ayah. Flower hit her across the face, and the woman was spun away with the tail of her hair whirling. Rupert shrilled, and Flower shouted, 'You dirty bitch!' The ayah ran, her sombre slender feet not seeming to touch the ground, and vanished beyond the wall.

Flower turned, and Crew was gnawing his nail, and Luksmi had appeared and picked up Urquhart in her arms, although he was clearly far too big for her.

'And you,' said Flower, red and sweating, 'which side are you on, you little toad?'

'I take care of baba,' said Luksmi.

Crew said, 'The little girl ain't one of them lot. She's Stiggins' get. She'll come with us, like.'

So Luksmi came with them, and they went into the fortress of the old barracks, and the black night seethed with what hurried towards them, seethed and heaved, and finally disgorged it.

Flower was watching from an upper window of the building. She heard a thrumming noise, like the sea. It was the crowd of people moving up on her through the dark.

Soon she heard the individual screeches, shouts, the banging of what she thought must be drums, or which were perhaps pots beaten together. It was as if the jungle came, and the beasts of the jungle.

Then, she saw the spots of light. They had torches, or rather they had bits of wood which burned, for though the flames of the cremation were out, the fire had gone on . . .

She had never before been so terrified—

In another room the herd of the station's children snivelled. The other women were fools. Flower thought, *I should have had a pistol. I'd show them*. But she shook, and she thought, *It's all very well for these men. They're not carrying a life*.

The mass of people swept down into the place beneath.

Faces – darkness – the face of the dark, repeated over and over, and the splashes of flame, and the banging noise, and the cries.

Then a man roared from below.

Flower realized it was her husband.

Hampton Smolte, buttoned in his uniform, in borrowed boots, the pistol in his hand, stood before the wave of night, the people out of the forest.

When he shouted, their shouts diminished.

He boomed, 'What is it you want?' And then again the same in Hindustani.

For a few seconds, perhaps a whole minute, a stillness or aberration went over them, but then they began to cry out again and Smolte shouted: 'Go back, or we fire. Go *back*, you bloody dogs. There are a hundred rifles on you. You know what a rifle is. Go back.'

But they furled and swayed. Their fires lit up the tops of buildings, leaning trees.

'I will count to three,' shouted Smolte.

And he felt, and *knew* an appalling strength, as if his lassitude and fever had been transmuted direct into another state, holy and sublime. He understood they would not move away. In a moment they would rush at him and tear him, and the men at his back, in shreds. As tigers or jackals would. What were they? Not human. Stone-age creatures, and they had led him into a wilderness. He had loved a demon, one of their own fiends, that could take any shape—

He counted, and behind and above him, he heard the rasp of readied fire.

On *three* they surged and came against him, and he raised the pistol and shot a man between the eyes.

Blood and matter erupted and behind the man was a woman, he saw her, masked in the gouted blood, and Smolte fired again and the woman went down and the mob sprawled over her.

Everywhere the guns exploded out their bees of death.

The wall of darkness was breaking and dropping asunder.

Smolte experienced flaming power, and he bared his teeth and pressed forward, and the other men were behind him, firing, reloading, firing, into the throng of beings who had come with pots and torches, old knives, and alien skin.

As they forged out on to the mall, the crowd broke and started to run away.

'Bring them down!' Smolte yelled.

And the men, grinning as he did, shot round after round into the pack of bodies.

Women fell in weaves of hair. And there a child, but it was a black child. Not a child at all.

The soldiers had come out of the barracks now, some had mounted up and rode along the crowd, stampeding and toppling, shooting into the midst.

The ground was a tangle of bodies, torches lying reflected in blood. Their blood was red. It should not have been. They were India. Smolte fired into the Indian heart, and presently, that heart stopped.

'Sir – some of the shit got away from us.'

'Go after,' he said.

Ten men galloped away. And then five more.

'Erskind, no, keep them here. Those things might try an ambush in the forest—'

'Not likely, Smolte. Look round. We've done for them.'

'The prince,' he said.

Erskind said, 'Yes, old Jarry was behind it.'

'Where are the native troops?' he said.

'Tied up tightly in the kitchens.'

'Kill them,' said Smolte. 'We'll leave ten men here for the women. Then we go up to the palace.'

Erskind suddenly was uncertain. 'He may be ready.'

'What with? His dancing girls? His fat bodyguard who cries? The slaves won't fight. We'll have forty, fifty men, and the guns. Let him complain.'

'What'll we do, Smolte?'

'Finish him,' said Smolte.

* * *

The native town was in chaos when they came to it. They fired it, and shot the men and women who ran out, and the goats and chickens.

In the palace, a cluster of red lights.

They went up to them, and he was there, Jarashan, in a warm and painted room, his retainers round him.

In his hands was an ancient gun, some present from a French- or Englishman of long ago. But this gun he pointed at Smolte.

Jarashan had mislaid his handsomeness. He looked *devoured*, like a leper.

'God is strong,' Jarashan said. 'He fears no rivals. All that is His will prosper.'

'Put down your bloody gun,' said Smolte.

'I will kill you,' said Jarashan. 'Or you will kill me.'

'So be it.'

Smolte fired at him. The bullet passed straight through Jarashan's silk-clad body, bursting the garland of pearls upon his breast.

The people in the room lay down on their faces.

The men they killed. The bodyguard who had wept for the elephant, who in any case had tried to stab himself. The fat taster who had bitten through his tongue from fear.

The women they had, or Smolte's men had. He did not want them. Ugly sooty sluts.

In the gardens they shot the squirrels, and the birds which rose in tumult out of the antique pavilions. They shot off the heads of marble carvings, and the peacocks, but they could not find the elephants, not one, which was a pity, for there was the ivory . . .

But the palace they despoiled. They tore out of it all it had. They loaded on the bullock-carts of the dead prince costly inlays, golden gods, ropes of rubies and topaz, and rent the diamonds from the ears and nostrils of young girls, as the men filled their mouths with mixtures of red wine, champagne and fine brandy.

It was dawn, first light, when they came away.

Out into the smoking amber air they rode, drunk and merry, with captive women and ebony chairs, and potted the birds that had woken in the trees of the forest. And they were amused that they were heroes, and Withers had missed it.

And much, much later, after the steamer had come and gone, and news had altered and amended itself, they were heroes without doubt, who had stopped a conflagration spreading across India. And Hampton Smolte was, of them all, the best, a gallant Englishman, who had made his fortune and would gain a title, and could now go Home.

Part Five

1

The cat ran through the house.

She had something in her mouth.

Up red-carpeted stairs and along green-carpeted corridors, oblivious, Kitty ran. Kitty came into a round tower, over a white stair, and scratched on a bedroom door.

Elizabeth Willow opened the door. She wore a silk shift stitched with little bones, and a bird's skull on the breast. She had been dancing in the pale morning speckles of light that drilled through the screens on to her floor.

'Here, Kitty, Kitty. What have you got?'

The cat leapt in. In the middle of the polished marble, she set down the live creature she had caught and carried upstairs. This creature was small and white.

'It's a mouse,' said Elizabeth Willow, 'clever Kitty.' The white thing moved a little. 'And it's alive! We can play with it.'

Elizabeth Willow dropped down on her knees and bent towards Kitty's tiny prey. She stretched out her narrow hand, with a thin gold bracelet on its narrow wrist, to bat at the mouse and make it dash in panic from place to place. Then Kitty would pounce again, and toss the mouse into the air—

Elizabeth Willow's hand stopped, frozen, before it reached the mouse.

The mouse was wrong.

'Ooh, Kitty,' said Elizabeth Willow.

She knelt there, staring, and Kitty, her lean belly lowered to the marble, slid forward, her wide eyes full of jewelry evil.

The face of the mouse ended in a tail. Two curved teeth stuck out of it. And its body arched up, its legs were like stems, quite straight. Another tail was on the end of it. It was very white, it shone more sheerly than the floor.

'What is it?' said Elizabeth Willow. She sat back, to see what her cat would do. She relied on Kitty's judgement in these matters.

Kitty sprang. But somehow the mouse-thing moved, and Kitty missed it.

Kitty pressed to the marble, tail lashing, ears laid flat.

And the atomy Kitty had caught turned about, and raised the serpent of its face. It blew a gust of air into the cat's mask so harsh that – absurdly – Kitty's whiskers were blown back.

The cat growled. She jumped backward now, and thrust a paw over her dark, lovely and malevolent face.

The mouse-which-was-not trotted across the floor and directly under the bed of Elizabeth Willow.

The girl and the cat dived after.

The girl scrabbled under the bed with her long pale arms, and Kitty followed precipitately.

There was a skittering and thrusting there, in the shadow, and Elizabeth Willow could not make out what went on, but suddenly Kitty ran out, and stood, fur on end, in the dapple of the sunlight.

Kitty would not go back, though coaxed.

And Elizabeth Willow, peering and poking under the bed with a long ruler left over from her childhood days, could find nothing.

'It's gone down a hole.'

Frustrated, the girl and the cat sat at opposite ends of the chamber.

The cat washed herself, and Elizabeth Willow, presently, began to lick her own arms.

Rose said, 'But it will be all right. You'll put him in a good mood.' And Annie said, 'Don't you know how I hate it?' 'Yes, but you must.'

And Annie got up and went through into the bedroom, where Innocent was lying, waiting, on the unmade bed.

Then she opened her eyes. She was not in Tooth Street, and Rose had not made her go to Innocent, to give him sexual pleasure.

Annie sat up. Her eyes were wet, and she rubbed them impatiently. As if Rose would ever have—

Someone knocked.
It was time for her nourishing, aristocratic luncheon.
Annie went to open the door.
Sometimes Divy came, or Burrow, or another of the housemaids. They treated her respectfully and unlovingly, and their eyes roved round her chintz room, and over the frequent indentation where she had been lying, sleeping in broad daylight, on the bed.
But now it was Luksmi, as also it sometimes was.
Luksmi entered and put down the tray of buttered toast and asparagus.
'I want to talk to you,' said Annie.
Luksmi attended quietly.
Annie said, 'How's Tiff?'
Luksmi hesitated, then murmured, 'They are saying her blood is poisoned. Some scratch from the garden, they think.'
Annie said flatly, 'No. I stuck a needle and cotton in her arm.'
Luksmi did not speak.
'Do you know why, Luksmi? She stole from me. Everything's done to me here. But why should I put up with that?'
Luksmi, again, did not speak, and Annie went on, 'And now I think you've stolen from me, too.'
'No.'
'No? That ivory thing I had. You gave me a chain for it. Now look—' Annie drew the thin black chain up from the table. 'It's broken, and the ivory is gone.'
Luksmi lifted her arm, and touched her hand to her forehead, where the mark was, between her eyes.
'It is so?'
'Yes it is. And who should I suspect but you? It was while I was sleeping in the night. Who could steal in, but you? Perhaps you gave me some draught, one of your potions, like you give to Mr Rupert when I've thrashed him.'
Luksmi said, 'Why should I steal from you?'
'You valued it. The elephant. It meant some queer magic thing to you.'
'But it was yours,' said Luksmi. Her face was calm and total. Nothing hid behind it, nothing ever did. 'You have enough to bear.'
Annie sat down. She shrugged. 'I believe you. Where is it, then?

It must have fallen somewhere. Not that I care. It was *that* started it. It's not lucky, it's cursed.'

Luksmi wore a drab dress, and her hair was pulled and scraped off her face. But Annie had come to see something in Luksmi's looks, something unusual, rare. And her figure was excellent. Rupert had told Annie that Luksmi catered to his brother's loutish tastes, when he wanted. And that was probable, for had not Luksmi once said, '*We are slaves*.'

'If you wish,' said Luksmi, 'I will search for the ivory elephant.'

'No, don't bother. I didn't like it. And when I wore it – it – made him worse. I had to – for longer.'

'The nurse,' said Luksmi, 'used to beat him. In the beginning he struck her, but then she got the better of him. She would smack him and then feed him opium, and in the end the opium was enough. He knew carnal delight through blows and drugs when he was three or four. But she did not mean to do harm. She was afraid of them.'

Annie sipped from the glass of red wine. She offered it suddenly to Luksmi, and although Luksmi shook her head, she smiled. Her smile was gentle, warm. *I wish I was far away from here, but I wish I'd known her there. I wish she was English. But then, she'd be different.*

Annie said, 'And what about the other one? Mr Urquhart.'

'He will have told you,' said Luksmi, 'that Mr Urquhart comes to my bed.'

'Yes. Does he hurt you?'

'Oh no. No, he is only greedy. There is nothing bad. No one has taught him to be kind, that is all.'

'I suppose you have no more choice than I do.'

Luksmi looked, for a moment, surprised. And then she said, 'Oh, but yes. It was my choice.'

'Then he rewards you,' said Annie, hard, wooden.

'There are gifts. But it was not for this.'

Annie ate a piece of the toast. She did not want it, but she must not waste this food. There would come a time when she would fly – oh yes, there must come such a time – and then she would starve and maybe die, and she must have the memory with her then that she had never, while she could, gone without.

Luksmi sat down on a chair. She was very straight. She had a royal look, and she folded her hands as a queen would have done under a weight of bangles.

'There was,' said Luksmi, 'a princess in my land. And she was so beautiful – oh, you could not imagine it, or I describe. She was like the evening of stars. Like a holy song. And I was born in her house, from the loins of one of her maidens. But my father was an Englishman.'

Annie forgot the food. Rose had related to her stories, once.

'And one day, my princess came to me, and she told me that a priest had spoken with her. He had revealed to her my former life, and that I had committed an error, which I might now put right, and so be free of it.'

Annie said, 'I know you believe your soul comes back and back. And you can be born an animal, can't you? But how many lives—'

'I am quite old,' said Luksmi. She smiled again. 'And in that former life, I should have acted better than I did. I was a village woman then, and I left my child untended. And he, running out, trod upon a snake, which killed him. Now the priest told my princess that this boy had returned, and was the younger son of the English captain. And if I were to go into that family, I might serve him, and so repay the debt, for due to me he had died.'

'And you believed it? But you were a child—'

'I was a child. But in the first year I saw the little mark upon his foot. Two little moles close together. The scar of the serpent's teeth. He was my son.'

'Luksmi . . .'

'Besides, if my princess had not sent me away, I should have died in her palace.'

'Why?'

Luksmi said, 'A shadow fell. Not one of my kind was left alive. But I was with the English. They are generous to me, as they know how. And I pay my debt.'

Annie looked into her past. She spoke very slowly.

'My sister murdered a man. Would your religion say then that she owed him a debt for his death? He was cruel and vile.'

Luksmi did not question her. 'Perhaps she does. Or perhaps it was he who owed her a death. Perhaps he drove her until she must take his life.'

'They hanged her,' said Annie.

'The world is pain and illusion,' said Luksmi. 'But there is much more than the world.'

'Then why live?'

'To learn,' said Luksmi.

'To learn what?'

'Only when it is learned, shall we know.'

'You talk the way Darius does.'

'He is a good man,' said Luksmi. 'I remember—' but she broke off. She said, 'You have much time alone now. It is not what you should have, for before, you had people with you.'

'I had my sister.'

'Go to Darius. Speak with him.'

'How can I trust him?' said Annie bitterly. 'I've seen what men are.'

'Not all men are cast from one mould.'

Annie said, 'Will he want me today, do you think? He's called for me twice in the afternoon. Once I denied him and he came to this room. He was rough – I made him lie on his face.' Annie went white. Her eyes blackened. 'I trod on him. I want to kill him. I want to tear him in *pieces*. Or – myself.'

Luksmi stood up. She stared at Annie. In the room, the light burned up hotly as the sun moved round towards the western side of the house.

'There is great strength in you,' said Luksmi.

'I'm *helpless*.'

Luksmi put her face into her hand. Her eyes gazed down into some depths beneath them, as if she saw fish move in a cloudy pool.

'You have only to ask,' said Luksmi. 'They taught me this. Knock upon the door, and it will open before you.'

'I beat on the door with my fists!' Annie cried.

Luksmi gazed now at Annie, and Luksmi's eyes enlarged. She spoke in her own tongue. Annie did not guess what had been said.

'What are you saying?'

'I do not know. But the goddess has touched you.'

'What *goddess*?'

'She is dark and terrible.'

Annie felt abrupt fear, unlike the other fear which, now, was always with her.

'I won't be frightened. It's some trick.'

Luksmi bowed her head. 'You are a bird caught in the storm, but the storm follows you. Tell me, tell me,' said Luksmi urgently, 'who gave you that ivory?'

'My father,' said Annie boldly. 'He left it for me before I was born.'

Heat so vast it hurt towered up over the English park of Sir Hampton Smolte. The sky was a dense and seamless blue that smoked on the horizons. The green grass was withering, and on the trees, by strange contrast, the leaves were ripe and lush as burgeoning grapes.

Down to the shallow river an animal picked its way. It was a deer, chestnut in colour. As it came up to the humping bridge that spanned the stream, you saw it was very small. It bowed a delicate head, and drank slowly from the water under the ferns.

A bird passed across the sky, and its shadow darted on the river.

The deer raised its muzzle and gave a short barking cry. Then sprang away into the woods.

Mrs Rope stood before Mrs Beare in the Den.

'I won't mince my words, Mrs Beare. There's a rat in my kitchen, and I want it out.'

'Come now, Mrs Rope.'

'I tell you. Several of my girls have seen it. Clarrie says it's white, a dark white, which means it's been in the flour.'

'*Dark* white. Is there such a condition?'

'I have enough on my shoulders,' said Mrs Rope, beery and red. 'I can't be expected to cook with rats running all over my tables.'

'I thought there was but one.'

Cross-eyed frump, thought Mrs Rope.

'One is one too many.' Mrs Rope bridled. 'God knows, Tiff may have got her sickness from a rat. Do you want them sick upstairs? They'll say I poisoned 'em, like that monkey.'

'Mr Churton shall be told. No doubt there is a rat-catcher in the county.'

'Let him be speedy,' said Mrs Rope.

As she went back to her kitchen and shouted for beer, Mrs

Rope felt a deep disquiet. The sweat beaded on her forehead and her brawny arms, and on the pale faces of her staff. This weather was a trouble for those that had to work.

And upstairs in the attic, Tiff lying in her bed, with a blue arm with a poultice on it, rambling about ghouls, screaming and falling into silence. Doctor Gry was to come, but Tiff being only the scullery maid, he had not bestirred himself yet.

A screech and a crash came from the larder.

Mrs Rope jumped up like an aproned haystack, and all the girls turned in terror.

Burrow ran out.

'I broke the pie,' she cried. 'It's there!'

Mrs Rope took up her rolling pin and marched through. A rat – she would brain it.

In the stone larder, a blessed cool, and there on the floor the blackberry pie in shatters. And there – there – under the shelf, behind the bin—

Mrs Rope bent low, and did not move. It was a funny rat. No, it could not be a rat. It was white as iced cream, and its tail was on its front—

Mrs Rope felt giddy and she straightened up.

'You lollocks, it's nothing but a mouse.'

Yes, that was what it was, a pair of mice, running together.

Mrs Rope sat down. It was that Rawlings' fault. He brought his spices in and spilled them. Or that pest of a gardener and his half-wit boys. A basket of potatoes with mice in them.

Burrow began to cry.

Mrs Rope flung an egg at her, then called Tiff to clean up the mess. But Tiff was not to be had.

At the Bird-In-Hand they were enjoying the sunshine at the day's end, the farmers and labourers in the tap-room, and the idlers on the meadow.

'I'll tell you, it's fair old hot along the road,' said one of Corry Pulger's customers as he supped his ale. 'And as I come by the Palace, there us a thing what nipped me – see—' and he showed a horrible blister on his arm. 'I upped and tries and squash the bugger, but he us off, and leaves me this.'

''Tis a mucky do,' said Corry, in congratulation.

But out by the river they were slapping the water with sticks.

'I say to you, Simon, 'tis as big as a whale.'
'And I says to *you*, you see it the wrong end of a pint.'
Along the grassy verge, as the slappers desisted, the water settled, lay smooth and polished as a dancing floor.
'There usn't no fishes.'
'No, 'tis a fact.'
'Something's eat 'em.'
'Then where's he gone?'
'Up-river on to old Smolte's land.'
'Then they can eat he in turn.'

The sun declined. It went swiftly down into a bank of darkness. Hot night soaked through the sky.
As she dressed for her dinner, Flower Smolte heard an odd noise out in the parkland. And going to her windows she thrust one up, and looked out between the lattice-work.
How black the night. She had never thought of the park in this way. The blots and surges of trees and slopes. Anything might be there. What had she heard? A familiar noise, and yet, not in this region.
It had been some other sound, distorted by heat and darkness.
It was so hot . . . Already the powder Luksmi had put on Flower's neck and face, bosom and arms, was sticky. Her corset cut. *I'm getting too big*. She thought, *I'm getting old*.
Flower pressed her gloved hand to her cheek in a sort of actual pain. Where had her life gone? What had she to show for it? What would she do tomorrow?
As she descended to the scarlet dining room, which had, by means of Smolte's money, been swiftly repaired, Flower tried schemes over to herself. She would have that poster framed and put up. She would make him take her abroad: somewhere European and clever; France, maybe . . .
At the doors to the dining room, Flower paused. She saw the area as if in a cameo of red and gold and darkness.
Her husband there, at the table's head, and there the other places, her son Rupert reading a book, and Urquhart snuffling up the bread. And the daughter, with the cat upon the table, among the linen and silver. And the gold plates, and the coloured glass. And all round, the Indian night of eyes.

In the park – what had she heard? Some animal in a trap? The raped shriek of a peacock.

She walked into the room.

No one spoke to her. But the men got up. Urquhart more speedily and fully than Rupert, and yet not even seeing her.

Is this my achievement?

Flower sat down.

The food started to come.

The pompous butler and his accomplices. The silver maid.

What blooms were they on the table? That sickly-sweet ridiculous smell, like frangipani – no, only roses.

'Move those flowers, Churton. They're too heady.'

The roses were removed. Flower ate her brown soup. Mulligatawny for Sundays. But not here. And already the whiff of Hampton's curry, and Rupert's too. She had got so used to it.

On her finger, the ruby shot out sparks. Like burning blood.

Elizabeth Willow spoke.

'Kitty caught an elephant today.'

Urquhart burst into enormous laughter like a series of belches.

Rupert only signalled for more wine. Smolte – did he even hear?

'Don't be stupid, Elizabeth.'

'No, Mama, Kitty's so quaint. She brought it to me. It was tiny. But I knew it was an elephant. Like the ivory one in the music room.'

Complacent, Elizabeth Willow pressed a morsel of anchovy on her cat.

Rupert said, 'Does this mean we are infested by bloody mice?'

Flower slammed down her fan. 'Don't use that language.'

Now Rupert laughed.

The curries were being served. She watched and saw her husband's liverish face dully light up, and Rupert sit forward in the chair. Urquhart received four mutton chops. Flower waved the dish away.

One is a pig and one a rat and one a cat, Flower thought. *By Christ, I believe that's what the silly little bitch is. Don't the Hindus say that? A man can be reborn as an animal. Then why not an animal as a girl? My daughter is a cat.*

Smolte saw his wife turning aside the food. Well, she was fat enough. It would do her no harm.

He looked away, and beheld the table on the elephant's leg.

His daughter was mad. She had soured in her mother when the mutiny occurred. It was that. India's last bane upon him.

Strange, he had thought he heard the noises of India tonight. The buzzing of insects and throb of frogs along the river as he rode across the park near sunset. And then, some chattering and whistling from the inmost sections of the trees. Had some creature escaped from somewhere? He could shoot it.

The stuffed panther gleamed. Its coat was very fine. And there, the wolves and jackals, tigers and bears, the horned deer. How their eyes shone.

He would take a gun and give himself a turn about the lawns tonight. He was not timid. He had been courageous once.

That night—

He could still recall the sense of power which his courage brought.

And in his brain behind his eyes, the black moon rose. Her face. He smashed it like a plate and black rain fell into the bowls of his eye-sockets.

She had wanted to see his wife. Of course, aware of his desire, she had wanted to see his wife to decide if Flower could hold him. He could not reconstruct her well, even though her face had reformed again. She would have been an eldritch stick by now, that one. They did not age well.

The curry was not hot enough. It was like . . . like the dishes of a raja's palace, too dainty for his palate.

Rupert read his book. Smolte could not be bothered to reprimand him. Smolte had never liked his children.

The dessert of ices and fruit was already melting and he did not want it. Flower began talking about the cities of France, and he did not listen.

Later, when Flower and Elizabeth and Rupert had gone, Urquhart sat on hoggishly drinking port with him.

'Don't you want to ride to hounds, Pa? I can arrange it.'

Smolte said, 'Damn your cheek, Sir.'

'Well, Pa. You know I'm in with the beggars. Flight and that pack. They've chased more foxes over your land than you'd credit. I should know, I was with 'em.'

'I hunted jackal in India,' said Smolte. 'And tiger. Look about.'

'Yes, Pa, I know. Because a fox wasn't to be had.'

'And wolves here, twenty years ago. Keep your bloody foxes.'

Presently Smolte left Urquhart the scarlet, pillared room, among all the sigils of Smolte's hunting. Taking a gun, Smolte walked out into the park.

The heat had not abated. It hung like a velvet curtain over the countryside. Above, the stars were dry and fiery; it seemed to him he had never seen them so large or well-defined, at least, not here.

He walked along the terraces and down the lawns, through the gardens. The lilies and the roses were overpowering, and the jasmin almost reeked, it was so strong. The gods and goddesses he had collected stood motionless for ever.

Smolte thought of Oxway's monkeys. Smolte had sent the fellow a bill for the refurbishment of the dining room. The curtains alone would have made him blink. But of course, Smolte had no conviction Oxway could or would pay up.

Where Krishna was playing his flute, recruited for the rhododendrons, something pallid rustled through the bushes.

Smolte halted, shifting the gun a little, then letting it be. For this thing was not very large, about the size of a weasel. And yet, it did not progress in a weasel's wriggling fashion.

He watched, not moving, and the whitish creature trundled off under the stalks.

A finger of cold felt of Smolte's neck, there in the boiling dark. He did not know why. He said, very low but aloud, 'Keep away from me, you bitch.'

Then he turned down and got into the yew walk, and went on and out into the valley meadows beyond the house.

As he did so a high thin cry rose up from the walls behind him.

He turned, and saw it, his palace. Its roofs and towers and minarets, some with golden windows, and some smoky red. And he thought how he had heard a woman laugh above him once, from a tower, elsewhere. But this cry – it was the sound of pain or intolerable pleasure. Was it that he had heard earlier, mistaking it for a noise from the land?

He knew the servant girls of the house were susceptible to his sons. Some of these women had been sent away. It did not concern him, it was Flower's province. That noise then, some girl fetching off.

Smolte spat into the dark.

He walked on through the tall wild flowers, and the burned grass that crackled as his passage broke it. Opening the gate he went out, and came to the river, and standing on the bridge looked across at the penis of Shiva pointing up from the north-west bank, pale on the dark. No moon tonight.

The river oozed below. It had shrunk to a thread. Frogs chorused from its shallows.

He gazed back again, through blackness, at the woods.

The trees were tall, and a roping wedded thickness lay on them. It was as if, rather than the oaks and pines of his estate, he saw before him the cypresses and bamboo and the giant sal trees of the Indian rukh. And as he thought it, he heard a distant scraping that he knew, but not here in this place, the sharpening of the tushes of a boar in a thicket. And then the shrill far-off chattering of the monkey tribe, lilting over the creeper-lanes of upper branches.

For a moment he was filled with reasonless savage joy, and raising his head, he let the sounds wash over him, and the resinous balm of the sal trees and the dense tindery perfume of the dry forest stretched to breaking before the rains.

But then he knew that all this could not be, he must be mad.

And as he came to this conclusion, in utter disbelief, a beast drove crashing and tumbling down through the woods towards him.

Smolte cocked the gun and raised it ready.

On to the ground before the bridge rushed a flailing panting ball. It was a boy. It was the fat gate-boy, Sebby, who had let Smolte in that very sunset.

'Stop!' Smolte shouted.

The boy gave a yell, and fell over on the grass.

Smolte lowered the gun.

'I nearly shot you, dolt. What are you doing out?'

'The Missus sent me,' gasped Sebby. In the moonlessness, he was all of black and grey, and pushing up his round grey face, he gobbled, 'Them woods us full of *things*.'

'What things?' said Smolte.

'Don't know. But they us.'

'You're a country boy,' said Smolte. 'You know there are creatures out by night.'

'Not these un,' said Sebby. He breathed and said, 'I usn't want to go. But Missus made me.'

'Why?'

'The cow's calved.'

'And so?' said Smolte. A silence pressed upon the world. A huge, limitless silence. One wished to keep one's voice to a whisper. Sebby whispered, and Smolte told him to speak up.

'It's wrong. It's white and got a hump. And the cow licks it. But Missus says I'm to tell them at the house.'

'It's nothing to do with me. Get the cow-doctor.'

Sebby blubbered, and out of the woods there rose a terrifying screaming. Sebby screamed in turn. He ran right at Smolte and dropped before him.

'Monkeys,' said Smolte.

He thought, *Oxway has had his revenge. He's turned them loose on my estate. Well, I'll shoot the damnable things.*

And then the silence swooped down again deep as a tunnel in the world, deep as memory.

'Don't make me go back through that there wood,' said Sebby.

And Smolte said, 'You can walk to the house with me. You can sleep with the gardener's boys. There.' And he smelled, over Sebby's terror, the resin and the tinder, and the clay of the river, while on his torso the small scars left from that night seemed to stretch tight, the bites of their knives, the lesion of a broken pot. But the moon of scar on his breast was warm, and he put his hand there, as he walked away, over the bridge, towards the shelter of his palace.

2

Wolves were not seen in those parts. Not any more. And so, well-dressed Doctor Gry, riding very early towards the Smolte house through the park, on his stout staid mare, was rather astonished to see one.

The mare had put back her dowager ears – that had alerted him. Normally she only reacted to the village washerwoman in such a way. Doctor Gry had been uninvolved in the faint sounds that laced the wood. There would be foxes too, for the hunt met today; the Satanic animals were in abundance.

Other things had caught Gry's attention.

The height of some of the trees, for example, the richness of the woodland. The number of squirrels springing through the branches. At least, he had assumed that they were squirrels. It struck Gry that Smolte had introduced a number of foreign species of plants into the park that he, Gry, had never noted before. Of course, it was an especially hot summer, and the flora would be flourishing, although, on Smolte's land, Gry began to consider drought. For the heat here seemed extraordinary, and Gry must remove his elegant hat and wipe his forehead over and again.

It was altogether a nuisance coming out for this.

Some scullery girl had got a poisoned cut or something of the sort. Lady Flower had sent for Gry and he had put off coming. He did not expect the family to recompense him in the same way they would have done with one of their own. Mr Rupert's winter coughs, for example, had been particularly satisfactory. And Mr Rupert himself, with his unwise craving for laudanum. When the young man began to see devils, Gry would be needed once more.

Where the trees began to open above the river, something went loudly through the undergrowth and the mare laid back her ears and jinked.

'Steady, you fool,' snapped Gry. But he turned to look.

And between the stems of a stand of tough gigantic grasses, the creature slid its way. It had four feet, and though its back was curiously domed – the head he did not glimpse – he knew from the size it must be nothing less than a wolf. And a white one, ivory white, albino.

'By God,' muttered Gry, wishing he had a gun, both to protect himself and to take a shot. For a pelt like that would rival bloody Smolte's Indian trappings.

By then the wolf had gone, vanished away under some large plumy trees whose nature Gry did not recognize.

'Damn it,' said Gry, relieved and sorry.

He wondered should he tell – for Smolte would be out after it in that case. Then again, Gry would not want, perhaps, to take on the beast alone. A summer wolf was not generally hungry, and so not often very dangerous, but company might not come amiss. Would the fox hunt flush it?

Gry sniffed the air. There was a strange scent to the woods he did not recall. And a bird cried somewhere within them in a voice that was new to him.

He rode on next and went over the bridge, and here at last his mare stopped her sidelong nervous motions and trotted straight.

He noticed the lingam across the bridge. Something like yellow paste was smeared upon it, that must be a fungus or moss . . .

He would say to Smolte: 'There's a wolf in your woods. Best take care of it.' Yes. Let the great Indian hunter have the hide. He, Gry, would be content with fleeces.

'She was screaming, Sir, all last night.'

Clarrie poised with her hands neatly folded on her apron, her small sensible mouth moving carefully.

'Oh yes,' said the doctor.

He did not have, for the staff, the consolatory manner he deemed needful with the Smoltes.

'And then near morning she was quiet, and I thought it was, she was better, but she's got such a fever on her. The sheets are like fire.'

'Yes, yes. I can see that, thank you, girl.'

Doctor Gry looked down without interest or compassion, but in some puzzlement, at the sick scullery maid. She was very ill, indeed. Blue blotches ran across her chest and red lines of deadly meaning showed like veins. The arm itself was a nasty mess; its homemade poultice he had flung away.

'She will have to be taken to the hospital.' He said, 'I must speak to Lady Flower.'

At this instant the patient opened her eyes.

They were small eyes, stretched with fear and delirium.

When they fixed on him, Gry however saw that she was lucid now, for she knew him. She knew him and was appalled, for a doctor spelled disaster, just as the hospital augured death. But she would die anyway, this one. They had called him too late. Besides, where had she got such poisoning? He had not seen anything quite like it.

'Head hurts,' said Tiff.

'It will,' said Doctor Gry. 'Now, lie still, and I'll help you all I can.'

'I'm twelve,' said Tiff.

'Yes.'

'I'm twelve, I oughtn't to be here, I want to be an upstairs.'

Doctor Gry turned away, and Tiff shrieked.

'Oh my God,' said Clarrie.

'Watch her until I come back,' said Doctor Gry.

'Fetch me Ember!' shouted Tiff. 'Ember us done it me. Fetch Ember. Make her come.'

'What is she saying?' asked Doctor Gry.

'I don't know, Sir. There's Annie, she's an upstairs, now, and Tiff is jealous—'

'Ember!' shrilled Tiff. She tried to sit up.

'Lie down,' snarled the doctor, 'do you want to make yourself worse?'

Tiff fell back fighting the bedclothes with her claws.

'Us done it me!' she squealed. 'Make her come.'

Doctor Gry's sly little pebble face was alert. 'Does she think this girl has poisoned her?'

Doctor Gry had examined the dire arm. There were no wounds, no marks of teeth – human bites had caused a death or two.

'Well, you'd better fetch this girl, if this one wants her.' He was very inquisitive now.

'I can't, Sir. It isn't my place.'

'I make it your place. Go along.'

Clarrie said primly, 'I shall have to go to Mrs Beare.'

'Then hurry up.'

As he waited in the overcast and sick-smelling attic room, Tiff lapsed back into confusion.

The doctor stood at the window, gazing at a wall with a pipe, and above the tip of a dome, like a decorated jelly mould. This house, it was a rascal's folly. Doctor Gry had nothing for it but a pleasant contempt.

He hoped Clarrie would be quick. He did want to see what happened when this other girl was brought . . . but he must soon get on to ailing Lady Flight, who, though her husband never paid a bill, was sure to bribe the doctor with some fine wine and French tobacco. And then he meant to catch the gentry's hunt – time was of the essence. The aristocracy of the county were the doctor's pastime. He liked them. And let such jumped-up knaves as Hampton Smolte provide the cash.

'I never meant to—' cried the girl on the bed suddenly. 'I never – I never – it us a jape, you know, you, it usn't nought. I'll give it back. I never spent it—'

Doctor Gry went closer to the bed, but Tiff was silent again. He tried her pulse. It was hopelessly fast. She would not last another night, and he must really make haste and show willing by having them send her off to the hospital.

The door opened, and Mrs Beare, the revolting housekeeper, came in.

'Good day, Doctor. I have brought Annie Ember, since you want her.'

Doctor Gry turned and took a good stare.

By God, a beauty. Heavy silk hair of acorn brown, creamy skin, smooth red lips, and great gems of eyes. And a slim, malleable figure, fragile yet strong. Dressed like a lady, too, though very simply, and with no jewels. What was she? Ah, but of course. She would be Flower's ill-kept secret, Mr Rupert's whore.

'Well, Miss Ember,' said Doctor Gry, fawning slightly. 'I'm sorry to trouble you. But we have this problem. The girl there is very sick, mortally so, I'm afraid. And she's been calling for you.

Perhaps you were kind to her . . .?'

Annie Ember looked at him. Her eyes were not gems but steel. Doctor Gry laughed placatingly.

Mrs Beare said, 'Ember has other duties. She rarely sees Tiff.'

Annie said, 'I don't owe her anything.'

'No, obviously not. Rather, it appears she thinks that she has done you some wrong—'

The horrible voice of the sick girl squealed out again. It seemed she had heard the tone she wanted, Annie's, and this had made her lucid once again.

'Ember—' called Tiff, 'you done it to me.'

'The girl is very ill,' said Doctor Gry. 'What she says is unreasonable, evidently.'

'I've done nothing,' said Annie Ember. She sounded like stone. And like a stone she went, unbending, to Tiff's bedside. 'What do you want, Tiff?'

Tiff's face was dark with congested blood and she panted. She was also plainly in dreadful fear.

'You usn't mind me, Ember. I us playing, like. Only playing, see? You can make me well again. I hate this pain. Take it off me, Annie. And I'll do whatever you ask me. I'll do anything you like. I'll be your slave, Annie Ember. If you takes my pain off from me.'

'Don't be stupid. I can't,' said Annie Ember. Her straight graceful back was to the doctor, and her mass of shining hair all piled up. It was a useful thing, thought Doctor Gry, that witchcraft trials were no more.

'Yes, you can, Annie. Oh please, lovely Annie, make me well,' whined Tiff. 'I'll bring it back, I never spent a penny of it, it us yours. And I'll bring you flowers. I'll be your dog. Make me well.'

Annie Ember turned away from Tiff. Her pearly paleness had now gone deadly white. She glared at Doctor Gry.

'Can't you help her?'

'She must go to the hospital.'

Tiff roared – an incredible vociferous hoarse bellowing – 'I see her! God – she's black and her hair us snakes and there's dead-heads on her and there's blood running off out of her mouth – *I see her!*'

Annie spun about and Tiff rose up straight as if pushed upwards by a pole.

'Lie down!' cried Doctor Gry. He shouted at Mrs Beare, 'Make her lie flat!'

Mrs Beare, with her hand to her throat, did not move.

Tiff screamed and blood and froth burst from her lips. She seemed impossibly standing up like a rearing serpent on the bed, and then she arched over, and her legs shot behind her as if she had no bones, no muscles at all, and the backs of her heels cracked against the back of her head.

'It's a convulsion,' exclaimed Doctor Gry. He thought he would have to take hold of the girl. But he waited, and she did not spasm again. She merely lay as she was, rigid, her feet up against her skull, like some preposterous exercise of an Indian fakir. He realized. She was dead.

Mrs Beare let out a quavering moan.

'Sit, woman,' said Doctor Gry, 'I won't have you fainting. There's enough for me to do. Miss Ember, are you well? Will you kindly go at once to Lady Flower.'

Annie left the room without a word, death-faced. In the passage, Divy was, standing all agog.

'Tiff's dead,' said Annie.

'Oh my stars!'

'The doctor says you must go and tell Lady Flower.'

Divy turned and flew, and Annie continued, down the stair, descending, descending, through all the looms and colours, the lights, and shadowed architecture of the unreal house, not knowing where she was or where she went.

I was in the street and somehow it brought me here.

That thing began it.

Ivory.

A journey.

Annie looked up and said, 'Something's been done to me. I'm under a spell. Something that was called up by Rose's board.'

'What's happened to you?' he said.

'What's happened? Everything that could. Almost everything. And it won't stop.'

'It will stop,' he said. He had a beautiful voice, so gentle, just as he spoke to the horses. Darius? It was Darius. What had she said to him? She should not trust him.

'I must go,' she said.

'Not at all.' And then, 'They said a girl was ill. Is it that?'

'Tiff's dead. I killed her. I stuck a sewing needle in her. I wanted to pay her back.'

'Then you've paid her, or will pay. Don't trouble with it now. Let it go from you, till you're ready. Tiff was a poor little soul, not formed yet.'

'Look at that,' said Annie foolishly.

They looked. By the great torrent of the geranium vine that grew up into the wheel of the warrior god, sat another red pot, that had in it another smaller blooming plant.

The horses made a sound, several of them, from the stables.

'Do they laugh?' she said.

'Of course they do. But that isn't their laughter. Can you feel the air, Annie? It's not right. The way it moves.'

A hot wind blew, worrying uselessly at the plant, and lifting up the thick fair hair on Darius' head. His forehead was high and broad, he had clear-water skin only lightly tinted by the summer. His eyes were dense with light.

Don't trust him. He had called her *Annie*. She had fallen. Now she was anyone's prey.

She turned to go. How had she come here? She could not recall.

'No, Annie. Not yet.' He took hold of her arm. Not harshly, but quietly, and the quietness laved all her strength away. She stood quite still, and bowed her head.

'Let us,' he said, 'go up through their garden to the river. I've meant to go. I've been hearing curious sounds, the sounds of other places, they were.'

'What do you mean?'

'And I don't know,' he said. 'But we can go and see.'

Nameless anxiety stayed her now. 'But what would be there?'

'Don't be wary of it,' he said. 'Like all things, it will be as you make it. Cry for the shadow, it will come. And for the moon, that too.'

'Luksmi said,' Annie murmured, 'that a goddess had – *touched* me. And Tiff - Tiff screamed out that I was black and blood came from my mouth and there were skulls—' Annie put her hands over her lips. But she had spoken calmly. The tumult would not come out, yet nor would it subside.

'Everything is illusion,' said Darius. 'See there, that clock of gold. It says that the hour is ten in the morning. But why do we believe the clock? You could if you truly would, bring instead the night. And for you, the goddess touches you as she touches everything, but the goddess herself is many things. Perhaps you have been the Dark Mother, but now you are soft and kind, with pearls in your ears, the Bright One.'

It was as if he laid a hand upon her head, and through his hand passed in a beam of mild cool light. Her eyes cleared and her heart began to beat in its proper rhythm. She thought, *Everything will do what it must.* She stopped resisting, she flowed, as if the summer wind blew her like a leaf on the vine. And like the leaf, though she was blown unresistingly, she was not torn away.

They went together into the upper yew walk, and back the way she had first, at the very first, come, and soon the mosaic of the house appeared above, on the left, caught in branches, scarlet and purple and white and gold. The ground rose, and they went by the gardens, and the gardens and the house did not matter, and they walked across the meadow and through the patterned gate and over there ran the river, with the stone shape on its bank the nasty child had said was a penis.

But—

'Annie,' said Darius, 'you'll take my hand. I think we should not stray apart, here.'

How green the wood, and yet not green, but cooked olive and sepia, and a low mist lay along it like a gauzy veil. Yet through the mist she saw into the aisles, and there a monkey, like the monkeys that had been brought to the house, and it had a yellow pod in its hand – and below a cobalt bird, bigger than a goose, spread out a fan of tail greener than the forest and bluer than the sky.

They walked forward, and there came a kind of shift in the air or the light. A beast growled deep in the depths of the trees, and some little deer-like creatures passed across the view. The lingam was there, only its head showing from the mist. Dyes and aromatics had been poured across it, and garlands of flowers encircled it. Ah, yes. If it was a penis, then it was the rod which created life, that was it, it was *magical*. It formed, from nothing, from thin air, the sorcery of a child, the phenomenon of Life itself. The gate of souls.

They had come to the bank of the river.

The forest had been close, but now it had drawn away. The river was wide, so wide, could she even see the farther shore . . .

The mist lay on the river, and the morning sun was in the mist like a drifting candle-flame. Below, the water mirrored it, pale cider mixed with milk, silken, dippered by the upside-down kingdom of the trees. Smoky, warm, the banks went up beyond the forest to a complex form, like a honeycomb – a temple balanced at the water's edge.

A crocodile lay suspended, far off, she knew it from remembered stories, with its armoured log-like punctuation of the water. But something else floated to them on the tide, skeins of flowers trailing from it, it was dark, a raft, and on this a heron stood, silver-white, with one upraised sail of wing.

Annie leaned forward involuntarily, and in that moment saw the raft was a portion of a body, burned black, the scorched bones stuck upward through a charred husk.

'Don't fear it,' he said. 'They cleave the skull and burn the flesh to let the spirit go free. It is done in pure hope, and loyalty. That floating there is nothing horrible. It is an image of true love.'

'What is this place?' she said.

'Oh,' he said. 'Everywhere. The past.'

She was not afraid, but she said, 'Can we go back, to the house?'

'Yes, I believe so. But see.'

A kingfisher flashed like a blue coin.

The corpse had serenely passed, with its sentinel heron.

'And if we don't go back?'

'That I think we must.'

They turned in unison, and the lingam gleamed in the mist, and beyond, the rukh ran away and away, with monkeys playing in it and the panthers sleeping.

'Is it a dream?' said Annie.

'The world is a dream. God dreams the world.'

The clasp of his hand on hers reminded her of some other time, and yet she could not recollect when. Whose hand had ever guided her so kindly?

They moved away from the river with a subtle regret and came out of the trees and there the house was below, burning brilliantly in the English sunlight.

'Don't glance back,' he said. 'Not yet.'

They went into the meadow, and among the flowers he let her go.

She turned and looked at him. She had never in her life seen a man that was like him. And he, on his side, looked back at her. They studied each other in silence, until, from Smolte's woods, there rose the eerie screech of a peacock, piercing up, fraying, done.

'Have I caused it?'

'It has come through you. But no. *They* have caused it.'

'What will happen now?'

'God knows,' he said, 'and only God.'

Annie turned suddenly towards the house.

'They're reaching after me. I don't want to go.'

'Stay with me here,' he said. He laughed. And Annie laughed. She had never known before that he was young. Young as she was, though maybe he was twice her age.

'I'll put flowers in my hair,' she said. 'And you can steal one of his horses, your favourite one. And the foal. And we can run away.'

'I'm bound to him,' said Darius. 'I would never have followed him, else. I must stay.'

'Then I must stay, too.'

'Poor girl,' he said. He looked at her now with such sadness from his beautiful and luminous eyes that tears welled up in her.

'Darius,' she said. 'Darius. Darius.'

He smiled. He said to her with a flaunting young man's human pride, 'It is the name of a king. Maira first gave it me.'

'King Darius,' said Annie.

But again there came a shift in the air, a faint darkness, almost like a trick of sight. And from below, the horses neighed insistently in the stable.

'They know,' he said. 'There's some weather coming. Go down to the house now, Annie. And stay indoors.'

She glanced away, at last, at the river, and the woods were green and the watercourse was narrow, although the garlanded flowers still shone on the Rod of Life.

Then Annie walked quickly across the wild lawn, not looking over her shoulder any more, at the river, or at Darius.

But he stood on alone, watching her, hearing the monkeys squabble in the English wood.

There were no laws now. The fabric of Maya, of solid-seeming unreality, was giving way.

Darius thought back to Smolte's return from India, the interview there had been, when Smolte had tried to slough him, and then imagined that Darius blackmailed him, and must be kept. For Darius had known. Saving Smolte's life, Darius had learned it all, from the marks upon Smolte's breast, from Smolte's fevered and unhinged dialogues with ghosts. And when the villages had risen, Darius had known too, why, and for what.

Once Smolte's powerful noisy little army, with its pain-quilled spine of busy rifles, had passed on to the palace of Jarashan, Darius had gone into the station mall, and moved among the wounded there, tending them as best he could, splinting, cauterizing, bandaging, ending swiftly, with his healer's hands or knife, those who beat on the door of death. And the child, Luksmi, had come after him, clutching the second bag of salves, watching without words all that he did. 'We are slaves,' he said to her, as he supported on his arm the head of a dying woman, held her till the life shuddered and fluttered away like a moth. Those that could had been making off, and taking, where they could, their dead with them. Oh, the stench of that street, its colours of blood and darkness. 'We are slaves.'

And he had been their slave thereafter, for almost twenty years. The servant of a rapist, murderer and tyrant, he, *King* Darius. And she, Luksmi, the slave of his family. And Annie. Annie.

The wind blew and the trees made a sound of bending low. The sky darkened over one iota more.

Urquhart had taken out the bay mare for his hunt. Darius did not like to think of her abroad in the storm. But what came now would come. Two decades and more it had been on the road towards them. You could not dissuade it, nor propitiate, nor hide. *Then let it be.*

Annie entered by the small side door. Above a minaret stretched sparkling. And inside, in the hot shade, Luksmi rose from a chair.

'He has called for you.'

Annie said, 'Rupert.'

'Yes.'

Annie thought, *It was a dream after all. What a bloody*

simpleton. That Darius – who was he? I can't trust him. They are all alike. And now – here is the truth. Rupert, the monster. What else?

But, his eyes had rested upon hers.

She thought, *No. That was the truth. And this, the illusion. Go on, then. Who cares? I'm not afraid. The burnt corpse is nothing. The soul is gone.*

'Very well then.'

She ascended the house now, behind Luksmi. And came to the door. And Luksmi went away.

Annie knocked.

No answer. She went through the gun room – the monkey was still on the table, not escaped into the woods – the second door, also closed. Again, Annie knocked.

Rupert's voice. 'Who the curse is there?'

'I,' she said. That was all.

'*You*? Oh. Come in then.'

And she went in.

He sat with his shirt undone, and some wine before him.

'Where the devil were you, you bitch? You're mine. You should be ready.'

She thought, *Am I ready?*

She thought, *He is nothing. What he does is nothing.*

Rupert said, 'You've been my mistress. But now I think you should be humbled. You *bitch*. Come here. Drink some of this.'

'No,' she said. 'You drink it.'

'I shall. All right. Go in the other room. Undo your hair and take off your clothes. You need tuition, Annie.'

He got up. In his hand was the flail, he had concealed it somehow until now.

'You hurt me last time,' he said. 'You need a lesson.'

Her stomach turned within her and she saw Tiff in her heart, hitting the back of her head with her heels.

Annie walked without demur into the inner room, which now she knew quite well, and better in her nightmares.

Will he kill me at last?

I've seen the truth. Let him try.

A good breakfast was served at the Bird-In-Hand before a meet. Boiled eggs and dishes of buttered toast, kedgeree, porridge, kidneys, and a sideboard of cold ham and beef. The gentlemen drank coffee and ale.

Urquhart Smolte had come for the breakfast, as if he could get none at home.

'The Old Wood is thick with foxes, so I hear,' said Lord Bobb, cheerily spearing a kidney. 'And Smolte's land, too. We'll have some work on our hands. And how is your fair lady?' he added to Flight.

'Oh, she has the megrims. A brisk gallop on a horse would cure her, no doubt of it. But she won't. She tells me I don't know what she suffers. Well, I'm heartily glad I don't.'

'Stout fellow,' said Bobb. 'The ladies must keep their mysteries.'

Urquhart laughed and filled his mouth with ham. He had been in Luksmi's room until dawn, and slept perhaps one hour. Luksmi's mysteries were all his. He would have married her if he could have had his way. Maybe one day he would do it, and get the county in uproar.

Along with Lords Flight and Bobb a handful of merchants had taken time to come, and with these some men out of town offices, who had begged the morning. In the fellowship of the hunt such participants were allowed. It was only parvenues – Hampton Smolte for example – who were not made welcome.

They ate heartily, and went out about eleven-thirty to the front of the inn, where the grooms were shining up the horses and checking their feet. Urquhart had brought the bay mare Jessa. Darius, that self-opinionated bastard, had tried to hold her back. 'They're not your horses, man,' said Urquhart. 'Are they not?' said Darius, insolent devil.

But she was in nice shape, better-looking than any horse there. And she had energy in her, unlike that stubby gelding Bobb had fetched, doubtless the only animal able to take his weight, and Lord Flight's wallowing grey. Indeed, Flight and Bobb had used other horses for the ride over, but Urquhart had not needed to.

In a field adjoining the road, the Master was riding up and down with his hounds, a brindle pack already wagging their tails in anticipation. There was Big Butter, the black-eared dog, whose teeth had met in the entrails of a hundred or more foxes, and there Tally, famous for the pulling off of tails.

Urquhart rode to pay his respects to the Master, who scowled at him. The Master had kind words only for his dogs, and for the foxes, whom he praised on their running, and referred to as 'Poor Reynard' after a successful kill.

'What do you think, Master? Shall we be lucky today?'

'I should say we will.'

'The Old Wood?'

'I should say so.'

'And my dad's land, too, I'd suppose. I saw a beggar there myself this morning. Took it for a pig it was such a great brute. And white – but the sun was on it.'

'Huhn,' said the Master.

'Doesn't believe me,' said Urquhart, and rode off on Jessa with a blithe heart, to where the cup was going round.

By five minutes to twelve, they were starting off, the hounds going first in a patchwork cloud of merry tails.

Bobb and Flight, and one of the merchants, pressed close, but Urquhart rode a little over to the right side.

They went downhill under the fierce sun, and came soon to the outskirts of mighty oaks and cedars. Riding here was not for the incautious, though later the wood spaced out. Even so, it was full of ditches and ponds, and there would be some jumps to see to.

'This weather,' said Flight, 'it's damned hot.'

'Hottest summer in memory, my old people say at the castle,' added Bobb.

Behind, some of the grooms came on more slowly, with the spare horses.

They went among the trees.

'Yes,' said Rupert Smolte. 'Now, let me look at you.'

He had sat down on a little hard chair in the inner bedroom, the flail across his knee.

Annie hung from the bedposts, her wrists held in the biting cords, her roped ankles together.

The heat in the windowless room was like pressure, a covering forced against her naked skin. But he, though he sweated, did not seem to feel the heat. Possibly he liked it. He had said that he did, once before.

'White skin,' he said. 'Do you know, Annie, how hideous I found white skin? For years I thought it was like uncooked dough. But now, I see it has its attractions. And it can be written on, Annie. Can't it?'

'Yes,' she said.

'You cut my shoulders open,' he said. 'You made a mess of me, my little panther. Did you like it, did you?'

'I would like,' she said, 'to see you torn apart.'

Rupert chuckled. He enjoyed this talk. It excited him further. 'How would you do it?'

'I'd change you into a fox,' she said. Even hanging there, she was far away. 'They'd hunt you and tear you open.'

'But,' he said, 'today you're the fox.' He got up and came to her and began to stroke her breasts.

Her heart gurned inside her. But she thought of the burned corpse she had seen adrift in the dream river. Free, the soul gone from it. He had not hurt her yet. He was working towards that hurt. Savouring each moment. He pinched her nipple painfully.

'Spit at me,' he said, 'the way you did last time.'

'That was last time.'

He slapped her face, not very hard.

'*Spit* at me.'

She looked into his eyes. He might have been blind.

'If I spit at you, you'll strike me. And if I don't, you'll strike me.'

'My Annie. Did you kill that scullery maid?'

A deep stagnant coldness sank through her, under the tons of heat. How did he know? *What* did he know?

'You shouldn't listen to gossip, Mr Rupert.'

'You can tell me. Did you poison her?'

'I called a god,' said Annie. She turned away from him and thought of Darius. But then she felt the edge of the flail brush over her hip.

A fox had been dug from cover.

Some of the forward riders had seen a slip of tawny red, and then the hounds were in the gap.

With a great hallooing and the yap of the horn, the huntsmen drove away along the eastern avenues of Old Wood, and turned towards the open fields.

'The thing's soon making a break. Let's hope there's some spirit in the red boy, or there'll be scarcely a run,' swore the thinnest of the merchants.

'Ah, did you want to leap all the ditches and hedges then?' inquired Lord Bobb. 'I'm not so sure your noble animal would be up to it.'

But the thin merchant bolted off, and Bobb cantered after.

Urquhart kept over to one side, and galloped steadily on Jessa. She had a heavy feel today, but took the first bank out of the wood very well, and three minutes later sailed over a hedgerow like a swan.

'Best girl!' cried Urquhart.

The horn pealed down the fields, and there beyond the rise the hounds were running in a spill, tan and cream and black, grunting and baying as they went.

'Just so,' said Flight, lumbering up on his carthorse grey. 'The fellow's making for the Palace.'

'They all go there,' said Urquhart.

'To see Sir Hampton's house, no doubt,' said Flight.

Urquhart took this in good part.

The fox it seemed had stamina, and now the hounds were running at full stretch. Urquhart pricked Jessa lightly with the rowel of the spur. Obedient, she seemed to wind herself up like an engine and then flung herself forward, taking the young wheat in her stride.

They cleared a ditch, and Urquhart had the loud pleasure there of seeing the thin merchant come off, headlong in the grain, and his horse standing shaking itself as if it had got rid of a flea.

'Bad luck, Sir!' howled Bobb, walloping past.

Diagonally across the next field then, came springing Doctor Gry on a wild hired horse that steamed from being ridden to catch up.

'Has it broken?' he shrieked.

'Going for Smolte's park,' said Flight.

'Damn me,' puffed Gry, 'your wife's much improved, my lord.'

'I'm grateful to hear it.'

'And so I came on here.'

'Well, you'll see the kill, if your animal can stand the pace.'

The riders went down the hill in a cluster, and sped along the untilled land towards the distant canopy of Smolte's wood. The gates of the park would be standing wide, in case the hunt should tend that way.

Urquhart, looking ahead, saw a dense pall above the park, like smoke, and yet unlike.

'Is something ablaze?' asked Bobb.

'No, it's a cloud, by God. Look there, Urquhart. Did you ever see such a thunderhead?'

'The devil, so it is,' said Bobb.

Urquhart shrugged. Jessa seemed heavy again as she mastered the rabbit holes in the meadow, and he kept his attention on that.

A warm wind blew, beating up at them from the east, where they were going.

'I was there this morning,' gossiped Doctor Gry. 'Sir Hampton's house. A kitchen girl dead. A funny business.'

Urquhart had ridden ahead of them. Lord Bobb listened to Gry as they pounded along.

'They have a curious record with housemaids, there.'

'One hears things,' said Doctor Gry, 'but one can't say.'

'And there's the fox!'

'He's gone for the park, by God.'

'Smolte's boy is right. They do run there.'

Doctor Gry remembered the wolf – but before he could speak of it, Bobb was away, and he, Gry, must use the stick on his horse to hurry it after.

Elizabeth Willow and her cat crouched under the window-seat in their tower.

The cat's fur bristled. Her ears were laid back.

Elizabeth Willow's human body could not accommodate such physical gestures. Instead she moved her facial muscles, a sort of grimace, over and over.

Against the four windows the hot wind pushed. The sky was the colour of a dark blue plum, and over it the birds pelted, then separated like tossed seeds, falling back into the woods below.

He had not used the flail. Not yet. He had begun with a bamboo switch. 'It's odd,' he said, 'some of my ivory things are missing. Did you steal them, Annie?' And the switch struck her across the buttocks, a shock, a second's nothingness, and then the bite of fire.

Let it end soon.

If only the world would end and end *this*.

No, it must never happen again.

She swallowed the iron water in her mouth, and said coldly: 'Now beg my pardon.'

But it did not work.

'Oh no, Annie. Not this time.'

Even so, he did not hit again, not yet, he traced her over with the switch, moving around her like a master sculptor, deciding where it was he should cut her next to make her the most beautiful.

The gate on the park's west side stood open, and the Master let his hounds pile through, after the fleeing red dart of the fox.

In groups, or singly, the hunting men slammed after.

As they rode into Smolte's wood, the trees pressed excessively near, the ground was dry and uneven, and the horses missed their step. Some sort of bird erupted away before Bobb and Flight, squawking.

'What the hell was that?'

'Some fancy duck of Smolte's—'

The woods were too close, and waterless, and no longer truly green. They were dark with a strange congested hollow gloom. Huge vines had tangled the trees, and huge flowers were caught there giving off an overwhelming sweetness that rolled into the riders as they passed. Had some peculiar experimental planting gone on?

It was not as they recalled.

Flight plunged among a stand of bamboo, and his horse protested.

'He's let this acre get out of hand—' shouted Bobb.

The horn yawled, off towards the river.

That was to the good, for in here, the cunning fox could get to cover once again, amid all this mat of undergrowth.

Seven or eight riders, of whom Bobb and Flight and Doctor Gry made three, careered down through a tunnel of ancient and savage trees, and so into a twilight blood-greenness that was nearer brown, and here a flock of things – starlings? – exploded from the branches and wheeled about the faces of the men, half-panicking their horses.

'*Bats* by Christ!'

'In God's eye, what part of the wood is this?'

The horn summoned them, and they dragged the heads of the horses round, waving off the bats, beating their mounts with crops and sticking in the spurs. 'Fight me, you fiend? Be damned to you.'

Urquhart, riding over to the side, with a pair of clerks on his tail who thought him more clever than the others, had seen, yet distinguished nothing properly bizarre, and now looked up, and beheld a spotted snake hung from a bough, but then it was gone.

The light was very dull, the light was not light. A guttural of thunder seemed to rise from the earth, and two or three boiling oily drops of water tapped on Urquhart's forehead.

Jessa baulked.

He slashed at her with the crop.

'Come on, girl. You know I won't stand bloody nonsense.'

They rushed the trees and tore through the curtains of creeper, and saw a long ride going down. The hounds were fully baying now, and close. And there, between the long-leaved plants that most of them had never seen before, there came the veer and glimpse of a tawny hide.

'The bugger's in there!'

They cannoned down the slope towards their fox.

But the ground was misleading, a tease, the barricade of verdure towered, and they must make it leaping, the unwilling horses going up into the trees—

Flower sat in her sitting room, with the posters of her youth and glory spread about her, on the sofa and the floor.

A plump and shapely girl with milky skin and strawberry hair, kicking up her heels. An artist's flattering impression.

'There I was.'

And here I am now.

Flower did not need to look into her mirror, she knew what she would see there far better than she recollected her younger self.

What would have become of her, if she had stayed as she was? Flower Bell . . . She would have married, probably, one of her own kind. And if she had grown larger, she would still have kept her figure. There would have been no children. She would have worked, playing with her audience – and at night they would have laughed, he and she, over the stout and gin, before they curled up together in their bed.

Did anyone ever think of her? No, the rotten wretches, they had forgotten her quite.

Flower got up and walked over to the mahogany jewelry cabinet. She took the key from its concealment, and opened the doors and drawers, and looked upon Aladdin's cave.

She had pearls, and she had beryls, she had rubies, sapphires, topaz, emeralds, diamonds. There they were, the sum of her, glinting very little now for the light had grown so dark, a storm coming, and besides, she did not really like them much, her jewels. Not much, really.

Rupert had twisted Annie's hair about his hand, he held her in this way, her head forced back, kissing with his teeth the arch of her throat, as he trickled the flail over her breasts.

'I've been so careful,' he said, 'not to hurt. But now I think I must. I must, Annie. It will be all right. Because you want me to, don't you? And you're so strong . . .'

I saw truth because of this. I was with Darius that moment because of this. He can kill me. He will—

Rupert held her, and drew back his other arm, flexing the limp thongs of the fanged flail.

A mewing scream violined out of the air.

She thought it was in the room.

But he said, 'Peacocks – the peacocks are crying—'

Then came a stupendous crash, like masonry collapsing, the house tumbling down. The room shook.

Rupert sprang away from her.

She opened her eyes, and she saw him go out of the door, and through the door came a blackness like utter night.

And then a rushing, like a million wires drawn across a gigantic rasp of silver.

The darkness danced. It was rain.

Annie stared up at her pinioned arms.

'Let me go.'

Nothing. She was held there. Rage stabbed through her brain. She tore her arms away and the cords broke like burning straws. The marks were on her wrists. She bent down and ripped apart the cords around her ankles.

At the first step she stumbled. Then righted herself.

She walked into the room beyond, naked still, and he was at the window in the darkness, gazing out at a wall of water.

'Annie,' he said, 'it's a monsoon.'

She said, 'You'll never do that to me again.'

Across her lower back, her buttocks, white-hot nails lanced into her nerves and muscles.

'What, Annie?'

'Never,' she said.

'Come and watch the rain,' he said.

Where they came down the ground was a drum. As the feet of the horses touched it, it gave off a colossal detonation.

The land rocked.

The two clerks were thrown at once, as their horses reared in terror.

No lightning. The sky was black.

Urquhart kept his seat on Jessa. She curveted, but did not stand up.

Lord Flight had hung on to the big grey, and Bobb was on his clown of a gelding, and Gry's piece was prancing but with Gry too somehow in place.

The stink of horse sweat, and the sweat of human fear.

And before them, the sea of hounds, roiling.

'Where is it? They've got the bloody thing.'

Rain dropped in slaps. And through the darkness and the rain, they saw as if through a smoked prism, a reddish golden thing part the world and come through.

It was not a fox. No, it was not.

'Now what—' said Flight – 'what is it?'

It was fifteen feet, from the mask of the face to the tail's black amber tip. It walked with the swagger of an enormous dog – that was also a king of cats.

'*Tiger*,' said Bobb. 'By the Lord God.'

And Bobb stuck his spurs and his nails and nearly his teeth into his horse, and it floundered around, and slipped, and came down, unhurt but clumsy, and Bobb fell off it into the rout of mud that was already what the earth had become. Then the horse got up, and Bobb lay there with one fool's foot up in the stirrup. 'Oh God,' he said. And the horse, drunk with the odour of tiger, which, even though it did not know it, it *feared*, fled, back into the wall of the trees. And Bobb was dragged after, through creeper and the mud, headlong. And he could not speak any more, his nostrils and mouth were full of the wet sludge, smothered in the mud—

One with another, orchestrated, the horses reared.

As they did so the men slid shrieking down their backs, and the hounds drew off in a broken ring, snarling and whimpering. And the tiger spoke.

The dogs went on their bellies. Several fell against each other, and tore each other open in their frenzy.

The tiger smiled. With the great canine face, the whiskers that could murder, bristling, and the small and peerless cat's eyes. Its teeth were white and clean. It glanced about.

The horses bolted, every one. Even Jessa. They stampeded through the alien wood, whinnying, their eyes rolling.

The Master lay in the mud, and he too had been torn, by thorns, and bled. Gry lay just beyond the circle of worship, where the dogs bowed to the tiger. He lay on his face and did not get up.

The merchants and clerks were gone. Things floundered and called among the trees.

Lord Flight muttered, 'I haven't a gun.'

And Urquhart, where Jessa had tossed him, on his knees in the bamboo, answered, 'You'd need to be a first rate shot.'

'No use, then.'

The tiger looked at them. It was the ultimate majesty. It looked, and looked away.

And then the Master shouted from the mud, 'Go Tally, Butter – have at the brute—'

And Tally, the taker of tails, fired herself like a bullet up into the tiger's face—

And the tiger took Tally, and snapped her neck with a single bite.

'Go, my boys!' ranted the Master. He heaved up on one elbow. '*Butter* – go – *go*—'

But Big Butter turned, and stood there, with his tail down in the muck, gazing at the hunt Master.

'My neck bone's broke for sure,' said Flight.

'Get off then,' said Urquhart.

'What will it do?'

The tiger looked at them again. It was like the core of a sun. And then it yawned.

Flight crawled, he went on all fours, like a beast, but backward, and not well. His head lolled. His jaw was cracked but he did not know that yet. His horse had cast him against a tree.

The tiger watched.

And then it turned and swaggered away, back under the brown-green fringes of the rukh, the mercury deluge of the rain, which closed upon it.

The dogs spread, and those that could ran in all directions. They fled, sliding and drooling, and coughing. All but Big Butter.

Big Butter came to the Master and leaned over him.

'You cowardly vermin,' said the Master.

And Big Butter bent low to smell the Master's blood, and then he ripped up the Master's waistcoat with his teeth.

'My fine best boy – good lad—' cried the Master.

But Big Butter's teeth had found the soft flaccid flesh, and they bit deep. They were practised.

Gry heard the screaming.

He lay listening.

He thought: *My arm's dead. Both are. My legs. Paralysis. My back's snapped. That dog will come for me too. And none of them will help. Is this what it is? I'm calm. I wish I hadn't been here. I wanted my lunch. I could have gone home.*

But Urquhart ran through the creepers and the rain. And the soaking foliage plastered over him and serpents hung down. And something was sliced from him, fell behind. As he ran he called, and suddenly he wept, holding his hands before him, so that soon they were gloves of leaves and spiders and water.

'Luksmi! Luksmi! Luksmi!'

The rain had frightened Flower. It glittered its reflections on her jewels like fires. They might only have been broken coloured glass.

Such a storm. She had never known such a storm since – then.

Then. The forests giving way, trees toppled, rivers swollen – floods – and all the snakes flowing out of their holes—

She stood up and marched to her dressing room, and pulled wide the doors.

And stopped.

For in the flickering light she saw she had a hundred beaded white wedding-dresses.

Flower did not go in. She reasoned, from the doorway.

Her clothes, the garments of her husband's bounty, the emblems of her years as his wife . . . Each and every one—

They were infested by white ants.

3

'Dinner won't be possible. They needn't expect it. They must see to this. How can they think I'd manage? It isn't right they should think I can manage. And you, you crew of radish-brained flies – what help to me are you?'

A ruined queen, Mrs Rope sat in her chair.

The range was out, black and torpid. A scent of smoke and turning food . . . The floor of the kitchen was awash, half a foot of muddy water, on which floated broken twigs, leaves, and various scums. In the great vampire warmth that sucked the life from their very bones, the rain lashed to the earth, a noise of throwings, ceaseless.

The flood had come in the night. They had found it here. Outside, in the stream of rain, the gardener had passed, bowed nearly double, and the dumb boy skittering after. No vegetables arrived. The vegetable maid had gone out, and come back crying, invisibly, wet to the skin, without vegetables.

Sometimes there was a vivid flash of lightning, greasy and brilliant. This lit the drowned kitchen, which otherwise had taken to oil lamps. The gas was not accommodating anyone. The upstairs house was also plunged in shadow.

There had been managed a breakfast, half-toasted bread, got from the spluttering range before it failed, cold meats, a salad. Such things would go up again for luncheon and for dinner. No one had sent a reprimand, but neither any help.

Mrs Rope said now, 'How were they, in the dining room?'

The silver maid said, 'Only Miss Elizabeth and Mr Urquhart were there. They looked odd.'

No one normally remarked that Elizabeth Willow always looked odd, but now Divy said, 'That cat had got two drowned mice. The cat was all wet and Miss Elizabeth was putting the mice on her plate. Maybe she meant to eat them.'

Pocks said, 'Mr Urquhart was jolly, but crumpled up. He hadn't changed his clothes from the hunt, and he was thick with mud. Mr Churton said Mr Urquhart came in without the horse. Darius met him and asked where she was, and Mr Urquhart just said, Oh, she ran off and left me, the jade. And then Mr Urquhart laughed. But he said—' Pocks glanced at Divy, and then shrugged. 'Mr Urquhart said, I shan't go back to school. It's too wet. As if he was a boy again.'

'Don't be a green goose,' flashed Mrs Rope. 'How could he say such a thing—'

'He did. Mr Churton heard him.'

Mrs Rope shifted. She drank her beer, no tea had been available. 'You go upstairs, Divy, you lazy sprat. You should be at work.'

Divy was uncomfortable. She said, 'I was upstairs, but the water's got in, there's damp, and there were beetles.'

'You pie-brain, get up with you and do your duty.'

Divy went off reluctantly. Clarrie said, 'There were seventy drowned moths in the water butt. I counted them.'

'Now don't you start with this flummocky mischief.' But Mrs Rope did not go on along this vein. She added herself, ominously, 'No one's come for poor Tiff.'

Clarrie said, 'I undid the window.'

'You stupid raisin. Then the rain will have got in.'

'Well better the rain, Mrs Rope. The smell wasn't nice.'

The door was opened and a brawny figure entered the kitchen, shiny with water, splashing vigorously in its great old boots. Cheerful, Rawlings took in the desolation of his enemy's sphere.

'Ho there, fat woman. Like the rain?'

'You lummock, you take yourself off. I've enough to do here.' Mrs Rope had a sudden lustre. She got up.

'Not doing much, though, are you? Well, you're in no worse pickle than me, except my spices are safe. I'll tell you what this is.'

'I know what it is. It's rain.'

'It's India, Fatness. That's how it goes there.' Rawlings smiled from end to end of his nut-brown face. 'I should know. Fifteen seasons I saw of it. Pouring water, and every insect on God's earth about. I'll catch you a big beetle you can shove in the stew. Make his white wife wink, eh?'

'Get off with you, you fiend.'

'I'll tell you what,' said Rawlings, splashing happily in the flood, 'there are things come up in the park I haven't seen since I was *there*. You go and take a look.'

'What time have I got for mollying about? You great loon, you get along.'

Rawlings saluted her, and splashed out. Mrs Rope flailed her arms at her kitchen maids. 'Move the food! Cover the joints! We'll do what we can. If you had a brain between the pack of you—'

As Rawlings waded away along the lower yew walk, he was full of wonder. He felt no premonition. He had abided by Smolte through vicissitudes and luck, and saw nothing wrong in anything that Smolte had done, except maybe his marriage, but then, a young man got ripe and they would twist you then until the ring was on their finger. Rawlings had had an Indian woman, and he had beaten her regularly. She died the night Smolte dealt with the Little Mutiny, and Rawlings had not missed her much. Her voice had got on his nerves and he could cook better than she. Besides, soon after, they came home and lived in style.

Rawlings himself did not want much. He had his frowsty and untidy room behind the curry kitchen, and here he played cards and looked at naughty pictures got from the city, drank his three nightly pints, or went off to Corry Pulger's for them, and smoked his hookah, a habit brought back from the East. The secret of Rawlings' joy in life was that he did not desire possessions, had no source of or need for beauty, or love, and got his fun from tormenting others. In Mrs Rope he had met his match, for she plainly enjoyed their battles. And though he would rather have procured an elderly cow than touch her, Rawlings had sometimes thought he would one day make her his wife, for she was as splendid a cook as he in her English way, and oh, the encrimsoned arguments they would have. But that was for the future.

The kitchen yards had been awash also, and the walk was slushy. On slightly higher ground, the hothouses were only caked into the mud, although looking up he saw a pane or two of glass had cracked at the impact of the rain.

A wind was coming and going too, blowing the blood-warm

waves of water about his head and shoulders. It did not bother Rawlings. He had known as bad, and worse – once at Kalachandra his whole kitchen had washed away.

Near the hothouse door he beheld a little brown snake squelching into the bushes. It was an Indian snake. But if the weather and the plants had come, then why not the beasts. It only tickled him. He was liking it.

Yet, as he opened the door, it creaked, and the sound reminded him of the voice of his Indian woman. She had died with a bullet in her throat, the silly sow, because she had gone running out in the mutiny, crying about the elephant idol, and the death of that raja's sister, of whom they all spoke as if she was a goddess herself. Rawlings had never seen *her*, but he had heard Flower's name for her, *See-the-Viper*. That had made him grin, then. Flower was jealous, jealous of a black woman.

The gardener sat on his stool along the lane of plants, smoking his dirty pipe, out of the rain.

'Nice day, Grandpa,' said Rawlings. 'Bet it makes you feel the rheumatics.'

'Uh,' replied the gardener, loquaciously.

Rawlings went to the bed where certain of his herbs were growing, and sure enough they were very spry.

'What would you say if I told you there was a panther in Smolte's park?'

'Buggered lie,' said the gardener.

'Well, there may be. I heard a noise like that at dawn. And the clink-clink bird going for all he was worth.'

'Buggered mad.'

Rawlings poked among the herbs. 'I'm not mad, Grandpa. The world is. You'd be surprised.'

Outside came a croaking and creaking. Like Ashira's tiresome voice again. Rawlings looked, and up through the glass and rain, he saw the tall trees shifting at the wind.

And then, looking down once more, he saw what had sprung up among the herbs.

'I'll be damned, I will.'

It was lal mustard, a kind of bhang, that Rawlings had only ever seen in India.

An instant plan came into Rawlings' head. With the plant's origins and sorcerous arrival he did not quibble.

'Now, Grandpa, here's a new herb here I've been trying. What say you give it a taste. You're the expert.' Rawlings nipped off a tiny shoot. 'You bite a bit of this.'

The gardener allowed Rawlings to approach, and without thanks, or hesitation, champed the shoot in his stained uneven fangs.

Rawlings could scarcely control a howl of mirth. Lal was potent stuff. Well, he might try a whisker himself.

As he did so, the trees creaked and made a sawing noise, and he saw quite suddenly Ashira standing in the doorway.

Rawlings did laugh now. He waved at her. 'Come back to haunt me, you black baggage? Bring the stick.'

She had made herself glamorous for him. She wore a sari of bright green – the hallucination was evidently based on the green of the wet world outside, and the brown of her arm must be the edge of the kitchen garden wall – and her hair was oiled and had jasmin in it. But she shook her head. She said to him, in Hindustani, 'Now I am here and you are to be sorry.'

Rawlings liked this. Her former subservience had always irritated him. He glanced over at the gardener to see how he was getting on, and there was a panther up on the tray of seedlings.

The animal was black as a satin dress, and its eyes were not yellow but just as dark.

'Go on, Puss,' said Rawlings, 'I know you're not really there.'

But the gardener was backing away, making guttural raspings.

'And what can *you* see, Grandpa? Don't get in a fuss. Not real, it isn't. It's what I gave you, you old broom.'

The gardener turned with a hoarse cry and ran full tilt into Rawlings, not seeing *him*. Rawlings went back into the plants and righted himself with an amused oath.

The panther winked out, and there was a column of pitch smoke rising up, and under it a heap of burning flowers.

Ashira said, 'It is the hour for your beginning.'

'Beginning what, Blackie?'

But then there came a thrust of the wind so hard that everything not held down moved along its ledges, and the glass of the hothouse sung. And next there was a huge heave of sound, like the noise of a ship's timbers straining.

'Look there,' said Rawlings, 'there comes the tree right over on us, Grandpa. But it's not real.'

The gardener let out a gout of terror from his mouth and his bowels, and then in through the roof fell the uprooted oak, over and over, smashing the glass cage in ten million sequins, its branches crushing everything, the plants, the shelves, the two brown men, broken, over and under and down into the flesh of the muddy earth.

She had not waited for Luksmi to come, nor for Rupert's permission. She had dressed, and left him there in his apartment, and he had not seemed to note her going, standing at the window as the vast rains tore down.

Annie went to her room, and there she found the little pot of blue salve Luksmi had given to her weeks before, and this Annie smeared upon her wounds. The pain brought scalding tears out of her eyes, but really he had not harmed her as much as he might have done. She was able to sit and stand, although each fresh movement brought a flower of agony.

She would not let this stay her. She was beyond it. And beyond them all. She was not a slave. If Darius must remain, then she must not go to him any more. She must take her own way. Besides, the moments with Darius . . . those were perfect, and the perfection could not last. He had not touched her beyond holding her hand. He had not said a word of wanting her. Had she been in error? No. He and she – those moments – but, they were gone. It was quite easy to forgo them, even. Because she had never in her life imagined that there could be anyone for her. Some frenetic liaison, perhaps, such as she had thought Rupert offered, something like that. But not a Darius. And that was why, of course, she had not recognized Darius from the first. Now she must try not to remember him.

Annie packed her own possessions into her box and tied it with the string. She did not put in the white dresses of Elizabeth Willow, but she kept the paper money Flower had gifted her, the sum of which had increased, in books, and under napkins, as the summer of Annie's humiliation and despair went on. Annie could use this money. It had only just occurred to her, so subjugated she had been, that it might be possible, after all, to survive.

She would wait for the morning, for surely the rain would ease. And if it did not, still she would go. She would walk to that inn they spoke of, and there hire some conveyance. And where next? God knew, and only God.

They would not pursue her. They did not dare. She could say very much, and they would not want that.

She was free.

She slept on her belly, to save her back, and dreamed that she grew out of the geranium pot, her hair and her arms wound up into the chariot wheel of Indra. She was not unhappy. She knew Darius would come and release her. But she woke before he did.

It was early, but the day had begun, hot as before, and the liquid noise of the rain seemed strange, for there was no cessation.

She got up and brushed and arranged her hair, and put on, despite her resolve, one of the white dresses – since she found her former clothing did not fit her. She had grown taller, and fuller at the breast.

Looking from the window she saw only the sea of rain, and beyond, the trees and hills were a swimming mass of green.

She thought, *I'll have to go back through the park*. The park had become the jungle, and would she be lost in it? But she thought, *It won't hurt me*. And then she felt herself grasp, for the first time, the unthinkable magic of what had come about, and she marvelled that she could not seem, even so, to be alarmed or disbelieving, or merely astonished.

Maybe it was not real. An apparition.

But it was real, she knew it. And in that instant it came to her also that everything had changed, she herself not least of all.

When she opened the door, she saw at once ten or so slender rivulets of water running down from the ceiling into the carpeted passage below.

Something made her leave her carefully packed box; she could return for it.

She went out into the Smolte palace.

Yes, something had happened, everything was changed.

Water ran from ceilings, collected in slow pools, eddied, meandered. In places it came up over her shoes. And everywhere, the notes of the water, like a tuneless melody. And on the walls, a thick green moss, a bluish mould, were growing.

Annie descended steps.

A palm in a brass pot had gone up and climbed over the ceiling. On the red carpeted stair, Urquhart was sitting, smiling, and Luksmi sat beside him.

'Do you know,' said Urquhart, 'the wood's full of dead people. The tiger did it. I expect some of them got away. Do you reckon so?' His face was bright, lighted by anticipation.

Luksmi said softly something in a foreign tongue. And Urquhart laughed. To Annie, Luksmi said, 'He is a boy again. He has forgotten how he grew up.'

'Silly old Dad,' said Urquhart, and then, hushed, 'Don't tell I said that.'

Annie said, 'What about the rest of them?'

'Lady Flower is locked in her room,' said Luksmi. 'And Sir Hampton is locked in his. I think Rupert will go out.'

'He'll get wet. Mama will shout at him,' said Urquhart. 'You'll tell her *I* was good, Luksmi.'

'Yes, I will tell her.'

Urquhart regarded Annie as she moved by him, down the stair, past an empty basalt stand, over the green moss that was the carpet. 'There's horses running about the park. And there's a white horse. I saw it. In the forest.'

'He will go too,' said Luksmi. 'He used to climb the pepul tree, or try to climb. I watched him, for there were the snakes. I must not let him perish a second time. But now, I have served him. I cannot stop him now.'

'Luksmi will let me do whatever I want,' said Urquhart. He flung his arms about her. A child's action, a man's arms and heavy weight, but Luksmi did not flinch. She kissed his temple.

Annie went on. She opened doors, and found the mould and the moss upon the pillars, and that creepers had entered on the ground floor. There were frogs in the music room, and on the dark blue walls veils of glittering water. The piano stood open.

As she poised there, Annie saw the ivory keys of the piano vibrating. They moved, but made no sound.

Otherwise, the ivory things were gone from the room.

Annie crossed to the glass door that led out to the garden and the park. She opened it. Rain like a blind mirror.

She thought, *Not yet*. It was as if the landscape spoke to her. *Stay indoors*, he had said.

She shut the door, and stole back into the house of rain.

Urquhart had made off from the hallway and Luksmi had gone with him.

Annie looked up the stair. The water dropped like a curtain, and there someone walked away, and Annie knew her.

Annie's heart contracted. She kept still, and then she hurried up the stair. Hurried, and halted, and thought *No*.

But at the turn of the corridor, there, she must follow, for everything was conceivable, even this.

Rose was sitting in the sewing room.

'Oh, isn't this lovely,' she said. 'Poor Annie, you couldn't enjoy it. But what we'd have given for this, you and I, in Tooth Street.'

All around, the room was the same, its couches and yellowish atmosphere, not tinged with green. And the sewing cabinet, with unique implements and rainbow cottons. Only the ivory things were no longer there.

Rose sat on a couch. She was dressed like a lady, but the clothes were elegant variations upon the worn garments she had had in life. A pink silk costume, and gorgeous pale straw hat with, pinned over it, roses that might have been real. But the lace gloves were her own. And Rose had pearls in her ears, and her golden hair was like an aureole, and her face was not tired.

'It's all right,' said Rose. 'Don't be scared, Annie.'

'I'm not.' Annie hesitated. She said, 'Can I touch you?'

Rose frowned, and then she smiled. 'I can make it so that you can.'

'No. No, it doesn't matter.'

'You've been brave,' said Rose.

'And you were dead.'

Rose giggled. 'Well, do I look dead?'

'You don't look the way you did.'

'No. It's better. I wanted to look my best for you.'

Annie said, 'Why are you here? Are you here to warn me?'

'Oh no. It's just I thought you should know. I saw Mother. At least, she isn't – but well. I did see her.'

Annie said, 'Eat more larks.'

'Oh that!' Rose giggled again. 'No, I really have seen her, Annie. And I have to tell you, something about your father.'

'Our father,' said Annie.

'No. Yours. My father was an army man. He died of cholera, poor boy. But your father – Annie, you mustn't be upset – your father was a demon.'

Annie thought, *This is, of all of it, a dream.*

As she thought it, Rose looked concerned. She said, 'It doesn't have to worry you. You can forget it if you like. But I'll tell you anyway. Mother was in the forest. And she met an Englishman. He was so handsome that it almost made her cry. And when he spoke to her . . . well, she couldn't resist him. But later she heard about the demons in the Indian woods. They can take any form. And then, there was you.'

'So what am I, Rose?' Annie demanded.

'You're you.'

Annie said softly, 'Do you remember the ivory elephant in my purse? The one that – made it happen?'

'No, I don't, really,' said Rose. 'That part's all gone away, somehow.'

'Then I can't ask you.'

'Yes, ask anything. Someone will tell me, and I can tell you.'

Annie said, 'The elephant has made things happen, but I couldn't see why it should choose me as its – vehicle. But then, even if I'm dreaming you, maybe – maybe it's only India. When I was small, I used to think India was alive, like an animal. Dark and shining.'

'Oh, Annie,' said Rose, 'you were always a good girl.'

'I'm glad I saw you,' said Annie. 'Are you going away now? It feels as if you are—'

'Yes. I mustn't stay. Or I could stay for ever. But that wouldn't be right.'

'You don't—' said Annie —'you don't have to see Innocent?'

Rose said, 'Not any more.'

Annie heard the rain, outside, and dripping through the room, as if, before, it had not been permitted a sound.

Rose took up one of the coloured cottons. She could hold it. She said, 'It's best if you go out.'

'Because you could just vanish.'

'Yes, and that might unnerve you.'

'Rose,' said Annie.

'Annie,' said Rose.

Annie turned and opened the doors and went outside and stood looking into the wall. Then she turned back, and Rose was not there, and the coloured cotton was on the table. Annie walked over to the table and took the cotton up. It was peach-colour. Annie clasped it in her hand, and left the room, shutting the doors. 'Our Father,' said Annie, 'which art in heaven. Hallowed be Thy name. Thy kingdom come, Thy will be done, on earth as it is in heaven.'

At midday, lit and drummed by the windows of torrential rain, they had gone to Mrs Beare's Den, but she was not there. And Churton did not appear.

A tree had fallen somewhere. They had heard it; been too uneasy to chance the deluge and see.

No work was done.

Clarrie went up to the attic room for something she forgot as soon as she opened the door.

The previous night, as well as undo the window, Clarrie had adjusted the sheet across Tiff's body, and then Clarrie had gone out to sleep with Burrow and Divy in another room.

Now Tiff had a new coverlet. And for a second, Clarrie thought Lady Flower must have come, and spread a fur on the body.

But it was not fur, it was feathers, and the feathers squabbled and fanned up purple and white wings.

The stench in the room was horrible, and Clarrie gagged.

Huge ugly birds had got in through the window. They were vultures, although Clarrie did not know. And they were hygienically employed, picking clean Tiff's corpse.

Outside the room, Clarrie fainted. Drops of water falling on her face revived her. She fumbled down to the kitchen and as she passed, clumps of painted plaster crumbled from the walls.

The elephant, which had swum the tears of Parvati, had swum the golden river, and had reached the sea. In the sea, the elephant swam, and the waves lifted him.

They raised him and cast him up against the mind of dreaming Hampton Smolte, so with a cry he woke in a wave of bedclothes, dense with the hot humid daytime sleep.

The rain swilled through his ears, and on the cornice above the bed he saw the mould, as he had seen it come in the rains to the colonial city mansions, in a day and a night.

He sat and swung his legs from the bed. They were veined and puffy now. He reached for the decanter, and far off, he heard the trumpeting of Jarashan's elephant, far off, miles away, and Smolte drank deep.

The rain stopped suddenly, the bath-taps of heaven turned off.

Looking from their window, the girl and the cat saw banks of trees steaming like a kettle.

Elizabeth Willow picked back to her bed, got up on it, and curled there, but the cat stayed in the window-seat.

A ray of bronzen sun gushed through the room.

The bed had not been made. Along the edges of the windows a fine green moss was growing. Elizabeth Willow was dressed inaccurately. No maid had come to assist her, nor her mother, who was wont to check over her daughter's appearance. Urquhart Elizabeth Willow had seen alone, and he had boasted that he had slept in the forest, but then he had admitted he had only slept in the garden. Luksmi had been there. She had made an offering to the Shiva across the pool, oil in a dish, which she had set on fire.

Elizabeth Willow thought of going out, into the garden or the wood.

She had seen the steward, Churton, go that way earlier. Churton had seemed bemused, but this did not distract Elizabeth Willow, who had never in her life once analysed or even considered a human emotion. So she had watched the big man amble uneasily away, as if drawn by an invisible thread, into the warp and woof of the rain, which now had paused.

That morning, Elizabeth Willow had eaten part of a mouse, raw.

There was a faint noise. From under the bed.

The cat turned, and her face became that of a gargoyle. She spat, and hissed, and her lashing tail brought off the green stuff growing by the window.

Elizabeth Willow sat up, and in that minute, the bed broke open at its centre.

Up through the mattress in a spume of feathers, through the ripped skin of sheets, a white and arching thing, like the limb of an unearthly tree—

The girl sprang off the bed and bolted away. She crouched again under the window.

And the bed erupted, seemed to *burst*.

A storm of feathers and frayed linen went up like a fountain, and the frame itself ruptured, splintered, and the sides split out. And through this blast the arching up of white struts went on, and then huge plates of breastwork, and head. It rose and stood. It was a thing of bones, dark white, gleaming in the gilt sun-shaft, corded together by some substance unseen. From the facial plates, two colossal crescent moons extended. The tusks. A skeleton, it had no trunk, its tail was a rail of little bones like blossom. Its body was like a baroque ribbed fruit. The scoop of the pelvis. Heavy leg bones, the toe bones flat upon the floor. Eyes empty.

The cat had flattened herself out. But Elizabeth Willow nipped across the room and pulled wide drawers. She brought out her tiny treasures, the balls of dead and desiccated mice, the skulls of birds. She brought them like flowers and laid them down before the faceless bone face of the elephant. She crept away.

The elephant shook itself, and its structure rattled. It grew, swelling, as if it must enlarge to fill some pre-ordained picture of itself inscribed on air.

It filled most of the room now. A cabinet, struck by the engorging carapace of skeleton, showered into pieces.

And the foremost tusk caught Elizabeth Willow's dress.

She cried out in terror wildly, wordless. The material tore up and away from her and she was in her bone-sewn shift, lying on the floor, as the top of the elephant's brain-case struck against the ceiling.

Plaster showered now soft as bloom. It powdered Elizabeth Willow, her cheeks and hair, and the fur of her flattened, quivering cat.

Enormous heat touched the chamber, a wing of fire.

All the bones of the beast gave way. They disintegrated, showering down, a cloud.

Elizabeth Willow hid her head. A single tusk, blushed opaque white, rolled against her foot, and she drew her foot away. The tusk melted into dust.

It was thick, that dust, on everything. The room was a room of dust, and the smell of burnt marigolds.

The sun streamed on the wall.

Mrs Beare had not been found, and Churton had not come to tell them anything. No bells rang for them. Steam from the wet hot world entered their kitchen bolt-hole, scented with loams and stinks and perfumes.

'Someone must go for assistance,' said Mrs Rope. She had drunk a lot of beer. 'There's Tiff to think of.'

Clarrie made a stifled sound.

In the corner, aslosh with water and the contents of a salad dish that had been spilled, Sebby toed the lettuce.

'There us a big bird on the pump. Big as a turkey.'

'Never you mind that.'

'It us got a big beak. I don't like the look of un.'

'Close your mouth, you nasty child!' cried Divy.

Clarrie said, 'They were all over her.'

'Shush,' said Mrs Rope. 'The boy can go for help.'

'Won't!' shouted Sebby. 'Can't make me! I us sent here.'

'You'll go with Pocks,' said Mrs Rope. 'You know the way better.' Her hands shook as she raised the beer. 'Will you go, Pocks? Be a doughty man, and do it?'

Pocks went very pale, and Divy too. It was Divy who said, 'Don't make him, Mrs Rope.'

'You be still, you rat's basket.'

Burrow said, 'She's been carrying on with him. That's why she doesn't like it.'

Pocks said, 'Prefer me to carry on with you, you bitch.'

Mrs Rope roared.

Subdued by habit, a moment's comfort of familiar threats, among the sewage water strewn with greens.

'You'll keep a civil tongue, Pocks. You'll do as I say. Get off, and take that lollock of a boy.'

'We should see the Master,' said Pocks.

Burrow said, 'He's locked his door. And she's locked hers, Lady Uppity.'

Mrs Rope said, 'They've no thought for us. Never did. They don't, such folk. You must go, Pocks.'

The vegetable maid began to cry. The silver maid went into the larder and hopped back with some gravy-coloured sherry kept for trifles.

'Yes, we'll have a drop of that,' said Mrs Rope. She scowled. 'This water's up over my boots.'

Outside, in the fecund sunny mist, things crowed and cawed.

Then a distant noise smote up like that of some instrument heard only in red-edged dreams.

'What is it?'

''Tis a bull,' said Sebby. 'I won't go.'

Annie moved through the Smolte palace, with the peach cotton held tight in her hand.

She had let down her hair.

She could do anything.

And for this reason, she found the door of Sir Hampton Smolte, and hesitated, and heard inside the door Smolte crossing the room, up and down, and the clink of glass. Further on along the emerald corridor she tried the door of Smolte's wife, knocking with the fist that held the cotton.

'Who is it?' said a voice. It was Flower; she sounded very young, or very old, bewildered.

'Annie Ember.'

'No, don't come in,' said Flower. And then, 'Yes, come in.'

Annie opened the door – it was not locked, if it had ever been.

In the sitting room, bugs were scuttling over the furnishings. They had eaten some of the pretty upholstery. And down the pillars water slipped, melodious, soft.

Flower was in the bedroom. Her hair was loose, a huge coarse unbrushed ginger bush, and she wore her dressing-gown of pink brocade, with drippings of lace and ribbons. But she had powdered and rouged her face and put on her diamonds, earrings and bracelets, a diamond necklace budded with ochre-green stones.

'We'll have to go away,' said Flower. 'Can't stay here. I went into the bathroom and turned on the tap, and yellow water came out and it had a filthy stench. Oh my God, I haven't smelled such a thing, not since then. We're bewitched. It's no good arguing with me. I've seen some funny things. When I was on the boards, we had a ghost. Oh, yes. Regular as the clock he was. And I've seen a chair move by itself. Ho, you can't be sure of anything. It's Hampton's business. I've knocked and called but he won't answer. I'll take my jewels. That's what's best. Leave everything, but take what you can carry. You'll help me, won't you, Annie? You're a sensible girl. I'll see you don't come to sorrow.' Flower laughed. 'You'll think I'm unhinged. Well I am, a bit. It's been a shock. And do you think my two sons have come to see how I am? Oh no. They're off to play. That Indian woman, I don't trust her. But how else can I manage? Ah – but there. That was then. Where am I, Annie? Am I there? Am I young, Annie? What shall I do?'

'I don't know,' said Annie. She looked at Flower coldly. 'You're right. Odd things happen now. I met my dead sister.'

'Well, there you are,' said Flower. She put up one hand into her hair. 'Luksmi hasn't come to dress me. It's not good. I was a mother to her, the slut. Little half-caste brat. I saw they taught her to read. And about Jesus.'

'My sister was hanged,' said Annie icily. 'But I expect you knew. She was a murderess.'

'Hung? Don't talk to me about that. I've got enough difficulties.'

There was a rushing, and both women looked up, and from a greenish patch the water ran down through the ceiling, thick and bright in the new sunlight.

'Hampton should stir himself,' said Flower. 'But he won't. How will we get through the forest? That idiot Withers has disappeared. But no. No. That isn't now.'

Annie said, 'You'd better stay where you are.'

'My daughter,' said Flower, 'is a cat. She won't mind.'

Annie went from the room and out into the corridor. A glass case of stuffed golden birds had been cracked. Beetles ran over the birds. Through a window, Annie saw a bird fly by. It was golden.

And deep down in the house there came the huge echoing chords of the piano. The ivory keys, *stamping*.

Annie thought, *It's come through me. Will it kill me? I don't care*.

She shouted out into the throbbing, piano-riven silence: 'Come on then! Come on, I'm game for it!'

Urquhart saw Pocks and Sebby standing out beyond the house, staring up at the rukh, through a field of wild mustard.

Urquhart knew that Pocks, whom he did not recognize, was

older than himself, and so, when he came up to Pocks, Urquhart was surprised to find himself the taller. The child, Urquhart instantly kicked. You had to show at once who was dominant.

'Don't do that, Mr Urquhart,' pleaded Pocks, as Sebby squalled. 'He's already scared silly.'

'Scared? What's he scared of?'

'Well, Mr Urquhart, I've never seen the woods like – that—'

They gazed. Even Sebby, blathering, gazed.

The trees rose high and wove together. An impenetrable green, steaming and smoking, sparkling with light. And through it, a splash of parrots, the more elusive shadow-movements of darker and more curious things.

'It's grand,' said Urquhart. 'I'm going hunting.' He showed the gun.

'You shouldn't carry it that way, Mr Urquhart.'

'Don't tell Daddy,' said Urquhart. 'I gived 'em the slip. I broke something. It was Rupy's toy. And he cried. He's older 'n me and he blubbed. Was an elephant. Daddy said, *Be a man*. I wouldn't cry. I never cry. I'm not scared of the rukh.'

'Is that what it is now?' asked Pocks. Sebby whimpered. 'Will you come with us, Mr Urquhart?'

'Bloody not,' said Urquhart. 'I don't know who you are. One of Daddy's riff-raffs. You watch out. There are rakshas in the forest.'

'Rats—'

'Devils. They can take any shape. But I'm not scared. Luksmi wouldn't let me go, but then she said, *No, I make you free*. So I'm free. I'm going to hunt a tiger. There is one. All the big men felled off their horses. But I'll shoot the rotten old tiger.'

Sebby snivelled, and wiped his snot on a fat sleeve.

They moved off, through the mustard, searing yellow as a colour new in the world.

The river, when they came to it, was quite wide, and very brown, like the disgusting sweet sherry found in the larder. On the bank of the river, where the boulders were, and Smolte's stone thing, they found Mr Churton's watch and chain, snagged up in a wreath of roses round the stone.

'Oh God, where's he gone?' said Pocks.

'Tiger's eaten him,' said Urquhart, good-humouredly.

'Mr Urquhart, Sir,' said Pocks, 'I think as how you've gone daft. Better get back indoors.'

But Urquhart only punched Pocks cheerily on the shoulder and ran suddenly off with the dangerous gun into the drenched viridian smoke of the woods.

Pocks entered the woods with a sad terror, helpless, looking round in despair. He had sometimes been this way on moonless nights, and seen the pheasants in the trees, or a dog fox prowling. But now the trees were so high, and huge ferns rose, and ropes of vine closed off the tremendous aisles that in spring had been frosted by bluebells, and which now had the odour of a swamp.

'Don't know the way,' said Sebby sullenly. 'It usn't what it been.'

'No,' said Pocks.

He looked up into the wheeling trees. The fronds against the sky seemed prehistoric, and squinting down at him was an eldritch black monkey face, heartless, indifferent to him. It was the way the Smoltes stared at you, but worse. The monkey screamed, and Pocks shuddered.

They went on, and the forest closed over. The river vanished away at their backs. Weird calls and trills rang through above, and somewhere someone – a blacksmith? – struck metal. But he must be a fey fellow, the blacksmith, very, very small, and the anvil a pebble.

'That girl's a witch,' said Sebby abruptly. 'She's done this. She said to me, look up my skirt and I'll give you a pound.'

'What girl? You're a nuisance.'

'And she put the queer eye on me. She did.'

They were in an avenue, and from the trees the flowers hung, crimson and orange. A shadow was in the hollows between the bushes. A dog, perhaps.

'Quiet, boy,' said Pocks.

But Sebby would not. 'Missus said *she* looks like a bad un. And she says to me, I'll bite you, Sebby, and drink your blood.'

Blood red, the flowers, Pocks gaped at them. The shadow slunk from tree to tree.

Sebby apparently noticed.

'Don't like it here,' announced Sebby.

Something bounded out from the trees. It was only the size of a big dog, but slim as a tube, smooth, black. A sort of cat. It leapt straight at Sebby and took him by the chest, jacket and shirt, and pulled him over in the rainy steamy grasses. And then it loped away, dragging him. Sebby called and howled, and Pocks stood there, watching Sebby's stricken face and the hindquarters of the big black cat, until they went together out of sight into the undergrowth.

Gradually the racket of Sebby's outcry was flushed away into the frightening music of the jungle, its sighs and purrs and tickings.

And then, Pocks was quite alone.

But Urquhart strode through the forest. He was not scared. His boots were on, and he had his father's gun. He would shoot the tiger.

He must show Luksmi, when he had done it. She would be stern, but he would convince her of his valour. She had made the offering to the Shiva, holding up the fire to her god, then breathing in the heat of the flame. When they grew up, he would live with Luksmi, and she would serve him, making him tea and washing his feet. But then, Luksmi was grown up. She was his mother.

Urquhart came into a clearing thick with bamboo, where there was a stream of tarnished water. He stopped, looking at it, and as he did so, something squat, with a huge head, came trotting over the slope towards him.

It was not the tiger. It was a pig. Not the white one he thought he had seen, but very dark, like chocolate, bristled, with pale coated tusks. And it did not trot. It was a kind of gallop.

Urquhart thought about this thing. Then he raised the gun and fired at it.

He was sure he had been precise. But instead of going over, the boar gave a horrible snorting gurgling cough, and thumped on faster towards him.

Urquhart all at once could not remember what to do with a gun. Probably it was not real, but a toy. He started to cry, and turned round, wondering if anyone was there to assist him. But only the jungle teemed about him, and overhead gaudy birds danced in the balconies of the trees, not caring.

Next second, the boar struck him. The impact was mighty, and flung him over. He rolled, and the boar's foul vegetable breath enveloped him. The dirty tusks went down, and dug up under him, going into his side.

Urquhart shouted. He thought Luksmi would come after all, and hold him to her, and a man would beat the boar to death with a stick.

But the boar stabbed him again, and now the blades of its rage went deep into his belly.

Urquhart tried to strike the boar away. It lumbered and waddled and went over him like a barrel and he heard his ribs snap under it.

High above, high as the topmost tree, a fan of golden light rested like a fallen sun. He saw it blaze and beam carelessly on him, brightening and glittering and then growing dim, as the boar gored and trampled him. And then he heard some thin shrill squealing, and the little children of the boar came hurrying to him also. Under his head he could feel the hotness of the earth. But the heat and the light went away in the blundering of the hard bodies that constantly knocked into and excruciatingly pierced him. He thought he would get up in a moment, and run back to the hut. But he did not do it, any more than he had done so the last time.

Hampton Smolte washed his face and hands, and shaved himself, and used some of the pomade on his sparse hair.

He dressed with attention, fresh linen and a good coat. He did not miss food, for the drink had given him nourishment and energy. The mould that had evolved on the walls he touched in one place with his finger. It was there, all right, viscous, mindless, a ruination.

'Well,' he said, 'well, you whore.'

But now she would not come. In his mind instead he saw a pale English girl, with long brown hair. He had glimpsed her in his house. A maid. Someone for the fool, Elizabeth.

Smolte went down through his mansion.

Slime coiled along the perimeters of pictures, fungus on carpets. Above, brass lights and bells with wisps of colonizing creeper somehow got in. The jungle. It smothered everything so quickly. The road, the houses, the courts of Jarashan's palace—

But he knew where he was. This was not India. Whatever

this was, he would not lose his sanity to it. He was here, at home. It had only pursued him.

He walked into the dining room.

The scarlet chamber, with its rounded red pillars, and ceiling of dark blue sky burdened by painted palms. A congealed remnant of a meal lay on the table, and there had been something else going on, as on the night of Oxway's monkeys.

The transparent boxes were broken. The wolves and jackals stood amid spears of lanced glass. And on the walls the bears' heads and heads of deer were askew. The skins had slipped and slithered on the floor, curling up, turned over. As if – as if the trapped souls had gone out of them, and smashed wide their way.

Smolte ignored these things. He went to the table on the elephant leg and picked up the brandy decanter and a leaf-green goblet.

As he raised the wine to his thirsty mouth, Smolte saw his elder son, Rupert, sitting by an open glass door, on the ground.

'Good day, Father.'

'Is it? Is that what you think?'

'Yes, I'm in love with it. Look, it's beautiful. Look at the gardens.'

Smolte glanced. The lawns were rife. Hedges sprang with rain as if with jewels, in a madness of growth. The ferns and flowers. Roses had spiralled up towards heaven. It was the rainy season, things grew apace.

The piano sounded, discordantly.

'Is that your sister?'

'My mad sister is out there,' said Rupert. 'The piano is playing itself. It's a poltergeist, Papa. But what the rest of it is, I couldn't say.'

Smolte beheld his son's face. He had never seen Rupert look happy before, many moods, but never that one. And so, Smolte did not grasp what it was.

'We have to keep a rein on ourselves. Our imaginations,' said Smolte, refilling his glass. His hand was perfectly steady.

'You think this is a vision, Father? I've had those. Due to Gry's impure laudanum. But this is real.'

'It seems to be.'

'My God, I remember it so well. The scent of the earth between the rain storms, the mulch of the rukh. And the warmth. I've been in the garden and seen the orchids, and the lotus in the pool. Mother won't like the snakes. And I saw a mongoose in the yew walk. The dumb boy was feeding it biscuits stolen from old Ma Rope. By the way, a hothouse has come down. There's a tree across it.'

'Perhaps there isn't,' said Smolte.

The piano gave again its twanging clangour.

Smolte said, 'And perhaps that's Elizabeth.'

'I'm going out again presently,' said Rupert.

'I shouldn't do that.'

'No, I don't expect you would. But no one will stop me.'

'Then I won't trouble,' said Smolte.

He filled up the goblet and was surprised when it dropped from his hand. It was as though someone had jostled him. But among all the shards of broken glass from the cases, it scarcely mattered. He took another vessel. Filled it, drank.

The piano again – no, not the piano. Smolte turned back and looked out beyond his house. Something in the woods. He had heard it earlier.

Obviously, if the beasts had come to be there, then there would be elephant too. He would go up soon and fetch the big gun. It had been kept pristine, and oiled, as if in readiness.

Rupert said, 'I've wasted all my life. Locked up in prison here, behind these cold walls of England.'

'Did you break those cases?' said Smolte.

'Did I? No. Something did.'

'Yes. Very well.'

Rupert got to his feet. He looked at his father, the creature whose scalding seed had begun him. He looked, then looked away, and walked out of the door on to the lawn.

Something happened – he did not object to it. The gardens were already gone, submerged in the opulence of the springing forest. The jungle had come down, over the river and the meadow, to the brink of the house.

He had only to stroll into it.

Rupert paused. He could see a woman now, just in among the trees. Slender and graceful, her black hair hanging down her left side in a plait. Her sari was apricot, streaked by shadowy gold. Could it be – yes, anything could, now.

They had called her *Ussi*, but that of course was not her name. His mother had coined it, presumably to rhyme with *hussy*. What then had *been* her name, the name of his nurse, his ayah, the minx-sphinx goddess with whom he had learned the first station of dark love?

'Ussi!' he called.

And she raised her narrow hand, the palm of which was like the inside of a rosy plum. She waved to him, as they had taught her to wave, mimicking the English lady. And she laughed. Her white teeth shone. And then she moved away, and the tail of hair whipped out and snaked behind her.

She swayed from him in that inimitable walk of the Indian woman clothed for her lord, the earth. Her rosy feet. Blue on her hair. The glimmer of light and shade over her hips.

Rupert lengthened his stride, and pushed off the wet reams of grass and creeper.

Insects bustled in the bushes, and animals disturbed the rain above, which fell on him, and he laughed, too. He laughed, and went after Ussi, now he was a man and might meet with her as a man.

A ruin passed. What had that been, or had the forest invented it? Bats clustered in the antique trees. He glimpsed the face of some emotionless god, before the vines had wrapped it up again. Above, in the foliage, a man seemed hung, made of leaves, with moss for a beard.

Ussi stood waiting in a glade. There in the green, her sunny darkness. She held out her hand.

Rupert ran to her. He ran and halted only when he was a foot away from her. He could smell her aroma of incense and flesh and the attar in her hair. The smell of the commencement, the scent of night in day. 'Ussi.'

'Lord,' she said. She composed her face. It was young still, it was just as he recalled. 'You are bad,' she said. 'A wicked man. Kneel down before me. Kneel to me.'

The start of sexuality in him was so intense it made a pain shoot through his heart.

'My love,' he said, 'I'll kneel to you. Punish me, Ussi.'

'I will, Lord,' she said.

So he knelt, and her hands came gently and undid his shirt, and at every whisper of her fingers, the ecstasy increased its pressure on him. 'Quickly, Ussi,' he said. 'Be quick.'

And her hand burned and raked him over, from his cheek to his navel, one long rending of thorns. And then again.

Rupert cried. He fell back, clutching her velvet body to him, so she fell too. And her claws went into him more deeply, bringing him to limitless agony and to impossible delight.

Her teeth met in his throat as he screamed in a hell of marvellous joy. Her paws disembowelled him and his entrails oozed out over the sunrise of her fur, as his semen sprayed against her impervious belly.

He was dead before his paroxysm finished, and the tigress, disdaining his offal and meat, let go of him and let him lie. She turned about and padded directly away, allowing the plattered rain of the leaves to wash clean her pelt. Combed with black, her tail swept after her through the grasses.

In the afternoon, Hampton Smolte rang the bell in the dining room. He did not believe anyone would come, his servants seemed now to be absent, but finally one of the house girls appeared. He did not know who she was.

'Where is Churton?' he said.

'I don't know, Sir.'

'And Pocks.'

'Mrs Rope sent Pocks to fetch someone. Someone for Tiff.'

Smolte did not know who she meant. He did not understand what she meant by 'sending' and 'fetching'. He had seen the forest come in over his land. Impenetrable. But perhaps the servants saw it differently. Or not at all.

'What do you think of all this?' he asked idly.

The dull girl looked at him, at the guns he had brought down, and the enormous elephant gun, whose ivory-work was, with the piano, now the only ivory left in the house. Then she stared away at the window. Again she said, 'I don't know, Sir.'

'What do you see?'

'The wood, Sir. It's got very big with the rain.'

'In your pantry,' said Smolte, 'you'll find Churton's spare keys. I want some brandy and some wine from the cellar. Bring anything. Anything will do.'

'Yes, Sir,' she said uncertainly.

'And I'd like some food. Mrs Rope hasn't seen to luncheon.'

'The kitchen's all water, Sir.'

'I see. Well, some bread and cheese and meat will do.'

The maid bobbed and went away.

They had not cleared the breakfast, but that was useful, because now he ate the wooden uncooked toast and the ham Rupert and Urquhart had left. And the girl did not come back.

Well, when the brandy was all gone, he could seek the cellar himself.

Out in the woods monkeys carolled. He had not heard the elephant, not for two or three hours, not since, in fact, he had brought down the guns. It had rained again, great plummets of water, but now once more the storm held off, and the sun shone and the rukh fumed.

Something would happen. It was only a matter of waiting.

A leaden misgiving coiled in Smolte's belly, and he drank another glass of brandy. His heart felt a bit flabby, as if the rain had got into it.

In India, he had been resistant to stories of spells and curses, omens, demons. The country was alive with it. And you saw things – tricks of magicians, coincidence, make-believe. Somehow there it had been easy to dismiss. But here, here he knew. She had come after him. He was only unsure why it had taken her so long. Nineteen, twenty years. Sitavaina.

When he realized what she had done – when he had learned she had died, he knew she had died through him. But she could have killed him too, what she had done to him. He perceived then that she was vengeful. And they said the ghost of the elephant came out of the jungle and burned with her, on her pyre. Lies, fantasy. And yet, now, he saw that perhaps it had been true.

She had hunted him down. She lusted for his life. But she had ruined his life. She had sucked the soul out of him. Wanting her, that had destroyed him. Courage and cunning, and the honour they brought, and the wealth, they were valueless.

He had only to remember her, the look of her, in the garden of peacocks, in the pool below the temple. And he could not properly remember, she had even taken that away.

She should have desired him. God knew what would have become of them, but they would have had their fire of life, and damn the death fire that came after. And damn her, damn her for what she had done, to him and to herself. Damn her for dying.

'Is it you?' he said aloud. He stared out into the smoking rukh. Wild mustard, jacaranda, sal trees ninety feet high. He felt a sudden lighting inside him. If she had not loved him, she had hated him, even after death. He had forgotten her face, but she had not forgotten.

He stood up, and the elephant trumpeted from lungs of bronze and steel, making the air tremble and every atom of the room vibrate.

Smolte reached for the gun. The beast was near. It was very large. Big like the tusker he had shot in the twilight in the forest. Like that elephant he had put down when the tiger scored it and it cried. The gun would settle it. If it was there, then the gun would be enough.

He had finished the brandy.

Go to the cellar now? There was no time. For all at once he heard the forest parting, separating like a sea, and things disturbed dived through it, he saw them, the leaping of squirrels, and birds that flew up into the sky. And then a tree fell somewhere and a tempest of leaves and branches showered out into the mist.

Smolte braced himself against the chair he had brought, and readied the great gun.

It was coming now. Silent but for the tread of its feet that shook the roots of the floor. By God, it was a giant—

And another tree fell abruptly straight down, shattering its green foam, and out of the vault of the rukh the elephant came walking, unimpeded, brushing aside the walls of the world.

His head and his hairs were white like wool, as white as snow; and his eyes were as a flame of fire; and his feet like unto fine brass, as if they burned in a furnace; and his voice as the sound of many waters.

Smolte lowered the gun. This was instinct. He raised it again.

The elephant – white as snow – was colossal. As it moved slowly on and forward, the structure of the house *thrummed.* The huge drums of the feet struck the earth.

So white. And on the whiteness, flowers of gleaming gold. Above the domed forehead, fringing the slender ears that were each the shape of India herself. About the massy neck. And the nails were golden as they trod down the land. The sun was in each of its eyes. His eyes.

'Now my beauty,' said Smolte.

But the gun weighed like the past. So heavy. So meaningless. For it could do nothing, yet he must fire the gun.

The tusks were the moon in two portions.

Smolte fired, and the impact of the gun dislodged him. He juddered back and went down on one knee and the gun crashed on the floor.

The bullet had hit the elephant. That much was obvious. For between the hillocks of the brow, a golden star appeared.

And that was all. Except that he spoke again, the beast of snow, spoke like the ghost of a mountain, and the golden voice rang round the dome of the sky and broke it. The sky turned black, and the smashed crystal of the rain thrashed down.

Smolte got up.

He walked backward over the red room, and reached its exit, and stood there, watching the gigantic white elephant come on to the ragged burnt lawn that was left before the house, and over this, and up to the glass doors, and there the elephant stepped forward again, and the doors showered like the rain and fell away, and the wall itself, with a growl, broke and spattered, bricks and plaster smoking off, as if the solid effigy were made of pie-crust, like promises.

Smolte turned round and went quickly to the stairway.

He climbed, and the drowned carpet sank under his boots. A frog bounced from beneath his feet, and then the treads gave way.

'No,' said Smolte.

He dragged himself up the dismembered stairs, sliding on the saturated carpet, the wood scattering.

As he did so, the wall behind him rumbled, and sighed, and then there came the second cascade of bricks.

He reached the upper floor.

Smolte had no thought for any other being. There were no others. Only himself, and the elephant. He found the door of his apartment in darkness, for the storm-night had dropped again. He tumbled through and stood in astonishment, there in the big plush chamber. The stair had given way. The elephant could not climb the stairs. Oh, they were clever, and could pick up a jewelled pin with the sensitive trunk, but no, they could not climb.

It – he – would rampage below, and then would tire.

And what then?

Smolte reached for the oil-lamp and lit it. A muzzy yellowish glow went up and made the room seem smaller than it was.

Silence, but for the rain, sizzling outside and inside. It struck in silver needles on a hundred surfaces. The window was black. Smolte walked to it and saw the cloud in heaven, the black elephant of the cloud.

Was it possible to pray? To what? To her gods only, and they would not listen.

He had left all the guns below. A mistake.

Smolte sat down with the oil-lamp in his hand and his body aching as if he had gone up a thousand steps. The rain slapped his bowed head through the bed's rotted canopy.

He thought, *If I went back, back to her, then, what could I do? I'd do it all again, the same.*

There came a dim groaning. He was reminded of a ship. And then a crunching dust flew upwards from the bedroom floor.

The bed tilted. Smolte sprang upright.

A fissure ran across the floor into which the carpet was siphoned. Then the panels of the floor folded leisurely up, vertical and strange. The head and shoulders of the mountain rose into the room.

The elephant had grown to twice his own extraordinary size, and now his whiteness flamed. He raised his face, and his old, old timeless dreaming seeing eyes were fixed on Hampton Smolte. Yes, the eyes were gold, and human, but profound. The sun burned on in each, eternal fire. And the tusks were each a death. And on the tusks were rings like pale amber, as a tree is ringed for every century, year and moment.

'What do you want?' said Hampton Smolte.

His terror was so vast he had not felt it, and did not feel it now. But nothing was left to him, not his gender or his personality, nor any memory. He did not now know why it had come to this. He did not know his own name. The words he uttered had no meaning.

But he felt inside himself a great heat. It ate him up. The eyes had set him ablaze.

He screamed out: 'Is it this then? You want this?'

And he dashed the lighted lamp across his bulky chest, over

the fine coat and clean linen, and the worn and bloated skin, and muscled soldier's breast gone to fat, the scar of the black moon where she had bitten him.

The chimney of the lamp broke. The oil and flame spilled out and wetted him.

He caught. Wreathed in brilliant fire, he suddenly saw himself alight, and began to try to beat out the flames.

The elephant watched him, writhing and screaming and flaming. The elephant watched with ancient eyes.

The fire curled and licked at Smolte's face, and lit his hair so there came the sweetness of dessert cookery as the pomade went up. And the odour of roasting.

Smolte fell. He rolled in the puddles of the indoor rain, under the taps of the ceiling of rain, and the fire smoked and smouldered and went out.

No longer to be known at all. A blackened husk, naked, its garments torched away. White bone peering through the tarry darkness. The mouth, continuing to scream.

The room all black now, only the elephant's head with the alabaster cobra of a trunk curled and still, and the golden eyes.

Smolte's screams were noiseless. His throat had been scorched out.

The door of the room opened.

Annie Ember stood on the threshold.

She too, a whiteness, but pale, muted before the incandescence of the creature. Her eyes occluded, shining, wide.

She saw. Smolte knotting and unknotting in his packaging of black leaves. And the face of the Infinite given form as an elephant. And on its forehead the mark of hate that had been made into a golden star.

And then half the floor gave way. Plunged in with a thunder, in clouds of debris, white for the storm and black for the black smoke of the burnt man. And as the cumulus cleared, nothing was there but the chasm in the masonry, and what was left of a man twisting about in agony, speechless, through the tinsel rain.

Down in the hallway, between the pillars of water, two or three of the servants were, and Divy was one of them, in tears like the rain.

'Someone was screaming,' said Mrs Rope, ruddy-pallid, and holding her apron to her bosom like a child. 'Horrible cries.'

Darius said, 'Yes, I know. I'll take myself up, and see.'

They let him by, and observed as he went with grace over the prolapsed staircase, emerging at the top of it and walking into the storm-shadowed recesses of the house.

Annie was in the corridor, and beyond her an opened door, which led to Smolte's rooms.

Annie said nothing. She shook her head, and showed him the way with her hand.

'What have you seen?' he said.

She tried to speak. Then she turned away from him.

Darius turned her gently back and held her against him. Like something frozen which thaws, she murmured, 'An elephant was there. But I never knew they were such a size. It was very big. And he's been burned.'

'Ah,' said Darius.

'But he's alive,' she said.

'Go down now,' he said. 'The stair will take your little weight. Go down with the others. I heard him call to me, in the quiet. The horses were all still as stones. There was the rain, and then his voice. He sounded as he did when he was a young man, and I a boy. *Come here, Darius*, he said. And here I am.'

Annie drew back from him. 'What will you do?'

Darius said nothing. She saw in that moment all the light within him, all the shade, and so she went away as he had said, down the stair, not aware of its condition, and Mrs Rope looked at her in alarm. 'Oh, Ember. What in God's name's to become of us?'

Annie felt soft, warm, at peace, silent. Meaning to comfort, she said, 'God knows.'

Darius waited by Smolte in the wreck of the bedroom, as Smolte came and went terribly in consciousness. And the sombre day dwindled. The clouds shone ruby, lined with mulberry, and behind the sky was washed to lilac. But the sun sank swiftly, and the dusk lasted less than a minute. And then it was night again, and the rain fell in jet beads now, and the jungle sounded and the thunder furled in the bowl of the sky.

Then Smolte managed to make a noise, a type of rustling and

crisping, and with his charred stick of hand, he touched Darius.

'I can't die, Darius. It won't let me die.'

Darius waited on.

Smolte said, 'Will you end it for me, Darius?'

'I will,' Darius said. He lifted up the pistol that he had found lying in the scarlet dining room, among the puddles and the towers of bricks. 'Shall it be now?'

'The pain—' said Smolte in his cinder-voice. His face was almost all blackness. He had no eyes. Only the red wound of the mouth. And then he said, 'Where shall I be tomorrow?'

'Safe,' said Darius. He put the lip of the pistol gently against Smolte's black forehead, and shot him, point blank.

The crack of the shot went up and up, like a bird that flew away. And then the night went on with its mantra of water and darkness.

4

In the hollow tree the two cats had been play-fighting, and one sat now, unconcernedly licking her scratches at her bark window. So she witnessed, a couple of feet below her on the ground, the people passing, and the horses, going on into the green. She made no signal. Perhaps they did not see.

Elizabeth Willow had lined the tree with her clothes, and sprinkled there the bones that had been left her, after the great bone creature had gone away. Here she and Kitty made their nest. They slept rolled together, and after the rain, went hunting. Both caught something, and these things they devoured. There was also fruit fallen from the trees, for monsoon and harvest seemed to have come together, and this the girl-cat ate, also, although her companion did not.

They were content.

If Elizabeth Willow recalled anything of her former existence as a human daughter she had only now to call down to the travellers in the wood. She did not call, and they went by.

'Did you see her, up in the tree?' Annie said quietly to Darius.

'I saw. Best let her be.'

They had all the horses, and the young horse trotted by its mother. Even Jessa had come back to the stable, and brought with her two or three others that had been roaming in the forest.

The house lay far behind, apparently struck by lightning in the storm, all its central portion laid open and the stairway caved in. Coloured minarets and domes had been tossed into the grass like marbles. A broken toy, the creeper was already clambering over it, and monkeys screeched and romped across the roofs with ripe mangoes in their hands. Marigolds grew thickly by the doors. In the distance, they saw Luksmi walking among these plants in the white sari of a widow. Had she kept it by her all this while, the sari? She plucked the marigolds and did not glance up.

Flower said, 'Go over, Darius, and make her come away.'

Darius said, 'No, Lady Flower, best let her be,' as he said later concerning Elizabeth Willow Smolte. But Flower did not notice her daughter as she had taken note of Luksmi.

Flower sat on Jessa, decorously and awkwardly, side-saddle. Flower was too feeble to walk. She wore a faded dress Annie had rescued from the ants, and into which Annie had assisted Flower. The dress was old and too tight, and Flower had cried when Annie did up her corset. 'Look at me. Fat old bag. Just look. Why has this happened to me?' And then she had asked Annie again where Hampton Smolte was, and Annie had said that he was with Darius, as Darius had told her to.

Presently, when Flower had been patched into her gown, and Annie had put up her hair, and the box of jewelry was hidden in a container, Darius came and knocked on Flower's door. Flower received him in her sitting room, among the lumps of moss.

'It's the weather,' she said. 'You can't trust those servants. They won't kill the beetles. The garden's flooded, you should see the mosquitoes. Is it my husband you want?'

'I've come to you about your husband,' said Darius.

'What's the matter?' said Flower. Under her rouge and powder she went grey and her cheeks fell in as if at the onset of death.

'The news is not good. I'm sorry. Your husband is dead, Lady Flower.'

'Oh, those animals!' exclaimed Flower. 'They set on him in the forest. Those fiends – they'll be seen to. But what's to happen now? I'm not safe. And the children – oh, what it is to be a woman cursed with brats. I must always think of them.'

'We'll find our way from the rukh,' said Darius.

'Yes, you can find your way anywhere,' said Flower. 'Yes, yes, they all say so. And then the river. To the city. We'll be safe.'

'If you will rely on me,' he said.

'What else can I do? You'd better be loyal, Darius.'

'There,' he said, 'when have you ever known me otherwise?'

Then there was another difficult passage, as Flower wandered the chaos of the smashed overgrown house, searching for Rupert and Urquhart. She opened doors on rooms of smoking greened furniture, where birds or rats hurried. She saw a monkey in a window and shrieked, a moment of macabre and terrible humour. She concluded the ayah had stolen her boys. She was angry, frightened and glad.

They persuaded her to come down, by another stairway which had half held, into the lower region of the house.

And here everyone was gathered by Darius, all who were left or could be found. Mrs Rope and Clarrie, the two kitchen maids, the housemaid called Burrow, and Divy, whose eyes were bruised by tears. The silver maid and the other girls had gone, like Mrs Beare and Mr Churton, as if the unprincipled green world had merely reached in and pawed them away into itself.

Elizabeth Willow of course they did not find. Rawlings and the gardener Darius had already located, wound in smashed glass and the arms of the fallen tree, already quick-bound by hungry vines. Hungrier vultures perched ready on the nearby hothouses. Two of the gardener's boys were in the kitchen, the dumb boy one of them, stroking the mongoose which sat on his shoulder.

Darius let out all the horses and tied them loosely together. Mrs Rope refused to be helped up on to the gelding.

'You've brought me my geranium,' said Annie. She took the small plant from Darius and stared into its leaves and boiling red flowers as if she might see the future there. Then she let him stow the pot away among the few things he had packed on the horses' backs. 'I don't want my clothes. The beetles will have eaten them. Ants have eaten the money they gave me. I went to look. But I don't want their money.'

Beyond, the forest gleamed with rain and sun. Its avenues melted into purple shadow. It was impassable.

Flower said, as they started off, 'I knew it would come to this. He'd never have listened. They told me, don't nag him. So I kept quiet.' Luksmi moved like a white spirit through the fiery marigolds. 'And there's the thanks I get,' said Flower. Then her face set, and became the Mask of Tragedy, elderly and wise with hurt, the hurt of many lives, which, like true happiness, is never really unremembered.

Darius led them in among the trees.

They went over the river, not wide but full of rain. Creeper had covered the lingam. Then the terrain was all unknown.

Darius, however, did not often hesitate, and then it was only as if he recalled some detail which would assist him.

He found them fruit on the trees, mangoes and peaches, figs, and there were certain leaves he made them eat, medicine he assured them. Divy wept and would not eat her leaf, and then Darius took her face in his hands and she became still, and did eat a little.

And Annie knew a cruel inappropriate jealousy. She thought, *He's the same with all and everyone. It's his kindness I've mistaken. I'm nothing special to him.* And walking through the sorcerous jungle, where tigers and panthers lurked, where green mantises sat like evil gems and hornets flew big as sparrows, she brooded on Darius and felt begin within her a new and sourceless pain.

Night came after the day. They were deep in the rukh.

They could only lie down in the moisture, on the humming and scuffling floor of the forest, pulling about them like weak cocoons the blankets Darius had provided for them.

Annie thought, *Was Rose truly there? She said my father was a demon. No, that couldn't be.* And she held the cotton in her hand, but in the sunrise it had dropped away and she could not find it. This was typical. To lose everything. She glared at the vastness of the impossible jungle, and went on.

Almost all of them went on. The vegetable maid had vanished in the night.

As they hobbled with trouble through the masses of the forest's undergrowth, Divy said, 'I think he's here. In this part.' She meant Pocks. Mrs Rope said, 'Don't you bother with that. We need all our blessed wits for this walking. I've got on my father's boots. There's a thing now, I can fit in them. But that's my luck, my big feet. Look at that poor woman,' said Mrs Rope, pointing at Flower up on Jessa. 'She's taken a blow, she has.'

At midday, a deer, dappled and unearthly, crossed their path. They watched it in awe. Nothing menacing had come near them.

When the sun went, the forest flushed with gold, then veiling itself in black, they crowded to Darius, and argued, and reviled him. But he only answered them mildly.

'She's been leaving a trail of rice,' said Burrow of Divy. 'She thinks he'll follow it.'

'But rats have eaten it all,' said Divy. She looked at Darius, changed by everything as he had not been. 'I'll go after him. I'll find him. Can I go?'

Mrs Rope slapped Divy. 'You panful of porridge. What can you be doing in that, there? You'll be eaten alive. Don't you think there aren't tigers. I've heard that Rawlings go on enough about them, and I know their noise, and I've heard it.'

Divy said, 'But I could find him.'

Darius said, 'I'm not your keeper.'

'Then I'll go.'

Annie watched as Divy went off into the darkness. Suddenly Divy began to sing in a high clear voice, like a child's. It was a country song and Annie could not make out the words. Divy disappeared into the night, and above them the monkeys hooted.

Annie lay under the trees and did not sleep all night. She heard the horses browse and shake their heads, and the others snore and doze and wake fitfully. Flower slept against a tree. She would not lie down. Things, she said, would get into her ears, or they would eat her hair. Mosquitoes would sting them, Flower said – this had not occurred – despite the smoky fire Darius made.

Near morning, as a kind of white veneer spread through the forest, Annie heard Flower calling to someone. Annie got up and crossed to Flower, and Mrs Rope came after.

'What's up, your ladyship?' said Mrs Rope.

'I saw Hampton,' said Flower, drowsily. 'He was there. He looked very smart, in his uniform and on the horse. Calling on that prince's palace, to show off the troops.'

'Oh, she's going,' said Mrs Rope. 'I knew she would. And all these bats asleep.'

Flower gazed at Annie. As the light came, Annie saw that Flower had lost a great deal of weight quite abruptly, and her face was no longer cavernous and fallen, but younger.

'It's a fact,' said Flower, 'I can't go any further. I've had enough.'

Annie turned to look for Darius, and he was there, standing up tall and pin-thin, with his hair like silver silk in the sunrise, and his eyes like darker silver.

'What is it, Lady Flower?'

'I won't go on. I'll stay here.'

Darius crouched down and took Flower's hand. She glanced

at this, and smiled. 'Saucy,' she said. 'You always were a nice-looking boy, for all you were so wild. Like a tree-spirit. I recall there was one like that in a play, but the wretch that played him was a great stout thing. He looked a sight.'

Darius had brought another blanket, rolled up. He said, 'Will you lie down now?'

'No, I can't lie down. It's this bloody corset. What a woman has to endure.'

Darius said, 'I'll go off a way. Annie can cut the laces for you.'

'No, no,' said Flower, quite bright, 'I'll die properly dressed.'

'Ah,' said Darius.

'Oh,' said Flower, 'did you think I didn't know? I'm not afraid of it,' said Flower. 'And that's odd, I always thought I should be. But I'm tired. I'm tired of being this ugly fat cow I've turned into. And I'll be something else next.'

Darius said, 'Yes, my dear.'

'Go on,' said Flower. 'If Hampton heard you, what would he say?' And then she smiled again. 'I feel all light now. I feel slim now. Am I slim?'

'Like a stem you are,' he said, 'my hands would meet about your little waist.'

'That's right,' said Flower. She closed her eyes. 'Perhaps I'll be a butterfly.'

After a minute Darius let go of Flower's hand, and that was the only reason that Annie knew Flower had died. Mrs Rope knew too, and began to sob furiously, saying Flower had been a good mistress, as they went, and it was a dreadful thing, in this heathen forest, and they must bury her, but who would do it, would Darius do it? Darius said if she wished he would do what he could. They had no spade, said Mrs Rope. Darius said she was not to fret. He put the blankets round Flower and took her up easily, despite her inert cumbersome weight, and carried her away. Then Mrs Rope began to decide Darius would not come back, and the horses, catching her alarm, shuffled in their lines. But Darius came back, alone. He did not say what he had done by way of obsequies, and maybe he had done nothing, but the forest itself, thought Annie, was like a temple, like a tomb. She felt lassitude, and when they went on, she moved in a deadly dream, beginning to forget herself, as if she would be the next to die.

On Jessa, the bag with the jewels in it hung down, and Annie saw it, and she thought, *They'll have turned to leaves and nuts.*

There were now Mrs Rope and Burrow, the two young boys, and Clarrie. That was all.

These last vestiges of what had been did not vanish away. They clung on, although in the sunset, the mongoose leapt suddenly from its perch and sprinted off into the trees and the dumb boy stared after it, wordlessly weeping. Darius walked over to the boy, touched his head quietly, and told him that the mongoose had left him only because now they were near the end of their journey.

'How can he know that?' demanded Mrs Rope.

'Oh, Dari's peculiar. He does know,' said Clarrie.

The horses knew also. They became frisky and pleased, and the young one played about, attracting the dumb boy so he stopped crying.

The monkeys did not roister any more. The trees were tall as ever, stuck together by the glue of darkness.

Darius said they would sit down and rest for one hour, and then they would go on and find the way from the wood.

Annie did not seat herself. She paced off a little way, and standing in the core of the dark, she understood. It was coming to its end. Everything was over. The power and the glory, the fear and the lawlessness. Unless she should choose, as the others had, to linger.

But that she would not do. It had engaged her. She would not trust it. She must have the harshness of reality.

And at the gate, she would lose him.

'Now, why are you here?' he said.

She turned about, and Darius was at her back, near as her thought, unless this was a demon . . . But that had been her mother's fancy.

'Where shall I go,' she said, 'when we're done with this place?'

'Where you want,' he said.

'Then,' she said, 'not with you.'

'Not with me,' he said. 'Unless you wish it.'

'And what do you want?' she said, bold and hard.

'I've lived enough that you might be my daughter,' he said. 'But the feeling I have for you is the feeling a man has for a woman. You're as lovely as the sky. You're in my heart.'

'Put down your head, Darius,' said Annie.
And when he did so, she garlanded his neck with her arms, and kissed his mouth. There are so many kisses. But lovers do not recollect.
He said, 'Now you belong to me.' She nodded. He said, 'And I to you.'

Before the darkness fell, Luksmi created the sun in the forest.
She had built a platform of twigs and vines, and on to this she had dragged his body, the partly eaten corpse of Urquhart, her son-husband. She had clothed him with marigolds, put a mask of flowers across his face. His skull she did not need to split.
Then she had used the ordinary matches and lit his pyre.
She sat by as he burned, and spoke for him some words. The essence of him rose, with the tang of meat, up into the canopy of the rukh. And there it had its liberty.
At length the wetness of the ground put out the fire, but he had been consumed. She took a handful of his ashes then, and bore them to the bank of the misty river, and there she let them go.
And then, as if it had waited, the marigold sun went down and it was night.
Presently, from farther along the bank, among the trees, someone called her name.
She was not afraid. She had never been afraid.
Luksmi went to the spot, and looking up, in the final trace of afterlight, she saw a being hung among the tree trunks, woven there. Roots and boughs had grown about him, and vines roped him in. Orchids spurted from his hair and moss dripped from his long beard, and from his genitals. He smiled at her. 'Don't remember me, eh? But I remember you. Little barefoot child. Flower making you learn about bloody Jesus Christ. Luksmi.'
Luksmi said politely, 'You are the Sahib Withers.'
'Just so.'
She made him a delicate obeisance.
Withers cackled.
'Can't return the courtesy, my girl. Can't move a limb. But I don't mind it. I'm cared for. I like it here.'

Luksmi seated herself beneath the tree where Withers was suspended. She heard him breathing, and then he said, 'I went after that sice, Darius. I thought he knew the temples. So I followed. But do you know, I think now I followed one of the rakshas. Or Krishna himself. He disappeared, or turned into a sal. And there I was, in the heart of the rukh. I couldn't find my way. I don't know what went on. But then I was here. I'd been starving, and so thirsty I'd have killed. I drank some water from a pool and it poisoned me. But then, once I couldn't move, the monkeys came. They brought me luscious fruit. They put it between my lips, so neatly. And later a mynah bird came and it talked to me. He still comes. We talk for hours. He knows the poets.' Withers laughed again. 'If you look at the ground, Luksmi, you'll see the jewels. Rubies as big as your hand. And opals, and emeralds, and there's a rough diamond there, well, it would break the bank. They bring them to me now. They know I like to see. Take what you want, girl, I don't mind.'

'No, Lord,' said Luksmi. 'I do not need such things.'

'No, you don't, your kind. Nor I don't, now. I have all I need.'

Luksmi got up. 'I will visit you in the morning.'

'Bring me some figs,' said Withers, 'there's a good girl. They never do. And it reminds me of the brandy, a fig.'

Over the river the stars had lighted, and seemed to float like candle-boats in the water. A jackal called across the spaces of the dark. The moon rose slowly.

As the rainy moon rose, they saw the bungalow of the gate-house, deserted, with blossom pouring from the roof. Just beyond, the pillared gate, topped by a crown, the iron twisted in lilies and peacocks.

In amazement then they paused, as if startled more by normalcy than by the curiosity of enchantment.

Darius led them on, and the horses went with ease, showing how it was done, the needful acceptance of everything.

Mrs Rope and Clarrie and limping speechless Burrow, the boys who were already downcast at leaving the rukh. Annie with flowers in her hair, which, coming to the gate, she drew out and laid by the way.

They moved through, one by one.

In the blue and filtered moonlight, the English rural road

stretched out for them, its big oak trees, its clumps of thistle and buttercups. A fox barked far away. An owl with a half-apple face sailed over the fields.

They did not look back, not one of them.

They did not look back.

Then, perhaps a hundred yards off, Annie Ember turned her head, she *looked* behind her. But in the darkness under the cloudy moon, you could not tell. If it had gone, the forest, gone away for ever. Or if it had remained.

More Fantasy Fiction from Headline:

ROGER TAYLOR

DREAM FINDER

The epic new fantasy from the author of *The Chronicles of Hawklan*

The City of Serenstad has never been stronger. Its ruler Duke Ibris is a ruthless man when his office requires it, but he is also a man of fine discernment; artists, craftsmen and philosophers have flourished under his care, and superstitions are waning in the light of reason and civilization.

For the Guild of Dream Finders this has proved disastrous. Since their leader Petran died, their craft has fallen into disrepute, and Petran's son Antyr is unable to fill the vacuum left by his father. Antyr finds himself growing bitter, without the stomach to pander to the whims of the wealthy, or the courage to offer them his skills honestly and without fear. His nightly appointments at the alehouse have lost him customers; and his quarrels with his strange Companion and Earth Holder, Tarrian, have grown increasingly unpleasant of late.

Then mysteriously one night, Antyr and Tarrian are taken to Duke Ibris, who has been troubled by unsettling dreams. It is the beginning of a journey that leads inexorably to a terrible confrontation with a malevolent blind man, possessed of a fearful otherworldly sight, and Ivaroth, a warrior chief determined to conquer the Duke's land and all beyond at any cost...

Also by Roger Taylor from Headline Feature:
The Chronicles of Hawklan
THE CALL OF THE SWORD
THE FALL OF FYORLUND
THE WAKING OF ORTHLUND
INTO NARSINDAL

FICTION/FANTASY 0 7472 3726 3

More Fantasy Fiction from Headline:

JENNY JONES

FLY BY NIGHT

Volume One of FLIGHT OVER FIRE

'An extraordinary book. A vivid original. There is something very special about Jenny Jones'
Michael Moorcock

Eleanor Knight is a child of her age: spoiled, bored, a stranger to commitment. From another world a desperate rite of summoning calls and she is carried on a whirling nightmare of hawkflight, out of her self-indulgent unhappiness . . . to the wind-lashed coast of the Cavers, worshippers of the Moon Goddess Astret.

The Sun God Lycias and His High Priest Lefevre maintain the Stasis which holds Peraldonia, an ocean away from the Cavers, in a summery land of light and eternal life. But the Stasis has a converse side and it is in ceaseless night that the Cavers eke out a barren existence – the rite of summoning is their final despairing attempt to break Lycias' hold on Time . . .

Disoriented and dismayed Eleanor wants no part of the Cavers' problems, but the Moon Goddess will not be denied. In the outsider's hands rests the fate of a people: the final heart-rending agony of choice will fall to her alone.

'Definitely something out of the ordinary, and something good' Michael Scott Rohan

FICTION/FANTASY 0 7472 3398 5

More Compelling Fiction from Headline:

DAN SIMMONS

CHILDREN OF THE NIGHT

'I AM IN AWE OF DAN SIMMONS' STEPHEN KING

Kate Neuman, a top American haematology researcher, is in Bucharest to help the orphans. Kate strives to save the AIDS babies and other abandoned children in a nation torn by revolution, stifled by centuries of oppression, and afflicted by superstitions reaching back to a dark and bloody past.

But it is one specific child who captures first her attention as a physician, and then her heart as a mother. Afflicted by vicious immune-deficiency diseases, seven-month-old Joshua's prognosis is bleak. But simple blood transfusions help the child to rally despite the prognosis and despite logic. Kate Neuman soon realizes that baby Joshua is nothing less than a miracle child. His genes may hold the cure for cancer and AIDS, as well as a clue to human immortality.

Helped by Father Michael O'Rourke, Kate battles the malevolent Romanian bureaucracy to adopt Joshua and return him to the United States, where only the most advanced medical technology can save the child and reveal the mystery of his amazing immune system. But just as the research promises an astounding breakthrough, just as Kate Neuman's life seems to be approaching fulfilment in her love for her son, terror reaches a cold hand from the dark forests of Transylvania to change her life forever...

'A mesmerising tour through the ghostly, gray tatters of Romania' *Publishers Weekly*

'His best novel ever' *Kirkus Reviews*

'Clearly good Simmons' *Locus*

Also by Dan Simmons from Headline Feature:
SONG OF KALI – Winner of the 1986 World Fantasy Award
CARRION COMFORT – Winner of the 1989 British Fantasy Society Award, winner of the 1990 Bram Stoker Award, winner of the 1990 Locus Award for Best Horror Novel
HYPERION – Winner of the 1990 Hugo Award, winner of the 1990 Locus Award for Best Science Fiction Novel
THE FALL OF HYPERION – Winner of the 1991 Locus Award for Best Science Fiction Novel, winner of the 1991 British Science Fiction Association Award for Best Novel
PHASES OF GRAVITY   THE HOLLOW MAN
SUMMER OF NIGHT – Winner of the 1992 Locus Award for Best Horror Novel
PRAYERS TO BROKEN STONES – Winner of the 1991 Bram Stoker Award for the Best Short Story Collection

FICTION/GENERAL   0 7472 3899 5